SOMETHING WILD

SOMETHING WILD

Linda Davies

HEADLINE

First published in Great Britain in 2001
by HEADLINE BOOK PUBLISHING

10 9 8 7 6 5 4 3 2 1

British Library Cataloguing in Publication Data

Davies, Linda
Something wild
I. Title
823.9'14[F]

ISBN 0 7472 7082 1 (hardback)
ISBN 0 7472 7080 5 (trade paperback)

Typeset by Avon Dataset Ltd, Bidford-on-Avon, Warks

Printed and bound in Great Britain by
Mackays of Chatham plc, Chatham, Kent

HEADLINE BOOK PUBLISHING
A division of Hodder Headline
338 Euston Road
London NW1 3BH

www.headline.co.uk
www.hodderheadline.com

To my husband, Rupert, and our sons, Hughie and Tommy,
loves of my life.

Acknowledgements

Some extremely kind, generous and knowledgeable people have provided me with information as I have researched this book. A thousand thanks to them all:

The rock stars.

David Pullman, inventor of 'Bowie Bonds' and guru of rock star securitisation. Jennifer Speck, producer, old friend, travel mate and wheeler dealer. Tommy Helsby. James Harman, entertaining entertainment lawyer, and his cohort, Paddy Grafton Green. Andrew Wilkinson, Paul Charles and Andrea Bartlett. Kati St Clair, visionary.

Most of all, I would like to thank my inspirations, my babies, Hughie and Tommy, and my husband, Rupert. Here's to research!

Chapter One

Buffalo River Valley, Wyoming

The wind blew the scent of terror into the horse's flaring nostrils and he began to dance and skip beneath his rider. She shortened her reins, just enough to let him know she was there, but not enough to provoke him further. Here in the wilderness, his instinct was infinitely better tuned than hers. He was not spooked by leaf shadows dancing on the rugged path, nor by the pulsing roar of the wind in the silver birch. The river in spate interested him, but warranted no more than a few cautious glances. She could feel his panic now, his flanks trembling, and she shared it. She attempted to fight it, tried to be the calm one, to offer quietude, but failed. Trying to divine the source of her mount's fear, she looked around, but the valley appeared unchanged. Then she heard it, coming from behind, a wild and throbbing sound – and knew it was the drumbeats of flight.

'Easy there, easy now, quiet boy, it's all right.' But it wasn't. A horse burst into view, galloping out of control, as if pursued by the hounds of hell. A rider clung desperately to its back, stirrups lost, reins flailing. The horse was going full pelt, heading for the trees half a mile away. There the rider would have no hope. He'd be flung off, hit a tree, break his back, snap his neck. Jesus. Sarah reacted automatically. She squeezed her knees.

'Come on!' The horse needed no urging. He leapt forward, off the broken path, onto the grass of the valley. Sarah guided him in the hope that he would intercept the other horse before the forest. If he could get there in time, if he could speed up, if he could catch the other horse. She squeezed harder. 'Come on, boy. *Faster.*'

Exhilarated now, he responded; Sarah felt his exhilaration, and his dread. If he stumbled, they would both tumble in a thrashing mix of broken bones. She was clear of the other horse, gift of her head start, but she was coming from an oblique angle. The horses began to converge. She could see the other rider's face now. White with horror. The horses eyed each other wildly. She felt hers quicken beneath her, saw the other horse respond. Jesus – they were racing! If she didn't stop them both, she *and* her fellow rider would be pulped in the forest.

The horses came closer, faster, closer still. Sarah fought her horse now, yanking on the left rein, pulling him in, battling his compulsion to run. Ten yards, eight, seven, six. She caught her breath, pulled her horse closer, saw the terror burn in the other rider.

'Hang on, brace yourself!' she screamed. Five yards, four, three, two. Now they were almost together. With one hand, she gripped her reins and the pommel, with the other she reached out and down, grasping for the flailing reins of the runaway. She glanced at the approaching forest, leaned out more, legs gripping her horse like a vice. An inch more and she'd slip. Please God, get the reins. The forest getting closer. One last lunge. She had them.

Now she hauled back, legs braced forward, feet jammed in the stirrups, reining back for all she was worth. She felt her horse bunch under her, abruptly shortening his stride. The other horse still tried to keep his speed. She fought being pulled from her saddle. She gave a bit of rein, then yanked back as violently as she could. The other horse bridled, bunched, tried to shake his head. Sarah inched in another handful of reins. Yanked it. Both horses tried to fight. She fought back. '*Easy now, easy now, whoaaa, whoooaaa.* Easy now, easy.'

Slowly, slowly, they began to come under her control. The forest loomed. Sarah pulled them to the right. They began to curve, slowly, easy now, not too violent or they'd tumble. The forest thirty yards away. '*Easy now, easy.*' And finally they slowed, putting the brakes on voluntarily, legs jarring forward, dust flying. Till they stopped.

Chapter Two

Sarah drove away from the ranch where she had hired her horse. Clouds of dust billowed in farewell after her. She had escorted the silent horseman back to the ranch where he was staying and handed him over to a worried ranch hand. The bolter, as she called him in her mind, referring not to horse but to rider, had said nothing all the way home, just gazed ahead, glassy-eyed. He was clearly in shock, which wasn't surprising. He'd nearly lost his life. Sarah had told the ranch hand what had happened, and suggested he call a doctor. Shock itself could kill, and the bolter looked like he needed something more than the local remedy – a double bourbon and hot coffee.

She felt disturbed as she drove, as the tendrils of trauma curled around her heart. The shadow of violent death had fallen over her again. This time, she'd outridden it – just – saved someone else's life, and narrowly avoided losing hers in the process. As usual, she hadn't thought about it twice, just plunged on, following instincts, genes, or some conditioning whose roots were so well buried as to be unknowable to her.

How many times did death have to stalk her before it claimed her? She had survived so far, in a life strewn with bodies. Her parents, killed in a car crash. The drunken driver who smashed into their car when Sarah was seven years old, shot point blank fourteen years later. Her best friend, Mosami. Her lover, Dante Scarpirato. Death had recently tried its best to take her brother, too, and now he lay encased in plaster in his hospital bed, waiting for her visit. Alex Jensen had been climbing Grand Teton in Wyoming when he'd fallen on a rock face. Some widget that should have broken his fall, failed to do so. He dropped a hundred feet before slamming into the rock outcrop that pulverised his body. Sarah felt tears course down her face as she thought of Alex as she'd first seen him, when she arrived dusty, exhausted and terrified after flying from London to be at his bedside. The bandages around his head seeped blood, his eyelids flickered but stayed shut. He had been unconscious for forty-three hours.

Sarah stared at her fingers, splayed on the steering wheel of her four-wheel drive. They were white and trembling. She pulled off the road with a screech of rubber, killed the engine, and sat for a while, resting her head on the steering wheel, until she felt some measure of calm return to her, then slowly, cautiously, she set off again.

Alex was reading a book, some tale of derring do no doubt, thought Sarah with a flash of sisterly despair, and was so engrossed in it that at first he didn't notice her standing in the open door. His hair was tousled, his face set into its habitual mien of curiosity. Although half of his body was immobilised by plaster, the energy emanating from him was tangible. Even the doctors, stepping briefly from their buttress of scientific rationalism, had admitted that the young man's life force was exceptionally strong. If he hadn't survived, Sarah wasn't sure she would have been able to go on. Orphaned as young children, their sibling bond went deeper than normal. Even though Alex spent much of the year away, travelling and climbing, their bond always united them. If one half of that current died, surely the other one would go too? She thought again about the bolting horse and shuddered. At that moment, Alex looked up.

'Hello there?'

'Hello, Al.' Sarah rushed forward and planted a large kiss on her brother's cheek.

'You all right?' Alex was looking at her askance. She never could hide anything from him.

Sarah sat down on the edge of his bed and told him about the bolter. Alex listened with horror creasing his features.

'*Je*sus! And I thought *I* was the crazy one. What happened then?'

Sarah gazed down at him with eyes full of love as he lay there, leg in sling, arms in plaster, the livid gash that gouged his left cheek almost healed.

'The guy couldn't speak. He wouldn't get back on his horse, just shook his head violently when I suggested it, so I rode, led his horse, and he walked, three hours back down the trail to this ranch by the river. I left him there with a ranch hand.' Sarah shrugged. 'That was it. I dropped off my horse, drove straight here.'

Alex took a moment to speak. 'You could have been killed, Sare.'

'That's rich, coming from you.'

Alex looked sheepish. 'Someone's got to be responsible for what's left of this family.'

'Yeah, well . . .' Sarah looked away, trying to force the spectre of loss from her mind. She turned brusquely back to Alex. 'Anyway, how's it all going? Doctors say anything?'

Alex looked suddenly pleased. 'Had a good check today. Arms should come off in the next few days, leg in a week.'

Sarah scratched at his plaster casts. 'That's great. They say anything else?'

'I think they want to take a look at everything when the casts are off. But I'll have to have extensive physio come what may.' An awkward look crossed his face.

'What?'

'Nothing bad, don't worry.'

'What then?'

'Bad financially. There's a place back home, in the country – a rehabilitation place. Apparently it's brilliant, best in Europe.'

'Then you'll go.'

'Costs a fortune, Sarah.'

'Nothing is more important than your full recovery.'

'They seem to think I stand a chance.' He paused as hope flared in his eyes. 'Two months there, then home, and regular sessions of physio and gym, all that. They say in nine months I could walk. Normally.'

Sarah dropped her head to her brother's chest to hide her tears. She quickly wiped her eyes as she straightened up.

'That's fantastic, Alex. That's the best news I've *ever* had.'

He smiled and took her hand. 'Sare, it's too much. Ten weeks here, two months in the clinic. It's not fair to you.'

She shook her hand free. 'That's what money's for.'

'Your money wasn't exactly easy come by. Now it's just haemorrhaging out on me.'

'As long as it's only money haemorrhaging, I don't care. You're my flesh and blood. You're all that's left of our family. You think I care about money next to that?' She made no effort now to hide her tears.

'How much cash d'you have left? I must be clearing you out. All this treatment, you'll have no change from a million dollars.'

'I've got a million.'

'Then what?'

'It's not as if I don't work. I'll get more.'

'You haven't worked since my accident.'

'I'll work when we go home.'

'I know how important money is to you. How you build up your security. You won't get a million back in a hurry.'

'Maybe I'll start playing the markets again. Anyway, I won't starve, Al – and you will go to this place back home, so let's drop it.'

Sarah drove back to Spring Creek. She'd been there two and a half months, since the day after the hospital's call, and still the view blew her away. Her cabin was on a hill, part of a holiday retreat, seven and a half thousand feet up, in Jackson Hole, Wyoming. Below it the valley curled in a huge bowl, fertile green and lush, and beyond that the Teton range towered up, craggy and snow-capped, framing the horizon as far as she could see. It was so peaceful here. There was none of the psychic noise that troubled her back home in London. There she sometimes felt she was walking through the streets of an Edvard Munch painting, past endless houses full of screaming occupants. Her skin was too thin, she knew it; could do nothing about it, would be flayed by life, if she allowed it. Wyoming, for all the terror of her arrival here, the image of her brother's broken body, was, now that he was healing, turning out to be a haven.

Locking the door of her cabin, she poured herself a glass of whisky and debated dinner. First she needed a shower. She smelled of horse and sweat, and while Alex would never complain of that, Sarah couldn't wait to get the dust off her skin.

She had just emerged, swathed in towels, when she heard a knocking at the door. Probably the hotel returning her laundry. Hadn't she hung out the *Do Not Disturb* sign? She pulled the towel tighter round her and opened the door.

A stranger stood before her, his face partially obscured by a cowboy hat. He said nothing, just looked at her. Sarah felt a sudden flash of fear, quickly followed by anger. She stuck her hands on her hips, striking an aggressive pose.

'Yes?' she demanded in a voice that really said: *Explain yourself pretty bloody fast, buster.*

The man smiled, and for some reason this infuriated Sarah more. She was just about to slam the door in his face when he spoke.

'I came to say thank you.' His voice was low, utterly self-possessed.

'For what?'

'Saving the life of my friend,' the stranger replied.

'Oh, that,' said Sarah, as if she did it every day. 'Well, what else could I do?' A cold blast of wind made her shiver. She hugged the towel around her and rubbed her arms. She expected the man to take the hint and excuse himself, letting her return to the warmth of her cabin, but he didn't. He just stood there, looking at her. She looked back, and for a while, they both remained motionless as the chill wind blew around them. Then Sarah turned, walked back into the cabin, knowing the man would follow.

She stopped in the middle of the room as the door swung shut.

'I'm going to put something on,' she said.

He just nodded.

Her fingers fumbled with buttons as she tried to do up her cardigan. She pulled on jeans, forced her feet into cowboy boots, combed out her hair, and walked back to him. He was standing by the picture window in the main room, staring out into the stormy night.

'Like a drink?'

He turned slowly towards her. 'Whatever you're having.' That low voice, the way he said it, turned her blood to smoke. She went into the kitchen, poured out two large whiskies, walked back to him and offered him the glass. He took it, drained half in one go.

'So,' said Sarah, back to her hands on hip stance, 'who are you?'

That prompted a laugh, seemingly of pleasure.

'I wasn't aware,' said Sarah coolly, 'that I'd made a joke.'

'Does it matter who I am?'

Sarah shrugged. 'What's in a name?' She took a long pull of whisky. 'You can take off that blasted hat anyway.'

He did as instructed, eyes on hers the whole time. Now she could see his face, the hard planed features, the scintillating grey eyes the colour of rock, the cold mouth.

'Ah,' she said. 'I see.'

Chapter Three

She lay in bed, restless as the storm. She must have eaten something bad, or perhaps it was some kind of delayed shock, because her stomach was upset and she spent half the night rushing back and forth to the lavatory. In the unquiet moments that she lay prone, her mind turned over, devouring the image of the stranger. She knew the facts, anyone within reach of a radio, a newspaper or a television did. John Redford was one of the reigning gods in the Pantheon of Rock, a man's man, a woman's man, the people's man. He was Thor and Pan rolled into one, with something of the golden sorrow of the fallen angel thrown in. He sang blue-collar diatribes against steel ghost towns, he sang hot-blooded torch songs that would have emptied convents, and he sang heart-rending laments of loss and loneliness.

He'd sold over one hundred million albums in his twenty-year career, and he was still only forty. Christened the hard man of rock by the press, he shunned the high-octane world he dominated for the lure of his ranch in Wyoming and working his horses. His hands were calloused, she had seen that, she guessed from manual labour, not from strumming his guitar, although he did that too, and God knows he did it well. His songs were part of her life. She had laughed to them, cried to them, made love to them. He had played her emotions like the master he was. Guitar and piano he played too, and he wrote all his own songs, from the heart. He laid bare his emotions in his songs, but the press always made much of the enigma of the man, accessible and totally inaccessible at once. He did no interviews, unless he wanted a platform to speak out against some pet injustice that you knew he really did believe in. But his views and his passions were disconcertingly unboxable.

John Redford was a conservationist who fought to keep factories open as keenly as he opposed opening new ones if they would plunder the environment around them. But he wasn't some reformed would-be saint.

There were stories of bacchanalian excess with his closest friends, one of whom was a famous Hollywood actor. He appeared to be supremely indifferent to his public image, said what he wanted with no kow-towing to political correctness, did what he wanted, and was lauded anyway. But always there was a slight wariness in the adulation, as if at any moment, the lion might turn and devour his admirers.

He was dangerous all right. That had been obvious from the second he stood outside her door. The danger was part of the most powerful charisma Sarah had ever encountered. She had met people who glowed with a light, bright, good charisma, but Redford's was not of this sort. Redford was a perilous journey, one that she had no intention of taking.

She'd known her share of dangerous men, taken some of them into her bed, one of them into her heart. Now he was dead, and she was responsible. Dante Scarpirato, with his dark regard, and smooth brown skin, had been her boss at the second bank she had worked for in the City of London. He had been the reason she had joined the bank. Her remit, in a complicated assignment worked out by MI6 and the Governor of the Bank of England, had been to investigate Scarpirato, who was suspected of masterminding a massive insider trading operation in the foreign exchange markets.

She had no qualifications for such a job, save her abilities as a foreign exchange trader, her beauty, and her appetite for risk, which is what MI6 and the Governor had counted on. And, God, she had not let them down. She was a spy in the house of money, but she had fallen in love with the object of her professional attentions. She and Dante became lovers and, in so doing, Sarah discovered that he was innocent. Then a kind of vicious fate put him in the wrong place at the wrong time, and he was murdered by a hitwoman sent after Sarah. What neither MI6 nor the Governor of the Bank of England had told her was that the Mafia were involved in the insider trading, and Sarah, unknowingly, had stirred up that nest of vipers. She had delivered the perpetrators to her secret taskmasters, but Dante, and her best friend Mosami Masimoto, were murdered for what they knew or what the Mafia suspected they knew. Sarah had survived only by doing a deal with the Mafia, and with the hitwoman sent after her. The ultimate trade: their freedom for her life.

She had seen her share of danger, and there was something in Redford's eyes that stirred some memory of it in her. But then what did it matter? She would never see him again.

Chapter Four

She drove to the hospital the next afternoon. Red-eyed and caffeined up, she perched on her brother's bed, telling her story.

'What did you do then?' asked Alex warily.

'Don't worry, little brother. I made some more polite conversation and showed him the door.'

'Hm. From the look in your eyes, I doubt very much it was polite conversation you made.'

'It was all I made, and all I ever will make. I'm not about to become a rock star's groupie.'

'The thought never entered my head. Methinks the lady doth protest—'

'Shut up.' Sarah aimed a good-natured swipe at her brother, skimming the air above his head.

An hour later, she got up to go. She bent over Alex and kissed his cheek. 'It'll be good to get home, won't it?'

Alex looked surprised. 'You're not in a hurry to get back to England, are you? I thought you liked it out here.'

'I do, but as Dorothy says in *The Wizard of Oz*, "There's no place like home".'

Looking back on that moment, she sometimes wondered if, like Dorothy, she could have spun round, clicked her heels three times and rematerialised back home right then, whether or not she would have done it . . .

Dusty again after another day's riding, Sarah drove back from the hospital. At the cabin she showered, and found herself vacillating over what to put on. When the call had come from the hospital ten weeks ago, she'd packed in five minutes, just hurled clothes into a bag. Now she wished she had her whole London wardrobe and half of Harvey Nichols to call on. Most of the clothes she had were in serious need of washing. Fragrant laundry seemed a bit irrelevant when you spent most of your days on a horse, your evenings visiting your brother, then dining alone in a log cabin with an audience of nothing more than cheeky chipmunks, sitting on your sun deck, begging. Dammit, what did it matter anyway. *Get yourself under control*, she thought disapprovingly, and settled on a pair of not too dirty jeans. The only top that was halfway clean and unsweaty was a vest. She pulled it on. Her bra straps showed. She pulled off the bra. Her nipples showed. Too bad. She allowed herself a grin, and walked barefoot back into the main room. The chipmunks wouldn't mind.

Pouring herself a whisky, she sat down with the latest Elizabeth George detective story. She must have lost herself in the plot, for the knocking on the door made her sit up with a jolt. She put down the book, swung her legs off the sofa, and padded across the room. Her blood racing, she opened the door. She had known it would be him. He stood there before her in his jeans, sheepskin jacket and cowboy hat. Six foot, weathered face, muscled thighs, one leg slightly cocked, half smile playing on his lips. She waited, echoing his posture, saying nothing. The moment of silence extended way beyond any normal comfort zone. Time inched by as Sarah stared at the stranger on her doorstep. She heard the wind susurrating in the aspens, she felt its cold touch on her cheek; she was preternaturally aware of every sensation of living. She could almost feel the blood moving in her veins. She smiled. 'You'd better come in.'

He gave the slightest nod, followed her in. She walked to the kitchen, fired up the kettle, poured two camomile teas. In all the time it took, neither of them spoke. Sarah went back to the main room, handed Redford his tea, and sat down in the armchair. Redford chose the sofa. They looked across the gap between them and smiled. Words suddenly seemed inadequate. Thought and emotion had run so far ahead. Play the game, Sarah told herself, seeking refuge where she could. Play the masquerade of words.

'Your friend ask you to come again?' she enquired, holding her mug to her lips, looking at Redford over the rim.

'He didn't ask yesterday.'

'So why did you come?'

'Curiosity.'

'Oh yeah?'

'You did something very brave.'

'Is that so rare?'

'Could have got yourself hurt, badly.'

Sarah shrugged.

'You weren't frightened?'

'Terrified.'

'Why'd you do it?'

'I didn't think about it. Your friend would have been mashed to pieces in the trees.'

'He would have been for sure, without you.'

'Who is he?'

'Strone Cawdor, my manager. So,' continued Redford, taking a slug of tea, 'what's your story? Why are you here, alone in a log cabin four thousand miles from home?'

'What makes you think you know where my home is?'

'You think I don't recognise that expensive London accent?'

Sarah laughed. 'Oh, please. You'll be calling me a Sloane next.'

'No. I've met a few of them.'

'And?'

'They're tame creatures. Different species.'

'So what am I then?'

'That's what I'm wondering.'

'Wonder away.'

'You haven't told me why you're here.'

Sarah fidgeted before answering. She looked out onto the mountains, snow cast red by the setting sun.

'My brother was out here climbing. He had an accident.' She retreated from the words.

'What happened?' Redford's voice, coming across the room, was suddenly gentle; his eyes, resting on hers, were full of compassion.

Sarah went to the kitchen, returned with two whiskies. She half drained hers before she resumed speaking. 'He was climbing Grand Teton, two and a half months ago – snow and ice climb. He fell.' Her voice faltered but she pushed on. 'He was airlifted to hospital with multiple fractures, one leg broken, six ribs, both arms, his face torn open. Oh Jesus.' She hid her face in her hands as her mask slipped. Redford watched her, waiting for her to recover.

'He was unconscious for forty-three hours. It was touch and go for a while.' She looked up. 'But he's a tough cookie. He survived and now they think, with major physio, he just might recover fully.' She gave a brave, weary smile. 'All he wants to do is be fit to climb. He's always loved it, more than anything else.'

'And you love him more than anything else,' observed Redford.

'He's my little brother, I've always looked after him, and yes, I do love him more than anything else.'

'Your parents?' asked Redford.

No, she wouldn't go there; she'd had enough pain for one evening with this stranger.

'What brings you here?' she asked, getting to her feet.

'I was born here, not in Jackson, in the mountains. I come back whenever I can.'

'Escape,' mused Sarah.

'Exactly. Gets a bit tiring, living on the road.'

'What, all that adulation, adrenaline, performance highs, worshipping crowds, not to mention the dollars pouring in. Yeah, it's a tough life.'

'Yeah, a real breeze,' replied Redford with heavy sarcasm.

'So what's so tough?' asked Sarah, goading him, unsure why she was persisting.

'Long story. One I'm not in the mood for, and you'd not be receptive to, if I'm reading you right.'

Sarah had the grace to smile.

'And what d'you do back home?' asked Redford, seemingly relieved to be moving on. 'Ten weeks is a long time to be away. Isn't there a husband, a boyfriend, a job, calling you back?'

'No husband. No boyfriend.'

'Why not?'

'That's my long story.'

'I'm not in a hurry.'

Sarah sighed, half of her relishing Redford's questioning, the unspoken understanding that seemed to be developing, the other half reminding her that however familiar his face might be, he was a stranger.

'There are men for love, men for sex, men for games, and companions. Fate has thrown plenty of the last three my way – I don't need any more of those right now – but it's been stingy with the men for love.' She smiled. 'Anyway, you just need one, don't you, one great love of your life.'

'And you haven't met him?'

'No, I haven't. Perhaps I won't till I'm ninety, but I won't sell out in the meantime.'

'What, no lovers between now and then?'

'Oh, there'll be lovers, but no one to stop me dropping my life and coming out here for ten weeks if I need to.' Sarah pushed the hair from her face to study Redford. 'What about you?'

'What? Am I married, hooked up, what?'

'Whatever.'

'I'm single. I have loved but I haven't met the one great love. I wish I could believe she existed.'

'You sing about her.'

'I fantasise, I dream about her. Then I wake up.'

'You're not that cynical, John Redford.'

He finished his whisky. 'Aren't I?'

Sarah walked up to him, tried to take his glass from him. He held on. She looked at close range into his eyes, at once hard and dazzling, all too aware of his own power, but harbouring too, a hint of uncertainty. Sarah had the feeling that with this man a woman could give no quarter.

'No,' she said, keeping her gaze unflinchingly on his. 'You're not.'

He released the glass. She refilled it and hers. She turned and put it on the table behind her.

'So where're you staying?' she asked, suddenly feeling the need to move onto safer ground.

'My little ranch. Just down the road.'

Sarah gave him a wry smile. 'Little? Yeah, I'll bet.'

'Not big enough for my purposes anyway.'

'Which are?'

'Space, freedom. Thousands of acres for the grizzlies to roam.'

'So buy more land.'

'Not quite that easy.'

'Why not? No sellers?'

'There are sellers, but the prices are crazy.'

'Excuse me sounding gauche here, but I wouldn't have thought that'd be an issue for you.'

Redford gave a wry grin. 'Yeah, all rock stars are loaded. You'd be surprised what we're left with after the record company, agent, manager, accountants and lawyers have had their fill.'

'Maybe, but even so.'

'You have any idea what a nice ranch with a view of the Tetons goes for?'

'Tell me.'

'One was sold a few months ago, two hundred acres, just down the valley. Twenty-five million dollars.'

'Jesus! That's insane.'

'There were over twenty people in an auction for that property. I had to drop out. Some tecchie guy from Silicon Valley got it.'

'There's a surprise. How come land's so expensive here?'

'It's the playground of the rich, summer and winter. It's incredibly beautiful, and less than three per cent of the land is available to buy; the rest of it's all public, protected lands.'

'You should do a securitisation,' said Sarah. 'Flog off your catalogue of hits to some bored institutional investors looking for something sexy to drop into their portfolios. You could raise much more than twenty-five mill. Look at Bowie.'

'Yeah, I've heard about the Bowie deal.'

'You're much bigger than Bowie. If he could raise fifty-five million dollars, you could probably raise a hundred mill.'

Redford looked unimpressed. 'You think so?' he said.

'Back home there's a bank called Goldsteins International. They're the best finance house there is. Hardworking, straight, aggressive, great rep. They'd practically kill for their clients,' she added, with a quick flinch at her choice of words. She moved on quickly. 'If you're ever in London, ask for a meeting with the chairman, James Savage.'

'Maybe I'll do that.'

Sarah got to her feet. Her mention of Goldsteins brought home the reality of life, cut short the night's fantasy. He was a rock star. She was a banker-cum-private investigator. Goldsteins employed her as a freelance, in both capacities, one acting as a superb cover for the other. After Dante and Mosami had been killed, Sarah had quit ICB, and fled to the Himalayas to join Alex. She lived there for one year, and travelled on with Alex to Peru for another year, before returning to the UK. Unable to think of anything to do with herself, stranded back in London without Alex who'd continued his odyssey, she'd joined Kroll Associates, the world's best private investigators, and learned her new trade. She made some great new friends, stuck corporate life for a year, then quit to set up on her own. Goldsteins were her best, now practically her only client. They paid well, well enough for her to work only half the year, and to pick and choose her assignments. All that would soon end, she thought, visualising the size of Alex's bill. When they returned to the UK, she would have to work solidly for a long time to rebuild her nest egg, and reclaim her financial independence. Some contrast, she thought, glancing at the man opposite her. *Out of your league*, said her silent voice.

'Will you excuse me,' she said. 'I have to eat then hit the sack. I've got a very early start tomorrow.'

Redford looked surprised. 'Not going back to England?'

'No. I leave when my brother does. I'm going riding, deep into the wilderness, three nights camping.'

'*Alone*?'

'Me, three horses, three mules, a guide and a muleteer.'

Chapter Five

'Take a *gui*tar? What're you, darn crazy?'

Sarah stared at the man in the chaps and cowboy hat, her guide-to-be for the next four days – *if* they ever set off, which was looking increasingly doubtful.

'What's this strummer friend a yours planning on doing with it? Knock a grizzly over the head, or play it and send him running fer cover?'

Sarah felt her temper quickening, but decided to hold her tongue and wait for the cowboy to grow bored with his own dubious humour.

'Bad enough you call me last thing, tell me there's gonna be one more; now he wants to pack a *gui*tar. What else he want, a ten-piece band?'

Sarah had had enough. 'Look, do you want our business or not?'

The cowboy grinned abruptly. 'Guess I rightly do. We're here now, ain't we, least you and I are. Where's that strummer boy?'

Sarah turned to her jeep. She could see the silhouette of Redford in his cowboy hat, talking on his mobile phone.

'He'll be along in a minute,' she answered, blocking the man's view of Redford and beckoning to the rock star. He appeared a minute later, just as their guide was gearing up for another verbal assault.

'Hi,' said Redford, extending his hand. 'Sorry to keep you waiting.'

'Hm,' replied the cowboy, disconcerted by Redford's charm. He turned his head sideways to study him. 'You been out this way before? You look kinda familiar.'

'Was born here.'

'Wheresabouts?'

'On the banks of the Snake River, just south of Moran.'

'What, literally born by the river?'

'Right there on the grass. River calmed my ma, apparently.'

'Don't say. Who was your ma? Still here?'

'We moved away,' answered Redford flatly. 'So, we going?'

The guide looked unsettled again, thrown by Redford's sudden shift of mood. 'Yep,' he said. 'Jest getting your *gui*tar loaded up.' Then the cowboy blew his nose with a vicious snort, and headed for the company of mules.

Redford raised his eyebrows at the man's departing back.

Sarah grinned. 'Bit like a horse himself, isn't he? Skittish, easily wounded – easily reined in, too.'

'Can you ride, strummer?' shouted the cowboy from across the corral. 'We're gonna be going right into the heart a grizzly country. Don't want any more accidents than we can afford.'

'That's a comforting outlook,' said Redford in an aside to Sarah. 'Just give me something sane,' he called out.

'Got just the horse for you, name a Tony. You're going on his twin, Wes,' the guide hollered over to Sarah. 'Pies both a them; sweeter horses you won't get.'

'Sounds good,' said Sarah.

'You got a name?' asked the cowboy, approaching Redford leading a piebald horse, just a touch over fifteen hands high.

'John. You?'

'I'm Dave.' He motioned at a wiry younger man in his early twenties who was crooning to the mules as he loaded them up. 'This here's Ash.'

Ash turned round and bestowed on them a shy smile. He shuffled forward in his chaps and shook Sarah's and Redford's hands.

'This is Sarah and John,' Dave told him. 'John says he's from here.'

Ash turned white as he paid attention for the first time to Redford's face. 'Mighty pleased,' he managed to mutter, before shuffling back to the mules.

They set out along the banks of the Buffalo River, brown and turgid with snow melt as spring advanced up the mountainsides. The horses picked their way delicately over the rough-hewn path, occasionally glancing from left to right, as if taking in the spectacular views themselves. They rode upwards through groves of silver birch, Douglas firs, and Lodgepole pines, pitted with eye-shaped gnarls, as if the spirits of the trees were observing them as they passed. The air danced with dragonflies and butterflies, and carried to them the smell of the pine, baking in the hot sun, pure and potent like incense. The wind blew sibilant through the shimmering emerald leaves of the silver birch. Wherever they went they were always within earshot of water, trickling, gushing, roaring rivers, and cascades, pooling streams where the horses would dip their soft muzzles and drink their fill.

As they rode into the bowl of a glacier-sculpted plateau, Sarah was amazed by the size of the sky, so enormous above them that she fancied she could see the curve of the earth in its brilliant blue. The meadows to either side of their rocky path were strewn with a profusion of blue and gold wildflowers that covered the grass. Bare stems of branch were budding all around them. Spring came to the high wilderness in mid-June. Sarah gazed at the summits of the distant Tetons and wondered if spring ever reached their snowbound mass. Fallen trees lay by the wayside, their barkless limbs stark like bleached bones. A lake glittered, radiant turquoise, brimful with snow melt; everywhere Sarah looked was potent with beauty, with life and death and renewal.

Redford rode up beside her.

'It's gorgeous, isn't it?' she said.

'Most beautiful place in the world,' he agreed.

'Lucky you to be born here.'

'Hm.' He reined in his horse and dropped back.

They turned from the plateau onto a winding track along the side of the valley wall. Suddenly the procession stopped as Dave pointed silently to a moose, standing about twenty feet away. The moose regarded them with limpid brown eyes, wary but unafraid. His head was huge and ungainly, but his long, floppy ears were soft velvet and, as he slowly moved away, his legs moved elegantly over the rough ground with the grace of a dancer.

'What an amazing creature,' Sarah said to Redford. 'Ugly and beautiful all in one.'

'Aren't we all,' said Redford. 'Apart, that is, from you. You're just beautiful.'

'Please,' replied Sarah, unsettled. 'You must have said that a thousand times.'

'Maybe, but I didn't always mean it.'

For a moment their mutual gaze lingered, each reluctant to break contact. Sarah was the first to look away. It still didn't seem real, Redford being here. When she'd told him what she was planning last night, he just asked, as if it were the simplest thing in the world, 'Can I come along?' And she'd answered, just as simply, 'Yes.'

They rode higher, coming into the snowline. The horses crunched through two feet of snow, stepping cautiously around the slender firs that reached a hundred and fifty feet into the sky.

The day passed in a rhythmic dream of hoofbeats and beauty and birdsong and warmth. They found the perfect place to camp high up in a copse of fir trees, overlooking a valley. Dave and Ash tethered, fed and watered the horses, then began to set up camp. They pitched tents. Two only. Sarah approached them.

'Need any help with the third tent?'

'Ain't no third tent,' replied Dave. 'You're sharing with the strummer, ain't you?' He caught Sarah's look and grinned. 'Put it this way – it's either him, me or Ash. Take your pick.'

'Pick of what?' asked Redford, approaching.

'Said she gets to double up with me, Ash or you,' answered Dave. 'So, who'll it be?'

Redford watched Sarah's face closely. She turned and walked away in silence.

'Hey! Before you go,' shouted Dave, 'give me anything scented or edible you might have on you.'

'Like what?'

'Like everything. Toothpaste, face cream, mints, mouthwash, anything with the remotest whiff of sweetness on it. Bears love it. We gotta string it all up fifteen foot from the ground. Better do it now.'

'What about when we cook dinner?' asked Sarah. 'The grizzlies will smell that, won't they?'

'Sure will, but they already know we're here, makes no odds. What we don't want is to attract them into camp when we're sleeping, and what we want even less is to leave something enticing in the tent for them.'

Sarah gave a worried grimace. 'Right.' She collected anything that might remotely tempt a grizzly and handed it to Dave in a plastic bag. 'What happens if a bear does come into camp?' she asked.

'Ash 'n' I'll take care a him, don't you worry.'

'How?'

'First off, he probably won't come in. Most a them keep their distance.

It's man that's the problem most times, not grizzlies.'

'But what if one does? What if one comes right up to me?'

'First off, don't run. Just stay where you are. And don't look at him; keep your eyes down. He might charge you, but ninety per cent of times it's just a mock charge, so stand your ground and he'll probably just screech to a halt then back off when he's lost interest.'

'Great, that's all right then,' she said faintly. 'What do I do if he doesn't back off?'

'Well, me 'n' Ash, we both got twelve-bores, and revolvers and pepper spray with a twenty-yard range. We'd start with a blast of that and it'll knock him down and he'll most probably move off.'

Sarah took a while to digest this. 'Have you ever seen a grizzly up close before?'

Dave nodded. 'That I have, and let me tell you, you'll never see a more magnificent creature on all God's earth.'

Chapter Six

They ate a cowboy's dinner, cooked on a camp fire; steaks, baked potatoes and, perhaps as a gesture to modern times, salad. They washed it down with beers chilled in the gushing brook that marked the right flank of their camp. Then John Redford brought out his guitar.

'You do requests?' asked Dave.

'Sure,' smiled Redford. 'What'll it be?'

'Well,' said Dave, shy now in revealing his favourites, 'since it's kind of a starry, starry night, how 'bout that one? Know it?'

Redford nodded, took his guitar in his arms, held it close, like a lover, thought Sarah. She watched him stretch his fingers over the instrument's wooden body, tapping it here, caressing it there, then, as if confident that it had warmed up with his knowing touch, he began to pluck the quivering strings. And then he sang.

When he finished and the last chords faded into the valley, he kept his eyes on Sarah. He had seen her rapture, seen the look that normally only a lover would see, and here, sitting with the animals and the cowboys on a lonely mountainside, the intimacy was greater than that even. A slow clapping broke the moment and they both turned to Dave.

'You sure can play some. Mighty beautiful, if yer don't mind my sayin'.'

Ash disappeared into his tent and returned with a pen. He took off his hat and approached Redford. 'Would you autograph my hat fer me?'

Redford took the hat and pen. 'It'd be my pleasure.' He signed and gave it back to Ash, who beamed like it was Christmas Day.

'Wait till I show my girlfriend. She'd never believe me if I said I sat out here 'n' listened to a private concert by John Redford.'

'John Redford? Jesus Christ!' Dave turned white. 'You're *John Redford*? Dang it all to hell. You might have told me.' Now his face turned red. 'Take off yer hat,' he choked. 'You don't look like John Redford hiding under there.'

The singer left his hat on, but he smiled and gave an elegant shrug.

'Dang it all. Well, how about you play us another song, since we transported that darn guitar a yours. Jesus, if I'd known it was you, I'd never have kicked up such a darn fuss. I thought you was one a these urban cowboys was gonna strum out a tune and torture us and the wildlife all to hell.'

'No reason you should know. What'd you like me to play?'

'Well, one a my all-time favourites.'

'Tell me.'

'That song a yours – "Something Wild". I always loved that.'

Redford took up the guitar. Again Sarah was transfixed by the sensuality of his touch. He sat cross-legged on the ground, mug of coffee by his side, guitar cradled in his lap, his hair gold in the setting sun. The wind in the trees and the tumbling brook were his orchestra, the whole of the valley, teeming with animals seen and unseen, his audience.

'You come to me like a hurricane, with storm in your eyes.
There is earth, wind and fire in your touch,
You blow me away.
There are no rules for you.
You're something wild.

You make the world your own, you stake your claim
To skyscrapers and canyons, to the rivers and sunrise,
To all God's creatures,
To my heart,
You're something wild.

What broke you down? What furnace hardened you?
Where did you come from, my lovely one?
You've burned down all my defences,
And left me hooked
On something wild.

For a while, no one moved, as if unwilling to let go of the song. Finally, Ash, Dave and Sarah tore their eyes from Redford, stared all three at some anonymous patch of earth, their faces shorn of protection by the beauty of his song, by his voicing of their dreams.

'That was for you, Sarah,' said Redford, his voice so soft, she wondered if she had really heard him. He was a sorcerer, casting a spell on her; she was trapped in it now, stripped of the will to resist. It was too beautiful, too perfect a dream to shatter with willpower.

Now another voice rose up through the gathering darkness, the long, rising howl of a solitary wolf. He was not far from them. As his voice died away, another howl travelled to them across the valley, from the distant slope.

'Two alpha males,' said Dave, voice heavy and grateful, as if he was glad to be back on familiar territory. 'One owns the valley, he's letting the other one know to keep his distance.'

Sarah went to her tent, the wolf howls following her as she slipped into her sleeping bag and zipped it up. She lay, listening to their wild cries, and to the wind fluttering the leaves of the silver birch, and to the mules and horses shifting and snuffling as they sought sleep.

When Redford came in some time later, she was turned on her side, face toward the wall of the tent, feigning sleep. She heard him unzip his sleeping bag, then zip it up again. She tried to make her breathing mimic the slow cadences of his sleep, wondered if he could hear the beating of her heart. She didn't know how long she lay there, bidding sleep to rescue her, but it must have done, for the next thing she was aware of was waking suddenly. A noise had disturbed her, a sharp, sudden noise that had disappeared before she had a chance to name it, but not before she had time to register fear. She pushed herself upright and glanced down at Redford. His eyes were wide open. Outside, the mules suddenly started braying and the horses snorting.

'What's going on?' Sarah whispered.

'I'm not sure.' Redford began to extricate himself from his sleeping bag. Outside, the animals redoubled their cries of alarm.

'Stay in your tent,' came Dave's voice, from close by. 'Get into the middle of your tent and stay there. *Do it.*' His voice was urgent.

'What's going on?' asked Sarah.

'There's a grizzly out here.'

'Oh shit.'

'It's all right. We'll deal with him – just you two stay put.'

'We're not moving,' said Redford.

'Aren't we?' asked Sarah, eyes blazing with fear.

'These guys know what they're doing,' Redford told her. 'C'mon, let's get closer.'

Sarah shuffled her sleeping bag into the centre of the tent. She could feel Redford's warmth as he moved his next to hers. The mules kept up their braying. In the snatches of silence between their fearful outbursts, Sarah and Redford could hear a calm voice speaking steadily, getting closer to them. Suddenly they heard footsteps, not human ones, heavy and purposeful. The footsteps came to a halt outside their tent. Sarah and Redford held their breath. Sarah felt fear course through her body, every sinew urging her to flee. As if reading her mind, Redford caught hold of her hand and gripped it hard. There was a loud snuffle, and then a great shudder and rending sound as their tent was ripped open. Sarah and Redford looked up and saw sky, and stars, and silhouetted against both, the giant head of a grizzly bear.

Sarah just stared at it, saw the long snout, the dark eyes looking into hers. Jesus Christ, where *were* Dave and Ashley?

'Easy, boy, easy there,' Redford spoke beside her. 'It's all right, you can go on your way now. We mean you no harm, we've got no food for you. Easy, boy, easy now. You can go now, you can go now, it's all right, it's all right.' As Redford kept up his gentle murmur, Sarah tried to tear her eyes away from the bear but couldn't. She saw something flicker in the creature's eyes. It seemed poised for some kind of action. She heard a gun cock; still Redford's voice spoke, calm, sinuous, gentle, and as he spoke, the great black head above him let out a huge vaporous breath, then moved slowly away. They heard the heavy footfalls, retreating now.

Sarah let out her own breath in a low hiss. She gazed up at the gaping hole in the tent.

'Jesus Christ!' she shuddered. 'We could have been killed – been scalped, been swiped into oblivion.'

'But we weren't, were we?' replied Redford, calm still. 'He was just curious, that's all. He meant us no harm.'

'Bloody hell! He eviscerated our tent.' Her voice was shaking.

'He wanted to see what was in here. Must have—'

'You two all right?' Dave's head appeared above them.

'We're fine,' replied Redford. 'Thanks.'

'We're not bloody fine,' said Sarah.

'Don't rightly think any of us is fine,' nodded Dave, 'but we're alive and we're uninjured, and that beautiful creature has gone on his way unharmed. Ash's keeping watch. I'll relieve him later, but the mules're our best early warning system. They'll let us know if he comes back.'

'D'you think he will?' asked Sarah.

'Nope, but it's always possible. Grizzlies are unpredictable beings. You did well,' he went on, looking at Redford. 'Stayed calm, gave him his space.'

Redford grinned. 'I'll never crowd a grizzly, that's for sure.'

'I'm gonna see to the mules,' said Dave. 'You two'd best get some sleep. I'm afraid there's not much we can do about the tent tonight, but you can have ours, if you like.'

'No, that's OK,' said Redford. 'Thanks anyway.'

Sarah lay back in her sleeping bag, the night sky arched above her, scattered with brilliant stars.

'You sure you're all right?' asked Redford.

'I feel a bit shaken up. I can't believe I saw a grizzly, eyeball to eyeball practically, and survived! He was fantastic, wasn't he?'

'Magnificent.'

'You charmed him,' she joked. 'I thought for one moment he was going to get right in here with you.'

Redford laughed. 'So did I.'

'It's hard to believe there's civilisation back there, that we just slipped from one life to the other.'

'What do you prefer?' asked Redford.

'Something wild,' replied Sarah. 'Every time.'

'What about me?' asked John Redford, taking Sarah's hand. 'Am I wild enough for you?'

Sarah left her hand in his. Her skin shimmered under his touch. He began to trace his fingers over hers in feather strokes, so light, so enflaming.

'You are too wild,' she said in a low voice. 'You're like the grizzly.'

'How so?'

'You are without doubt one of the finest specimens on God's earth, but I'd rather see you from a safe distance.'

Redford smiled. 'You mean it's too close here, in this tent, in the wilderness, with the stars gazing down on us, the wind singing in the trees, just the two of us.'

'It's much too close.'

'For a beautiful woman who's an island.'

'I *am* an island. I enjoy being an island. I don't like anyone to come ashore.'

'But your brother has?'

'That's a given – that's like the sun rising. I have no choice.'

'There's always a choice.'

'And you're trouble, John Redford. I didn't choose you.'

'No, you didn't. We were on a collision course.'

'You're saying fate threw us together?'

'Didn't it?'

'Who says I have to dance to fate's tune?'

'Don't we all? You dance toward it or away, but you still dance, babe.'

His fingers caressed her hand. Still their eyes held, while her mind said *run*. As she said this, silently, like a mantra, like a plea to some greater force to save her, she reached out and picked up his free hand. Her fingers traced the brown skin, the fingers she had watched pluck the strings of his guitar. We're all alone, she thought. This is one of those moments in time, complete in itself. A moment in time when everything is perfect, with the wind dancing in the leaves of the silver birch. Just one night, Sarah promised herself. One perfect night, and nothing more.

She could smell the earth below them, she could smell his skin, like fresh bread and honey. She kissed his wrist, she licked the warm flesh, taking his taste into her. They moved slowly, finding each other, finding their fit, lip to lip, breast to chest, his thigh between her legs; freed of clothes, freed of inhibition, they moved against each other, starlight gleaming in their smiling eyes. They laid down the weapons of their own, unending battles, abandoned their solitude and made love all night. They slept as dawn crept over the towering mountains and woke as the sun kissed their tent, lying in one another's arms, breathing the same sweet air.

Chapter Seven

Sarah faced down the matron of the hospital, a friend made during her long hours of vigil. 'Is he ready to leave, or isn't he?' she demanded.

'He can leave, sure he can. Not ideal though. Should by rights have another two weeks, get the casts off. I thought you were cool with that. What's happened, girl? You come marching in here, after visiting hours are finished, and say you want to take your brother back to England on the first flight. We done something to upset you?'

'You've done nothing. Nothing's happened. I just want to go home with Alex. If it's safe for him to travel, I'd like to fly out tomorrow.'

'What's your bro say about this? I know you're picking up the tab, but how does he feel about it?'

'This has got nothing to do with the tab. He's ready to leave.'

The matron gave an almighty sigh. 'All right, girl. Have it your way. Fly away home.'

Now that nothing stood before her and flight, Sarah wavered. But the more she wanted to stay, the more she knew she had to leave. She refused to have her heart broken by this man, and that would surely happen if she stayed. He was not the kind of man that you got over with a yawn and a few bottles of Chardonnay. He had marked her already, with their one perfect night. *Run now, quit while you're ahead.* It wasn't just the trader in her speaking, it was the woman who had gone on alone when those she loved had left her or, more accurately, had been torn from her by violence. Redford must have had thousands of nights like the last one. He would be inured to them, could walk on easily. She was too raw to be spared so lightly. She had no choice but to go.

She signed the closing bill, suppressing a feeling of nausea as she wrote out the figures – seven hundred and forty-three thousand dollars and eighteen cents. Healing really *was* a luxury in this land of opportunity.

'Can I stay in the hospital tonight?' she asked the matron. 'I've got all my luggage in the rental car, parked out back here. It'll make it easier to set off tomorrow morning.'

The woman gave her a probing look. 'You doing a quick split on Spring Creek?'

Sarah laughed. After months in the town, she was familiar with the family mafia. 'If I remember rightly, your cousin's the reception guy. It was him I paid. Ring him, you doubting missy.'

Matron laughed with her. 'All right, girl, I believe you. You can stay. I'll waive the charge, you've paid enough.' She looked thoughtful for a moment. 'You know, this is none of my business, and you can tell me to shut my mouth if you choose to, honey, but it worries me to see a girl like you have to pay up so much money. Can you really manage it?'

Sarah pulled her hair off her face, a nervous habit she'd developed these last months. 'It's practically wiped out my savings, but I've still got a house I own outright, and some rather dubious skills I'll always be able to use to make money. My clients like me. They're loyal.'

'Jesus! What are you, girl – a hooker?'

Sarah chuckled. 'No. A banker.'

The next morning, through a cloudless sky, the plane lifted off, soaring high above the Tetons, carrying Alex and Sarah home, carrying Sarah away from the wilderness, away from John Redford, who sat alone in his ranch, waiting for a woman who had said nothing about leaving him. Sarah gazed out of the window, feeling her fear lift with every mile she put between them. She hadn't sought love. She was not ready for it, didn't want it, would *not* dance to its tune.

Chapter Eight

Carlyle Square, London, eighteen months later

Sarah woke to laughter as the sun sloped in through the window of her four-storey house in Chelsea. She lay in bed for a few moments, luxuriating in its warmth, listening in bliss before slipping from the sheets, pulling on a long T-shirt and padding through to the next room. She gazed down as a fusillade of giggles and smiles greeted her.

'How are you, my sweetheart? Have you any idea how gorgeous you are? Have you?' She bent down and kissed the satin skin, almost swooning with pleasure at his scent, his eyes. There was no passion like this. She reached out her arms, ramrod straight toward him. 'Want to come to Mama, do you?'

Her son giggled again and, mirroring her action, reached out his arms back to her. She picked him up and he used all his baby force to fling himself against her; one little hand grabbed her hair, the other patted her. Sarah spoke against the creamy skin of his neck. 'How are you, my sweetheart? Did you sleep well – did you, my love-child?'

She changed his nappy and took him through to her bedroom where she breastfed him. When he was dressed for the day, she put him back in the cot to play and took a quick shower, stopping the water a few times just to listen out, make sure Georgie was OK. After smothering cream on her face and breasts, she dressed in jeans, jersey and trainers, picked up Georgie and headed down two floors to the basement kitchen. After a prolonged cuddling session, she put the baby down on the newly installed kitchen carpet with a selection of toys, and began to prepare their breakfast.

She loved this room. Sunlight streamed in through the east-facing French windows that opened on to her small and lavishly tended garden. Adjoining the kitchen was the family room, with deep sofas, bookcases, a huge television and a Bang and Olufsen CD player, which had been cutting edge five years ago, when Sarah was still pulling in nearly half a million pounds a year as one of London's top foreign exchange traders. She put Lauryn Hill, one of Georgie's favourites, on to play. She should probably be playing him Mozart or Beethoven, but he seemed more than happy with Lauryn.

Breastfeeding gave her a ravenous appetite, so she cut five huge slabs of organic brown bread, toasted it well, smothered it in butter and a selection of jams and honeys. She cooked up some porridge for Georgie, added a mashed banana, and set it aside to cool slightly. Then she brewed up a large pot of camomile tea, looking longingly at her espresso-maker, neglected by her since she discovered she was pregnant with Georgie and destined to be ignored until she gave up breastfeeding him, which she had no intention of doing for a long time. She gathered up Georgie, deposited him in his high chair, and set to feeding him and herself.

A herd of stampeding wildebeest sounded on the stairs, heralding Alex's appearance. Sarah smiled. That he could walk down the stairs, let alone run, was a small miracle.

Her brother appeared with a swirl of energy and well-being. 'Hi, Sare.' He blew her a kiss, and headed for Georgie. 'How are you, you little rascal? Did you give your mother a good sleep?'

'Not bad,' replied Sarah. 'Up just once last night. No need for you to get up now, with us larks.' The clock on the wall showed six-thirty. Alex was loath to appear before nine in London.

'I smelt toast, didn't I,' he said with a grin. Sarah felt both warmed and saddened by his lie. He was off in a week, for his first expedition since the accident, and she knew he was trying to spend as much waking time with her and Georgie as possible before he left.

He was a wonderful uncle, more like a father really. He would have been up half the night with Georgie if Sarah had let him. She did in the early, early days, when the exhaustion was at its most brutal, but after that she insisted on doing it herself. She refused anything that resembled a crutch. She had to go on as circumstances dictated, as a single mother. But Alex had done everything he could. He had driven her to hospital when her contractions started, and he and their beloved Uncle Jacob were the first people outside the medical staff to see Georgie. Both had fallen passionately in love with him. Her baby was lucky, Sarah told herself. He had two besotted uncles, and that surely made up for the lack of a father. Her thoughts turned involuntarily, as they so often did, to Redford. Where was he? What was he doing? Did some strange stirring ever waken his consciousness to the existence of someone who shared half his blood, half his genes? Sarah felt the old yearning, that to her discomfort had never gone, waned slightly, but still burned in her.

After polishing off breakfast, Alex headed for Sarah's study, spread with his route maps and scribbled notes for his next trek in Peru. For Sarah and Georgie, it was walktime. Sarah got her baby ready, put on his hat, and together they headed out in the summer sunshine. Sarah pushed the pram through streets both familiar and fresh. She and Alex had only just returned to London, after nine months in the country. They had come back briefly when she gave birth to Georgie at St Mary's Hospital, but after that, they returned to the cottage she was renting deep in the Dorset countryside, where their Uncle Jacob was a frequent and longstaying visitor. Sarah was excited to be back, yet nervous, too. She glanced around. Sooner or later, she would bump into someone she knew, and her secret would be out. So far only Alex, Jacob, and her cleaning lady and mother of five, Mrs V, knew of Georgie's existence. She gazed down at the child, stopping impulsively to bestow kisses on him. He smiled and squirmed and she laughed with joy.

'You are my little secret, aren't you, my love-child? I suppose I'll have to share you with the world one day soon, but just for now, it's the two of us, no one else.' Georgie gurgled, as if he understood completely and was delighted with the prospect.

Sarah wheeled the pram proudly, negotiating the streets and traffic until they reached the haven of Battersea Park. There she walked for an hour in the warm sun, before heading home as Georgie's lunch beckoned. Alex had gone off for his workout when they returned. He exercised six days a week, relentlessly trying to regain his fitness and strength. Sarah knew he was doing well, but she knew too that he kept the pain hidden. Only the odd grimace that escaped before he could tame it betrayed his continued suffering. The doctors said he was 80 per cent recovered. Alex maintained he was ready to trek the high mountains again. The doctors had cautiously given their assent, although they warned that another fall on his shattered leg, still held together by pins, and he might have to kiss goodbye to trekking for ever. But Alex would always live life to the full. Not for him the slow seepage of compromise. Like his sister, if risk stood between him and what he wanted, he simply leapt.

Sarah picked up one of his discarded jerseys, folded it and put it on the dresser. She settled herself in the kitchen armchair, and took Georgie to her breast for his after-lunch feed. She had just put him to bed for a nap when the doorbell went.

'Shit, who's this?' she whispered to herself, creeping from the room so as not to wake Georgie. She headed swiftly down the stairs before they could ring again, and pulled open the door.

'Eva Cunningham!' she exclaimed.

'Bad time?'

Sarah shook herself. 'What? Yes – no, sorry.' She pulled her hair off her face. 'I'm just a bit flustered seeing you. I thought you were somewhere in the South Pacific.'

'Sarah Jensen flustered? Now *that*'s a novelty,' said Eva in her icy purr. 'I was in the South Pacific – we got home a week ago. Look, am I going to tell you my life story here on your doorstep, or are you going to invite me in?'

Sarah grinned, looking a bit more like her old self. 'I'll keep you out here all day if it means getting your life story.'

Eva grinned back. 'Yeah, dream on, babe.' She came inside and headed towards the stairs, making for the kitchen, their usual haunt.

'No, it's a real mess down there,' Sarah said hurriedly. 'Let's stay up here.'

Eva gave her a probing look but said nothing.

'What'll you have?' asked Sarah. 'It's too early for champagne to celebrate your return.'

Eva narrowed her eyes. 'Has your mind gone soft? I don't drink, remember?'

'Ah yes.' Eva Cunningham was an ex-heroin addict, that much she had told Sarah.

'Coffee then?'

'That'd be great, but don't let me stop *you* drinking.'

'Don't worry, I'm not drinking either.'

'Now that really does surprise me. What's going on? Drying out?'

'I never drank that heavily, Eva,' replied Sarah testily. 'I'm just taking a break. Right – let me get your coffee,' she said in a rush, giving Eva no time for questions. She headed downstairs to the kitchen, leaving her friend ensconced in the toy-free drawing room on the ground floor. A few minutes later, she returned with coffee for Eva, camomile tea for herself.

Eva studied the camomile suspiciously. 'You drinking horse pee?'

'Very droll.'

'So what's up? You look different.'

'Tell me about your trip,' said Sarah, fingers snaking into her pocket to check the baby listener was still on. 'I want to hear about the South Pacific. How could you possibly bear to leave it?'

'Well,' Eva said wryly, 'Andrew gave up his job, followed me out there, and we lived there on and off for two years. He was beginning to go stir crazy, so it was only fair I go his way now. We've come back to start up an investigations firm – corporate checks, individual checks – you know the kind of thing.'

'The same stuff you and I used to do for Kroll?'

'Exactly. You still working for them?'

'Uh, uh.' Sarah shook her head. 'Did it for a year, but I've never been the corporate type. I set up on my own, freelance, working for Goldsteins mainly, but I've had a sabbatical for a while now.'

'So what're you doing? How do you pay the metaphorical rent?'

Before Sarah could answer, sleepy cries rose from the baby listener in her jeans pocket. Eva's eyes opened wide.

'Excuse me, but I think your jeans are crying.'

Sarah got to her feet, face bare of concealment. She went upstairs to Georgie, picked him up and hugged him to her. She carried him downstairs. Eva was standing when she entered.

'Bloody nora, Sarah. You're a mother.'

Sarah grinned.

'Who is this little person?' asked Eva softly.

Sarah turned sideways on so that Georgie and Eva could see eye to eye. 'This is Georgie. Georgie, this is Eva.'

'Jesus, Sarah. I'm not much of a maternal type as you know, but he's *beautiful*.'

Her friend beamed. 'He is, isn't he? The most beautiful thing I ever saw. He's the love of my life, the most precious thing on earth.'

'Wow, you've got it bad,' Eva commented. 'I'd never have thought it of you, of all people.'

Sarah sat down with Georgie in her lap. 'I've no choice in the matter. I really would die for him. You hear people saying that and you think, how over the top, but it's true. Let me tell you, maternal protectiveness is the most powerful force on the planet.'

'I can well believe it,' said Eva, sitting down opposite them. 'So, where's his father? I didn't know you'd settled down.'

'I haven't.'

'Ah. We *have* got a lot of catching up to do.'

'There's not much to tell.'

'What? You got pregnant and he left you?'

'No. I left him before I even knew I was pregnant.'

'Did you tell him after?'

Sarah shook her head.

'So who does know?'

'Hardly anyone.'

'That explains all the secrecy when I arrived. I thought you had a lover downstairs.'

Sarah grinned. 'I haven't had a lover for so long, I've almost forgotten what it feels like.'

'It feels pretty good, I have to say.'

'Huh, don't worry, it's a long way from my current list of fantasies. If it's a choice between sleep and sex, sleep'll win every time.'

'Can I ask you a question?' said Eva gently.

'What?' asked Sarah warily.

'Well, when you found out you were pregnant, you had a career, you had a life, you seemed to have it all worked out. Against that, it's still hard to have a child alone, even post millennium, especially for women like us – you know, supposed careerwomen. What made you go ahead and have your baby?'

Sarah kissed her son's downy head and hugged him closer. 'What can I say? I followed my heart, not my head. I was terrified when I found out I was pregnant, absolutely petrified, but I made myself slow down, I gave myself time to feel through the terror, and you know, it was as if this little being was speaking to me. I felt his presence, he was living inside me and

I knew I had to give him a chance of life. And after what happened to my own family, so much death . . . the chance to start a family of my own – how could I not go with that? But there was more to it than that. I fell in love with him even then, when he was a tiny foetus, too small for the eye to see.'

Eva nodded. 'Has it been hard?'

Tears came spontaneously to Sarah's eyes. 'The hardest thing I've ever done. Let me tell you, getting up three times a night to breastfeed, and six times a night to comfort him is a million times harder than doing all-nighters at the office. The exhaustion is something you wouldn't believe, and you cannot get up and walk away. This little thing depends on you absolutely and utterly for life.'

'That would get me, the total responsibility.'

'One hundred per cent responsibility. For ever. It still terrifies me. I always thought, if I ever had a child, that it would be on my terms, that I would be able to control the experience, compartmentalise being a mother, keep the old me going, but it's impossible. You're made anew. Maybe it's like a religious conversion, only I suspect it's infinitely more powerful. When your child is born, you're born again too. There's no going back to the old life.'

'Do you hanker for it, ever?'

'Sometimes.'

'Would you rewrite history if you could? Never have become pregnant in the first place?'

Sarah shook her head vehemently. 'I wouldn't change a thing. There is nothing like the look of love in his little eyes, when I walk into his room and he sees my face; there is nothing like holding him, and feeding him, and the moment when he was born and I was lying there and they handed him to me . . . well, words can't describe it. We wait all our lives for something bigger than us to happen, to be truly transported, to see magic, to witness a miracle. This is the biggest one of them all. I'll never forget it.' She brushed her lips over Georgie's face. 'Nothing will ever compare.'

Eva fell silent. This was a language she couldn't speak, but she could see its power. The strength of Sarah's love for her child moved her almost to tears. She wondered if she would ever feel a love like that.

'You're very lucky,' she said slowly. Sarah gave her a radiant smile, overjoyed that Eva had seen what she felt, what life was for her now.

'I'm as lucky as it's possible to be.'

'One more question,' said Eva. 'How come you got pregnant? I mean, you're not exactly careless.'

'I was on the pill,' said Sarah. 'I thought it was safe. But I'd had a bit of a gippy tummy. Forgot about it at the time. I think the pill must have gone straight through me before doing its job.'

'Aha. Last question.'

Sarah guessed what it might be, felt the dread at its coming.

'Am I allowed to ask who his father is?'

Sarah smiled and shook her head.

'Just tell me what he's like then.'

Sarah sighed. 'He's amazing – the most charismatic, totally sexy, gorgeous man I ever clapped eyes on.'

'So why walk out on him?'

'For all those reasons. I told myself I wasn't going to be a slave to love.' Sarah laughed. 'And look at me now.'

'Do you think you'll ever see him again?' asked Eva.

Sarah shook her head. 'I doubt it. Our paths crossed once in a lifetime. It would be too much to expect them to cross again.'

Chapter Nine

The telephone rang the moment Eva had left. Sarah rushed in and picked it up, Georgie cradled in one arm.

'Sarah, James Savage.'

'Gosh, hi James, how are you?'

Georgie gurgled.

'What was that?' asked Savage.

'The radio,' said Sarah. 'Hang on a sec, let me go and turn it off.' She took Georgie next door, put him on the floor and placated his immediate outburst of tears with his favourite toy, a yellow bunny. She hurried back to the phone. 'Sorry, James.'

'Hm. Never knew it took so long to turn off a radio.'

'Well I'm here now.'

'So you are, and sharper than ever, it would seem. You still interested in working? I know you said your sabbatical should be over around now. Had a nice time?'

'Like you wouldn't believe.'

'Ah, that's the life, young, free and single.'

Sarah stifled a yawn. 'Yeah, tell me about it.'

'So, would you like some work?'

Jesus. Sarah felt her whole body gripped with panic. She wasn't ready to work, to enter that world again. It was so alien to her now. What had once been her domain was now frighteningly inaccessible. She didn't want to leave Georgie. She didn't want to take on a nanny and hand him over, but she had known that this moment would have to come, sooner or later. She needed the money. It was as simple as that. After bailing Alex out she was hard up anyway, but now she had a child to support. Like millions of women before her, she had no choice but to go back to work. However, she was lucky. Her job was lucrative. She could work for a few months then take time off. She took a deep breath and fixed her resolve.

'All right. I'll do it.'

'Don't you want to know what it is?' asked Savage, surprised.

'Just tell me where to be and when.' What difference did it make? Work was work. It paid, that was the point now. She didn't have the luxury to choose what was interesting, what was palatable, to reject anything she didn't fancy.

'My office. Tomorrow at eleven.'

How quickly and disconcertingly our outlook can change, reflected Sarah. Work had always been a kind of passion for her, loved and hated, a necessary therapy, and a distraction. Now it was a way to pay the bills, and no more. She had always supported Alex. He tried to earn money. He wrote the odd article on mountaineering, but his payment would hardly buy him a pair of new boots. He was a dreamer, and a born climber and explorer, and Sarah had always been happy to finance his choices, but now she had Georgie too. The mountain of her future financial responsibilities towered above her. She didn't need the distraction that work used to provide. She wanted to be home with Georgie. She had a reason to exist now; she didn't need to justify her existence by competing in the workplace. She had been one of the best FX traders in the City, had earned the money to prove it, and while she was still proud of her achievements, the old mind-set that went with them was now a foreign language to her.

She wondered what assignment Savage had lined up for her – trading or private investigation work? Would she be able to do either any more with her mushy brain and lack of zeal? She had learned her PI tricks at Kroll, with Eva Cunningham as her mentor. Eva had worked for seven years as an undercover agent for MI6, her cover going so deep that she had started to take heroin to substantiate it, before quickly becoming hooked. Her years of addiction were now well behind her, as were her days at MI6, but she had used what she had learned to teach Sarah a whole battery of tricks that you'd never find on any sanitised private investigator's course. Sarah tried in vain to summon any of them to memory, wondered how the hell she was going to con Savage.

The soft closing of the door stirred her. Georgie looked up with interest from his nest of cushions on the floor as Alex breezed in with sweaty hair plastered to his head.

'Hi there.' He picked up Georgie and cuddled his nephew boisterously.

'Am I knackered. Think I'll have a shower and a lie-down.' He rested his eyes on Sarah and his lighthearted smile faded. 'What's up?'

Sarah pulled her hair back off her face and held it in her fist. 'James Savage just called. He wants me to go into Goldsteins tomorrow. Got some kind of job for me.'

'Ah.' Understanding flooded Alex's face.

'I'm not ready yet,' said Sarah, hunching her shoulders. 'I'm still breastfeeding. I've never been away from Georgie for more than a couple of hours. How'm I going to cope with some bloody meeting in the City? How's Georgie going to cope? What am I going to say? I've scarcely spoken about anything more taxing than which brand of nappies to buy for the past eight months.'

Alex smiled. 'You're not that bad.'

'Not far off, though. And who's going to look after Georgie? You have to go to the gym.'

'I could miss it for one day, for goodness sake.'

Sarah shook her head. 'Maybe I'll ring Jacob,' she said.

'You know he'd be delighted to help out,' said Alex.

Sarah smiled. Georgie and Jacob loved each other to bits. 'Yeah. I'll give him a call. It's probably just a one-off anyway. When Savage catches on to my atrophied brain he's bound to send me packing before you can say cut your losses.'

Chapter Ten

Sarah awoke the next morning gripped by panic. What would she wear? She was still twenty pounds over her normal weight. What would she say? Her mind really had turned to porridge; she'd become forgetful about anything that did not revolve around Georgie, and completely uninterested in anything other than him. She had no idea what was going on in the world at large, let alone in the markets. She didn't watch the news, didn't read the newspapers, she didn't read anything!

In the old days, she could have bluffed her way, but her confidence had flown, she wasn't sure where, why or how, just that it had gone. She began to pace around and chant, 'You're bright, you're successful, you have a Cambridge degree, you've earned millions of pounds in your life, you've tangled with some seriously dodgy characters and outsmarted them, *you can do anything*.' It didn't work. She lacked even the ability to convince herself.

When Jacob arrived at nine, Sarah was still in her nightgown, hair and eyes wild. Georgie picked up his mother's panic and cried heartily.

Sarah kissed Jacob as he started to gurgle at the baby. 'Hello, Georgie. Hello there! Helloooo, Georgie.' He gave him huge smiles, soon returned by Georgie, who bestowed his ultimate approval by straining away from Sarah toward his great-uncle.

'Come to your Uncle Jacob, come on then.'

Sarah handed him over. Jacob hugged Georgie to him, speaking over his shoulder to Sarah. 'You go and get yourself ready, sweetie.'

His niece shifted from one foot to another. 'I don't think I can do this. I can't go back. It's too soon – I'm not ready. I don't want to go, Jacob. Why should I go? It's not fair, it's not—'

'Steady there, sweetie, easy now. You'll go and you'll be fine. You've faced much bigger challenges than this in your time.'

'Have I? I can't remember. Anyway, that was the old me, she's gone.'

'No, she hasn't. She's always there, just waiting for an outing. Give her a chance. Go to that meeting and sock it to them. Look, always remember my trick. If ever I was nervous, feeling a bit intimidated, I'd always imagine whoever was making me feel like that was naked, on the loo.'

Sarah burst out laughing.

'It works,' her uncle said. 'Try it.'

The trio of Jacob looking resolute, Alex sleepy still in his pyjamas, and Georgie looking puzzled waved Sarah off. She sat frozen in the back of a black cab, studying the changing nature of the streets as they took the interminable journey to the City. If she looked hard enough at the suited bodies scurrying to and fro, perhaps she'd be able to pick up a few of her old tricks as if by osmosis.

They were all there waiting for her, faces turned towards her, watching her walk into their midst. At the head of the table sat James Savage, chief executive of Goldsteins, and the man responsible for recruiting her. He leaned back, arms folded behind his head of silver hair, resplendent in a razor-sharp navy pin-striped suit. His eyes were narrowed. He smiled, not with affection, but with pleasure. He enjoyed Sarah; she produced results but, more than that, he savoured her dangerous unpredictability. He knew of her reputation. The Governor of the Bank of England had recommended her to him, but with the caveat that she was the wildest of wild cards. Savage, who fancied himself a renegade beneath the pinstripes, felt an immediate affinity. Felt more than that, if he was honest.

He eyed her quickly. She had put on weight, was wearing a baggy pair of trousers and a loose tunic top with clumpy flat shoes. Her skin was in high colour, her cheeks glowing. She looked incredibly voluptuous, the curve of her breasts all too visible through the thin fabric of her tunic. Sarah Jensen was a walking incitement to lust. Today she seemed a little tired, preoccupied, but she was smiling determinedly. How she kept that lightness, that touch of grace, Savage couldn't fathom. He knew only part of her story, and that bit alone would have clouded the sunniest of souls. He knew she had been orphaned as a child, that the body count had risen around her during her short time at InterContinental Bank, that she had been in grave peril, but had somehow walked from it, only to flee to the Himalayas. The shadows must hang long over her, but here she was, apparently so gloriously, determinedly carefree. He could only guess at the courage and the faith in life that took. The only hint of the tragedies she had suffered, the battles she had fought, showed in the lines around her eyes, which were too deep for one so young. She couldn't have been more than thirty. He had seen the odd flash of her sorrow, but only during those rare moments when she left herself unguarded.

Dick Breden, a private investigator used by Savage for broader investigations than Sarah conducted, welcomed her with a somewhat ambivalent smile. He tended to view Sarah as a rival, but could never quite summon the full forces of his competitive spirit to use against her. On the one hand, Goldsteins' business was too valuable to risk losing, but on the other, his work and Sarah's was more complementary than competitive. Besides, her blithe, devil-may-care attitude tended to diffuse any rivalry. He knew she could get up and walk away at any time, that she treated most things as a game. For that reason, he always considered her the lightweight to his heavyweight, albeit one who Savage clearly believed could punch significantly above her weight.

Breden got to his feet, elegantly uncoiling, and stood to attention with a soldier's formality. Ten years after leaving the army, he still had a lean, muscled body.

Zaha Zamaroh, the head of the trading floor, *summa cum laude*, Harvard, brain like a mainframe computer, body of a Rubens nude, stayed in her seat, legs crossed, black hosiery gleaming. She unashamedly looked Sarah up and down, checking out the wardrobe and the woman, as she did every time they met, looking for a chink, and, judging by her triumphant look, finding it. Zamaroh was perfectly turned out as always; her outrageously curvaceous body swathed in a tangerine-coloured Chanel suit, her raven hair fluid and shiny as a slick of oil. Zamaroh was a predator, a big, glossy black panther, sinuous, brilliant and powerful. To her, Sarah was sport, good sport because she enjoyed a fight and fought well.

You bunch of predators, thought Sarah.

Each one of them had something to hide, she could see it in their eyes. Savage was too confident, too slick. No one reached his position and stayed there without accumulating secrets and misdeeds. His defence was the perfectly cut suit, the clipped delivery, shorn of politeness, to demonstrate his power and superior status; public-school vowels corrupted by the occasional American intonation and jargon, just to show he was of the zeitgeist; a hardass who worked for his money, but still expected a gong at the end of it.

Savage loathed the press, more than was fashionable or reasonable. As a result the press pursued Goldsteins with a more than average ferocity. The year before, *The Word* had published a story written by an aggressively anti-City journalist called Roddy Clark, alleging financial shenanigans at Goldsteins. Four weeks later, the paper had published a retraction and paid what they admitted were substantial damages, but, strangely enough, none of the traders implicated in the scandal worked for Goldsteins any more. In fact, they had left the City altogether. Savage had survived, however, as had Zaha Zamaroh, who was the suspect traders' boss. She had grown more brittle though, thought Sarah, almost as if she herself had suffered a near-miss. She seemed more confrontational, as if her sense of injustice, of rage against the City and the world was stronger than ever. Sarah found her fascinating. This woman had shattered the glass ceiling, but the shards still stuck to her and Sarah was careful not to get too close.

As for Breden, he was the repository of other people's secrets, and who knew how many trades he had made to obtain those secrets? The more you know, the more you can sell. Goldsteins was his major client, but there was something of the mercenary about him. The habitual detachment, the flashy gold watch, the Aston Martin. He loved money more than was healthy, thought Sarah.

But then who was she to judge any of them?

Chapter Eleven

They sat around a polished board table, while a secretary poured coffee from a silver pot. Savage drained his espresso then clinked the cup back in its saucer. The telephone beside him gave a chirp. He picked up the receiver and listened impassively. 'Show him in.'

Sarah drank her mineral water, looking up as Evangeline, Savage's secretary, entered, eyes shining. Sarah was holding her glass high, draining the liquid as the father of her child walked into the room.

She wanted to choke. She struggled to keep the water in her mouth, finally managed to swallow it with a gulp. *Keep calm, keep calm. You won't die, this isn't life, this isn't death. Breathe, girl, deep, slowly. Calm down, don't blow this, you will* not *blow this.* She could feel her breasts leaking milk into the cottonwool pads with which she'd lined her bra, just in case, but at this rate, the whole of her top would soon be sopping. Oh God, not even her body was subject to her control. She searched for a sliver of ice in her soul, some steely self-control, then gave up and tried Jacob's trick, imagining everyone naked and on the loo. The effort of holding hysterical giggles at bay sobered her, gave her just enough self-possession to gaze ahead levelly, as if she had never met this man, never made the sweetest, most passionate love with him, never created life with him. Oh no, she shouldn't have thought that way. Georgie sat before her, in full adult beauty. Her son's face was writ so large and clear in John Redford's that it was almost too much to bear.

She could hear Savage going ahead with the introductions. 'This is Zaha Zamaroh, she's head of the trading floor, and this is Dick Breden, who'll be helping her.'

Redford took a seat, face cold, as if he too were in shock. He did not shake hands with anyone, just glanced in their direction as they were introduced.

'And this is Sarah Jensen, another trader who's also on the team,' Savage was saying. When Redford turned to her, it seemed to Sarah that he gave her just a glimpse of emotions battened down; too many, coming too fast to say what they were. In return she gave him the curtest nod. Redford hardened his eyes again, as if to say, *So this is the way it will be*. He spoke for the first time.

'Hello, Sarah. It's a pleasure.'

She nodded, unable to speak. She kept her glass in front of her face, as if cooling her burning cheeks.

Evangeline withdrew, reluctantly. Sarah glanced round the room. Savage seemed uncharacteristically unsure of himself. Zamaroh was trying hard to look blasé, and Breden, despite his English understatement, was looking mildly interested.

'You're on time, and you're alone,' said Savage, summoning a droll smile.

'And why shouldn't I be? Look, can we cut this rock star shit?' Redford said irritably. 'I'm a normal businessman, like the rest of your clients. My product happens to have a lot of baggage with it, but only in people's minds. Drop the baggage, life gets simpler.'

'Is your music just a product to you?' asked Zamaroh with surprise.

'Of course it's not,' replied Redford with quick disdain. 'Music's the biggest part of my life, but that doesn't make me some airhead artist who can't also see it from a business perspective. I can play that game too.'

'But not when you sit down to write your songs?' continued Zamaroh.

'No, not then,' he admitted. 'I couldn't give a damn at that point about the business, about how many discs I'm gonna sell. All I care about then is what I'm trying to say, getting across the emotion that I'm feeling, taking people with me.'

Like a snake charmer, thought Sarah, or the Pied Piper, leading the children away. It was a nasty image that came unbidden, and she rebuked herself as she looked into the features of Georgie's father. As his passion lit his face, he showed just a flash of the vulnerability underneath.

'Can we get you a coffee?' asked Sarah, relieved and delighted to have found her voice, but frightened too. She felt as if she were operating outside herself, outside of self-control, social boundaries and convention. It didn't help that the whole meeting had a weird air, as Zamaroh strayed from the balance sheet to philosophy.

Redford seemed surprised by Sarah's voice, and her question, and she wondered for one horrible moment if she had asked him something else altogether.

'Yes, of course. Do excuse my manners,' Savage was saying, to Sarah's vast relief. 'Coffee, tea, mineral water?' He gave a rakish grin. 'Whisky, gin, vodka, whatever.'

'A mineral water would be great. Still, room temperature, no ice, slice of lemon.'

Savage blinked, pushed a button on an ornamental cockerel and Fred the butler appeared, resplendent in a tailcoat. He took their orders, pausing momentarily over Redford's, then disappeared like a wraith, thick soles moving silently on the plush carpet.

Everything in this room whispers *money, position, privilege*, thought Sarah. Savage, Zamaroh and Breden, and she herself, she supposed, all looked refined, tempered. The air-conditioned office with its hermetically sealed double glazing seemed a million miles away from the bloody business of making money, from the dreams, sacrifices, the victories and the losses that lay behind every fortune. Perhaps that was why people thought the money-makers in the City never deserved their fat rewards. The pin-striped elegance and refinements of butlers were a disguise, a relic of the days when making money was like illicit sex, something hidden, conducted behind locked doors. Yet, just a few floors down, the trading floor thrashed, writhed and sweated cash.

'Would you like to see something?' Sarah found herself asking Redford. 'See what we're really about here?'

Redford's eyes widened.

'The trading floor,' she explained. 'The guts of this place. You want to see the deals being cut, money being made and lost, emotions running riot . . .?'

'Yeah. I'd like that,' answered Redford, eyes lingering on Sarah's.

Savage looked on with worry; Zamaroh glared. Sarah had just publicly smashed the unwritten rule. Don't show clients the abattoir, where they are the carcasses on which the traders feed. Zamaroh didn't see in Redford what Sarah knew was there – the raw ambition, burning still in a man supposedly at the peak of his profession. She could see that the plush carpeting and butler switched him off, that the only way they would win him as a client would be to show him that they too could be raw, that they too were hungry, even though they appeared fat and self-satisfied.

Leaving the silent sepulchre of the boardroom, they all headed for the lift. Redford waited for Sarah and Zamaroh to enter first. He stood alongside Savage, with his back to Sarah as they cruised down three floors. Redford wore black wool trousers and a tight-fitting fine wool jersey. Sarah could see the cleft of his backbone, and the musculature that swelled to either side. She remembered tracing those contours with her fingers, then with her tongue. She recalled the smell of him, the taste of him. The doors to the lift drifted open and Savage strode out. Redford stood back, allowing Zamaroh and Sarah to exit before him. Sarah kept her eyes straight ahead and moved past him, so close she could almost touch him. She walked towards the entrance to the trading floor, conscious of his eyes on her.

Zamaroh waved her electronic pass at the doors to the trading room; at her command, they opened. The roar was the first thing to hit them, the raised voices of five hundred traders, the hiss of their terminals, the electronic beeping of phones, the shouts of anger, of triumph. Zamaroh led them deeper into the room. Snatches of conversations vied with each other:

'I'll take a ton at forty-nine twenty.' 'You bastard, you screwed me on the Entox deal. I'd soon as trust you as fuck you.' 'Yeeeeeaaaas! I'm ten miles up and cruising. Am I the greatest or what?' 'Shit, the whole fuckin' thing's going south so fast I got the bends.' 'Give it to me baby, the whole nine yards!'

Redford turned to Sarah. 'This is where you worked?'

'For seven long years,' she answered. She saw the question in his eyes. 'With a few breaks here and there.'

'And are you good?'

'What do you think?' She saw the amusement flare in his eyes before he quickly pushed it down and resumed his poker face.

Back in the boardroom, Redford took the initiative.

'So,' he said, 'securitisation. Tell me how it works.'

'First of all,' said Zamaroh, 'tell us exactly what you want. How did you come to hear of Goldsteins?'

Sarah and Redford looked at each other. She feared in just that one moment that everything would be detected in the gaze which passed between them.

'I'll take over here,' rasped a voice from the doorway, claiming everyone's instant attention. A man in his early fifties stood leaning against the door jamb, with one hip thrust forward, in a pose half casual, half aggressive. The man was lean, jeans-clad, with a leather jacket slung over his shoulder. He had short, thick grey hair which covered only the sides of his head; the centre was a shiny desert. His nose was long and full, his lips thick. His eyelids were heavy, giving him a jaded air. It was the man on the runaway horse, restored now, it would seem, to his habitual arrogance. Sarah blessed his timing, cursed his arrival. Now her masquerade *would* be blown.

'Can I help you?' Savage got to his feet.

'I'm Strone Cawdor, John Redford's manager,' he announced with a self-congratulatory smirk. Sarah wondered briefly and unworthily whether saving him had really been such a good idea. Evangeline stood mute beside him.

'You're late,' said Savage.

Cawdor looked surprised. 'Late?' he asked, as if the concept were either novel or irrelevant. 'Well, I'm here now, aren't I? So let's get started. As I said, I'll take over from here.'

Sarah checked Redford to see how he was taking this. The rock star was watching Cawdor with patience and a tinge of amusement.

Savage performed the introductions with steely correctness. Cawdor nodded in return. When it came to Sarah's turn, she expected some reaction, a show of acknowledgement perhaps, but it seemed that Cawdor didn't recognise her. Admittedly it had been a year and a half ago; when it happened, he had been in shock, she had worn a cowboy hat over a brown dusty face, she had been a stone and a half lighter, and she had been part of an episode that he probably tried hard to forget. An obvious control freak, out of control. Not one of his finer moments. So she was the banker, an anonymous suit, and that was just fine by her. She let out a silent sigh of relief.

'We've checked your credentials,' stated Cawdor, taking a seat beside his star, 'and so far, you've got a good rep.'

Zamaroh snorted. Cawdor turned to stare at her. Zamaroh stared him out. 'You're part of a beauty parade,' continued Cawdor with relish, clearly enjoying the City term and the concept. 'We'll be speaking to other banks as well as yourselves, so,' he took off his gold watch and put it on the table, 'tell me why we should come to Goldsteins.'

Before any of the Goldsteins team could react to his ticking time bomb, Redford spoke.

'We've come,' he said, staring at Sarah.

'Say again?' demanded Cawdor.

'Goldsteins has my business,' Redford said evenly.

'You've just walked in the fucking door.'

Savage flinched.

Redford shrugged and said nothing more. As an elegant display of who held the power, it was flawless.

Zamaroh grinned. Sarah watched, struggling to remain impassive. Breden looked bored, a guise which Sarah knew concealed deep interest.

Cawdor took a deep breath. He turned from Redford as if the rock star did not exist. 'Right. Got any coffee?'

'How would you like it?' asked Savage crisply.

'As it comes from the bean. Black as the ace of spades.'

Savage buzzed his ornamental cockerel. Fred arrived seconds later, unable to resist stealing covert glances at Redford. The gossip in the kitchens, Sarah knew, would be rife.

Cawdor drained his coffee and seemed to regain his composure. 'Right then. This is the way it goes. Bowie does it. Iron Maiden does it.'

His accent puzzled Sarah. He was American, but had a strange Mid-Atlantic inflection, like a Brit trying to be American. Iron became *Iaarn*, Maiden was *Mayden*. Sarah reckoned he modelled his voice on Mick Jagger. Not that she'd ever met Jagger, but she'd heard him being interviewed.

'Securitisation is where it's at. We got twenty platinum albums – that means each has sold in excess of one million copies,' he added with a patronising smile. 'But each album has sold considerably more than one mill. Total album sales are some way north of one hundred million. John's had seven consecutive number one albums in the States, four of them simultaneously with the UK. It's been calculated that he accounts for three per cent of all the singles, albums and tapes sold annually throughout the whole world. He is *it*. He's at the very apex of his profession and poised to stay there for years. We want the benefit of all that now, up front. An asset working hard for us, a bond issue, securitisation, the whole works.'

He sat back, his City vocabulary exhausted. Interesting, thought Sarah. He never once mentioned the word *money*, the one thing that drove this whole meeting. His aggression was poor camouflage. Sarah guessed that in his usual dealings with the record company, with lawyers and accountants, he was used to being in control, being the one with the power, but if there was to be a successful deal here, it would be on Goldsteins' terms.

Savage waited until the silence became uncomfortable before he spoke. 'Let us tell you both a little about the process, about what we could do for you, and about what we would need from you. Then we'll see if we're compatible.' He gave Cawdor a brief, cold smile.

Cawdor laughed in disbelief. 'Compatible?' he said with derision. 'What are you – an escort agency? It's not like we're gonna go to bed together.'

Redford glanced at Sarah. They held one another's eyes as Savage responded.

'On the contrary,' said the chief executive, 'in financial terms, that is *exactly* what we are going to do. If we decide to do business together, we become partners, very close partners. You rub off on us, we rub off on you. We need to find out as much as we can about each other now, take a view on whether or not it will work. For both our sakes,' said Savage emphatically as Cawdor tried to interrupt. 'I don't really think you would want to appoint a bank who took on clients without undertaking a thorough review, would you? That would hardly be in your client's best interests, would it now?'

Redford took his eyes off Sarah. 'Would you mind,' he asked Savage softly, 'if we just got on with it? Tell us what you propose, ask us what you need. We'll try to help.' He flicked a glance at Cawdor.

'May I?' asked Zamaroh. Savage gave the faintest nod.

'What we would do is this. Collect all the data on your sales since you first started out, and run projections on likely sales on the existing back catalogue over the next seven to ten years. We would need to know what percentage of cover price goes to your record company, what to wholesalers and retailers, and what to you. What we have to play with is the money that goes to you. That's our starting point. We work out from that what level of interest burden your income could support, at a range of different interest rates, then we calculate from that the principal sum you could raise, on the different rate assumptions. As part of that process we have to decide how you would repay the principal sum in, say, ten years. You could pay off a portion each year, or do it in a bullet in year ten. To see what would work best, we'd have to take a view on the quality of your earnings, how volatile they have been, how volatile they could be.' Zamaroh paused for a while. 'This is where it becomes sensitive. We have to be as sure as we can be that you will do nothing over the period of the bond issue to harm your reputation and your earnings.'

'Like what?' asked Redford.

'Oh, I don't know,' said Zamaroh evasively.

'Any crimes which might outrage the record-buying public,' filled in Sarah, turning to Redford. '*Your* record-buying public, to be precise. I'm not putting a value judgement on this,' she continued, 'and don't dream of quoting me outside this room because I'd deny it, but drugs wouldn't be a big issue, if they were just for personal use and didn't get in the way of songwriting and performing. The same goes for alcohol, but crimes against the person, that's a different matter. Figure it out for yourselves. Look at what happened to Michael Jackson's sales after the allegations against him.'

'Are you suggesting—' Cawdor began to bluster.

'Oh, drop the act and do us all a favour,' snapped Sarah. 'I'm not suggesting anything of the sort. I'm trying to explain something as explicitly as I can. None of us is here to impugn your client, so why don't you stop acting like a rabid Rottweiler. I know you're trying to do your job, but it's just getting in the way here.' Redford watched Sarah, patently trying to conceal his smile. Cawdor stared long and hard at her, his look of outrage fading gradually.

'You are one hell of a piece of work,' he said to Sarah. He seemed to ponder something for a while before turning his attention back to Zamaroh. 'All right,' he said more calmly, 'it just so happens that my client is totally above board, but why get uptight about all this crap?'

'Let's say something *did* happen that made the public stop buying his records,' replied Zamaroh. 'There wouldn't be enough income to repay the bond holders, and the chance of raising more money through another bond issue or equity issue would be zero. You'd be in default, and if you had undertaken a personal guarantee of any or all the proceeds of the bond issue, something I wouldn't recommend by the way, you could end up bankrupt.'

'It'd never happen,' said Cawdor.

'Maybe not,' replied Zamaroh, 'but it *could* happen, that's the point. What we have to assess is the *likelihood* of it happening, the *risk* of it happening, then we *price* and *structure* the issue according to that risk. The higher the risk, the higher the interest rate and the lower the sum you'll be able to raise. At a certain level of risk, the deal isn't viable. The lower the risk, the lower the interest rate, the more money you can raise and keep. The people who'd supply the money, who'd buy the bonds, are sophisticated institutions. They make minute calculations of risk and return, but they also put a lot of store by Goldsteins' name. They know that if we are representing a client, unless we've made a monumental mess-up, the deal is good.'

Savage spoke up. 'That's what the Goldsteins name buys you, but before that, we have to ensure that our reputation isn't in jeopardy. As I've said, and Miss Zamaroh indicated, our reputation is our most valuable asset. So, if you do decide to go ahead with us, we have to do what we call "due diligence". We have to check you out, as we do every client. So you have to be prepared to go down that road if you appoint us.' Savage let his words hang in the air.

'We've got nothing to hide,' Cawdor said. He gazed around the table, then got to his feet. 'Anything else you want to know, John, seeing as you appointed these people?' he asked.

Sarah glanced at Redford. He was looking directly at her. He smiled at her, nodded to Savage, Zamaroh and Breden, and walked from the room. Cawdor followed him out. He paused at the door.

'We'll be back in one week.'

Chapter Twelve

'Why the hell did you take him down to the floor?' yelled Zamaroh.

'What?' asked Sarah, subsiding slowly into shock, now that Redford had gone.

'Shut up, Zaha,' said Savage. 'It switched Redford on, we all saw that.'

'Now everyone knows he was here, they'll guess it's about securitisation,' she retorted.

'If Redford's word is his bond, we've got the deal,' said Savage.

'Hah! You'd trust a rock star?'

'I wouldn't necessarily trust him, but I think he has his own reasons for giving us the deal and he's unlikely to change those.'

'And?' probed Zamaroh, glancing angrily at Sarah.

'I don't know what they might be,' replied Savage, and it seemed to Sarah he was studiously *not* looking at her, 'and it doesn't really matter, does it? Fact is, he's awarded Goldsteins the deal.'

'But can we keep it?' Zamaroh demanded. 'How do I control things now after Sarah's little sideshow?'

'Oh, for God's sake stop bitching,' snapped Sarah, emerging suddenly from her reverie. 'I took him down to the floor because he was bored stupid in the boardroom. Makes you wonder why they called it *boardroom* in the first place, doesn't it? And I thought the floor would appeal to him. He's visceral and he loved it.'

'It *was* a great idea,' said Breden, with rare appreciation.

'It was,' concurred Savage.

'Thank you,' replied Sarah.

'We have one week to become experts on rock securitisation,' said Savage, all business now. 'It's a new product for us and we can't afford to be out of the marketplace. We missed the Bowie deal and the Iron Maiden deal. We're supposed to be the pre-eminent investment bank in the world, a market leader, not a follower. This will be a high-profile deal. It's sexy. It's different. We'll get coverage where we never got it before. Goldsteins' name will be spread around the globe. We're going to win this deal with a signature as well as Redford's word, and we're going to keep it.'

'I thought the two were synonymous,' said Sarah, puzzled by Savage's diatribe.

'So did I,' spat Savage. 'What you don't know, and what you must keep absolutely to yourself, is that over the past six weeks we've lost four deals we thought we'd won, worth fifteen million in fees. Only those of us in this room know about this, but some bastard in Goldsteins is handing *our* deals to the opposition. We've got a leak that's threatening to turn into a haemorrhage. If we appear to win this deal, only to have it snatched from us at the last minute, we will become known as the Teflon bank. No deal sticks. We will not let that happen again.' Savage paused, letting his words grow heavy with threat in the silence.

'Assuming there's a deal to be done, the only people to know about this deal until it's signed and sealed will be those of us in this room. So, if there is a leak, I'll know it's one of you three. Sarah, I want you to work on the deal at home. You have one week to become an expert on the securitisation of rock stars' back catalogues. Work out if Redford's back catalogue can be securitised, and if so, do a preliminary deal structure, and proposal.'

Sarah felt like she'd been punched in the stomach.

Zamaroh filled the breach. 'Why should Sarah do it?' she demanded. 'I've got ten people on the floor who could do that with their eyes closed. They work fulltime in the markets, they're infinitely more plugged in than a freelance.' Zamaroh shot a glance at Sarah, then turned back to glare at Savage.

'The choice is you, or Sarah,' replied Savage. 'I'm not trusting another bastard in your nest of vipers downstairs until we find and fire the Leaker. I am not prepared to lose this deal, is that clear, and if having a freelance prepare the ground is what I have to do then I'll do it happily. This is your problem, Zamaroh. One of your people is a Judas, and I'm giving you a temporary solution.'

'You're assuming I'm happy to do the work,' said Sarah, finding her voice.

'Why wouldn't you be?'

Oh Jesus, you have *no* idea. 'Like Zaha said, I'm a freelance. And she's got all these fulltimers.'

'You can outperform them in half a day if you decide you want to.'

Zamaroh sucked in her breath.

'So make me want to,' said Sarah.

Savage got to his feet. He glanced at Breden and Zamaroh. 'Excuse us.'

He led Sarah into his private bathroom. She sat on the marble sink, cooling her hands on the cold stone. Savage closed the door behind him with a back kick, then slouched against it.

'Thousand a day plus expenses.'

'Not enough, James. On that rate your fulltimers would be paid two-forty K a year and you and I both know that's peanuts. Your top performers'll get ten times that, so don't try my patience. Freelancers get paid more too.'

'So what ludicrously astronomical sum will you find acceptable?'

'Three and a half, plus expenses.'

'That's absurd. You're pricing yourself out of business. Don't you want this work?'

No, she felt like screaming. *I do not want your bloody work. My breasts are bursting, I want to get home to feed my baby and never see your face again, never enter this godforsaken place again.* She said nothing, just stared angrily at the floor.

'You've got me over a barrel here, Sarah. I won't forgive you for this.'

'It's a market, James, like any other. Take it or leave it.'

'Jesus Christ, you've hardened up. I don't know what's come over you, Sarah. You're different.'

She smiled.

'All right. Three and a half plus expenses.'

Shit, shit, shit, shit, shit. She'd never thought he'd go for it.

'Don't look so miserable,' said Savage in disbelief. 'Anyone would swear I'd just consigned you to slave labour.'

'No, just to prison.'

Savage gave her a look of total incomprehension and led off back to the boardroom. Zamaroh was talking on the phone, businesslike, urgent, but taking her time just to make the point. Breden wore a mild look of amusement. Zaha hung up with an instruction to her invisible serf to *just get on to it*, as Savage took his seat, glaring at her invasion of his territory.

'Trading floor never sleeps, James.'

'Insomniac trading floor. What a fearful thought. All right, here's my game plan. Sarah will help out with the deal. She'll do the initial structuring and research work. Have it ready in a presentation package. Redford and his manager are coming back in a week. I want to hook them on us and on our preliminary proposal, get them to sign a mandate letter as soon as possible. Once the mandate letter is signed, or we find our Leaker, whichever is sooner,' he turned to Zamaroh, 'we can get your people on to the deal.'

Sarah felt flooded by panic. It would be an awesome amount of work to complete in a week, without back-up, with Savage ready to hang her out to dry if she got it wrong. She'd have to work practically all day and night, she'd have to stop breastfeeding Georgie during the day, find someone to look after him, find the energy reserves in her exhausted body. She felt tears burn her eyes, brushed them quickly away.

'Zaha, you direct Sarah in this,' continued Savage, 'but not over the phone. Meet in person in the office, or outside it. I'll leave that to you. Ensure there's nothing on paper anywhere in Goldsteins about this deal, that no one overhears a word.'

'Silent as the grave,' said Zamaroh.

'What happens when news of Redford's visit spreads?' Breden asked.

'The Leaker probably knows already,' replied Savage gravely.

'Exactly,' said Zamaroh. 'Taking him down to the floor was idiocy.'

'Oh, shut the fuck up!' shouted Sarah. 'Don't you think his visit would have been broadcast anyway? How many people will have seen him on his way up here? Doormen, anyone passing through Reception, anyone in the lift, anyone walking around the floor here. Fred. Going in and out he'll have been seen by upwards of thirty people. You think they're going to stay schtum?' Sarah leaned across the table toward Zamaroh, anger feeding on itself. 'You know what your trouble is? You're used to bullying people who rely on you for their bonus. That doesn't work with me. I can walk away from this without a backward glance, so if you want me to help you out here, you'd better learn to handle yourself. Got it?'

Savage and Breden watched in silent awe.

'So do me a favour. Walk,' spat Zamaroh.

'All right,' interjected Savage. 'That's enough. Shut up both of you. Can we try to be constructive for just a second? We were trying to work out what to do about our Leaker. Can we focus on that?'

Sarah and Zamaroh glowered silently at each other.

'Make a virtue out of the gossip,' suggested Breden.

'How?' asked Savage, interested.

'Set a trap to catch a thief. This deal will be like gold dust. The biggest rock-star securitisation yet. Every investment bank in the City'd kill to get their hands on it. If our Leaker is being paid to deliver, his price will go sky high on this one.'

'*His* price?' asked Zamaroh, eyes narrowed as she focused on some imaginary betrayer. 'You have any idea who it is?'

'None. Yet. We could use this deal to flush him out.' Breden turned to Savage. 'What do you say?'

'I say if we appear to win another deal, only to have it stolen from us, all your jobs are on the line.'

Fear and greed, thought Sarah miserably. Nothing's changed.

'So let's catch him,' urged Breden.

'How?'

'Give Sarah an office on the floor, use her involvement as bait. Hide a movement-activated camera in her office, bug the phones, have sound-activated voice recorders, be ready to bug the home phones of anyone I suggest. Let's go nuclear on the bastard.'

Savage smiled. '*Great* idea.'

'It stinks,' said Sarah. 'I'm going to be just a tad busy as it is.'

'You can work on the securitisation from here, as long as you lock up your documents when you leave your office. I think it's brilliant,' said Savage.

Sarah felt a wave of despair. Everything was moving way out of control here.

'I don't like it,' she insisted.

'God Almighty. What do I have to do to convince you?' asked Savage.

'I don't think you can. I'd be working virtually twenty-four hours a day and those days are long gone. I don't buy that trip any more. I've got a life.'

'Well, put it on hold.' Savage passed Sarah a note. It said: *£5,000 a day. Final offer.*

Sarah wrote back: *Plus fifty bonus if I find your Leaker.*

Savage read her note, his face carved in a kind of impressed fury.

'You are beyond belief. I always thought sabbaticals were a bad idea.' He scrunched the note up, put it in his pocket and turned to Breden. 'Dick, you work with Sarah on the mechanics.'

Sarah felt a momentary warmth as she thought of all the money that would soon be pouring into her bank account, before falling back into silent hysteria at the wave of work about to engulf her.

Breden inclined his head graciously.

'Zaha, you join in if you have any suspicions,' added Savage.

'I suspect everyone,' she replied. 'I find it repugnant and unthinkable that *any* of my team could be betraying me, so I suspect them all.'

It's always personal with her, thought Sarah. Life as war.

'Narrow it down,' suggested Savage. 'Give Sarah and Dick something to work on. Watch your people like a hawk when news of Redford's visit goes out.'

Zaha smiled. 'Have no fear.'

Sarah felt as if they had all thrown a huge net over the trading floor and its five hundred occupants. Like the rest of them, she was trapped by it. She was to be hunter and captive.

'I know nothing of all this. Do what you have to do,' said Savage briskly.

Sarah glanced at her watch, stifling a sigh. She was desperate to get home. Georgie was due his pre-nap breastfeed half an hour ago. She'd had no idea the meeting would go on so long; an hour and forty-five minutes already. She'd expected just a quickie, a half-hour proposal, Savage's usual style. The wretched Leaker had extended the meeting and given her more work than she'd ever be able to handle.

She could stand it no more. She got to her feet. 'I've got to go,' she told them all, then rushed from the room, slamming the door behind her.

Savage, Zamaroh and Breden gazed after her in surprise. Zamaroh expelled her breath in a slow hiss.

'Where does she get off, that woman? Saunters in here and runs out like she's late for an audience with God. And who the hell is she? Just a burned-out trader scrabbling round for work.'

'The best trader there ever was,' said Savage, with an unaccustomed wistfulness.

'*Was*. Past tense,' hissed Zamaroh.

Savage gave her a wry smile. 'She's the hardest negotiator I've ever met in my life, and she seems to have some new steel in her. I wouldn't make an enemy of her if I were you.'

'I can take care of myself. *Nobody* worries me.' Zamaroh was outraged.

Savage smiled. Zamaroh was almost unbearably arrogant. Her saving grace was that, compared with her, most people were intellectually challenged, and there was something rather magnificent about her conceit. She carried herself like the Iranian princess she was by birth, and would be to this day, had not the Shah been exiled and her own tragedies unfolded. Savage could, and did, forgive her a lot.

'Do you want this deal?' he asked.

'You know I do.'

'Then work with Sarah. As well as being an awesome trader, past *or* present, she's also one of the best judges of human nature you'll ever meet.' He drained a second espresso and gazed out of the window.

'Strange though. Something's come over her.'

Chapter Thirteen

Sarah raced home in a taxi. A flustered-looking Jacob was holding a screaming Georgie, rocking him frantically to the strains of Lauryn Hill.

'How are you, sweetie?' he asked, struggling to be heard. 'How'd it go?'

'It was a nightmare,' said Sarah, taking Georgie and immediately hitching up her top.

She settled with him into her rocking chair and began to feed him. Silence fell like a benediction. For five minutes Sarah said nothing. She just sat with Georgie, gently stroking his hair, both of them recovering themselves. Jacob busied himself, loading the dishwasher, boiling the kettle, getting lunch together. By the time Sarah had fed, burped and put Georgie to bed, Jacob had pasta and fresh tomato and basil sauce ready. Sarah sat down wearily, placing the baby listener by her plate. She perked up as she began to tuck into the pasta.

'So?' asked Jacob. 'What happened? You looked in a state of shock when you got back.'

Sarah gulped down some water. 'They want me to work on not one, but two assignments.' She felt herself faltering as her mind turned to Redford. How the hell was she going to hide the role of this man in her life from Jacob? Only Alex knew. No one else would ever know – *if* she could hold herself together in front of the man who, after her brother, knew her best in the world.

'And?' Jacob waited patiently, head on one side, studying his niece with a puzzled look on his face.

'They've got a Leaker, someone dripfeeding details of deals they've almost won to the competition, who then go and steal the deals out from under them. Savage is apoplectic. Zamaroh wants someone's head. I'm supposed to find the culprit.'

'Tricky, but not impossible for you. What else?'

Sarah took a minute to empty her plate. She got up to load it into the dishwasher, speaking with her back to Jacob.

'There's this rock star, someone called John Redford . . .' There, she'd said his name. 'He wants to do a bond issue, securitising his back catalogue. Because Savage doesn't trust anyone on the trading floor not to leak this deal, I'm supposed to do all the research, come up with a preliminary structure and present it in a week.' She turned round. 'That's of course when I'm not working on finding the Leaker.'

'Oh sweetie,' said Jacob. 'That's a *lot* of work.' His worried face mirrored Sarah's.

She came back to the table and slumped into her seat.

'I know. How can I do it? I can't – not with Georgie. I'd have to stop feeding him. I'd have no time to be with him, take care of him. I wouldn't see him.' Tears burned in her eyes. 'They trapped me. Savage trapped me. I asked for so much money I thought he'd have to throw me out, but he hired me instead.'

'You can always back out.'

Sarah looked at Jacob, her eyes filled with misery. 'No, I can't. I need the money. I need to start working sooner or later, and this'll pay me so much I might not need to work again for six months. He's giving me five grand a day, plus expenses, plus another fifty grand if I find the Leaker. If I do, say, a fortnight, three weeks max here, and find the Leaker, that's a hundred and twenty-five grand. I can't afford to turn that down.'

She got up. 'Forget it. I can't do it,' she decided suddenly. 'I can't leave Georgie, and anyway, there's no one to take care of him.'

Jacob cleared his throat. 'That's not strictly true.'

'What's not strictly true?' Alex poked his head round the door. He dropped his gym bag on the floor and headed for the pasta cooling in the saucepan. 'God, am I ravenous,' he said, scooping up a handful of pasta with his fingers.

Jacob smiled. 'When are you not?'

Alex turned and grinned, mouth full of food. 'Fair point,' he mumbled. 'So what's not true?'

'That Sarah has no one to look after Georgie.'

'Absolutely. We can look after him, can't we?' he said to Jacob. 'We'd love it, you know that,' he told his sister. 'You wouldn't get a look in.'

She smiled. Alex swallowed with a sudden gulp. 'I'm losing my mind.

How'd it go with Goldsteins? You got the work?' he asked.

She grimaced.

Alex looked worried. 'No go?'

'Lots of go. Too much,' she answered bleakly. 'Savage wants me to work on two assignments.'

'With a rock star,' said Jacob, impressed.

'Which one?' asked Alex casually, eyes on Sarah.

'I've never heard of him, of course,' said Jacob. 'Redburn. John Redburn, isn't it?'

'Close enough,' answered Sarah, bending down to scratch her ankle. When she looked back up, her brother's eyes were on her with a concern she refused to acknowledge.

'And?' asked Alex.

'He seemed all right,' answered Sarah. 'For a rock star.'

When Jacob left fifteen minutes later, Alex went and quietly sat next to Sarah on the sofa.

'So what's going on?'

'With what?' she asked, attempting lightness.

'You know what.'

Sarah heaved out a massive sigh. 'I'm sitting there in Goldsteins with Savage and co, and in he walks. I nearly had a seizure.'

'God, Sare. You OK now?'

She looked at her brother gloomily. 'No. I'm in shock.'

'You had no idea he'd be there?'

'Absolutely none.'

'What did Savage and co make of it all?'

'Nothing,' answered Sarah. 'I hope. We played it cool. Pretended we didn't know each other.'

Alex pulled a disbelieving face. 'So why's he here?'

'He wants to securitise his back catalogue.'

'Why now? Why Goldsteins, why you?'

'*J*esus. I don't know. Of all the bars in all the towns . . .' she quoted, half angrily.

'He had to choose yours,' finished Alex. 'Pure coincidence?'

Sarah raked her hair off her face. 'I don't know. I mentioned to him, back in Wyoming, that he ought to do a securitisation. I said Goldsteins were the best bank in the world and gave him Savage's name. God, I've thought no more of it. It was just a throwaway line. I never knew it'd come back to hook me.'

'And has he?'

'What?'

'Hooked you again?'

'No, Alex. He hasn't.' She rubbed her eyes. 'You don't think he can know anything about Georgie, do you?' she asked suddenly.

'How could he?' Alex answered gently.

'I don't know. It's just my nightmare – that he'll somehow find out, and come and try to take him away.'

'He couldn't do that, Sare, even if he found out, which he won't.' A frown crossed his face.

'What?' asked Sarah quickly.

'Well, working on this assignment with him might bring him too close for comfort.'

Sarah shook her head. 'I'm going to do this bloody work for Savage, but that's it. I'll keep the mother of all Berlin walls between me and Redford. He won't get to me. What happened happened. It's in the past.'

Chapter Fourteen

Vera Vernon had for many years attempted to impose order on Sarah's house, cleaning, ironing, shopping, dropping off the dry-cleaning, dispensing advice as she went. As a mother of five, now grown-up children, it was hardly a leap to chief bottle-making teacher.

'All right, this is how you do it, now concentrate. Watch me.' Vera, alias Mrs V, poured eight careful ounces of freshly boiled and cooled Evian water into a sterilised bottle, then doled out eight level measuring spoonfuls of formula milk into the bottle. She secured the top, gave it a violent shake with her powerful wrists, and put it in the fridge. 'Now for the next one.' She handed Jacob the bottle. 'Your turn.'

Sarah watched, holding Georgie in her arms. He seemed to find the preparation of his bottles an amusing spectacle, breaking into his habitual giggles, wriggling in his mother's arms, trying to grab any and all constituent parts of the paraphernalia.

Mrs V turned to Sarah, hands planted on hips. 'Not exactly the best way to start weaning him off the breast, is it? Several feeds in one go. You'll suffer for it, the both of you, him with withdrawal, you with all those flippin' hormones flying around. Not to mention your boobs'll feel like Zeppelins.' Her eyes took on a distant look. 'I remember it. Bloody awful.' She smiled. 'Bloody wonderful too.' She refocused on Sarah. 'Don't you worry, luv. I'll be here all day. You'll survive, the both of you. Go'n get yourself ready now. Give me your boy.'

Sarah hesitated.

Mrs V reached out her arms. 'Come on now. More you linger, worse it'll be. Get ready, and go without a backward glance.'

'Is that what you did?'

The cleaner laughed. 'Do what I say, not what I did. Go on, luv. I know what you're going through, but you'll only make it worse spinning it out. For you and your little one.'

Sarah did linger, strung it out till the last possible moment, relinquished a screaming Georgie with a gut-lacerating stab and ran upstairs. Had no time to shower. Just slipped out of her nightie, splashed cold water on her face, rubbed in moisturiser, hung her head upside down as she brushed her hair and pulled on a navy wool suit. The skirt refused to do up. She turned the zip to the back, hid the gaping gap under her jacket. Pulled on high navy slingbacks and slid her finger into Jacob's huge ruby ring, her talisman. It took her eight minutes to get ready. She passed Georgie's room as she tiptoed down the stairs and stopped, ignoring her own admonitions. Jacob was lying on the floor, allowing Georgie to play with his white moustache. Man and boy were both giggling, oblivious to her look, to her longing, to her pain. She gasped in misery, hurried on and out the door.

She got to Tatsuyo, a Japanese restaurant in Broadgate Circle, fifteen minutes late, but she was still the first to arrive. She felt hot, sweaty, and unkempt. Get a grip, she told herself. Walk like a queen and you will be one. She was shown to a table for two downstairs. When eyes followed her progress, she felt a quick flash of gratification. So she still had something.

At twelve-fifteen, the restaurant was already close to full. Sarah ordered a green tea and tried to cast herself into work mode. Her old role which, pre-Georgie, she had assumed so effortlessly, now felt as unfamiliar as if it had belonged not to her, but to some distant acquaintance. She gazed around the room, searching for other impostors, seeking out their disguises.

Everyone in the restaurant could be classified as either buyer or seller. The seller always seemed to speak with the louder voice, the faster delivery; sell or die. They all bought into it. If only they could pretend for an hour, to the courted buyer, that they did not need them so desperately; if only they could play hard to get with themselves and with their product; if only they could speak slowly in a soft voice, they would make the killing of their dreams.

Play the game, Sarah reminded herself. Aim for substance, but never forget style. It was so easy to see how everyone else should do it. *Witch doctor, heal thyself.*

Into the den stalked Zaha Zamaroh, twenty-three minutes late, even though Goldsteins was only three minutes' walk away across the Circle. As the waiter was seating her, she reeled off her order without the benefit of a menu. Only then did she acknowledge Sarah.

'I'm in a hurry. You know what you want?'

Sarah leaned back in her chair with an amused smile. 'Hello, Zaha.' She glanced up at the waiter. 'Could I have a menu, please?'

He returned two minutes later, menu in hand. Sarah took another two minutes to study it and make her order, calm and poised under the missiles of Zamaroh's eyes.

'You're late,' she said, breaking the silence. 'Don't be late again.'

Zamaroh looked for a moment as if she would explode with rage, but she must have had a sense of her own powerlessness, since she managed to rein herself in. For a while she just stared at Sarah, as if searching for a more appropriate weapon than intimidation, but she seemed to come to an impasse, for all she did was summon the waiter and call for more tea.

'Since Goldsteins is paying me by the day, perhaps we might start,' said Sarah.

'Why don't we?' replied Zamaroh, as if picking up a gauntlet.

The waiters brought their lunch on a tray; miso soup, sashimi and a seaweed salad for them both.

'I'd like an inconspicuous office,' said Sarah, taking a sip of the soup, 'but not too inconspicuous. Let's make it look as if you're trying to hide me, but bluffing, too. I've got to be bait, but not too obvious. Our boy's a tricky bastard I reckon, keen on head games.'

'How so?'

'You said it yourself yesterday. What he, or she – I'm keeping an open mind – is doing is a betrayal, and I'll bet they're getting one hell of a kick out of it. What they're doing is closet and taboo, so let's play with that. They think they're smart, let's make it *just* difficult enough to flatter their ego. I want to give them a real red herring. Let's set up a phantom deal and call it "Gravadlax". Perhaps they'll think it's going to be a takeover of Volvo. Code-names are always giveaways. People choose a name which their subconscious links to the name they're trying to conceal, so Gravadlax is good; it'll point him in a certain direction, make it easier to track if anyone starts trying to do something unusual with any Swedish corporates.' Sarah could see the beginning of a predatory gleam in Zamaroh's eyes.

'I'll mock up a false trail,' she went on. 'I want to occupy the office as soon as possible. That means Breden will have to get his people in there tomorrow first thing, posing as cleaners, to do a sweep of my office for bugs, and yours, and all the conference rooms as well. If they find bugs, I want them left there; we'll use them in our favour to talk about Gravadlax. I want a good PC, big, strong and fast, twenty-one inch—'

'You talking man or machine here?' interjected Zamaroh.

Sarah burst out laughing at Zamaroh's unexpected shot of humour.

'I wish. So that's a twenty-one-inch *screen*, screen-protector; I want ISDN, and I want NEXUS. My computer speaks to no one in Goldsteins. I don't want any other PCs eavesdropping on mine. You and I will have to meet outside the office to talk about Redford, whom I shall codename Tatsuyo.'

'Name him after a restaurant?'

'It's perfect. What possible connection could there be between a megastar and a Japanese restaurant?'

'True,' acknowledged Zamaroh with a faint smile. 'How do I describe you when people ask?'

'Just say I'm doing some freelance work. That should tantalise our Leaker. I'm going to get Breden to bug my office and yours with sound and vision so we can check if anyone tries to go through our papers after hours.'

'My phones?'

'Your phones and any conversations you have in your office.'

'That is an unacceptable invasion of my privacy,' declaimed Zamaroh with staged offence.

'You have any on the trading floor? If you do you're doing better than I ever did. Look, it's just for a week or two, until we catch our thief.'

Zamaroh grimaced.

'It's not as if we have much choice. You can't afford to lose any more deals, Zaha.'

'Shut up, don't remind me.'

'You need reminding.'

'Is there anything else?' Zamaroh asked, tight-lipped.

'Yes, there is. Who do you think it might be?'

Chapter Fifteen

Sarah had forgotten quite how visceral the trading floor was; the winning and the losing, the measurement of people in terms of pounds sterling, the gamesmanship, the Schadenfreude. And most of all, the envy.

It was a catwalk she sauntered down to her borrowed office. She knew it was not just her looks that attracted attention. Any new person drew unconcealed scrutiny, as would a strange hyena skirting round the pack, but Sarah already had a certain notoriety. Acknowledged as one of the top traders in the City in recent years, she was known too as the woman who had walked out from amidst the bodybags at ICB, only to disappear for two years. Even to the uninitiated, Sarah Jensen seemed to carry an air of danger and exoticism.

Let them talk, she thought, watching the buzz through her glass walls. They're talking about someone they only *think* they know. Her mind lurched back to Georgie, as it did about every ninety seconds. Perhaps he'd be sleeping now, or maybe he'd be fretting without her, objecting to the formula milk that had been thrust upon him without warning. She looked longingly at her phone. Her call, like every other on the trading floor, would be taped. And if the office were bugged, there was no point in using her mobile. Jacob had her number. If there was a problem, he'd call her. Yet she could rationalise all day for all the comfort it brought her.

Karen, Zamaroh's secretary, knocked on her door.

Sarah looked up. 'Yes?'

'Zaha wanted me to give you these.'

Personnel files, Zamaroh's suspects. Sarah took possession of three inches of files. 'Thanks.'

She began to plough her way through the realms of paper. After an hour and a half she'd finished them. She made her way to Zamaroh's office, slid through the open door and took a seat opposite the Iranian.

'Thanks for the files,' said Sarah. 'Tell me why you suspect these three.'

Zamaroh let out a dramatic sigh. 'What can I say? I have no hard evidence, or I'd have fired them straight away. I have no soft evidence either, just a feeling, just the look in their eyes when I talk to them. You must understand that,' she added with uncharacteristic respect. 'You and your fabled instincts.'

Sarah smiled. 'I'd like to see them. Can you point them out, discreetly, please.'

Zamaroh studied Sarah in silence for a few moments before rising to her feet. 'Follow me.'

Zamaroh strode to the floor, with Sarah at her side. Backs stiffened, voices shrilled and bond calculators took a bashing as they passed. In between exhortations, admonitions, frowns and a few treasured hellos to her stars, Zamaroh discreetly pointed out her suspects to Sarah. There was Petra Johnson, government bond salesman, selling Gilts and Treasuries into Europe – the most boring job on the trading floor as far as Sarah was concerned. Government bonds were safe as houses and about as sexy as a semi in Deptford. There was practically no margin, minuscule volatility, you really had to squeeze hard to extract any profit from that business. PJ, as she was known on the floor, must have been persistent as hell, a real grinder.

Sarah recalled her file as she studied the woman. She was thirty-five, with a degree in history from Bristol, minor league boarding school, salary last year £75,000, bonus £100,000. Next of kin listed as her father, Julian. She'd taken an extravagant, by trading-floor standards, twelve days off sick last year. PJ was blonde, expensively so, made up, smart clothes veering towards tarty. The brilliance of her hair clashed with the red tones in her face, exaggerating her naturally choleric air. She was a woman in a hurry. She talked fast, as she got up to consult another trader on a price, she walked fast and, when she didn't like the price, lost her cool fast. Sarah bet she spent fast. She was single, boyfriendless as far as Zamaroh knew, but Sarah doubted that anyone on the floor confided in Zamaroh, so she didn't set too much store by that.

Then there was Miles Churchward, bulldog salesman, selling UK corporate bonds to UK institutional investors. His file revealed him to be thirty-six, educated at day school in Jersey, then Exeter University. Salary last year £80,000, bonus £120,000. Next of kin his sister, Claire. No days off last year. Sarah didn't see why Zamaroh could have objected to him on any of the usual grounds. On the basis of Sarah's casual examination, and the faith she put in physiognomy, he appeared to be a thoroughly nice person. Six foot tall, mature, elegant, almost too refined for the trading floor, he seemed kind, considerate, amiable – all qualities that marked him out as an oddity and perhaps for that reason alone he was worth further analysis. Churchward fitted the category of *the last person you would ever suspect*, another black mark.

By contrast, Jeremy St James, known as Jezza, looked far too obvious, which on the basis of double bluff, made him a good candidate too. Thirty-three, Eton and Oxford. Salary last year £200,000, bonus £1 million. Next of kin blank. Eight days off sick. He was flash, ambitious, loud, a little too well dressed. He was Eton-made-good on the trading floor. As he switched between phones he alternated between cut-glass vowels and down and dirty with the barrow boys. Sarah guessed he was whoever he wanted to be, with whoever mattered to him. He was clearly a natural mimic, a crowd-pleaser, but Sarah doubted that anyone on the trading floor sought him out as a friend or confidant. He did not exactly have 'trust me' writ large on his face. Whether or not he had a hidden integrity that he chose to guard from the hyenas on the floor she couldn't tell, but in a strange way, she suspected he might have. It would have been in character, for the trading-floor persona was often a screen, protecting something finer. It also just as often hid emptiness.

Sarah returned to her office and pondered the suspects. All chosen by Zamaroh on nothing stronger than instinct, a latent dissatisfaction with them, or else perhaps just pure dislike. Zamaroh was not, in Sarah's eyes, a good judge of character. She was too caught up in her own rage and pain to be sensitive to other beings. She rated them on the basis of the profits they made for her and Goldsteins, on whether or not they gave her a smooth or rocky managerial ride. Peripherals such as personalities, private lives, hopes and traumas did not register. Zamaroh's take on them was just Sarah's starting point. It was time to talk.

Jezza was the best place to start. He traded foreign exchange on a proprietary basis, using Goldsteins' own capital. Sarah had done exactly the same at Findlays and ICB, so that gave her a natural way in. She planned to amble by for a casual chat about the markets, but Jezza beat her to it.

'Sarah Jensen, queen of the FX markets. Don't say you've joined our humble ranks.' He stood in the doorway, lanky frame propped against the jamb, eyes full of mockery and mischief.

Sarah eyed him carefully. 'Let's just say I'm on loan from the real world.'

'Oh puhlease.' He strode forward and stuck out a hand. 'I'm Jeremy St James.'

Sarah shook his hand. St James's handshake was cool, at odds with his smiling face.

'I trade prop. FX,' he said, swagger in his voice. The proprietary traders were at the top of the trading-floor food chain. He might just have announced he had a twelve-inch penis. Sarah continued to say nothing.

'You still follow the markets?' asked St James.

'In my own way.'

'And what way's that?'

'Sporadically.'

'Follow cable?'

'A bit.'

'Wanna take a punt?'

'Depends what it is.'

'It's one sixty-four sixty-five now. Close up or down today?'

'What's the stakes?'

Jezza pondered that, a slow smile forming. 'A bottle of vintage Krug. Tonight, at Corney and Barrow.'

It was a pretty meaningless punt. Sarah had never been unduly interested in the daily movements of any index, regarding them as erratic, drunken staggers. She preferred to gamble on monthly trends, where some underlying logic came into play, and as for delaying her return to Georgie to spend two hours with an egomaniac, drinking bad champagne which would turn her breastmilk to sour fizz and give her the mother of all hangovers . . .

'It's gonna close down,' she said, with sublime and genuine indifference.

Jezza came back at five. 'Get out your wallet.'

Sarah looked up from the papers she was studying. 'Just a sec.' She called up her screen, checked the closing prices and burst out laughing.

'You lying bastard. You honestly thought you could get away with that.'

He grinned. 'Always worth a try.'

'You thought I wouldn't check?'

'You looked supremely bored by the bet.'

'I was, but not so bored that I'd trust you.'

He shrugged. 'My bluff usually works.'

'Not with me, buster.'

She made a quick call to Jacob on her mobile from the loo. 'How's it going?' she asked urgently.

'Fine, sweetie, don't you worry.'

'Bottles OK?'

'Drunk every last drop.'

'He's been OK?'

'He's been grand.'

'Not been crying?'

'Well, now and then, but nothing much really.'

'Good.' Sarah felt a wave of relief mixed in with another, less clear emotion which she didn't want to analyse too much. She frowned. 'He's not missing me, then?'

'Course he's missing you, love. Pining, but not pining too much, OK?'

Sarah took a deep breath. 'Look, I won't be home for a few hours. Can you manage?'

'I'll manage fine. You just do what you have to. We'll be here.'

'Right. I'll keep my mobile on. You have got the number? Remember, it's pinned up in my study.'

'It's pinned in my mind, now get on with you.'

Sarah stared at the breast pump in her bag and wondered whether or not to take a little off the top of her agonised, bulging breasts. I'll start a flood, she thought, and if anyone comes in and hears the noise they'll think I'm in here with a vibrator. Jesus, bursting mother mistaken for sex maniac, sublime to the ridiculous in one buzz. She put the machine away and hurried out to meet Jezza.

They squeezed through the gathering crowds at Corney and Barrow to take pole position at a corner table. Jezza peeled off to the bar, where he stood, head and shoulders above the throng, darting eyes trying to hook the barman. Sarah scanned the room. Edgy traders coming down after a tough day, hard drinking, heavy smoking. Jesus, what a life. Four years ago, she'd have been at it with the best of them, soothing away the day with legal drugs. Now she was counting the minutes till she got home. Fifty grand if you get the Leaker, she reminded herself, as she glanced longingly at the door. Her breasts felt as if they were about to burst. She'd gone through what felt like a pack of breast pads already. If anyone was about to leak, it was *her*. She began to giggle, caught halfway between hysteria and the absurdity of it all.

'What's so funny?' asked Jezza, depositing a magnum of vintage Bollinger on the table.

'Lord above, you don't expect me to drink that, do you?'

'What have you got to stay sober for? You're not trading for us, are you?'

Sarah smiled. 'Research.'

'Aw, come *onnnnn*. Think I'm stupid?' He began to wrestle with the cork.

'I thought they did that for you at the bar,' observed Sarah.

'Always pop my own cherry, darlin'.'

The cork flew out of his hand and ricocheted off the ceiling, coming down to land on a neighbouring table. Envious eyes flickered from their own bottle to the magnum. Sarah wondered again what the hell she was doing there.

St James quickly filled two glasses to just below overflowing, as pleased as if he'd tamed a foaming horse.

'To winning,' he said, raising his glass high, clinking it with a flourish against Sarah's.

'To winning,' she replied, miming a sip.

'I like your ring,' said St James, eyeing Sarah's ruby.

'Thank you.'

'From a lover?'

'From my uncle, actually. Not that it's any of your business.' Not her real uncle, but Jacob had forever been an honorary uncle.

'Got a lover?'

'Have you?'

'Aw, how d'you even begin to start counting, darlin'?'

'A harem of eager ladies – ah, I see.'

'A harem of ladies.' Jezza warmed to the idea.

You're gay, said a voice in Sarah's head. Why don't you just come out? Because his life would be made hell on a trading floor where conformity was king, where minorities, of whatever type, were sport.

'Jezza, you couldn't get me a bottle of Evian, could you? It's hot in here.'

'Yeah, sure.' He got to his feet, disquietingly eager to please, and disappeared. Sarah glanced around, then emptied her champagne into the half-full bottle of Evian hidden in her bag. By skipping to the loo twice, emptying her glass in the sink each time, Sarah disposed of three glasses of champagne, while Jezza drank four. He appeared unaffected.

She rejoined him with a smile. He had polished off another glass in her absence.

'So, tell me, who's who on the floor?'

Jezza smiled. 'Well, the biggest of the big swingers just has to be *moi*.'

'Why?'

'D'you know how much I made for Goldsteins last year?'

'Tell me.'

'Fifteen mill.' He toasted himself, threw back his head and drained his glass. Sarah studied his bulging Adam's apple, riding the champagne torrent. He looked so vulnerable, with his bare throat.

'Not bad. And this year?' she asked, plunging the knife in.

His head snapped back. 'Who's counting? It's only September.'

Zamaroh had told Sarah that St James was eight million down, close to out. Zamaroh was giving him one more month to begin the turnaround, but Sarah doubted he would make it. His bluster was too desperate, his eyes too full of fear. When a trader lost his nerve, he was dead meat in the City's sea of sharks.

'So it is,' said Sarah gently. 'So who's the second biggest swinger?'

Jezza went through a roll call, down through the pecking order. If she'd asked a dozen other traders from Goldsteins, she hazarded they'd have picked pretty much identical lists from the floor of five hundred traders. It was not by accident that it was called the jungle, but Jezza, despite his noise, was never going to be the alpha male.

After a few minutes, Jezza came to Miles Churchward. His verdict was damning personally, but offered no clue to any hidden criminality.

'He's *boring*,' shouted Jezza. 'But what d'you expect of someone who comes from Jersey? Born and brought up there, speaks French like a frog,

French girlfriend, came to last year's Christmas orgy. She's the best thing about him.'

'You didn't make a pass at her?'

'What if I did? About time she hooked up with a player.'

Sarah laughed. 'I thought he *was* supposed to be a player.'

'He's *sort* of a player, I suppose, but more like the Invisible Man, in fact. Comes to work, does his job, pisses off, never see him, never has a drink after work, never has a drink, full stop.'

'A teetotaller on the floor, that's a novel concept.'

'A mind-numbingly *boring* concept, you ask me,' spat Jezza.

'Good for consistency.'

'Mr bloody Consistency, that's what he is. Makes one and a half mill for the firm every year, year in year out, once made two I think, last year – crack open the champagne.'

More names, the roll call went on, Jezza cruising on the oxygen of gossip, Sarah swaying in her seat with exhaustion. Then Petra Johnson's name cropped up.

'She has to be on the way out,' said Jezza, high on Schadenfreude. 'Used to be good, all she thinks of now is catching a rich idiot and retiring.'

Sarah stirred herself, hiding her agreement. 'Oh, come on. Don't do that every woman over thirty is desperate lark, it just isn't true.'

'I'm not saying that, but it is true for her.'

'Couldn't she just retire on her own savings? You say she did well for a time.'

'Fast living, babe. Taste for the good things.'

'Like what?'

'Like what we all like.'

'Jesus, Jezza, I've got no idea what you like, let alone her.'

'Good flat, right address, real jewels, right friends, good holidays, right places, good—'

'I get the picture.'

'Where d'you live?'

'Carlyle Square.'

'Flat,' announced St James.

'House,' corrected Sarah.

'Jeez. Daddy?'

'Me.'

'You must have been good.'

'I was. I know the pressures. I feel sorry for PJ.'

'Don't be. She knows what she's doing. The flat, the clothes, the lifestyle, the frightful friends, all an investment, isn't it? She's not going to meet Mr Fifty Mill in Tesco's, picking up her ready meals.'

'I never realised it was such hard work,' reflected Sarah.

'It isn't, is it, for the likes of you?' This was said with just a hint of bitterness which the bluster couldn't disguise.

'What's it to you?'

'Golden girls, stride into life like you own it, you and Zamaroh. Everything comes easy, doesn't it?' The drink talking at last.

'Yeah, right, and you've got it hard.'

The eyes narrowed and glared into hers from about four inches away. 'You've got no idea.'

'So tell me.'

A quick flash of hatred and Jezza lumbered to his feet. 'Aw piss off, why don't you.' He weaved through the crowds, trawling in annoyed and indulgent looks as he made his way out.

Sarah searched for a taxi on London Wall, puzzled by Jezza's violent mood swing. Once safely ensconced in a black cab, she wished she could affix a police siren to the roof and speed home through the traffic. She tried to stay calm, but felt as if she hadn't seen Georgie in a month. She and her body, which in many ways these days seemed to operate as a separate system to her mind, craved her baby.

Once reunited with Georgie, she released Jacob with profuse thanks, fed and cuddled her son, put him to bed, and made one quick telephone call.

'Teddy? It's Sarah Jensen. I know, it's been a very long time. Feels like a lifetime. Look, I've got something urgent. Can we meet tomorrow? It's really urgent, I'm afraid. Don't be busy, please. Good. What time?' She groaned. 'OK. See you there at ten.'

She hung up, fed herself, and went to bed, before exhaustion claimed every last cell in her body.

Chapter Sixteen

Jacob arrived at nine the next morning with a huge casserole dish in his arms.

'Lunch and dinner. No time to take care of a baby and cook something decent, at least not while I'm still a learner driver. And as for your brother's cooking, let's say I hope I never see another baked bean in my whole life.'

'Huh,' said Alex. 'They taste pretty delicious twenty thousand feet up a mountain, let me tell you.'

'So would bread and water, I imagine,' retorted Jacob.

Sarah smiled and took a whiff of coq au vin. 'Oh Jacob, you're a star.'

'Bet you didn't eat much of anything last night.'

'I didn't, but I'll make up for it.'

'Doesn't work like that, the digestive system. You should know that.'

Sarah offered up an apologetic smile, as if it were Jacob's, not her own system, that she had offended.

'We'll sort you out,' he said, swapping the casserole dish for Georgie. 'Be an angel, put that in the fridge, and go get yourself dressed.'

Sarah kissed them goodbye, wondering if the parting from Georgie would get any easier. She got to her office at ten-fifteen, just as Zamaroh was swinging by. The Iranian's eyes flared with predatory glee.

'Ah – we have arrived. Good afternoon. I thought you were worried about Goldsteins paying you by the day? No time to waste.' She hissed on the S, just like a snake. An anaconda, thought Sarah.

'I wouldn't waste my worries so lightly, Zaha, and, as it happens, I've been up since five-thirty, when I rather imagine you were slumbering in your lair.' Sarah gave her a sweet smile.

'Now, if you'll excuse me . . .' She turned pointedly to the open files on her desk. She felt Zamaroh's eyes on her long after the Iranian had headed back to her own domain, felt her sizing up the navy suit, worn for the second day running. Now she'd have to shop on top of everything else, waste precious time and money on buying a suit two sizes bigger than normal, which hopefully would be consigned to the back of her wardrobe in a matter of months. And all because she had to look the part, feel secure in her body armour. That was what really annoyed her – being held hostage by her own looks, image, call it what you will. It shouldn't be so, but it was. She'd always taken her beauty, her previously perfect figure for granted. Now that both were challenged by childbirth and exhaustion, they suddenly mattered.

She glugged back a long, skinny, decaffeinated cappuccino, turned on her computer and started to surf the net, trawling all the information she could on rock-star securitisations, then she logged on to NEXUS and read through over a hundred press cuttings. Savage was right. Rock meets finance *was* sexy. The press couldn't get enough of it:

The Real Price of Fame – celebrity bonds are designed to turn hot talent into a great investment, but will Wall Street bite? Rock solid investment? Forget about the Footsie, consult the pop charts instead. Ain't too proud to sell a piece of Rock. Bowie's banker sings new tune. Motown hits are still golden. Pullman rolls in with the bandwagon for the perennial rock stars. Can Bowie banker avoid falling to earth? Stars unearth rock of gold. Brown Bonds. Papa's brand new bonds. Heavy metal becomes new currency. Iron Filing. Iron clad. Iron Maiden run to the tills. Iron Maiden places earnings in Bondage.

The headline writers did their worst. The commentary spanned the spectrum from finance, through straight news, to the entertainment press: *Time*, the *Wall Street Journal*, the *Financial Times*, *Business Week*, the *New York Times*, *USA Today*, *The Times*, *Rolling Stone*, *Variety*, *Billboard*, the *South China Morning Post*. The interest was huge. Sarah could see Savage's vision; Goldsteins' name writ large where it had never been before, and writ larger where it had been. *If* they won the deal. *If* the Leaker didn't wreck it for them.

It was twelve-fifteen when she finally took a break. She rubbed her eyes and gazed out over the floor. It was braying with the usual cacophony of voices, human, computer and telephone, and seething with the same old emotions, exhilaration, despair, greed, envy, terror. So easy to be seduced, to get hooked on the buzz, to have to search harder for the ultimate kick, but the Leaker still seemed to Sarah to be someone motivated by revenge, not by kicks for their own sake, although those too no doubt played a part.

She timed her next move carefully. As PJ hurried across the floor, heading for the double doors, Sarah followed at a distance. Sure enough, PJ disappeared into the ladies. Sarah went in after her, took the quickest pee of her life, and emerged from her stall at the same time as PJ. As they washed their hands at adjacent sinks, Sarah caught PJ's eye in the mirror, and waited for the other woman to speak.

'You've just joined us?' asked PJ.

'Yes,' answered Sarah, drying her hands. 'Yesterday.'

'How's it going?'

'Oh, early days are always a trial, aren't they, in more ways than one.'

PJ paused, hands on hips. 'How's that?'

'Oh, you know, all the usual stuff, figuring out the lay of the land, who's good, who's bad, who you can trust, who to avoid, who's nice, who's psychotic.'

PJ laughed. 'The answer to *that* one is about half the floor. Do you have your own office, or are you attached to a desk?'

'Research.'

'Ah. Which area?'

'New products.'

'Any in particular? I mean, you must have *some* area of expertise.' Hm, the first dagger thrown.

'What's yours?' asked Sarah.

'Governments.'

'Ah.' What the hell could she find to say to that. 'Enjoy it?'

PJ barked out an incredulous laugh. 'Yeah, I just love it, don't I?'

'So why d'you do it then?'

'Why d'you think?'

'There's more than one way to pay the rent.'

'Yeah, well, you find a better one, you tell me.' PJ wheeled on her high heels and ricocheted out.

Sarah's next target was Miles Churchward. She contrived to stand behind him in the sandwich queue at Birley's. He turned to her and smiled.

'Aren't you new at Goldsteins?'

'I am.'

'No one's taking you out to lunch?'

'No, but it's fine. I've got a lot to do, so I can't really spare the time. I'd rather work through lunch and get home at a reasonable time in the evening.'

'My sentiments exactly, and I've developed quite a taste for Birley's. Best sarnies in the City.'

'Yeah, not bad, are they?'

The queue edged nearer to the counter.

'So what d'you do?' asked Churchward.

'Research.'

'Aha. Into what?'

'New products. How about you?'

'Boring old Bulldogs. Salesman,' he added, almost apologetically. Salesmen were a poor second to traders in the trading-floor hierarchy, but even so, Churchward seemed a tad over-apologetic. Their turn came up. Churchward collected his bag and disappeared with a friendly wave. 'See you.'

'Yeah, bye.'

On impulse, Sarah headed into a men's outfitters. She fingered through the suits until she found three she liked. Then she picked out six shirts, two each in white, pale blue and pink, and piled them on the suits. A salesman approached, smiling. It was rare to see a woman shopping for suits for her man and he clearly approved.

Sarah pointed to her pile. 'I'd like to try these, please.'

There was a surprised cough. 'I'm sorry, madam?'

'You heard me. I'm not a reverse transvestite. I'm a lactating mother with a figure shot to pieces and I thought these would be just the ticket. May I try them?'

If the man's eyes grew any wider, they'd roll back in their sockets, thought Sarah, stifling her grin.

She walked out with three suits, and six shirts, all of which fitted her perfectly, thanks to men having large waists and chests.

Jezza made his appearance as Sarah was tucking into her sandwiches back in her office. She was trawling through more background info on securitisations, when he popped his head round the door. She hit screen switch and swimming fishes came up on her monitor.

'Hi.' He shifted from one foot to another, reading her for clues, trying to suss how to play her. She gave away as little as possible. Let him sweat.

'Boy, am I hung over,' he said, propelling himself into the office and into a chair opposite Sarah. 'Don't normally drink that much.'

'Don't you?'

'Well, empty stomach and all that. Was I a bit boisterous? Can't remember.'

Like hell, thought Sarah.

'How about some dinner?'

'Hm?' asked Sarah, hoping she'd misheard.

'Tonight, Momo. I can always get a reservation.'

'Sorry, Jezza. I'm busy.'

'Tomorrow, then.'

'Busy too.'

Jezza leaned half across the desk. 'Day after, then?'

Did this man never give up? 'Can we play it by ear?'

'Yeah, suppose we could. I get booked up early though.'

'Then I'll just have to take my chances.'

Sarah downloaded some of the rock-star info she hadn't yet read to her home PC and locked up her desk. She left the floor at six, weaving her way through the labyrinthine desks, conscious, as she went, of Jezza's eyes following her to the door.

Georgie was asleep when she got home and the house was quiet. Sarah gave Jacob a quick kiss on the cheek, then hurried upstairs to the baby's room to take a peek at him. He was lying on his back, arms thrown out, mouth relaxed, breathing softly. He gave a blissful sigh as Sarah stood watching him, listening to his breath. His rosy lips formed the most perfect cupid's bow. His long, dark eyelashes fluttered against his silken skin. He was the most beautiful being Sarah had ever seen. She felt her heart glow. She stood there for a good five minutes, drinking him in. She thought of his father, recalled the sensual beauty of his face. Was he here in London? What was he doing, at this very moment? Did he feel there was a little bit of his soul somewhere, sleeping peacefully, watched over with love? Georgie was his too, thought Sarah, with a pang of possessiveness.

She tiptoed downstairs to Jacob. Alex had gone out to meet some climbing buddies.

'How was it?' she asked, pouring him a glass of red wine.

He took the glass with a smile. 'Good. He was a little angel. He's such a good boy. You're a lucky mother.'

'I know it.'

'I tell you, though, I don't know how these single mothers do it with three kids on the go and no one to help them. Mrs V came in for a few hours today and I practically jumped up and kissed her.'

'Steady on. But seriously, you're not getting too tired, are you?'

'I'd be a liar if I said I wasn't absolutely cream-crackered, sweetie, but it's a long time since I've felt so satisfied. Me and George, we get on fine; we have an understanding. You know, I adore that boy. Spending time with him is a privilege.'

'Oh, Jacob. I really don't know how to thank you.'

The old man grinned. 'You just did.'

When Georgie woke up, hungry and crying hard, Sarah fed him, then took a long, luxurious bath with him. She dried him, dressed him in his sleepsuit, herself in jeans and white shirt and sat him on the floor beside the kitchen table in his nest of cushions. Jacob laid out two plates of steaming coq au vin and Sarah fell upon hers as if she hadn't seen food for a week. She moaned with pleasure.

'This is delicious.'

She finished it quickly, got to her feet and stooped to pick up Georgie. She rocked him to her. 'I should be back in under two hours,' she said to Jacob. 'When you go to bed, just park the listener in the doorway. I'll pick it up when I get back.' With all the babysitting Jacob was doing, they'd decided it would be easier for all of them if he slept over in the spare room for a while.

'Who are you off to see then?' he asked.

'My man in a dirty mac.'

'Ah, one of those. How's it all going?'

'Got three suspects. One's riddled with bitterness, one's an angry control freak, one's nice and normal, so it's got to be him.'

Jacob grinned. 'How's your rock star?'

Sarah started. 'John Redford?' she asked vaguely. 'I'm mugging up on all the securitisation stuff. God only knows when I'll get it done.' She glanced at her watch. 'Oops, sorry, Jacob, got to go.'

She kissed Georgie gently, and put him to bed. Then she hurried to her safe and took out a large plastic envelope, bulging with cash. She counted out £1500, rolled the notes into two fat sausages, secured them with an elastic band and stuffed each one into her socks. She took a file from her briefcase, shoved it into a carrier bag, pulled on a denim jacket and trainers and headed out.

It was eight-thirty; the summer streets were alive with people dining and drinking in the pavement cafés spilling out onto the King's Road. Sarah caught a cab to Camden, which was even more packed than the King's Road, but with a poorer, edgier crowd. She was glad she'd dressed down. She headed for the Rat and Parrot and wove through a crowd of drinkers; they were quieter than the City brigade the night before. People came here for relaxation, not to convince themselves and everybody within earshot that they were having the best time.

Teddy was already seated at his favourite corner table, nursing a pint of bitter. He, too, had dressed down.

Sarah made for the bar, ordered a Virgin Mary, and went to join her friend. He smiled. 'Hello, dearie. Good to see you after all this time.'

She smiled back. 'Good to see you, too, Teddy.'

'What have you been up to? Haven't seen you in an eternity.'

'Oh, this and that,' she answered.

'You look well on it, whatever it is.'

'Thanks. You're a gent.' The charmer. He was so smooth, with his velvety camp voice, the well-groomed hair, evenly dark, brushed back. Even his jeans looked pristine.

'Sorry to drag you out,' she added.

'If anyone has to drag me out, I'd rather it was you. Besides, I've been to so many of those things, I could practically write the script of the evening. I'm not missing much.'

'That salves my conscience.'

'What can I do for you this time?'

Sarah took the file from her plastic bag. 'Three names. They all work at Goldsteins. These are details from their personnel files. I want the works on them, asap. Credit card, bank, telephone statements.'

'It'll cost you, if you want it yesterday.'

'I do.'

'When don't you?'

'Never.' Sarah bent down and extracted the sausages of money from her socks. She palmed them to Teddy under the table. 'There's fifteen hundred. Let me know if it's not enough.'

'I will. I'll ring you tomorrow, dearie. Count on it.'

'Thanks, Teddy.' Sarah drank her tomato juice and headed for the street. Teddy Skelton, senior partner at Spinnacres, the leading City law firm, watched her go, with a smile.

Chapter Seventeen

Sarah made it to Goldsteins by nine-thirty. She was tucking into her second breakfast of the day, when Savage's secretary knocked on her door.

'Fed-Ex for you.'

'Thanks, Evangeline.'

Sarah slit open the package. It contained all the financials on John Redford, mixed in with realms of verbiage. Sarah went straight for the numbers.

Redford had written seventeen albums and over five hundred individual songs. His best-selling album was his most recent one, *Fire Walk*. Each album sold more than the last. His first album sold one million, one hundred and ninety thousand copies, his latest five million. All together, he'd sold one hundred and eight million albums. He'd done ten sell-out world tours, grossing one hundred and twenty million dollars. Total merchandising receipts were eighty million dollars. Each year he seemed to earn over one million dollars in what was called performance income, the fee payable to him each time one of his records was played on the radio. Over the last three years, he'd made a total of eight million dollars from licensing his songs to appear in television ads. His 1999 single 'Something Wild' had been licensed to Ford for ninety days' use in TV ads, for which he was paid five million dollars.

'Sweet Jesus!' Sarah announced to herself.

The man's achievement was phenomenal. He was a modern-day prophet, singing to millions who listened to his words and paid for more, who escaped from their worlds into his voice. This man who had strummed his guitar and sung for her in the wilderness, sung for her and given her a child.

Sarah got to her feet, suddenly dizzy. She turned from her desk and gazed out of the window at the City skyline. Early autumn rain blew horizontal against the glass with strange savagery.

She raked her hair back from her face. She couldn't hide in the numbers. It was impossible to handle this as if it were just another assignment. However hard she tried, Redford kept intruding, her son kept intruding. Everything blurred together – love, secrets, longing, the memory of desire. Any hope of objectivity was a myth. She would have fired herself in an instant. Savage would, if he ever comprehended the truth. What would the old Sarah Jensen have done? she asked herself. *You can pretend you are her*, she insisted silently, *just for a fortnight.*

She sat back down, tried to immerse herself in the figures again, but conflict and confusion assailed her still. She felt like a voyeur, flicking through the business life of the father of her child. Redford's actual income was difficult to discern. He seemed to pay out deductions at every turn, to managers, agents, promoters, accountants, lawyers, his record company. He was at the top of a very long food chain, supporting a cast of what seemed like thousands of takers. After all his payouts and deductions, his gross income was in the region of twelve million dollars a year.

God, this stuff would have been great ammunition in another mother's hands, someone who might want to claim maintenance. A combination of pride, possessiveness and her habitual secrecy meant Sarah would never do that. She could and would support Georgie herself. She didn't need any of Redford's millions, dramatically laid bare before her but, despite herself, she felt a quick pang as she learned of the true extent of his earning power. A few million from him, and she'd never have to work again. What was the going rate? What did Mick Jagger allegedly bung the Brazilian mother of his alleged latest love-child? Ten million dollars, hadn't she read somewhere? She tasted the temptation for a moment, before spitting it out.

She worked for a while longer before locking the papers in her desk, then going to the loo, to the water machine. She left the dummy Gravadlax papers on her desk, partially, temptingly concealed, a strand of hair stuck to them to test for molestation, but when she returned the hair was in place, the papers untouched.

After three hours, the numbers waved like snakes before her tired eyes, but she managed to put them into some kind of order. She paused for a brief lunch of Birley's sandwiches, then opened up her laptop and began to build a picture of Redford Inc, history and future.

Playing with numbers in this way still gave her a real kick. Financial structuring was indulging the art of the possible, fortune-telling with a computer chip and a brain and, like all the best fortune-tellers, she added the ability to perform some gymnastics of time-travel, to see and to know what was real and what was not. All the best financial brains could do this – Nicola Horlick, Warren Buffet, George Soros – all the out-performing fund managers. For many of the rest of them, stock-picking was just a random walk; a monkey could do it just as well.

Sarah's excitement grew as she filled pages with numbers and calculations. The quality of Redford's earnings was spectacular, more or less recession proof. When recession hit and people cut back, they seemed to regard the dreams and sorrows of which John Redford sang as necessity, not luxury.

Her telephone rang.

'Sarah. Evangeline. Could you drop by James's office, please?'

For a moment she felt breathless, gripped by an irrational fear that Savage had found her out. She wondered if she would ever lose this fear of being caught out, for simply just being herself, even without secrets. She walked up the back stairs to the sixth floor, her heels clicking out a weary tattoo on the marble steps.

She found Zamaroh and Breden in attendance in Savage's office. Breden was telling Savage and Zamaroh about the bugging.

'All the offices we tested were clean,' he revealed. 'Zaha's, yours, James, Sarah's temporary office. What I'd like to do now is bring forward our monthly sweep. Better to do it at a random time like this now and then, anyway.'

'Fine,' said Savage. 'You surprised the offices were clean?'

'Not really,' replied Breden. 'I think we're dealing with a sophisticated individual, someone who knows we'd be de-bugging offices. It's such an obvious way of extracting information. *Too* obvious.'

'And not at all fun,' observed Sarah.

'Fun?' asked Breden.

'Yes, *fun*. Our Leaker is doing this chiefly for kicks. I'll bet you a case of good red wine, a humidor of Havanas, whatever your own private vice is, that's his motivation. Bugging's too impersonal. No real theft or betrayal there, in his eyes.'

'And what, may I ask, makes you so sure of this?' challenged Zamaroh.

'Profiling,' responded Sarah simply, 'and instinct.'

'You have anything concrete?' asked Savage.

'Not yet.'

'What about my suspects?' asked Zamaroh, in the voice of a queen asking about her prisoners.

'Nothing yet.'

'You've done nothing?'

'Not quite. I have nothing to report.'

'What on earth have you been doing, then?' the other woman demanded.

'Saving you time. I could fill you in on everything I've been doing, but that would waste my time and yours. I know you set great store by posturing on the floor, you'll excuse me if I don't.'

'Tell us about securitisation,' said Savage, trying unsuccessfully to conceal his grin.

'Arse,' said Sarah.

'I beg your pardon?'

'RSS,' she replied slowly. 'Rock Star Securitisation. The bonds are known as Bowie bonds, because he was the first rock star to be securitised by this American whizz called David Pullman. They are typically issued for a ten- to fifteen-year period, on a single A rating, but paying one to two per cent more than comparable single A corporate bonds. Often there's some form of credit enhancement, a guarantee from the music publisher, but if the quality of earnings from the rock star is good enough, you don't need guarantees.

'Bowie sold around a million CDs a year, year in year out. His deal, which raised fifty-five million dollars, was backed by royalties on his first twenty-five albums. What gave Bowie an edge was that he owned the songwriting, publishing and recording rights to his music, so he got royalty streams from all three. Often artists just own the recording rights.

'I believe John Redford owns all three rights, like Bowie, and that makes him an excellent candidate. He's put out seventeen albums, and has sales of over four million CDs a year on average, so that's another tick in his favour. There are a whole load of technical issues, like proving he owns the copyright to his work, but assuming they can all be got around, and I imagine you'll have teams of lawyers crawling all over that, on the basis of quality of earnings, and his wit in writing his own material and holding on to as many rights as possible, Redford should be the perfect candidate for an RSS.'

'What would you rate him?' asked Savage.

'Single A.'

'Yield?' barked Zamaroh.

'Say around four hundred and fifty basis points over base, to give a current yield to maturity of around nine per cent. On that sort of rate, given Redford's apparent annual income of around twelve million dollars, he ought to be able to raise a hundred million or thereabouts with a coverage ratio of one point three three. Tight, but do-able.'

Savage, Zamaroh and Breden were stunned into collective silence. Even Sarah was impressed by herself. Maybe my mind hasn't completely atrophied, she thought.

'Fees?' asked Zamaroh, recovering.

Sarah started from her reverie. 'We could probably charge an arrangement fee of around five per cent, clear a cool five million, enter a new business area, arrange the biggest rock-syndication deal yet, and emerge as market leader.'

'Sounds pretty sexy to me,' said Savage, smiling at Sarah. 'You seem rather keen on Mr Redford.'

'It's a good deal,' answered Sarah, fearing that her cheeks were colouring.

'Why's he want to do it?' asked Zamaroh, inadvertently saving Sarah. 'That's what I want to know. What's the rationale? How are we adding value?'

Sarah laughed. 'Since when have you given a damn about that? What happened to take the money and run?'

Zamaroh glared at Sarah as if she'd just lifted her skirt.

'Ah, I see,' said Sarah. 'The new spirit of political correctness. You're among friends here, Zaha, or fellow conspirators at least. You don't need to pretend.'

'Spare me the lecture, just answer the question, if you can.'

Sarah smiled. 'An RSS means the rock star is essentially borrowing money and paying it back out of future royalties. It's much better than getting the record company to pay him an advance on future royalties, because, one, the record company discounts future royalties at a higher rate than investment banks pricing an RSS do, so the rock star gets more money up front if he does an RSS, plus he receives a higher royalty rate from the record company which doesn't now have to pay him an advance. Second, whereas an advance from the record company is treated as income and taxed accordingly, the money received up front by the rock star doing an RSS is viewed as a loan. The interest on the loan is tax deductible, so the rock star can actually reduce his tax burden by doing an RSS. Third, once the bonds mature, the rock star retains ownership of the catalogue that generated the royalties. If the royalties are greater than expected, the bonds get paid off early, so the rock star gets all the upside.' Sarah finished her recital, grateful for the series of extremely well-written articles she had read the day before, outlining all the pros and cons of the RSS.

'Who are the buyers?' asked Zamaroh.

'Insurance companies, normally. The Pru bought all the Bowie bonds, the whole issue. You can see why that's attractive to someone like Bowie; it means only one institutional investor gets to pore over all his confidential stuff, not a string of twenty. It's something I think we should seriously consider ourselves.'

'What, eat a hundred million dollars' worth of Redford bonds?' demanded Zamaroh.

'If we want to win the deal we might have to,' replied Sarah, looking to Savage for his reaction.

'That'd be a big position to carry,' answered Savage, 'but if the numbers back it up, and if it appears we have to buy the deal to win it, we do it.'

'Ups the stakes,' said Zamaroh. 'If we get it wrong, we take a hundred mill bath.' She eyed Sarah slowly. 'That'd be one hell of an error.'

She's Salome, thought Sarah, watching Zamaroh, and, for some inexplicable reason, she wants my head.

Chapter Eighteen

Jacob had set off to Golders Green for a night of poker with his chums, Alex was in Sarah's study pursuing his love affair with maps, and Georgie was sitting on Sarah's lap, playing with tendrils of her hair when the doorbell rang. She jumped, and Georgie let out a little howl of surprise.

'It's all right, my darling.' Sarah put him down on a blanket on the floor, where he immediately burst into tears of rage and abandonment. She closed the drawing-room door behind her and made her way to the front door, wondering who it could be, hoping Jezza hadn't tracked her down. He knew she lived in Carlyle Square. It wouldn't take much to narrow it down to the right house.

She peered through the peephole and relaxed when she saw it was a motorcycle courier. She opened the door.

'Jensen?' he asked, his voice muffled by his visor.

'That's me,' replied Sarah, glancing round the empty square.

'Sign here, please.'

She signed, took the package, and closed the door behind her with relief, upset by her own jumpiness. Georgie's tears soon subsided in her arms. She tore open the thick envelope and saw bundles of bank, credit-card and telephone statements. Teddy had moved fast, as promised. There was no acknowledgement slip from the senior partner at Spinnacres. Teddy Skelton had one of the best little black books of dodgy, subornable contacts; better still, post the Data Protection Act, when investigators and litigators became a bit more nervous about obtaining such information, he had a wholesaler who could do his dirty work for him. Whoever that mystery man was, he had done a great job, and Teddy Skelton's sign-off was a typed note saying *U owe another half grand.*

Sarah settled down with a sleepy Georgie in the rocking chair and started with PJ. Petra had a gold Visa card that sucked the cash from her current account. For the past four months, she had been overdrawn, the balance rising each month to stand at twelve grand under. Monthly spending on her card averaged four grand over the past year. Sarah ran through her spending, picking out patterns. The woman shopped at Harvey Nichols, at least once a month, sometimes once a week, then she drank, expensively, at Harvey Nick's fifth-floor wine bar, a pick-up joint if ever there were one, thought Sarah. PJ ate at Vong, Momo's, and Alberto's, a local Italian by the sound of it, in South Kensington, close to where she lived in the Little Boltons. These were probably girly meals, where she paid for herself, or they were Eurotrash gatherings, where everyone but the trophiest girls went Dutch. The only oddity, besides her living beyond her means, was that she took out over fifteen hundred pounds a month in cash, always at the beginning of the month, and always from the same Old Brompton Road cash-point.

Churchward typically spent less than fifteen hundred a month, spread between Visa and Amex, with no apparent logic for the distribution between the two cards. He was a subscriber to *Country Life*, *The Week*, the *Spectator*, the National Trust, *The Economist*, Condé Nast *Traveller*, the retired Seamen's Benevolent Fund and Red Hot Dutch. Conscience and desire, aspiration, dreams of bucolic bliss, intellectual, armchair traveller, real traveller.

The only aberration in his conservative spending was his holidays, each one a blow-out; nine grand to charter a sixty-foot yacht for a week. Six grand heli-skiing for two weeks in Canada, eight grand scuba diving for a fortnight in Tortola; they were all action holidays, no romantic weekends in Paris, few dinners in expensive restaurants. Churchward was more interesting on paper, with all his contradictions, than, at first sight, in person.

Sarah turned to Jezza's credit cards. Eight grand a month split between Visa and Amex. John Lobb shoes, two thousand pounds, Oswald Boateng suits, three grand, long weekends in Venice and Cairo, seven grand, dinners at the Ivy, three hundred quid, drinks at the Met Bar, five hundred quid – the man was quite the entertainer. The only oddity was the occasional, more prosaic evening; regular meals at an Indian restaurant off the Brompton Road. Sarah jumped as the telephone rang. She dropped the papers on the floor and, cursing, hanging on to Georgie with one hand, reached out for the phone with the other.

'Hello!'

'Good evening, Sarah. Dick Breden.'

Sarah looked at the phone with horror, praying Georgie would keep his peace. If she put him down to go to another room he would scream his head off. If she kept him in her arms he might gurgle or let out one of his famous roars of happiness. She picked up the remote and switched on the television to distract him.

'Hi Dick, how're you doing?'

'I've got some info on our people. I wondered if I could come round and discuss it with you?'

'Now?'

'Is it a bad time?'

'Can we do it tomorrow?'

Georgie let out a happy gurgle as a favourite advertisement came on the televison. Sarah coughed heavily, trying to drown the sound.

'You all right?' asked Breden. 'Sounded very funny there. A sort of gur—'

'I'm fine, thanks, Dick. Where shall we meet? In the office?'

'I'm trying to stay out of the office for a few days. Can we do it at home? I can come to you.'

'I can meet you in Oriel – you know, Sloane Square?'

'Breakfast?'

'What time?'

'Seven-thirty?'

No chance, thought Sarah. She'd be breastfeeding. 'I'm busy till nine-thirty.'

Breden had the good grace not to ask why. 'See you there.'

Chapter Nineteen

Sarah had had a rough night. Georgie had woken not his usual once, but three times. She arrived at Oriel twelve minutes late, feeling weak and haggard. To compensate, she'd put on one of her new suits and shirts, teeming it with high navy, sequinned mules which, she hoped, drew the attention away from her face.

'Hi, Dick. Sorry I'm late.'

He nodded with his customary grace, letting it ride. 'Can I get you a coffee?'

'Camomile tea, please, and four pieces of toast with honey.'

When the food arrived, Sarah polished off all four pieces of toast, scarcely drawing breath.

'You miss dinner?' asked Breden.

'Hm?' asked Sarah, wiping crumbs from her face with a napkin. 'No, just hungry.' She ordered more tea, then waited until it had been served before reaching down into her bag and pulling out her growing files on the suspects.

Breden flicked through the papers and looked up, his eyes lingering on Sarah's face. 'You've been busy.'

'Yeah, pretty much.'

'Any preliminary thoughts?'

Sarah drained her tea and settled back in her chair. 'Jeremy St James, alias Jezza. Expensive tastes, generous entertainer, an image to maintain, flew high, now he's about to crash. He can see it coming and he's desperate. Possibly has a problem with alcohol, mildly misogynistic, latent homosexual, in denial and that makes him vulnerable. Poor family ties, pent-up anger, swings from that to remorse and guilt.' She told Breden about her drinking session with him. 'As I expected, he avoided me yesterday morning, then finally plucked up courage to breeze into my office, play it all down, wait for me to shrug and give him absolution. Then he asks me out. Not the type to take no for an answer, could get nasty about it. I really wanted to tell him to piss off, but I might be able to get something useful out of him, so I defused him, told him I'd play it by ear. A flat *no* and he'd be my sworn enemy.'

Breden nodded, watching Sarah closely.

She went on. 'Problems with intimacy, commitment, likes to live life on the fly, buzz here, buzz there, never settle. Like most traders, low boredom threshold.'

'Fancy him?'

'As our Leaker? He fits the profile all right. Needs the money, fears being fired so, selling information, wounding Goldsteins in the process, revenge in anticipation, all that satisfies him. Leaking is sneaky, makes the Leaker feel one up and Jezza's big on that, a real status freak. Likes to think he's number one on the floor.'

Breden chuckled. 'I imagine Queen Zaha would have a few words to say to that.'

'Wouldn't she just? But she's more like an empress, so Jezza could still fancy himself first-born prince.'

'How d'you rate the others?'

'Churchward sounds too good to be true; boring, consistent, keeps to himself. Prudent financially, lives within his means, only extravagance is his holidays. Likes porn. Strikes me he has a game-plan and is sticking to it. Does his job well, keeps his head down, everyone dreams of glory, he's not immune. Perhaps he wants to set up his own business, working hard for the capital. Maybe he wants to retire in a few years, sail round the world. He's from Jersey, he lists sailing as his hobby on his CV. But I doubt whether selling Goldsteins out would net him enough to compensate for the risk. He's got no other motive, far as I can see. No revenge, no sense of injustice, although, thinking about it, perhaps he reckons he should be better rewarded, that he suffers from being a nice guy, that if he were louder, nastier, he'd go further, which is almost undoubtedly true. He's the archetypal grey man. Rebellion within? Who knows.'

'And PJ?' asked Breden, calling the waiter over. 'Another black coffee, please. You want anything?'

'Yeah, Evian, please. No ice. She's bitter, angry, running out of time and money. High spending, overdrawn, big user of cash. Withdraws fifteen hundred a month, could be interesting, could be drugs. She's got motive, and I get the feeling she's a nasty piece of work. She could definitely get a kick out of betrayal. Trouble is, if I analysed the whole floor, I'd come up with a hundred people with motive and the right profile. Trading floors attract selfish, avaricious, loud, competitive people. If you're not that way when you arrive, you will be by the time you leave. They also foster feelings of injustice. People know, or fancy they know, what everyone else earns, and of course, no one reckons that the biggest hitters deserve what they get. Everyone thinks they're underpaid by comparison. It's like a prison, a whole load of inmates bunched up together for twelve or fourteen hours a day, pumped up on testosterone, women included, cut off from the outside world. You've got a pressure cooker and someone's going to pop. Trying to find our Leaker's going to be like looking for the proverbial needle.' She sighed and rubbed her eyes.

'You want me to have some of my people take a look at the phone records?' asked Breden.

She jumped at it. Poring over the phone records, ringing up, identifying people called by the unholy trinity of suspects would be back-breakingly boring, time-consuming, but delicate work.

'Oh yes *please*. I would *love* it.'

Breden smiled. 'Hand them over. Any chance of copies of the bank and credit-card statements?'

'These are all extra copies I ran off this morning. They're yours.'

Breden cast a quick glimpse over them, then put them in his briefcase.

'Thanks. Where d'you get them from?' he asked casually.

Sarah smiled. 'You don't honestly expect me to answer that, do you?' The new, more vigorous Data Protection Act made everyone more cautious about protecting their sources.

'No, but you might give me a clue. Wholesaler, retailer et cetera.'

'A man with an extremely well-stocked black book.'

'A wholesaler. What d'you pay him?'

'Him, nothing. His contacts, two grand.'

'So what's in it for him, unless he cuts himself a share of the two grand?'

'He wouldn't. That'd be peanuts to him.'

'So?'

'I saved him a lot of money in his divorce.'

'Ah.'

'Ah, indeed. So, what've you come up with? By the way, you can take your jacket off, you know. You don't have to be formal at ten a.m. in Chelsea.'

'Is that a fact?' Breden slipped easily out of his jacket. He was wearing a black long-sleeved cotton T-shirt which clung to his well-muscled frame. Sarah's eyes lingered for a moment and, much to her amazement, relief and horror, she felt a jolt of sexual desire.

'First off, the floor's clean. We did a wide sweep. No bugs found anywhere, let alone in Zamaroh's office.'

'Hm. So it has to be someone with close access.'

'Looks that way.'

'But that still rules in five hundred people on the floor for starters,' said Sarah.

'It does, but we're watching them. Zamaroh's office is now wired for sound and vision, as is yours.'

'Oh joy. I won't be able to pick my nose in peace. I pity the poor bugger who's got to monitor the tapes.'

'I would say it'd be quite a perk in your office.'

Sarah laughed. 'Anything on our gang of three?' she asked.

'A little bit of background. Jezza lives in a rambling house at the bad end of the Fulham Road. Has a taste for antiques and the purveyors thereof. Had a sleep-over last night – young brunette, pretty, works for Sotheby's, seems to be a nice girl. Er, he drives an Aston Martin.' The minutest flicker of discomfort crossed Breden's features.

Sarah couldn't help herself, she burst out laughing. 'I wouldn't necessarily hold that against someone, would you?'

Breden managed a grin.

'Younger model than yours? Bigger, faster?' Sarah asked.

Breden was watching her in a way that suggested he'd like to put her over his knee and give her a good spanking.

Sarah giggled to herself. 'So the man's got a big engine, what else?'

Breden gave her an acid smile. 'PJ is boyfriendless as of about seven weeks ago, smarting by the sound of it. Giovanni di Castiglio. Minor aristo, lots of family dosh. She'd been with the guy three years, probably banking on marriage, probably feels three invested years have gone to waste. She's thirty-five, unmarried, a tad bitter I'd imagine.'

'Needs a new game-plan,' mused Sarah, half her mind with PJ, appalled by their way of evaluating her, the other half grinding forward with an investigator's politically incorrect but remorseless logic. 'How's she live?'

'Basement flat in the Little Boltons, backing onto a garden, lots of well-tended plants.'

'Funny, never had her down for green fingers.'

'Me neither. Drives a navy-blue BMW convertible. I'll tell you more tomorrow. It's me on night shift tonight, watching her.'

'Hence the black coffee. Stoking up. Churchward?'

'Churchward lives in a two-bedroom mansion flat off Kensington Church Street. Drives a company car, unlike the other two. A Nissan Micra.'

'A Nissan Micra? What's with this guy? You know he really has to be saving for something major. No man drives a Nissan Micra unless he has to. Most men I know like big, powerful, thrusting cars that—'

Breden cut her off. 'To go with his car, he had an evening in reading and watching telly. The guy really does seem too good to be true.'

'God, we're warped,' said Sarah.

Breden looked at her with interest. 'Does it bother you, what we do?'

'Sure it does, delving into people's lives, gouging around for their weaknesses. It bothers me if they're innocent. If they're guilty, all's fair. But, you know, you gotta pay the rent somehow, and there is part of it that's pretty interesting. I've always been fascinated by people's hidden lives. Does it bother you?'

'It's a job. I dissociate.'

'You certainly do. When do you engage, Dick Breden? What *does* bother you? What do you do it all for? It can't only be the money, can it?'

Breden just smiled.

Chapter Twenty

Sarah returned home to her office and spent most of the day working on the securitisation proposal. The meeting with Redford was the next day, and she wasn't close to finished. Working from home was infinitely preferable to trekking into the City. She could see Georgie every hour or so, but there was torture in that too, just five minutes of him while she and he craved more. She interrupted herself to feed him his night feed, and to feed herself, then she hid away in her office. She left Georgie with Jacob and Alex who had rented an old black and white video about early Everest climbs.

The telephone rang at eight.

'Sarah. It's Zaha.'

'Hi, Zaha.'

'Why didn't you come in today?'

'Is there a relevant point to this phone call?' asked Sarah. 'If there is, could you please come to it. If not, goodbye.'

'Have you done the proposal?'

'I'm working on it now.'

'Not finished?'

'It'll be ready when it needs to be.'

'I need it now. I have to check it.'

'There won't be time to check it, Zaha. Unless you feel like coming here to pick it up in the middle of the night, which'd be a waste of time, because I don't propose to change anything anyway.'

Sarah could almost hear Zaha mouthing silent Farsi imprecations. 'Did I just hear you correctly? I mean, I can't believe I did. I can't believe—'

'Good night, Zaha. Believe or don't. It's all the same to me.' Sarah hung up with a feeling of euphoria. God, the last word was delicious. The euphoria wore off as she worked on, determined not to give Zamaroh anything to criticise, finally finishing at three in the morning. She fell exhausted into bed.

As if by telepathy and empathy, Georgie let her sleep undisturbed until seven. At eight Jacob took him from her, and she was left with herself, and her impending meeting. She couldn't fool herself. She was excited and disturbed by the prospect of meeting John Redford again. She tried to convince herself the sick feeling in her stomach came from nerves about presenting her proposal. Perhaps one tenth of it did.

She stood naked before her wardrobe and picked out her new dark grey pin-stripe suit, and a pale pink shirt. After slipping on a pair of black leather loafers, she squirted two generous blasts of Fracas behind her ears. A pair of diamond stud earrings followed, and then her lucky ruby ring. She checked herself in the mirror, slicked on lip gloss and mascara, combed her hair through with her fingers, wondered what John Redford would think, and instantly reprimanded herself for caring.

Alex had awoken and was walking stiffly downstairs as she emerged from her bedroom. He gave her an appraising look.

'You look nice.'

She smiled. 'Thanks.'

'Your big meeting?'

'Yep.'

'Good luck, Sare.'

'Yeah.' She took a deep breath in.

'Take care, won't you,' said her brother, and Sarah knew he wasn't warning her about jumbling her presentation.

She arrived five minutes late for the meeting. Savage, Breden and Zamaroh were waiting in the boardroom.

'Glad you managed to make it,' said Savage, eyeing her clumpy masculine loafers.

'You're late,' said Zamaroh pointedly.

'I know. I was shagging my boyfriend and it took a while to get cleaned up afterwards.' Sarah flashed a smile. 'You know how it is.'

Savage and Breden guffawed with laughter. Zamaroh, out of the bank, would have laughed too, but here every line was a competition, and she wouldn't acknowledge Sarah's victory.

A discreet cough sounded.

'May I come in?' John Redford stood in the doorway, beside Savage's secretary, Evangeline. He looked tired, but fit. Sarah's eyes were drawn to his sensual lips, curved now into a gentle smile of amusement.

Evangeline withdrew. Savage rose to his feet.

'Mr Redford, delighted.'

Redford shook his hand. 'It's John.'

'John,' said Savage, as if trying it out. 'You remember Zaha Zamaroh, Dick Breden, and Sarah Jensen?'

Redford acknowledged them all with a polite smile. The look he gave Sarah suggested that not only did he remember her extremely well, but that he had heard her quip.

Sarah felt her cheeks flushing red. God, what impeccable timing she had. What a great start, guaranteed to get her off on the right foot.

She fiddled with her jacket cuffs.

'Nice suit,' said Redford, a teasing look still in his eyes.

Sarah gave him a thin smile, not keen to encourage bantering that she knew would be minutely scrutinised by Savage, Zamaroh and Breden afterwards. Trying to pretend she'd never met this man was agonising. She could only hope that Redford would continue to collude in the pretence. His teasing suggested otherwise. Oh Jesus, should she just own up now, jump up and announce to the table that she and Redford had been lovers, for one blissful, fateful night.

'Sarah?' Savage's voice cut through her reverie. She dragged herself back to attention. 'You will present our proposal to Mr R—, I mean John.'

Sarah smoothed her thighs and looked up brightly. 'Of course. Would you like me to start now, or shall we wait for Mr Cawdor?'

'He's not coming.'

'What? You're not having any representation?' asked Sarah in disbelief.

Redford shook his head. 'Nope.'

'What about a lawyer? I mean I'd really recommend—'

'Don't worry, Sarah. I'm a big boy. I won't be lured off the straight and narrow by you. Anyways, I'll give all your stuff to my lawyers later. Does that make you feel better?' His eyes smiled at her, his voice was languorous. He was gorgeous and infuriating in equal measure. She was conscious of Savage, Breden and Zamaroh focusing on the exchange. She could only hope that they'd put his teasing intimacy down to rock-starry immunity to the normal social laws.

She pushed the document she had so carefully worked on into the night across the desk to Redford. She wondered briefly what he had been doing at 3 a.m., and felt a flash of jealousy, for his lifestyle, for his money, for his freedom, for any unnamed lover that lay in her place. Jesus, woman, get a grip. She *had* no place with him.

'Right,' she said firmly, nodding at the document. 'What's in there is the technical verbiage and a bunch of numbers. To paraphrase: as we currently understand, and you'll have to get used to these legalistic inserts, your numbers would support an issue of around a hundred million dollars. You could probably secure a Single A rating with Moody's, Fitch, or Duff and Phelps. That means you could borrow at a cost of around four and a half per cent over base rates, say around nine and a half per cent. We would charge a fee of around five per cent on that, and—'

'Jesus,' interrupted Redford. 'What the hell d'you do for that?'

Sarah smiled. 'First off, we charge what the market will bear, OK? I'm not going to bullshit you about that. Other banks will charge around the same. Lesser banks might cut the fee, but your deal might suffer, and anyway, I'm sure your advisers wouldn't think it good for your profile to associate with second-tier banks. Now, what we do for the money is this. We start off by giving you an engagement letter which we both sign. In this, Goldsteins International undertakes to, one, securitise a specified part of your catalogue – that is, issue bonds backed by the income stream on that part of your catalogue – two, obtain a rating, and three, place the issue. Goldsteins will grant ourselves an option to purchase all or a portion of the bonds at our discretion.'

'How long's it all take?' asked Redford with a frown.

'Typically, a one-hundred-and-fifty-day engagement, although that can vary enormously depending on the complexity of your own operation. There's normally thirty days for due diligence, verifying your income streams, splicing and dicing them, extracting all the relevant statistics and convincing ourselves that they're all kosher. Then there's thirty days to size, price and structure the deal, a sort of mathematical orgy. Then there's another thirty days to write the document, that's a legal and descriptive orgy, and to write the investor book, basically a sales document telling everyone why they'd be incredibly lucky to get their hands on a Redford bond. Then there's thirty days for closing, that's when everyone gets hysterical and shouts at one another and threatens to call the whole thing off. And we normally factor in another thirty days for contingencies on the "what can go wrong will go wrong" basis. All the while, the rating agencies are working on your rating, the lawyers are setting up your Special Purpose Vehicle, we're doing a copyright search to check all your records really are yours, we're checking Lexus-Nexus to confirm you're not a criminal, we're getting a tax opinion, a corporate opinion that your SPV is of good standing, and a bankruptcy opinion which states that even if you go bankrupt, your SPV and all its dedicated income stream will remain immune. If you survive all that, then we launch the issue to great plaudits and huge institutional appetite, and you go home to Wyoming a hundred million dollars richer, minus all the fees of course.'

Redford smiled, and Sarah could see in his eyes that he was also thinking of their tent in the wilderness.

'Very impressive,' he said, eyes still on her.

'That's the Goldsteins machine,' said Zamaroh, as if she, not Sarah, had just delivered the proposal. 'That's what Goldsteins International can do for you,' she continued, in hard sell mode, also seeking to remind Redford, noted Sarah, that this was about team Goldsteins, not about Sarah Jensen, at whom Redford was still smiling. Sarah smiled back, allowing herself just the smallest lapse. She'd done well in her presentation, she could feel Savage beaming beside her, and this was her reward; five seconds of Sarah the woman, responding to Redford the man. And all the while, there was her son's face looking back at her in her lover.

'So,' said Savage, inadvertently breaking the moment, 'do you have any questions?'

Redford's eyes became distant once more. 'Nope, not at this stage.' He got to his feet, slipping the presentation file under his arm. 'I'll give this to my lawyers right away,' he glanced back at Sarah, 'before I do anything rash with it.'

'Where will you be, if we need to contact you?' asked Savage, looking at Sarah with a puzzled frown.

'Back in the States,' answered Redford.

'Whereabouts?' asked Zamaroh, annoyed by his vagueness.

'All over. I'm on tour.'

'You broke your tour to come here?' asked Breden.

'I had a few days off. Besides, it's worth flying to London for a hundred million dollars, wouldn't you say?'

'I would,' replied Breden, 'and excuse me if I'm being impertinent, but why you in person? You could have sent any one of a legion of advisers.'

Sarah shifted awkwardly in her seat. This was becoming dangerous.

'That's why people like me get in trouble,' said Redford, with slow emphasis. 'They leave everything to a team of advisers, then they wonder why they've been screwed.'

Breden nodded, conceding the point. 'But why London? You could have gone to our offices in New York. It'd have been much easier.'

Redford cocked his head slightly and scrutinised Dick Breden. 'Where're you coming from, here? I don't get you.'

Breden shrugged. 'I'm curious. I like to know why people do things.'

'Jesus. Go ask my shrink.' Redford walked to the door. 'I'll be in touch.'

'What on earth got into you?' Zamaroh demanded of Breden, the moment the door swung shut. 'Quizzing him like he was a convict?'

'That's my job.'

'You *were* a bit persistent,' drawled Savage. 'Like a rather elegant terrier bothering a bone.'

'Something doesn't ring true,' replied Breden. 'I'm not sure what it is, I just know it's big.'

'Like what?' asked Zamaroh contemptuously. 'He'll be back in New York in a few hours. It's nothing to a rock star to get on a plane. Don't be so provincial, for God's sake.'

Breden turned his gaze upon Zamaroh, regarding her as he might a laboratory experiment. Sarah watched, saying nothing, hiding behind her silence. Then Breden fixed his gaze on her, stripping away her veil.

'What do you think?' he asked politely.

'He's a rock star,' she replied, 'and I'd say they operate on different rules to the rest of us. We should factor that in before we judge anything as odd by our standards.'

Breden looked at her for a while, pondering her answer, before giving a musing *hm*, and turning away.

'I think it went rather well,' said Savage, on his own trajectory. 'Don't you?' he asked the table at large. 'You mugged up pretty well, Sarah. I think we might just have a deal here.'

'Do you have copies of what you just handed him?' asked Zamaroh.

Sarah opened her briefcase and handed out three sets. Zamaroh pounced on hers. 'It sounded all right, but I'd like to check.'

My God, thought Sarah, approval from Savage, and praise, of sorts, from Zamaroh. She must have done a good job.

'I think we should be ready to move this on,' said Savage.

'How?' asked Zamaroh. 'The ball's in his court now.'

'Let's assume for a moment that we get this deal,' replied Savage. 'Before we get carried away, we need to establish if there is any reason why we might not want to add John Redford to our illustrious list of clients. I know we've got some real shitheads on our list, but they're discreet shitheads, they're establishment shitheads, or they're boring shitheads that are about as attractive to a journo as a brown paper bag. Redford is a rock star, for God's sake. He's supposed to be bad. I need to know just how bad he is. There's acceptably bad, and there's smearing shit all over our name and reputation bad. Dick, you think there's something fishy. Follow it up.'

Oh Jesus, the best private investigator in London hunting out Redford's skeletons. Sarah was still reeling from this when Savage turned to her. 'You work on this together with Dick.'

'I'm sorry?' She tried desperately hard not to understand what Savage was asking her.

'What's the big deal? Good God, woman, you look like I just asked you to walk through fire.'

Sarah just stared at him, in shock, struggling for composure.

'This is part of the work, going forward. You will get on with it if you want this assignment and, may I say, if you want your rather hefty fees to continue. And don't even think of asking. You will get no more, understand. Do *not* push me.' He turned to Breden, ignoring Sarah, who watched him in silent fury, tears raging, waiting to spill.

'You do the broad brush stuff,' Savage said to Breden. 'Background, where and how he grew up, what he's done since, with whom, financial arrangements, embarrassments, hobbies, homes, the works.' He turned back to Sarah. 'You have a week of grace. If in a week's time, I'm happy with all the preliminaries, then we have a deal and your private game starts. You delve into the man's soul, find out what's there, what he loves, what he hates, what he can't live without, what, if anything, he'd kill for. You rattle him and his cage until the skeletons come tumbling out and you be there to catch them.'

'And how do I manage that?' Sarah managed to say.

'You'll find a way.'

Chapter Twenty-one

Sarah spent a blissful, but poignant weekend with Georgie, Jacob and Alex. Her brother was flying off on Sunday for Peru, and they all tried to make the most of his last few hours in London for what would, if all went well, be more than two months. They walked the baby in the autumn sunshine, lay with him on the grass in Carlyle Square's communal garden, with Sarah reading and Georgie tearing up her papers. Eva Cunningham joined them for lunch on Saturday, arriving laden with goodies. Takeaway Chinese for the adults, the latest fashions from Baby Gap for Georgie. Eva played happily with Georgie, a wistful smile on her face while she gossiped with Sarah. On Sunday, Alex checked the last of his packing and shared an emotional goodbye with his sister, nephew and uncle.

Sarah took his face in her hands and kissed his forehead. 'Good luck, Al, and keep safe, eh? Promise me.'

He mirrored the gesture back at her. 'I will, don't you worry about me.' His eyes took on deeper intent. 'You keep yourself safe too, in every way.'

She took his meaning loud and clear and smiled with a reassurance she didn't completely feel. 'I will. Don't you worry about *me*.'

Sarah held Georgie tight as he waved away his uncle with a puzzled frown. She felt sorrow mixed with pride as the taxi bore Alex off for an adventure they had all doubted he would ever be well enough to take. Sarah still had her doubts and fears, but Alex had fought with every sinew to repair his body, and although it was unlikely he would ever fully recover the strength and mobility of old, he was still extremely strong and fit by most people's standards; enough to keep him safe on what would essentially be a trekking, not a climbing holiday. At Heathrow he would meet up with Eddie, his old travelling companion and an ex-boyfriend of Sarah's. Eddie's presence was a great reassurance to Sarah.

Also, after Georgie's birth, Alex had stopped being her *de facto* child, and the relationship between brother and sister had shifted on its axis.

Alex had always been protective of Sarah, but now she sensed in him a new measure of responsibility that involved a scaling-down of the risks he was prepared to take. Added to which, he was not quite so fey with money any more. He had been quietly earning, writing articles and interviews with top mountaineers and, despite Sarah's protestations, he had begun the tortuous process of paying his sister back the nine hundred thousand dollars which his uninsured hospital treatment had cost her.

Now he had gone, she would have no one to confide in about Redford. She'd have to bottle up her secrets even more than normal. With luck, the entire episode would be over and Redford out of her life by the time Alex came home.

She tried her best to keep Redford from her thoughts. That Sunday night, after she had put Georgie to bed, Jacob set off for Golders Green and a night of independence. Sarah heated up the meatloaf he had left her, then sought the refuge of sleep. Georgie was sleeping better now. He'd woken only once on Friday night, sleeping through the entirety of Saturday and Sunday nights, leaving her undisturbed with the dreams and fears which always seemed to ambush her under cover of darkness.

Monday morning saw Jacob reinstalled as babysitter and Sarah back in Goldsteins on the Leaker quest. Perhaps if she did find the culprit, she could take her fifty grand bonus and refuse the Redford assignment. Dreaming of it, she ran into PJ again in the ladies, this time by accident. As Sarah entered, PJ, who was in the process of applying mascara, caught her eye in the mirror.

'Hi,' said Sarah lightly. 'How're you doing?'

PJ studied her for a moment before answering. 'Shit, actually,' she replied, with surprising candour. 'My boyfriend dumped me a few weeks ago.'

'Ah,' said Sarah. 'That is shitty.'

'You might know him,' said PJ, turning from the mirror to face Sarah.

'What's his name?' asked Sarah, as if she didn't know.

'Giovanni di Castiglio.' PJ spoke the name with contempt, and longing.

Sarah shook her head. 'Why should I have known him?'

'You live in Carlyle Square, yeah?'

'Yeah, I do.' *God*, news travelled fast here.

'So does he. Number eighteen.'

'Opposite side of the square,' answered Sarah. 'Amazing how you can live so close to people and have no idea who they might be. Or what they might be up to.'

'Not if you keep your eyes open,' replied PJ, with a hint of a smile.

Sarah cocked her head. 'Meaning?'

'Well, as it happens, I live down the road from our noble chief executive.'

'*Do* you?' asked Sarah with interest. 'And?'

'Let's just say I've observed that Mrs Savage has something of a penchant for afternoon tea. Particularly on Wednesdays.'

Sarah puzzled that one for a moment, before hazarding a guess. 'You mean afternoon delight?'

PJ smirked. 'You said it, not me.' She dropped her mascara into her make-up bag and snapped shut the clasp.

'Just as a matter of interest,' mused Sarah, 'how would you know?'

PJ gave her a dismissive look. 'You never taken a sickie?'

Sarah smiled. 'I've lost count of how many.'

The day passed and PJ's comments faded. Sarah was extra vigilant in her search for the Leaker, but got nowhere. Tuesday and Wednesday came and went and neither she, nor the cameras, delivered the Leaker. Savage and Zamaroh grew increasingly nervous, and irritable. Both dictators in their own way, they took out their bile on those around them. On Thursday, short of inspiration, sick of office politics, Sarah decided to stay at home. The sun was shining, the garden square was radiant, and she felt like having a day lounging on the grass with Georgie.

She diverted calls to her mobile, praying it wouldn't ring. It stayed silent until just before lunchtime. She grabbed it up, before it could wake Georgie, sleeping on a blanket under an old oak, and moved a few yards away.

'Yeah?'

'Sarah? James here. Great news. John Redford has signed.'

'That's fantastic,' replied Sarah with wildly mixed feelings. 'We've got the deal you wanted. The biggest rock-star syndication yet. We've beaten the Leaker.'

'I hope so. He's been like a shadow. I've been imagining him everywhere, Zamaroh too. I hope we've seen the last of him.'

'Breden's cameras turned up anything?'

'Not a thing.'

'Maybe he's got bored, gone on to torture someone else,' suggested Sarah, not believing it. 'Got a good contract with Redford?'

'Pretty good. Fourteen pages of legalese, which boils down to Goldsteins undertaking to structure, price and lead a bond issue backed by the catalogue of his hits. He, in turn, has warranted that he knows of no prior incident, encumbrance or claim which could threaten the viability of the deal from execution to redemption of the bonds,' recited Savage.

'Has he?'

'You think he has something to hide?'

'Who doesn't?'

'You know what I mean.'

'He's a performer. He'd hide it well, wouldn't he?'

'We're all bloody performers. Will you take the job?'

Sarah said nothing, still unable to come to terms with what Savage was asking her to do.

'I know you have your doubts,' Savage went on. 'Care to tell me what the problem is?'

Oh Jesus. 'My problem is it's a set-up, and I'm almost guaranteed to fail. The worst skeletons are the best buried.'

'Like what?'

'God, I don't know. The man's got to be a real pro at protecting his private life. Nearly twenty years at the top and he's probably had his privacy violated so many times he's become an expert at concealment. It's not necessarily anything sinister for him, just a way of life, I'd imagine.'

'Perhaps, but I sincerely doubt there are any dark secrets lurking there.'

'Breden's turned up nothing?'

'All fine so far.'

'You've decided he's kosher?'

'Enough to sign a mandate letter and certificate of undertaking. If we, or you, find anything along the way we don't like, then that becomes a condition adverse and we pull the deal. It'd be embarrassing, but not disastrous. What *would* be a disaster is to miss something and have it come out while we're launching the issue, or during the life of the bond. Especially if we decide to hold it all ourselves.'

'Will you?'

'That depends partly on what you come up with.'

'That's what worries me, James. There's too much riding on this. Rock stars aren't exactly my field of expertise.'

'Reading people is your expertise.'

'I don't know, James. It's *so* messy. So easy to get it wrong, and it'd be my ass on the line.'

'Come on, Sarah. It could be a great deal. A first for Goldsteins and for you. You're always saying to give you something interesting, something sexy.'

'This is at the pornographic end of sexy. So hot someone could get burned and that someone is usually me.'

'You've never cared about that in the past. The riskier the better as far as you were concerned, if I remember rightly.'

'Maybe I've lost my appetite for risks.'

Savage laughed. 'I'll believe that when I see it.'

'I don't want the job, James. Can't you just accept that? Dick'll do it fine. You really don't need me.'

'Dick won't be able to get the access you will.'

'I don't see why you should assume that. Besides, he'll find a way. He always does.'

'Not as good a way as I've got for you.'

'What d'you mean?' Sarah asked, suspicion and panic mounting. Savage paused. Sarah felt the energy crackle between them.

'You go on tour with him for two weeks.'

'I do *what*?'

'Before we signed I told him and his manager that you'd need to spend many hours going over the business in general, and picking apart all his contracts, to assure Goldsteins that there were no liens there shouldn't be, no side agreements that affect the disbursement of his income, no other claimants, the works. You'd already laid that groundwork rather cleverly in your presentation. They said fine, but where were they going to get the time for that? They are in the middle of a world tour. I left it with them, made it pretty clear they would need to find the time. Cawdor rang back, said you were invited to join them for a two-week leg.'

Sarah couldn't speak.

'New York, London, Paris and Venice with one of the sexiest men on the planet, or so I'm told, and five thousand pounds a day. What more could you want?'

Chapter Twenty-two

One hour later, Sarah and Georgie arrived in Golders Green. Sarah carried a sleepy Georgie from the car, through the gate that Jacob deliberately left squeaking, as part of his early warning system. Jacob's garden welcomed them with scents of honeysuckle and jasmine. He was at the door to meet them.

Sarah looked with love into his face. This man had been a surrogate father to her and her orphaned brother. When Sarah and Alex's parents were killed in the car crash in New Orleans, the children were brought back to London by Sarah's father's sister, Isla. They came to this place, Rotherwick Road, in North London, and Jacob was their next-door neighbour. Isla was a Professor of Chemistry at London University. She was kind, but too cerebral and caught up in her work to give the children the attention they needed. Jacob provided warm meals and kind hands to tend their bloodied knees and broken hearts.

His wife had died the year before Sarah and Alex arrived in Rotherwick Road, giving him something new to live for. The children's hearts never did heal (you never got over that kind of loss, merely learned to accommodate it), but they learned to love again. Jacob was their love, their friend, their mentor, their security. He sat with Alex, pored over atlases with him, read stories about the great mountaineering expeditions, fired in the young boy a love for adventure which he never lost. He had helped nurture Sarah's anarchy, her unconventional morality. Jacob was a retired safe-cracker. He'd worked for thirty years and, at Sarah's insistence, retired before he got caught. Sarah had also pestered him until he'd passed on some of his skills to her, and although she was a tad rusty, she reckoned she could still get into most basic safes.

Sarah looked into Jacob's weathered face and thought about the people she had loved, and lost to violent death. Her parents, her best friend, and her lover. Jacob had been her salvation. She couldn't imagine life without him. Isla had moved to the States when Sarah grew up, and Sarah had adapted easily enough to life without her, but she feared the loss of Jacob more than her own death. He was seventy-eight, still sprightly and good-looking, but his ageing terrified her, and every new sign of it rent her with pain. She stroked the back of his head and kissed his cheek.

'Hello, sweetie.' He stood back and checked her face, noting her extra tenderness with suspicion. He turned to Georgie, who was waking up rapidly, fuelled with excitement by Jacob and his new surroundings.

'Hello, my beautiful boy.' He kissed Georgie's forehead, and the baby squirmed and giggled as his soft whiskers tickled him. 'Come on in. I don't know about you, but I'm starving.'

He led Sarah and Georgie into his house and Sarah felt once again the balm that had saved her childhood. His cat, Ruby, wound herself round Sarah's ankles, and purred when she bent down to stroke her. There were roses on the kitchen table, in a simple vase, a chicken baking in the oven, turning crisp and golden, and a bottle of red Burgundy breathing on the sideboard. Jacob took out two of his giant glasses.

'Like one?'

'Love one.'

Jacob had taught her about wine, about cooking. She could feel him scrutinising her. She put Georgie on a mat on the floor with a selection of toys and took a seat at the table.

'So where're you off to then?' asked Jacob, handing her a glass.

Sarah sat down at the kitchen table and took a mouthful of wine. 'Is it that obvious?'

'You ring up and announce that you're coming round. You're fizzing with excitement, and trepidation, trying to act cool, as if you should know better. I can practically see a phantom suitcase by your side. So what is it? Trip with some new boyfriend?'

'No new boyfriend,' said Sarah, gulping her wine. 'No old boyfriend either. I'm going to New York. With the rock star.'

'What? That Redfern fella?' Jacob sat down opposite Sarah, and leaned across the table toward her.

'Redford.'

'Is that supposed to mean something to me? Who the hell is he, and what's he want with you?'

'He's a client, Jacob.'

'I know that.'

'He writes and performs rock music and ballads. It's beautiful, wild, poignant music. He's sold hundreds of millions of records around the world, and he's signed with Goldsteins.'

'And what're you supposed to do with him?'

'Check him out. Shake him till his skeletons come rattling out. If there are no nasty ones, Goldsteins do this deal for him; if there are, we pull out.'

'You'll be popular, won't you? He's a rock star, sweetie. They're all raving loonies.'

'Well, let's hope not. Savage rang an hour ago and asked me if I'd go on tour with Redford for two weeks.'

Jacob got up and busied himself with the cooker. A few minutes later, he doled out chicken and roast potatoes. He didn't speak until they both had steaming plates before them.

'What about George?'

Sarah grimaced. 'I don't know. I want to go and I'm frantic about the thought of leaving him. I'm torn and I don't know what to do.'

'What did you tell Savage?'

'That I'd get back to him.'

'Two weeks is a long time.'

'I know. I'd try to come back for a few nights, but it'd still be horrible.'

'So why do you want to go?'

Oh God. *Because part of her loved John Redford, had loved him from that first passionate night in the wilderness, loved him all the more for being the father, albeit unknowing, of her beloved child; part of her craved him, part of her felt she was following some strange path fate had carved out for her.*

'Because I feel I have to, Jacob.'

The old man gave her a long, probing look.

'I know I can't tell you what to do with yourself. No one ever could, even when you were a little girl, so I won't say don't go, but for my sake and your son's, look after yourself. New York with a strange man . . .' Jacob gazed off worriedly into the distance.

Sarah felt a sickening mixture of elation and agony. She'd handed Jacob the dice, and he had thrown her fate. She would leave her baby for two weeks, to be with a man. To work, she told herself, to earn money. The lover and the mother rose up in her, in clamouring, denouncing opposition.

'I'll be careful,' said Sarah. 'Don't worry. His manager'll be there as well, and a whole entourage, no doubt. Safety in numbers and all that.'

'What's he like?'

This was agony. To have to lie repeatedly to the one man on the planet, besides her son and her brother, to whom she owed the truth.

'He seems nice, sensitive, thoughtful, intelligent – quiet, almost.'

It was on Jacob's lips: *And what would your mother have said about the quiet ones*? But he swallowed his words.

'Take care of yourself, sweetie, and I'll take care of your son.' He paused for a moment, looking down at his food with a sudden lack of appetite. 'When do you have to leave?'

Sarah pushed her full plate away from her. 'Tomorrow.'

Chapter Twenty-three

The following morning, Sarah breastfed Georgie for the last time. The finality of it left her utterly bereft. It marked a cut-off, a rite of passage along the journey of separation from her child. She feared he would no longer be her baby in quite the same way. This was something she could do for him that no one else could. It was her unique bond, and now she was losing it.

After she'd finished feeding him, she took Georgie downstairs to Jacob, and left him in his arms. Then she returned upstairs to her room, threw herself on her bed and howled for five minutes. Later, she picked herself up, and began to pack her suitcase, moving dully like an automaton. She switched on the CD player, turned the volume up high. John Redford's voice filled the room, blocking out all else, as if the two of them were alone together. He played emotions as expertly as he played the guitar, but he was better at pain than at joy. Where did it come from, all his pain? He was singing a ballad, a lament to lost love:

'Run away, run away, run away, run away.
Words can't hold you, touch can't hold you,
eyes can't hold you, love can't hold you.
You're a prisoner of my heart,
Run away, run away, run away, run away.

Go now before you kill me,
Kill me with your words,
Kill me with your touch,
Kill me with your eyes,
Kill me with no love.
Run away, run away, run away, run away.

Stop pretending, sweet love, stop pretending,
I can see your love's gone,
Your touch is cold, your eyes are absent,
You're somewhere else, with someone else,
And I'm dying without you.
Run away, run away, run away, run away.

Sarah turned off the music and walked downstairs to Jacob and Georgie. She took her son in her arms, held his head to her lips, breathed him in.

'I have to go away, my love. But I'll be back. I'll think of you all the time. I'll send you love all the time. I'll . . .' she faltered as tears threatened to overwhelm her. She would not cry in front of him, frighten him with her sorrow. She fought for composure, and when she had found it she held her child away from her so that she could see his eyes. 'I love you, my sweetheart. Mama loves you.'

Jacob watched her, tears flowing down his own cheeks. He wiped them away, hoping Sarah hadn't seen them, and lifted Georgie from her embrace. A door slammed outside, footsteps sounded on the stairs and the intercom rang. Jacob answered it.

'She'll be out in a second.' He turned to Sarah. 'Taxi's here.'

She kissed Georgie one last time and headed for the door.

The telephone rang, freezing her. She grabbed it up from the hall table on her way out.

'Yes?'

'Sarah, it's James. Just been speaking to this entertainment lawyer at Theodore Goddard,' he announced portentously. 'Says to look out for women. They could be Redford's downfall. Mothers of his love-children, waiting in the wings with their palimony and paternity claims, trying to argue that they co-wrote his songs, that the copyright's not really his. Sarah? Are you there? Sarah? *Sarah*?'

Chapter Twenty-four

Sarah surfed through the music selection as the plane flew her across the Atlantic. It didn't take her long to find John Redford. He was singing a cover version of Van Morrison's 'Queen of the Slipstream'. He sang into her headphones as if he were whispering into her ear. She fell asleep dreaming of fountains of lies, and dreams made visible in the face of a child.

Her flight touched down at JFK at twelve. She made her way through the thronging airport, immigration, customs, baggage claim, out onto the chill forecourt where the taxis lumbered up and sped away. Pulling her coat tight around her, she waited her turn, casting covert looks at her fellow travellers. The sun hung bright in the sky, making her squint. It always seemed to be sunny in New York. Each time she arrived, she had been welcomed by radiant sun, summer or winter. There was a faint shadow, too, of a quarter moon, set to outwait the brilliance of the day.

Sarah's turn came. She dumped her luggage in the boot, sat back on the cracked plastic seats of the cab, and, for the first time in her life in the city, obeyed Eartha Kitt's injunction not to be evil and fasten her seatbelt. She smiled wryly to herself. Georgie the puppet-master, unwittingly twitching her strings. Her cab took off like the space shuttle, bearing her to Manhattan.

The SoHo Grand looked strange, redbrick, very modern, almost like an unimaginative apartment complex in Marylebone. This impression was immediately dispelled as Sarah walked into the ground-floor foyer. It made her think of Batman's underground lair, with its brickwork, industrial metal and glass stairway, watched over by a pair of bronze dogs which looked at once frightening and comforting, depending on whose side they were on.

She padded up the stairs to the first-floor reception area and gazed about her as she waited to be checked in. The other guests were, for the most part, as hip as the hotel. They tended toward casual dress, as befitted the SoHo location. There was a profusion of beige jerseys, worn tight over well-tended pectorals for the men, while the women favoured anything by Prada. Lovingly aged leather pouffes and well-padded sofas marked the lounging area to the right of Reception. Lavish palms with blunt-cut leaves cast Far Eastern shadows. The effect, for all its trendiness, was incredibly soothing, as well as glamorous. Sarah felt as if she had stepped back into the Jazz Age.

The receptionist straightened when Sarah announced her name and handed over her passport to check in. There was a quiet stir, and she was immediately escorted to her room. The guest relations person, Deborah according to her name tag, pushed the PH button in the lift, and appeared to wait expectantly for something from Sarah. The lift shot upwards and opened onto a soothing coffee-toned hallway. Sarah snaked left, trailing the other woman. They stopped before a distressed metal door, which Deborah opened with a flourish. Sarah stepped over the threshold, into her room. Correction, into her penthouse suite.

'Enjoy your stay,' exhorted Deborah. 'Let us know if there's anything at all we can get you.'

Sarah nodded, wondering what was included in 'anything at all'. She dumped her handbag and walked excitedly through a huge sitting room, flooded by light, to a French door opening onto the biggest roof terrace she had ever seen. She let herself out, gasping as the chill autumn wind whipped around her. Manhattan stretched before her, midtown straight ahead, the East River to her right. She had an almost complete three-sixty view. A wooden sun-lounger lay next to an arrangement of mini firs and decorative cabbages. If the weather turned, she could sunbathe naked, overseen only by helicopters.

Gazing down at the hustle and bustle on Canal Street below, Sarah felt rarefied, cosseted. This surely ranked fairly high on the scale of compensations. She let herself back into her suite. The bedroom was deliciously cosy and snug, with a burnt-orange blanket folded down over the bed, chocolate walls, and another great sun-drenched view. There were striped taffeta curtains, crisp to the touch like a debutante's ballgown. A golden margarita floated in a bowl of water, black and white photographs adorned the walls. Wouldn't this be great, if only she didn't have to work! The realisation brought her down with a bump. No such thing as a free lunch, she mouthed to herself, as she finally acknowledged the glowing message light on the telephone.

There were four messages, all from Strone Cawdor, asking her to call him. Take a laxative, she thought crudely, hanging up. She quickly grabbed up her bag and coat and quit the balm of the hotel for a bit of street New York. She loved this city. The energy, the anonymity, the thrilling possibility that lay behind every secret smile and tinted window.

She couldn't meet Redford yet. She wanted just a few hours alone with her dreams and illusions, before she set about destroying them all. She started walking, not knowing where she was heading; it didn't really matter. She was wearing her black Todds, her 'urban commando boots' as Jacob called them, and was ready to walk for miles. On Broadway, the full force of the wind assailed her. God, it was brutal here. For all the comforts of the life here, nature would not be tamed.

She paused by a street sign – Worth Street. Written underneath was 'The Avenue of the Strongest'. She smiled to herself. She was in the vicinity of Wall Street. *Were* the Wall Streeters the strongest, or was there some more subtle reference she was missing?

She returned to the hotel in time for an exaggeratedly late lunch. Back upstairs, she took out her electronic key and let herself into her suite. She paused on the threshold, senses screaming. Something was wrong. She felt a presence; the air vibrated with it.

Movement caught her eye.

'At fucking last. Where the hell have you been?'

Strone Cawdor sauntered out of the bathroom, shaking water from his fingers. He walked rudely past Sarah and sat down with his back to her. 'Didn't you get my messages? I left four.' He reached out and took a handful of peanuts from a silver dish, rained them into his mouth one by one. Finally, he turned to look at Sarah.

'Get out of my room,' she said, her voice low. She stood completely still, her face devoid of emotion. Something in her tone made Strone get to his feet. Then, as if remembering his cool, he spat back at her.

'*What* did you say?'

Sarah took a step closer. 'Get out. Now.'

Strone forced out a laugh. 'Did I hear you say *your* room? Two thousand dollars a night, with my signature on your bill, did you say *your room*?'

Sarah walked to a side table and picked up a phone. She tapped out three numbers. 'Security? Yes, you can help. There's a man in my—'

'Shut the fuck up!' screamed Strone. He leapt over the sofa and slammed his fist on the telephone, cutting the connection. 'Stupid bitch. If the press got hold of this . . . Ring them back now – tell them it was a mistake. They'll be here in seconds, they'll—'

'Better get out, then.'

Strone made a stabbing motion at Sarah with his index finger, then rushed from the room. She slammed the door behind him, then leaned back against it, breathing hard, shaking. She looked at her suitcase, propped against the wall, not even opened yet, and contemplated picking it up, walking out and flying home. The doorbell rang, and walkie talkies crackled outside. She peered through the peephole; Security. She opened the door and two men rushed in.

'You had an intruder, ma'am?' asked one, eyes scanning the room, while the other crossed it in three long strides.

'He's gone,' said Sarah. She contemplated giving out Strone's name, for Goldsteins' sake decided not to.

'What happened, ma'am?' asked one while the other got on his walkie talkie. 'What did he look like?'

'It was a misunderstanding,' Sarah found herself saying. 'Someone I knew. Playing a trick on me.'

She managed to convince the clearly sceptical security men that she was fine, the victim of nothing more than an error of judgement. Just as she closed the door on them with many thanks and more reassurances, the phone rang.

'Sarah?'

Her heart jumped. 'Yes?'

'It's John. I'm really sorry about what happened. Can I come and see you?'

Chapter Twenty-five

Redford was wearing faded sweatpants and a white T-shirt. His hair was unwashed, combed only by his fingers. There was a sheen of sweat glistening on his face. Sarah could smell him. She could almost taste him.

'Sorry about the gear.' He gestured to his outfit, walking into Sarah's suite. 'I just came from the gym.'

'You must have caused a riot.'

He laughed. 'They have a private gym in my suite.'

'Oh. How lonely.'

Redford looked surprised. 'It is,' he said simply. 'Half the point of the gym is forcing yourself on to impress the chicks there, and the other guys.'

Sarah remembered every inch of his body, knew it was worked to perfection. She tried to push the memory from her mind.

'Look, Sarah, I'm really, really sorry about Strone being in here. He thinks because we sign the cheques the room is his, and he—'

'No,' said Sarah, 'he thought that *I* was his, that because you might be paying Goldsteins a fee, he owns everyone who works for them. Let me tell you something . . .' She paused. 'No, wait. Let me tell that asshole himself.'

Redford shrugged. 'It's your energy. Go burn him, if you want.' Sarah slowly sat down, her temper still blazing, but checked.

'He's a hot-head,' said Redford quietly, 'but he's got a good heart. Problem is, way we live, it's easy to lose touch. He needs a reality-check. We all do. We've been on tour over a year now, and the pressure gets to you. I'm not excusing him, I just want to ease this over.'

He saw Sarah looking at her suitcase. 'You're not thinking of running again?'

'Absolutely I am. If this is the way it starts out.'

'Come on, Sarah. Give him a second chance. Please.'

'Why?' she asked, resolutely unmoved.

'Because everyone makes mistakes.'

'So? I don't have to suffer his. You know I really wish I'd just let his horse bolt into the forest.'

Redford smiled involuntarily. 'I know. I feel that way about him sometimes too.'

'He comes across as *soooo* cocky, but I've seen what he's really like when he's scared. He's like a little boy.'

'That's his nice side.'

'I mean, the bastard doesn't even recognise me!'

'He was in shock when you delivered him back to the ranch. And the whole thing was an episode he'd rather forget. He flew out on the first available flight, back to New York, back to urban safety, and he's never mentioned it since. Denial, it's called. Let me tell you, ain't nothing worse for a control freak than losin' it on a bolting horse.'

Sarah burst out laughing. 'Probably did him good.'

'It would do, if he ever confronted it.'

'How do you stick him?'

'He's actually a nice guy under the bluster. You've got to have a lot of front to do what he does. There's so many people trying to rip me off, he has to play the hard man. He has to be in control the whole time.'

'Yeah well, not of me. I don't see why I should suffer him.'

'All right. How 'bout this deal's important to me?'

'Why's that?' she asked softly.

'You *know* why.'

They stared at each other, searching one another's eyes, for one brief moment dropping their act. Redford's question was all too visible. *Why did you walk out on me*? Sarah turned away and went to the window. She looked out over Canal Street as a stretch limo crept up to the kerbside.

Redford came up behind her. 'What do you want? How can I make this right?'

Sarah turned to face him. Her face was less than twelve inches from his. She skirted round him, took refuge behind a chair, gripped its back.

'*I'll* sort it out. I'll get the pass key from that bastard and I'll pay for my own suite. If he tries to get in here again, I'll bypass Security and ring the press myself, and what's more I'll tell them he's a scaredy boy ninny who can't ride a horse for shit.'

Redford smiled. 'All right, you've got a deal. But look, there's no need for you to pick up the tab. These rooms cost a shitload of money. Even I'm not so out of touch I don't know that. How can you possibly afford—'

'I'm not an impoverished banker, John, even if there were such a creature. I work freelance for Goldsteins, on special deals. I work only out of choice, not necessity,' she lied. 'I long ago earned myself the luxury of working only when I choose. You think rock stars have egos, that rock-star managers have egos – well, traders'd give them a run for their money. Strone had better treat me with kid gloves from now on, and if he doesn't I'll kick the shit out of him before I trample him on my way out. No one owns me – got it? If I stay, it's for Goldsteins' sake, because James Savage wants this deal, and because it's important to you.'

'So you will stay?'

'For now.'

Sarah pulled back her hair from her face and paced. Redford watched her and waited. She paused by the sofa, gripping its back, keeping it as a barrier between them.

'Can I ask you a question?'

'Yeah, sure.'

'Does Strone know we know each other – *knew* each other?' A blush spread over her cheeks.

Redford shook his head. 'No, he doesn't.'

'Didn't you tell him you'd gone over to thank me for rescuing him? I mean, he was still staying with you after all.'

'He'd flown out before I went to look you up. The ranch hand, Earl, told me you told him you were staying at Spring Creek. Strone didn't even know that. Earl also told me that Strone said you'd rescued him; Strone couldn't even tell me that himself. All he ever said to me was that he hated horses, wasn't ever going to set his ass on one again, then he upped and went back to the city. Wasn't any point in talking about you. Besides, some things are private.'

Sarah needed the full explanation, felt relieved he'd given it so gracefully. She flicked a glance at him. He was watching her as if searching for a clue. She turned away.

'I'm assuming Goldsteins don't know we knew each other,' he said softly.

'No,' replied Sarah. 'They don't.'

'Well, no point telling them now, is there?'

Sarah met his eye, grateful. 'No, there's not.'

'Good. I'm glad we sorted that out.'

Sarah felt adrift. Redford's intuiting what she needed and giving it to her so elegantly that she was spared any appearance of having shown her hand, disarmed her. She didn't want him to be so reasonable, or so generous.

'Look, I've got to clear my mind, have a cup of tea, calm down.'

He took the hint, raised a hand in farewell. 'I'm gone.'

Sarah watched the door closing behind him. Why did he have to be so damned sensitive? He was a rock star, for God's sake. He was supposed to be a selfish egomaniac. He must want this deal very badly, she thought badtemperedly, to be so nice to her.

The bell rang five minutes later. A bellboy handed over a room key, and an envelope. Sarah bent the plastic key double, and threw it into the bin. She sliced open the envelope with a fruit knife.

Dear Sarah,

Would you like to start the information process? We can meet you at five-thirty in my suite, if that suits you.

Strone.

No explicit apology, but the uncharacteristically conciliatory tone was probably as close to an apology as Strone could come. Sarah picked up the phone.

The manager answered with a bored-sounding, 'Yeah?'

'I'll see you in twenty minutes.'

She hung up and walked to the wall of window. She dropped to her belly and lay, nose to the cold glass, gazing out at Manhattan. She loved this city of dreams, or reinvention, of brutal fantasy. People were prepared to believe in whatever illusion you created, as long as you believed in it yourself, and carried it through with sufficient trappings and flair. So, who was John Redford? Who was *she*?

Chapter Twenty-six

They sat round a glass and steel table. John Redford had showered and changed into faded black jeans and a black polo-neck jersey. Strone Cawdor wore jeans and a perfectly ironed white shirt that looked made to measure. Sarah wore brogues, black wool trousers from her new men's suit collection, a sky-blue long-sleeved T-shirt and a tight black cardigan. She wore her huge ruby ring, and a waterproof Swatch.

Strone looked over at her. He had swung between relieved and edgy since she had walked in. She wondered what Redford had said to him.

'Would you like something to drink?' he asked her.

'Espresso would be nice, and a bottle of still water.'

He dialled room service and recited their orders. Redford had still mineral water, room-temperature, with lemon.

'How un-American,' observed Sarah. She recalled him ordering the same thing at Goldsteins.

'What, exactly?' asked Redford, eyes sardonic.

'Americans normally have lashings of ice.'

'Freezes your digestion.'

'Into healthy living?'

'Aren't you? You look like you are.'

'I like to mix it up a little,' said Sarah. 'Stops me becoming too obsessive.'

'Are you obsessive?' asked Redford with interest.

'By nature.'

'About what?'

'Details,' said Sarah with a smile. 'Shall we start?'

Redford leaned back in his chair, giving Sarah a faint grin, as if to say, round one to you.

'How do we do this?' asked Strone.

'It's like a tango,' said Sarah. 'Only I'm the man.'

'Meaning?'

'I lead and you follow.'

To his credit, Strone didn't flinch.

'Lead on.' He gave her a slow smile, head tipped to one side, scrutinising her. But before she could speak, he held up one hand as if to halt her. 'You know, it's really bugging me. I'd swear I know you from somewhere.'

Sarah felt the blood rush to her face. Strone's eyes were on her, Redford's too. She could not afford to blow this. She tried to imagine her face bathed in ice.

'Really?' Her voice came out light, bemused. 'Where from, do you think? Because I have no recollection of ever meeting you.'

He shook his head. 'That's it. I'm damned if I can remember.'

'I've been back and forth to New York a lot in my time,' answered Sarah smoothly. 'Perhaps we just passed in the street, or sat next to one another on the plane.'

'Yeah, that's probably it.' Strone shrugged, as if it were of no consequence, but Sarah could see the curiosity still burning in his sharp eyes.

'Well, shall we get on?' asked Sarah. The two men nodded.

Sarah turned to Redford. She paused for a moment before she spoke, gathering herself, adopting her impersonal banker persona.

'I need to know who you are, who you were, who you will be, who buys your records, for how much and where. I need to clarify your figures, sales, royalties, any and all deductions, down the line till the money comes to you. Some of this I've seen, but I need a deeper explanation. I'll need to know all about all your contractual professional relationships, the contents of your different bank accounts, details of your assets, homes, cars, shareholdings, why you need the money, why you want a public deal. I need to know what your plans are for the next ten years, professionally, personally, if it's relevant. I'll write a worst-case scenario, a mid- or most-likely-case scenario, and a best-case scenario. What can go wrong, what can go right and why. I need to know if there's anyone who might make claims against you, or your catalogue, claiming *they* wrote or co-wrote your songs, or claiming anything else that might give them rights over Redford Inc.'

'Jesus.' Redford raked his fingers through his hair.

Sarah wondered if she'd overdone it, mixing in too many of the private investigator's questions with the banker's.

'Get used to the intrusion,' she said evenly. 'I know it's not pleasant, but I'm not doing this for fun, or from curiosity. I'm doing this because the investors demand it, and because Goldsteins have a duty of care to provide all the relevant information. If we don't and something goes wrong, we can be sued, and our reputation seriously damaged. Sorry to sound so pompous. I just want you to realise this isn't personal.'

'It's personal to me,' said Redford.

'I know, and I'll try to be as sensitive as I can.'

'Is this really necessary?' asked Strone. 'Isn't there another way, a less intrusive way?'

'Not if you want this deal to work,' replied Sarah. 'Any decent bank would require the same information. Any outfit that didn't wouldn't know their job and would consign the deal to failure because the investors down the line will require this information and they will go through all the minutiae with a fine-toothed comb until they're satisfied. Believe me, there's no other way.'

'All right. I don't like it, but I'll buy it,' said Strone. He turned to Redford. 'Yeah?'

'Yeah.'

Then he turned back to Sarah. 'John Redford started writing songs when he was fourteen. His grandmother taught him piano; he sang and accompanied himself.'

Sarah suddenly had an image of a lonely child singing out his dreams.

'Ah, you don't want the nostalgia,' said Strone, utterly misreading Sarah's faraway look. 'Let's stick to the numbers, then. John Redford has made a series of deals with record companies over the years, getting better and bigger all the time. But, believe it or not, it's hard to make money in this business if you're a performer.' Strone paused. 'You look surprised, but let me tell you where all the money goes before the last bit trickles down to the artist.'

He bent over and pulled a CD and a calculator from his briefcase. He banged the edge of the CD on the table. 'Cassandra Wilson. Jazz I happen to like, but let's say it's John Redford, selling in the UK.' He took his calculator and plugged in a number. 'Start off with the price you pay if you walk into, say, W.H. Smith. £14.99. Take off £2.62 for VAT, that leaves you with £12.37,' he said, rapidly tapping out more calculations. 'About thirty per cent of that, around £3.71, goes to Smiths. That leaves £8.65. Ten per cent of that, 86 pence, goes to the music publisher and songwriter, both of whom, happily, is John, leaving £7.79. That's your royalty base. John, because he's at the very top of his profession, gets a twenty per cent royalty, that's £1.56. That works out at ten per cent of the retail cost of the CD. But if you think that goes in his pocket, you'd be wrong. Let's say he sells a million copies of the CD – he actually sells a hell of a lot more than that, but let's keep the sums simple. On a million sales, that's a total royalty of let's say, one and a half million pounds to John. Out of that comes what's called the "free goods factor", supposed to cover the CDs the record company gives away free to promote the album; part of it does go on that, but the rest is basically just another rip-off the artist has to pay. That takes fifteen per cent, or £234,000, which leaves John with £1,326,000. Then he has to pay another rip-off deduction to the record company. This one's called a *reserve*, supposed to protect them if they've done their sums wrong and have given him too much. The reserve takes another twenty per cent, or £265,200, leaving John with £1,060,800, plus his publishing royalty, which would equate to £860,000, giving him £1,920,800. His agent takes five per cent, that's £96,040, leaving £1,824,760. Then I take ten per cent as his manager and business manager, that's £182,476, leaving £1,642,284. Then the record company deducts a hundred per cent of the recording costs, which would be around £200,000, and fifty per cent of the video production costs of £50,000. Legal, accounting and other business costs take around another £200,000, and that leaves John Redford, superstar, with £1,192,284 net on a gross sale of £14,990,000.'

Sarah let out a hiss of breath. 'Let me get this straight. One million albums, selling in the High Street for nearly fifteen million pounds in total, leaves John with –' she took out her own calculator and tapped out the sums, '£1,192,284, which amounts to only 7.9 per cent. That's outrageous!'

Strone smiled. 'And *that's* before tax. Also, you have to remember, it's very unusual that an artist is also the music publisher and songwriter. Without those royalties, John's percentage-take of the whole CD price would be closer to five per cent.'

'The penniless rock star,' said Sarah wryly.

'It's more common than you think,' said Strone. 'Course, John sells throughout the world. One million per album's just his UK take, so he has the volume to bring in the big bucks, even if the percentages are small, but it makes the point.'

Sarah nodded. 'Presumably the tours bring in a lot of money?'

'Now they do,' replied Strone. 'Coca Cola sponsors them, picks up all the costs, and that makes a real difference. When we wind up this tour, we estimate 3.4 million people will have come to fifty-nine John Redford concerts. With an average ticket price of forty pounds, that grosses 136 million pounds. From that, the deductions run as follows.' Strone recited all the facts and figures from memory.

'How do you organise all the financials?' asked Sarah. 'Do you have receipts coming in to lots of subsidiary companies, all held by one holding company?'

'Yeah, different companies for different tax jurisdictions.'

'Could you get copies of all the back-up information, all the sources of those figures you've just quoted me, to Goldsteins in London?'

'What'll they do with them?'

'They'll use them as a reference point for writing our internal book with all our details on historical financials, and they'll form the basis for future projections.'

Strone looked uneasy.

'Is there a problem?' asked Sarah.

'There're over forty different companies.'

'We're used to paper mountains,' Sarah said breezily, filing away his concern. 'If you could have someone supply me with the summary you've just given me, sales figures, royalties and so on, I can start to play around more with the structuring.'

'You do that stuff?' asked Strone.

'What do you think I do?'

'Ask difficult questions.'

'I do that too. That's stage one. The structuring's stage two.'

'I thought the rocket scientists did that,' said Strone.

Sarah laughed.

'That's what they're called, isn't it?' asked the manager.

'That's what they're called,' replied Sarah.

'So you do it?'

'I do it.'

'Don't think me rude,' said Redford, 'I'm just curious. How did you get into all this? What qualifications do you have?'

'A Double First from Cambridge in mathematics and philosophy; eight years in the City. Will that do?'

'You don't look like a mathematician,' said Strone.

'Jesus,' said Sarah, 'and I thought the City was sexist. Well, my brain cells *think* like a mathematician, which is what matters.'

Redford was glaring at Strone.

'What do you think I'm here for?' Sarah asked. 'Do you think I'm some wide-eyed innocent who has come along for a bit of PR? That you could flash a smart hotel suite at me, give me a backstage pass, a few good dinners and I'd go home and say, "Hey guys, had a great time, we've got to do this deal"? I'm sorry, but it doesn't work like that in the City, and it doesn't work like that with me.' Sarah got to her feet.

Redford stood up too. 'Hey, calm down. Don't you think you're overreacting a little here?'

'Are you so used to sleeping with groupies you can't get your mind round the concept of a woman with brains?' Sarah asked coldly.

Redford stared at her in anger. 'That's a trashy stereotype.'

'Exactly,' said Sarah. 'Get the point. See how you like it.' She walked to the door. 'That's about enough shit for one day for me. Get me the numbers, would you please, get me your mundane press releases, your hagiographies and puff stuff, and perhaps tomorrow we can do something real.'

Back in her suite, Sarah cursed herself. She sat down heavily on the bed, head in hands. How could she lose her temper so easily? The fabric of her self-control seemed to have burned away, leaving her naked and defenceless. What had happened to her poker-player's sang froid? She got up and stumbled to the bathroom, where she splashed her face with cold water, then she returned to bed, pulled the covers up around her and rang Jacob.

'How's everything?'

'Hello, sweetie. Everything's just fine. Little one's missing you, keeps searching round, but I'm keeping him amused. So far so good.'

'I miss him so much it hurts,' she said. 'Give him a huge hug and kiss from Mama, will you?'

'I will. He's kipping like a good 'un, you'll be pleased to hear.'

'Oh good. Bless him.'

'Now, tell me. How are things your end?'

'Horrible. I want to come home.'

'Aw, sweetie.'

'I just picked a fight with the client. I knew I should rein myself in, just couldn't help myself.'

'Sounds to me like you're looking for an excuse to pick a fight.'

'You're absolutely right.'

'Look, you don't have to stay. You can always walk away – you know that.'

'Yeah, in theory.'

'In practice. Why don't we toss for it?'

Sarah giggled. Jacob could almost always joke her out of a mood. 'You *are* joking?'

'Never been more serious.'

'My God, you are too.'

'Got a quid in my hand. Heads you stay, and you shut up and like it. Tails you quit. I spin.'

'How can I trust you?'

Jacob snorted. 'Ready?'

'As ever.'

Sarah heard the phone handset clunk down, change rattled, then a coin was slapped down on a table.

'Heads,' said Jacob sadly. 'You stay.'

There was a knock at the door.

'Hang on a sec, Jacob.' She uncoiled herself from the cocoon of her bed and headed warily for the door.

John Redford stood on the threshold. 'Am I interrupting?'

Sarah spun around. 'Come in,' she said over her shoulder. She picked up the phone in the sitting room. 'Sorry Jacob, gotta go. *I'll* toss next time.' She hung up and stood behind the sofa, observing Redford with a critical eye.

'You'll toss?' he asked.

'A coin.'

'What for?'

'To decide whether I stay or go,' she answered with provocative nonchalance.

'Stay here?'

'Absolutely.'

'You make decisions on the fall of a coin?'

'My whole life's a game of pitch and toss. I'm a gambler. Don't take it personally.'

'Dammit, Sarah, I do take it personally. This isn't a game to me.'

'Well, wise up then.'

Redford rammed his hands in his pockets. He paced across the room, staring at the carpet. 'What *is* your problem?'

Sarah raised her eyebrows theatrically. 'Where do I start?'

'So you're off?'

'I'm staying, actually. I suppose I really ought to see you in concert tomorrow night.'

'Don't do me any fuckin' favours, will you?'

'I wouldn't dream of it.'

Redford took a deep breath, reining in his anger.

'What I'd come to say was, let's try and get off to a better start. Will you come out to dinner with me tonight?'

Chapter Twenty-seven

Redford's black Range Rover dropped them somewhere on the Upper West Side, Sarah was too preoccupied to notice where. As they walked into the restaurant together, Sarah felt nervous, anticipating a re-run of her performance that day. At first she didn't notice the reaction in the room. Voices of even the most determinedly blasé New Yorkers dipped, faces turned, eyes tracked their progress like radar. Poses were struck, envy launched at Sarah like missiles. The couple took their seats in a banquette at the back of the room. They could see out, but were reasonably well hidden from the legion of onlookers by a lavish arrangement of pussy willow.

'Jesus,' breathed Sarah. 'This happens all the time?'

Redford nodded.

'How d'you stand it?'

'I hate it, but it goes with the territory. It's more difficult for other people who are with me.'

Sarah shook her head. 'If looks could kill, I really would be dead. I don't think I've ever been the subject of such envy.'

'D'you like it?'

'What? Are you mad? I hate it.'

'Some women love it.'

'I'm not some women. Don't take this the wrong way, but reflected glory isn't my thing.'

Redford laughed. 'I'm glad we got that straight. I only wish more women felt like you.' Just then, a woman sashayed past, ostentatiously flipping a business card onto their table. Redford ignored it.

Sarah picked it up and read aloud the written message. ' "Call me for the fuck of the century." *What*?'

Redford tore it up and dropped it in their ashtray.

'That a common occurrence?' she asked.

'You wouldn't believe just how common.'

'You know what it feels like to be a woman then.'

'To be a very beautiful woman, maybe, with more propositions than you could handle in a hundred lifetimes.'

'Is that how it is for you?' asked Sarah.

'Isn't that how it is for *you*?'

'Not quite.' She fiddled with her watch, growing wary.

'Please don't get all offended,' Redford said with feeling, 'but you're one of the most beautiful women I've ever seen. You must get propositioned ten times a day just walking down the street.'

Sarah looked at him in disbelief. 'I'm two stone overweight, I don't sleep well, I have permanent black bags under my eyes, and my skin looks like second-hand tinfoil.'

The lights were dim, a candle flickered on the table between them, Sarah's skin glowed peaches and cream. Her feline eyes shone, the curve of her cheekbone and the fullness of her lips gave her a voluptuousness that threatened to spill over. She still wore her black trousers and cardigan and men's loafers from Lobbs. Her tousled hair fell down her back. She smelled of tuberose and trouble.

'You're looking in the wrong mirror,' said Redford softly.

Sarah smiled. 'Talking of which, I must go to the loo.'

She picked her way across the restaurant, garnering more than her usual share of looks on the way. The ladies' room was done up like a boudoir, with large, ornate gilt mirrors and a red velvet chaise longue, on which a starvation blonde was reclining angularly, discussing her waiting date on her mobile with a girlfriend who was probably similarly positioned.

'I mean, why *shouldn't* I?' whined the blonde. 'It *is* the second date, after all.'

Give yourself a medal why don't you, thought Sarah, ducking into the loo.

When she came out, the blonde had gone, resolved upon a night of passion no doubt. The door suddenly swung open with force. For some reason, Sarah jumped. A tall, rakishly thin woman with waist-length red hair walked in. She looked to be in her thirties, with the prettiness of extreme youth matured into a hard beauty. Her eyes alighted immediately on Sarah. Sarah looked back, expecting the woman to look politely away, but she just kept on eyeing her. She brushed past, knocking Sarah's handbag from its perch on the sink. She immediately bent down to pick it up and turned slowly back to Sarah, holding the bag at arm's length.

'Clumsy me,' she said, with a tight smile and in-your-face insincerity.

Sarah took the bag in silence, mystified by the pulse of animosity given off by this stranger. It was almost as if the woman had issued her with a challenge. *Let it go*, she thought. *Don't waste your energy.*

'Why do you go out at all,' she asked Redford back at the table, pushing the redhead from her mind, 'if you get all this attention?'

'Should I order room service for the rest of my life? I thought you might like to go out, sort of neutral territory, that we could talk, like normal people. Not rock stars and bankers.'

'Sounds good to me,' replied Sarah, appalled by the prospect.

'What will you drink?'

'Some red wine would be lovely.'

Redford scanned the list. He suggested a 1983 St Julien. 'You like red Burgundy?'

'Love it, and that one in particular.' Thanks to Jacob's education and plenty of application over the years, Sarah knew the wine was an exceptional one.

The wine waiter brought the bottle, uncorked it and went through the offering and pouring ritual. When he'd disappeared Sarah and Redford sipped for a while in silence as if collecting themselves.

'I'm sorry about today,' said Redford.

'What was it all about?' asked Sarah.

Redford looked puzzled. 'Strone was an asshole, going into your room, treating it like it was his, but the rest of the stuff, I don't get it. I'm thinking you're a little bit sensitive?'

'Of course I'm bloody sensitive, but that doesn't get you two off the hook. You just don't talk to people that way.'

'Did we really behave that badly?'

'No, you didn't,' said Sarah. 'But what annoyed me was the principle. You both acted as if you could say what you wanted, with no need for consideration. I was trying to tell you I wouldn't put up with two weeks of that.'

Redford nodded thoughtfully.

'Look, there's nothing deep or mysterious about this,' said Sarah, puzzled.

A profound weariness seemed to settle over Redford.

'What's wrong?' asked Sarah. 'What have I said?'

Redford gave a weak smile. 'Something that no one else has said for a very long time.'

'Meaning?'

'Meaning that no one speaks straight to me, no one tells me where to get off, because they all want something from me. They take the shit so they'll get the goodies, and they take as many goodies as they can get to make you pay for the shit. So you dish out more shit 'cos you know you're being taken for a ride, for a fool, and next thing you know, it's normal and all relationships are like that. You start forgetting how it should be.'

'Other people *must* talk to you like I do.'

'I wish they did. You're a major pain in the ass, but you're a good pain.'

Sarah laughed.

'How come you manage it?'

'Well, I suppose you said it yourself. I don't want anything from you.'

'Nothing?' asked Redford, slowly.

'What might I want?' asked Sarah, wariness mixing with the thrill of it all.

'Heck, I don't know. Jewellery, money, an apartment, a record deal, a scalp.'

Sarah chuckled. 'I've got jewellery – jewellery that means something to me. Without that, it's just hydrocarbon. I have a beautiful house, I have money, enough to enjoy life, not so much that I don't have a purpose. I couldn't sing to save my life, so a record deal would be a touch fanciful, and as for your scalp . . .'

'Yes?'

'Don't even joke about it. I should warn you, my mother had some Indian blood. She was about one-fifth Cheyenne.'

'You're kidding me.'

'It's the truth.'

Redford looked at her, head on one side.

'I see it now, your colouring, your high cheekbones, that long, glossy hair. Mm. I had better be careful, hadn't I?'

Sarah said nothing.

'How'd she get to Britain?' he asked.

'She didn't. She was American.'

'Where from?'

'New Orleans.'

'Now *that's* a great city.'

'It is.'

'You lived there?'

'Till I was eight.'

'What then?'

'I moved to London.'

Redford looked puzzled. 'Just you?'

'Me and my brother.'

'Your mother? Your father?'

Sarah looked into her wine glass. 'They were dead.'

'Oh Sarah, I'm sorry.' He took a gulp of water. 'How?'

'Car crash.'

He turned pale, like he'd seen a spectre.

'What is it?' asked Sarah, alarmed. It didn't seem possible that her pain could affect him the way it seemed to.

'My mother was killed in a car wreck. When I was twelve.'

'Oh John.'

'Might as well have killed my father too. He hung on for four years, then blew his brains out with the rabbit gun.'

Sarah reached out and grasped Redford's hand.

He turned his eyes to hers. The pain in them lacerated her, a broken mirror of her own torment. For a long while neither of them spoke.

Chapter Twenty-eight

Dick Breden sat across from Savage and Zamaroh. He wore a look of casual triumph.

'Let's have it then,' said Savage, his interest cutting through his habitual guise of boredom.

'Drugs,' said Breden. 'Cocaine. He spent three months in a rehab clinic in Arizona, three years ago.'

'And?' interrogated Savage.

'He was a heavy user, apparently.'

'I don't wish to do down your efforts, Dick, but I would have been surprised if he hadn't been into drugs or alcohol or excess of some kind. He's a rock star, for God's sake.'

'A rock star with a habit that probably made him unstable. Most drug addicts have to give up alcohol too, but he still drinks. Raises a question mark.'

'He *had* a habit,' said Zamaroh. 'And maybe he can handle the booze without succumbing to drugs. Besides, worst case, lots of drug users can perform to a high enough level, providing they keep getting their fix.'

Savage wheeled round. 'We haven't got any coke heads on the trading floor, have we?'

Zamaroh studied him for a fraction too long, scarcely able to conceal her incredulity at his uncharacteristic naivety. 'Of course we haven't.'

'We bloody well better hadn't. I can just imagine them, building up a position they're convinced is invincible, living in never-never land.'

'There's no such place on the floor, James, you know that. It's Judgement Day every day.'

Savage smiled. 'And you're God. I know.' He turned back to Breden. 'Wouldn't it be common knowledge if John Redford were on drugs? I mean, it's practically obligatory for rock stars.'

'There were rumours, suspicions. I confirmed those.'

'And now? Is he clean?'

'I could find no evidence that he still takes drugs.'

'And the rumours, the suspicions?'

'That he's clean.'

'Good,' said Savage. 'So far. Anything on the Leaker?'

Breden shook his head. 'Lots of legwork, but nothing to report.'

'Maybe the Leaker's given up,' said Zamaroh, 'in which case, perhaps you could remove the cameras and the listening devices from my office. I can tolerate a one hundred per cent invasion of my privacy for only so long.'

Breden turned to Savage. 'You think we should give up?'

Savage shook his head. 'Not until we find the bastard. We lost four deals worth over fifteen million pounds to this character. He has to pay for that.' He glanced at Zamaroh. 'Sorry, Zaha. The cameras keep running.'

Zamaroh sighed angrily. 'Maybe we should have them on in *your* office, see how you like it.'

'It's not necessary,' replied Savage curtly.

'Why not?' asked Zamaroh, head cocked, awaiting with interest Savage's self-justification.

'Because I say it isn't. People don't stroll into my office the way they do yours.' Savage turned to Breden. 'You have anything else?'

Breden examined his hands. 'I did find something else, from Redford's background check.'

'Do tell.'

'His mother was killed in a car crash when he was twelve. His father killed himself four years later. Blew his brains out. Redford found the body.'

'Jesus.' Zamaroh looked sick. Savage gave her a surprisingly compassionate look.

'Are you all right, Zaha?'

She took a few seconds to answer, and replied in a quiet, dignified voice, 'I'm fine. Thank you.' She got to her feet and walked out. Savage and Breden watched her go.

'What's up with her?' Breden asked incredulously. It was the first time he'd ever seen Zamaroh show vulnerability.

'The ayatollahs hanged her father,' answered Savage.

Zamaroh returned ten minutes later. 'What have I missed?' she asked. Her voice was level, but the bluster had gone.

'We were discussing whether or not we have a problem with any of this. Do you?'

'No, I don't,' she answered quietly. 'The guy had a drugs problem, he cleared it up. Well done him. He's overcome personal trauma, gone on to rise to the top of his profession. He's a survivor, he's a star. No, I don't have a problem. Do you?'

'It'll be interesting,' mused Savage, 'to see what Sarah Jensen comes up with.' He saw, to his pleasure, the flash of competition in Breden's eyes.

'She'll come up with nothing,' replied Zamaroh dismissively.

'You really want this deal, don't you?' observed Savage.

'So do you. We've been chasing this type of business for years.'

'I do want it,' said Savage, 'but not at any price.'

'Don't worry, I'll keep the price payable,' retorted Zamaroh.

'Goldsteins won't suppress information, no matter how uncomfortable it is,' said Savage. 'It always comes round to bite you in the arse in the end.'

Does it, wondered Zamaroh, pondering her own experience, still unsure. She lived under the sword of Damocles. And Sarah Jensen could come along at any moment with her cool scrutiny and cut the thread. Although she would never admit it to a living soul, scarcely to herself, Zaha lived in fear of Jensen. She desperately needed something on Sarah to balance the scales, to bargain with.

Chapter Twenty-nine

Sarah woke late, with the lingering sense that a nightmare had assailed her sleep. She could remember nothing of her dreams, but the echoes of something unpleasant still reverberated. She lay in bed for a while, going over the evening before. She was horrified by Redford's loss, for his own sake, and because it somehow united them even more.

She pushed herself out of bed with a groan. She had missed last night's breastfeed, and this morning's, and her breasts were rock-hard with engorgement. Physically, she felt as if she would burst, and mentally she felt herself almost implode with longing. She thought about her boy, wondered how he had passed the night, and what he might be doing now. She shook her head and forced herself into the comfort of routine. She took a long shower, dressed and refocused herself on business. She rang Strone at ten. He sounded abstracted.

'When shall we get together?' Sarah asked.

'No can do today, sorry.'

'Oh,' said Sarah, pausing. 'Why's that?'

'It's concert day, Sarah. Do you have any idea of what's involved?'

'None whatsoever. But I'd love to find out,' she said with genuine enthusiasm. 'Perhaps I could shadow you for the day. I'd keep quiet, I promise. You wouldn't even notice I was there.'

Strone laughed. 'Yeah, really. All right. I've got stuff I can't share for most of the day, but why don't you come early to the Beacon with me, see the stage and the set-up, sound check and all that jazz. I'll pick you up at six. How's that sound?'

'Like a deal.'

Sarah hung up and glanced around her room, suddenly adrift with nothing to do. She would go out, she decided, have brunch in the Village, get away from her role for a while. She grabbed her handbag, reached for her purse to take out some cash to stuff into her pocket. Her purse wasn't there. Dammit, where had she put it? She searched her suite. She tried to remember the last time she had seen it. Last night, she'd taken it to the restaurant. She'd wanted her cash in case she decided to bail out on Redford. Always have your running away money. She looked round wildly. No wallet. No money, no credit cards, no drivers licence. *Shit.* Where *was* it?

Half an hour's frantic searching, clothes strewn everywhere, and there was no mistake: her purse was gone. She felt a murderous impulse toward whoever had taken it. Could it have been a maid? But she'd always had her bag with her when she left the room. Someone delivering room service while she was in the other room? Possible, but highly unlikely. Then it came to her. The bitch in the restaurant, the redhead who knocked over her bag. She had stooped to pick it up with her back to Sarah. How easy to slip the wallet into a pocket before turning and handing the bag back to Sarah. She remembered the woman's sarcastic, 'Clumsy me,' and the odd look in her eyes. *Damn* her!

Sarah searched for her reserve of calm. There was no damage to life and limb, just property. But calm didn't come. Her wallet was too personal, her feelings about money too precarious to shrug off its loss. She felt stranded, shorn of her power, of her independence, and she hated the feeling. She'd have to ring her bank tomorrow, get a pile of money wired over. She remembered her rash insistence about paying for her suite herself. Oh Jesus! Her pictures of Georgie – they were all in her wallet, too. She felt bereft without them, as if her son had somehow been torn from her. Tears burned in her eyes. She rubbed them away angrily. Now the bitch had the photographs; Georgie in her arms, Georgie in the bath, Georgie seconds old in hospital. Those images were a glimpse into her heart and soul. That a stranger should possess them was a kind of violation.

She forced herself to breathe slowly and rhythmically. Focus on practicalities. She raided her pockets, the money she left lying around to hand out as tips. She garnered twenty-five dollars; enough for a frugal lunch. She suddenly laughed; stranded in a five-star hotel, under the aegis of one of the richest men in the world. Money, money all around . . . She rang the operator and got the number of Visa and AMEX. She reported the theft of her cards, hung up and headed out.

Chapter Thirty

At six-thirty Sarah and Strone arrived at the Beacon Theatre on the Upper West Side. Redford's picture, a black and white study of an enigmatic gaze, watched them as they entered the building. Strone nodded to a black-clad, sharp-eyed security man, who wore a tiny mike and an earpiece.

'Everything OK?'

'Yeah. No hassles.'

'Good.' Strone swept on. Sarah slowed and gazed around her. The Beacon was a rococco paradise with scrolling, gilt, a mural of a neo-Classical utopia, a balustrade, and stained glass more reminiscent of a church. Strone had nearly disappeared from sight. Sarah quickened her steps to catch him up as he walked backstage. The air smelled of fried food and beer. About forty people hurried purposefully back and forth across the stage, tending to a series of wires and electronic boxes, undertaking a whole variety of esoteric, in some cases almost invisible, but undoubtedly essential acts before disappearing stage left and right. They wore jeans and combat trousers, long hair, ponytails, heavy boots. Men and women were dressed identically. Many wore headpieces with small microphones into which they whispered almost constantly, as if conducting conversations with a lover. At Strone's appearance, the busyness turned to frenzy. Strone stood still like a centurion watching his troops prepare for battle. People came to him, and conducted hurried conversations.

'This is the Get In time for the rig,' Strone explained to Sarah. 'Tonight's show'll be a miniature of a normal John Redford set. He's done five shows at Madison Square Gardens over the last two weeks. Twenty thousand seats a shot. Tonight's his goodbye to New York for this time gig. Intimate, you know. Real. Two thousand people. It's—'

Strone fell silent. Sarah followed his eyes to a woman with long blonde hair and high black boots who was approaching purposefully.

'Hello, Zena,' he said wearily.

'Don't *hello Zena* me. Don't you even speak to me.'

Strone turned on his heel. 'Oh, OK then. Great. I won't speak to you.'

'Hold on, you jazzed-up jerk.' The woman put her hand on Strone's shoulder. Sarah half expected him to explode; she would have done, but the manager just gave a sigh, gently removed the offending hand and turned to face the diatribe.

'You promised me Ray would get a hike three weeks ago, and what do I see in his pay slip? Diddly squat, that's what. You know he plays bass like an angel. He *carries* the show. Jake got a rise and he can barely strum.'

Strone spoke into the fusillade of words. 'Zena, Zena, Zena. No one doubts how good Ray is. We all know he's a genius. That's why he plays for a genius.'

Zena opened her mouth and looked as if she were going to lunge at Strone. The manager raised his hand in a pacifying gesture. 'Now just calm down. I do what I can. I'm subject to all sorts of constraints you don't see. I—'

'Oh bullshit. You do what you want to do, you're the all-powerful Strone.' Her voice leached sarcasm. 'Mr Potent, don't we all know it.'

Strone's voice dropped an octave. 'Now you're overstepping the mark. I'm busy. Please leave us.'

Sarah watched with interest.

Zena wasn't about to be dismissed so easily. 'Don't you threaten me.'

'You'd know it if I threatened you. You're just a sad little groupie who got lucky. Now disappear and do what you do best. Quit hassling me.'

The blonde's eyes filled with tears of rage. 'You bastard.' She spat her words at Strone before turning on her high heels and running off.

Sarah looked around. Quite a few of the roadies had stopped work to watch the exchange. Strone glared at them and they reluctantly got back to work.

'Stupid bitch,' said Strone. 'If I could cut the domestics out of my life I'd be just fine.'

'That happen a lot?' asked Sarah, still reeling from the viciousness of the exchange.

'All the time. You wouldn't believe the pecking order here. Jake, the lead guitar, gets a rise. Stupid prick blabs about it. So now Ray wants one, and if I give him one, all the other musicians, and their groupie girlfriends'll come clamouring.'

'You don't seem to have a very high opinion of the people in this business,' observed Sarah.

Strone gave her an appraising look. 'For the most part, they're either bastards or fools.'

'So which are you?'

A lithe, totally bald man, who looked to be in his forties took Strone aside before he had a chance to answer. Sarah wondered who the man was.

Strone returned a few minutes later, white-faced.

'What was that all about?' asked Sarah casually.

'Huh?' Strone affected vagueness. ' 'Scuse me a sec, honey. Got to piss.'

Eloquently put, she thought, watching his tight jean-clad figure marching off. She stopped a passing roadie with a broad smile.

'Sorry to bother you, but who's that man?' She pointed out the baldhead.

The roadie gave her a puzzled look, as if she came from an alien planet. 'That's Jim O'Cleary. Head of security.'

Sarah cocked her head, feigning puzzlement. 'Funny. I'd swear I know him from somewhere.'

At this point the roadie gave her an extremely wary, and curious look before rushing off.

Sarah wondered why her words had provoked such confusion. She mooched about, hands in pockets, trying to look as if she belonged in this world. Driven by hunger pangs she headed for the catering cart and, against her better judgement, bought a hot dog. She leaned against a huge metal trunk and tucked in.

'So who are you then?' asked a friendly voice.

Sarah turned, mouth full, and studied her interrogator. He was a man in his forties, with long wavy hair, and brown, amused eyes. Sarah swallowed her mouthful.

'Who are *you*?' she countered. The man seemed momentarily disconcerted, but then quickly regained his smile. 'I'm Ray Waters.'

'Ah.' Sarah took a flying guess. 'John Redford's bass guitarist.'

'The one and only. And you're his latest tottie.'

The tone was still friendly, and Sarah thought she must have misheard. 'Excuse me?'

'Tottie. T. O. T. T. I. E.'

'My God,' said Sarah, pausing to subject Waters to a lengthy scrutiny. 'You're surprisingly literate for an arsehole.'

Strone reappeared silently at Sarah's shoulder. 'I see you're getting acquainted.'

Sarah jumped and turned on Strone with anger. 'Don't *do* that. You nearly gave me a heart attack.'

'That's his style,' said Ray in the same friendly voice. 'In-tim-id-ation. Makes him feel the big man.' He turned to Strone. 'Zena told me about your run-in. I don't appreciate you bad-mouthing my woman.'

'Perhaps you ought to watch your own mouth then,' said Sarah, in Ray's same benign, duplicitous tone.

'Where's the fun in that, Tottie?' He grinned and walked off.

'Seems people can be both idiots *and* bastards in this business,' commented Sarah.

Strone gave her a rueful look. 'Ignore him. He likes to stir.'

'Is that how I'm seen, as John's tottie?' Sarah asked incredulously.

'Think about it,' said Strone. 'You share the same hotel, you're on the same floor of the same hotel. And you have no other reason to be travelling with him that they know of. I mean, we can hardly announce you're his banker checking on his figures. And *please*, don't be offended, but you don't exactly look like these people's idea of a banker anyway. Seeing as the deal's confidential, tottie's a pretty good cover for you. Don't knock it.'

'I do knock it,' she said in irritation.

'Many women would leap at that position, real or imagined.'

'Many must fulfil it, I would have thought.'

Strone gave her a hard stare. 'Well, I'd say that was John's business, wouldn't you?'

Sarah shrugged. 'Why's it such a big deal to stay in the same hotel as him, and why specifically the same floor?'

'Why d'you ask?'

'Because of the way you said it, as if it were remarkable.'

'None of the band or the entourage are allowed to stay in the same hotel. Just me.'

'And tottie,' said Sarah, still fishing.

Strone didn't bite.

'Why do the band stay in a different hotel?' she asked.

'Privacy – to get away from being John Redford twenty-four seven, I suppose. You've met Ray Waters. Some of the other band members are better than Ray, some're worse, but they're all gripers, all bar one – the keyboard player, Stevie Charlton. He just lives to play. He's wonderful.' Strone gave a snort of appreciation. 'Doesn't care what he gets paid, or who has the biggest hotel suite or all that shit. But the rest of them gripe nonstop. John doesn't want to get ambushed by his band or their loony girlfriends.'

'Doesn't he get on with the band?'

'He's not close to them, no. He does his thing, they do theirs. They come together on the night and it works. Offstage the chemistry's different. He doesn't want to see them weaving and screaming down the hallway towards him at one in the morning.'

Sarah smiled. 'Having met Ray and Zena I can well understand that. But why break a rule and put me in the same hotel?'

Strone shrugged. 'Beats me.'

His eyes moved to the stage as Ray Waters and, presumably, other band members from the deference afforded them, took their positions.

'Sound checks,' explained Strone. 'The sound engineers are king at this point. Each instrument has its own amplifier, and the sound engineer can make bass practically blow you out of your seat, or tone it down to oblivion. There's a real skill to getting the balance between the instruments right. There's politics too. Poor bloody engineers have to stand up to Waters and co insisting that they amp up their own instrument. Ray'd drown out John if he could.'

'Where *is* John?' asked Sarah. 'When does he do his own sound check?'

Strone studied Sarah for a moment. 'Who knows? He's a man of mystery, isn't he, our John.'

Was he taunting her? Did he know something, or was it just an innocent tease?

Sarah had to get out from under Strone's gaze. She made her excuses and headed off to the ladies. The loos were a cool haven after the engine room of John Redford inc. She pushed Strone from her mind and thought about what it was to be John Redford. All those people on the payroll, all the gear, all the preparation. How did Redford cope with the responsibility of it all?

Behind the circus atmosphere, the apparently free-living roadies, were wives, children and mortgages. Under the stardust and greasepaint lurked bills and the spectre of unemployment. Redford Inc was a one-man show. There was no substitute if he turned in sick, if he didn't feel like going on. He was trapped in something much greater – the Show – and it had to go on. This was carnival, this was circus, and it had all the pathos of play today, pay tomorrow, the ephemeral pleasure of performance, all the creation and the tearing down, the before and after, repeated in a hundred different cities over eighteen months of a marathon world tour. All the leaving and arriving, the rootlessness, the entourage in one hotel, the star apart in another. No wonder the atmosphere was isolating, nihilistic. There was no longterm consequence to anything; hit town, move on. Like a raiding party.

Sarah shook herself, tried to free herself from something that felt almost sinister.

Chapter Thirty-one

The strobe lights scanned the auditorium like weapons of war. The crowd smelled of sweat, the base chemical of perfume long evaporated with excitement. Their eyes flickered back and forth to the stage as the hour approached. Sarah could feel their anticipation, verging on hunger. It was a yearning, sexual in part, but more than that, a craving for the man himself.

She studied the people around her. A woman in tight jeans, high black suede boots and a pink tank top. Heavy make-up, scent, lust in her eyes, all dressed up and ready for a night with her lover. A girl, no more than fourteen, long fair hair, faded denims, hope and wonder in her eyes, trying to guard her longing from her mother's jaded sophistication.

The crowd hushed as three black backing singers in short, tight, sequinned dresses undulated onto the stage and took up their places. They shimmied together to an almost inaudible beat.

Sarah jumped as John Redford walked onstage. The crowd surged to their feet around her, roaring and screaming. Adrenaline pumped through her as if she and the crowd were plugged into a common source. Redford wore jeans and a white T-shirt with cowboy boots. His face was radiant, wild. He raised his hand and a chord of music rose from backstage. His band came on, and took up position at drums, keyboards, lead guitar, bass guitar, alto sax, tenor sax, trumpet and violin. The spotlights played on all the different performers. When the roar of the crowd finally faded, a roadie ran forward, handed John Redford his guitar. Redford stepped into the spotlight once again, and began to sing 'Come to Me', an anthemic rock beat, whipping up the crowd.

Redford sang, roared, ran across the stage. There was something intensely sexual about the way he played the guitar. It hung at groin level, and the movements of his fingers plucking the strings conjured memories and fantasies in equal measure. Sweat began to slick his arms, run down his face. Sarah could see it from her front-row position, she could see it shine on his face. She remembered how it tasted.

For the first time, Redford looked at the crowd. His eyes ranged out over the sea of faces. She felt herself yearning for his glance. She was so close, perhaps ten feet away from him, but whether by accident or design, his eyes did not alight on her.

'Good evening,' he said with a complicit smile, voice low, seemingly utterly confident. The crowd roared back.

'It's great to be here, somewhere intimate, like the Beacon. Means you can see me, but you know what?' The crowd roared back, a slavish puppy taking up the game.

'It means I can see *you,*' replied Redford to more roars, 'and not only that, but I can hear you too.' He smiled, gently parodying. ' "He looks good, looks younger. What's he had done?" Or, "Look at his muscles. He really is the hard man of rock. I wonder if he's hard *all* the way down?" Or, "Can he really do it for seven hours?" Well, lemme tell you, I've given up tantric sex,' he announced. 'I now do tantric shopping. Shop for seven hours and never buy anything.' The crowd erupted into laughter.

This was where passion met the business of rock. Redford was the performer, the artist; all those vaguely effete titles suddenly became meaningful in the person of John Redford, striding the stage like a colossus, giving out what the audience so desperately craved. There is always a moment once a performance starts, when it could go one of two ways. The audience watches, breath bated, waiting to see if the performer is worthy of them. It is the Christians and the lions and Ancient Rome all over again. If the performer beguiles and seduces, he can live. If he is a free man to start, then as he beguiles, he enslaves his watchers. If he fails to assert his mastery over them, the audience will turn and rip him apart with barbs of derision. So great was Redford's reputation that his fate never seemed to hang in the balance, not even for a few tense seconds. But it was the man, not the image or the reputation which carried the audience forward from their initial respect to slavish devotion.

Sarah watched him pace to the side of the stage and drink long and hard from a pint glass filled with what looked like water and lemon slices. She felt a pang, seeing him do something so prosaic. He returned to centre stage and sang three more rock songs, fast paced and furious. The stage was a force field. What Sarah hadn't expected was how all the individual instruments and performers lived within the whole. On a CD, however good the quality, the music always sounds canned in comparison, flavourless. But once live, all the instruments found their own voices and what they made was an alchemy of sound.

Onstage, all the performers, even Ray Waters, achieved a kind of nobility, but Redford still stood above them, undisputed King. Sarah wondered about the long road to his superstardom, the days when he was establishing himself, about the self-belief and the doubts, about how a boy with his history of pain could have cobbled himself together enough to hold a stage. It was something she could never do. There was too much ambiguity and too many shadows in her.

The stage was suddenly plunged into darkness. When the sole spotlight came back on, Redford stood centre stage, alone with his acoustic guitar. He launched into the first of his ballads, 'How'. He moved slowly, dancing by himself, his voice low and almost rasping with pain as he sang. '*How could I do what I did? How could I say what I said? How could I kill our love*?' Sarah watched his torment, felt his pain, wondered who he was singing for.

She watched those closest to her, saw them stripped of their defences. Faces raised to the stage were screens where emotions flickered unhindered, undefended. Their naked vulnerability was strangely affecting. '*How can I win you back? How I'm going to love you this time, just give me one chance.*' It was a seduction, slow and masterful and knowing. Every chord a caress, every word a kiss, and as word and music and movement slipped together, it was a consummation.

Sarah rarely went to concerts, had instinctively stayed away. She was suspicious of groups – of churches, of aerobics classes. Perhaps because there was something in her that she feared was over-susceptible to a mass seduction. But she, as much as anyone, had a longing for oblivion, to be held in the arms of someone who understood, who sang out her pain, who drew it out and turned it into something beautiful. And now she gave herself up to it.

Now she could see that the hunger of the crowd was for meaning, for the world John Redford created, for the places he took them. He showed them their souls, he showed them their hearts, he ennobled their emotions, spoke the words they couldn't. He lived the life some of them dreamed of. He was their prince, their messiah, but also a man of the people. He had lived their life, dreamed their dreams, experienced their sorrow. There was no such thing as gold-plated pain. His money, his success, his talent – nothing separated him from them. He could have led them anywhere.

Sarah felt a secret thrill that she knew this man, that a part of him would be forever hers in the form of her son. At that moment, Redford looked directly at her. She tried to look away but couldn't. His eyes held her in a current of sexual energy so pure and electrifying she almost felt as if she could come there and then. His eyes still on her, he began to sing '*One Perfect Night*'.

'One perfect night you came my way,
With your uncertain smile,
You stopped awhile in your wild flight,
And you spent it with me.

Just you and me and the singing wind,
The wolves for guards,
The stars lit our way,
And you left me with shards.

You smiled on me, you kissed my face,
You let nature go her way,
And you left without a trace,
Leaving me with nothing but the memory,
Of one perfect night.'

Sarah must have heard the song a dozen times without listening to the words, but tonight Redford seemed to sing with an extra clarity, for she picked out every one, as if it had been meant for her ears alone. Her face burned. He *had* to have been singing about their one perfect night. She wanted to believe it and reject it at the same time. Every nuance of his words conjured up the memory of their night together. As the last of his guitar chords faded away, she was lost in her recollections.

She jumped as someone tapped her on the shoulder. Strone stood beside her. 'Come with me,' he mouthed. He grabbed Sarah's arm and pulled. Sarah was grateful for the propulsion Strone provided. She felt as if without him, still stuck blissfully in the beauty of her dream, she would have been powerless to move. Security men made way for them. Strone took Sarah to the side of the arena, round the stage, up a flight of stairs, to the stage itself. She could smell dust cooking in the stage lights. She could smell velvet as she stood beside curtains eighty foot high. She watched Redford as he sang his encore, 'Run Away'.

Backstage, she gazed out at the sea of faces behind the lights and saw for the first time what Redford must have seen a thousand times or more. A huge stage, an empty, lonely expanse. Thousands of people, all there for you. The hunger and love of the crowd was focused here, on one small person, who filled the theatre with himself. He fed the crowd, he filled up on their worship. Sarah raked her hair back from her face. How the hell did he keep sane?

Strone was watching her.

'You see it now, don't you?' he asked. 'What he's all about.'

Sarah nodded. She felt like she was in a dream, trying to run from danger, her feet stuck in treacle. She didn't want to be naked, like the crowd. She didn't want Strone to see her emotions. She tried to run in her mind, back from abandonment to some kind of sanity. They stood watching Redford together until he'd done two encores. He finally walked offstage after a heroic two-and-a-half-hour performance. She gazed at the space he had filled, feeling almost as if she had performed somehow alongside him. It was a sense of catharsis, as profound as any of the ancient philosophers could have aspired to. She felt exhilarated and drained, too. Strone's hand gently touched her shoulder.

'It's all right. We've all been there. First time I saw John in concert I felt like I couldn't speak for a week. He brought me to tears. But I must have got some words out because I signed him up that same night.'

Sarah turned to him, her eyes shining. 'Did you? When was that?'

'Long story. C'mon. I'll buy you dinner and tell you all about it.'

Chapter Thirty-two

Soon they were heading over Brooklyn Bridge.

'I'm going to take you to Pierre's. Does the best steak and chips in the city and has a fantastic wine list.' A horrified expression suddenly crossed his face. 'You're not vegetarian, are you?'

'Carnivore, through and through.'

'Thank God for that.'

Sarah sat opposite Strone. She drank exquisite red wine for the second night in a row. Tonight there was a welcome anonymity to dinner. No one paid them any more attention than Sarah was used to.

'What about John?' she asked Strone. 'Don't you have to go to him? He can't be alone after that.' She stopped herself with a brief, awkward smile. 'I suppose he's not alone. He's probably got fifty thousand lovers to choose from, just from one city.'

Strone laughed. 'Don't go believing that old cliché. The rock star and his groupies.'

'Why not? Clichés usually have some grounding in fact, and look at Mick Jagger.'

'Yeah well, John's grown out of that.'

'So what does he do now?'

'Normally does a load of meet 'n' greet. Record company execs, friends, journos, but not tonight. He did this show just for him, for the fun of playing in a small venue rather than a zoo. So tonight he comes down alone. Meditates. Does his yoga and breathing, drinks a pint of carrot juice and goes to bed.'

'Alone?'

'He doesn't have a girlfriend at the moment, so yeah, he goes to bed alone,' Strone replied patiently, giving Sarah a curious look.

'It seems so lonely,' she said, heart soaring involuntarily, 'after performing like that, all the love of those people, singing your heart and soul out for them, then you go back to an anonymous hotel room, alone.'

'It *is* lonely. Why d'you think I love the guy? Why d'you think I'm here now, alone too in the relationship sense, when I could be home somewhere cosy, with a wife and kids?'

'You love him?' asked Sarah with surprise.

' 'Course I love him. I found him when he was a boy – sixteen years old.' He smiled. 'I was practically still a kid myself; twenty-six. Anyway, there he was, singing his heart out in a bar in Jackson Hole, Wyoming, and I literally got shivers up and down my spine. I knew he was *it.* Since then, I've seen it all. His ups and downs, I've seen his ambition, his courage. I've seen his talent, raw and wild, I've seen him hone it into the magic you saw tonight. You've never seen anything like him, right?'

Sarah shook her head. 'It was beyond words.'

'We've been there for each other through it all,' continued Strone. 'I see all sides. I see the glory and the worship and I see the pain and the loneliness and the sacrifice.'

'What sacrifice?' asked Sarah.

'The mind-fuck,' answered Strone impatiently, as if the answer were obvious. 'The whole totally insane roller-coaster ride called rock and roll.'

'Why mind-fuck?' asked Sarah.

'Because it's dangerous. It takes your sanity, drives you absolutely nuts sometimes.'

'You and John?'

'Me and John.'

'How does it show?'

Strone looked at her and then away, concealing his answer behind veiled eyes.

'So why do you both do it?' asked Sarah. 'Why doesn't John just retire?'

Strone laughed. 'You saw him up there. You saw what he saw, felt the crowd. Can you imagine what it feels like, to be the performer? The kick, the power, the high. That's the sweetest drug you'll ever take, the greatest love you'll ever feel.'

Not even close, thought Sarah, her mind on Georgie.

'Tell me exactly how you met him,' she asked, biting into a forkful of bleeding steak.

Strone took a long sip of wine and his eyes became wistful. Sarah marvelled at the transformation in him. Redford's performance had exposed another side to Strone; perhaps he felt freer to show it because he could see how Sarah had responded to his star. It was as if she had gone through an initiation ceremony and was now part of the tribe.

'It was twenty-two years ago. I had been an accountant for five years and I couldn't stand it any more.' He saw Sarah's look of surprise. 'I know, I know, I don't seem like an accountant, but then does anyone look like what they are? Please don't chuck your wine over me,' he said cautiously, 'but as I dared to mention earlier, you don't look like a banker.'

Sarah smiled. 'Point taken.'

'Anyway, I couldn't stand accounting on its own, so I thought I'd try to use it to get me into something more up my street. I'd always loved music, so I kind of had this dream that I would find a star and manage him. Or her. One day I just upped and left, quit my job in New Jersey, set out for the Wild West. If ever there was a place where dreams come true I thought it would be here. So I just travelled, went anywhere the fancy took me, not really focusing on where the talent might be, just wandering. Anyway, after about a year I shipped up in Wyoming, in Jackson. I was nearly out of cash, so I was sleeping in barns, living on breakfasts in truckers' cafes and peanuts in the bars. One night I went to this joint, sawdust on the floor, roughnecks at the bar, and across the room I saw this boy, weaving through the tables, carrying a guitar, on his way to the stage. I'd found what I was looking for. I knew it before he even opened his mouth, before he even played a chord. He just had something. He was young and beautiful and he had this wildness, but a great pathos in his eyes, as if he understood the world, aged sixteen. And then he opened his mouth.' Strone smiled and shrugged as if he need say no more. 'I approached him afterwards, introduced myself, used practically my last dollar to buy him a drink.'

'What happened then?'

'I told him I could make him a star. He asked who the hell I was, where did I come from? What was I doing in Jackson, where was I staying? I took a risk and told him I was dossing in barns. He burst out laughing, said that was good. Anyway, he must have seen something in me too, 'cos I scribbled a contract on the back of a napkin and he signed it.'

'Impulsive,' mused Sarah.

'Yeah, he was, but you've got to understand, no one had told him he was good at anything for a long time, and he had nothing in Jackson, no reason to stay, save his brother, and he came along with us.'

'His parents were both dead,' said Sarah.

'He told you?'

Sarah nodded.

Strone gave her a sharp look. 'He doesn't normally talk about it.'

Sarah shrugged. 'Yeah, well. He didn't go into detail and I wouldn't have asked him to. How old was his brother then?'

'Fourteen.' Strone was still watching her suspiciously, as if she'd breached some kind of defence.

'So where'd you all go?'

Strone smiled. 'To my mother's house in Jersey City. We all needed feeding, some TLC. My mother was very good at that.'

'Was?' asked Sarah gently.

'Cancer. Last year.'

'Oh God, Strone. I'm sorry.'

He waved his hand, eyes tight, but he didn't speak. Sarah helped him out. 'So then you went to Melody, Music, Entertainment.'

He nodded. 'John sang and played guitar for the MD. I insisted he see him in person, no demo tape. He had to see John himself.'

'How did you manage that? You were an unknown ex-accountant with an unknown teenager.'

'I was very persuasive.' He smiled. 'I usually get what I want.'

'Usually?' probed Sarah.

'I was discounting trivia. When it counts, I *always* get what I want.'

'Yeah, right. Don't tell me, you're immortal too.'

'There's only one goddess here,' he responded.

'Not me,' said Sarah. 'I lost my illusions of immortality long ago.'

Strone smiled. 'Who would miss you, if you went? That's what we should all be asking ourselves.'

Sarah thought of Georgie and to her dismay, her eyes filled with tears. Strone reached out his hand across the table, took hold of hers.

'Hey, I'm sorry,' he said, with appalled concern.

Sarah pulled her hand free and brushed away her tears. 'It's OK, I'm just a bit over-emotional. It's not you, don't worry.'

Strone gave her a gentle smile. 'Not quite the tough cookie you come across as, huh? Whoever you love that much is a lucky guy.'

Sarah turned away. This was getting too close. Redford, via his concert, had opened her up, as only he had the power to do, and she was frightened what might be visible.

Chapter Thirty-three

Room service woke Sarah with breakfast at 6 a.m. Bleary-eyed, she pulled on a towelling robe, let them in and signed the bill. Beyond exhaustion, she felt out of sorts. Her breasts still ached, and she could feel the edgy light-headedness which heralded some kind of hormonal assault. Mrs V had been only too right about dropping breastfeeding too rapidly. Fat lot of comfort, thought Sarah. She looked longingly at her plate, piled high with pastries, but before she tucked in, she made herself ring her bank in London and arranged for the emergency transfer of fifteen thousand dollars. With her suite at $2000 a night, she had no intention of running out of money here, or in Paris, their next stop.

She rubbed her eyes, poured a coffee, and rang Jacob. Everything was fine. Georgie even gurgled at her down the line. Sarah spoke for five minutes then hung up. She bit her lip, got to her feet, paced back and forth, staring unseeing out of the window at the Manhattan skyline. Then she made herself sit down, pour another coffee, bite into a croissant and start work on Redford's financials. She managed an hour, then she rang Savage.

'What've you got?' he asked.

'On the bad side, nothing. On the good, he is an *incredible* performer. His concert last night was amazing – two thousand people spellbound.'

'Has he converted you?'

'I'm a heathen, James, always was, always will be. What have you got for me?'

'Drugs,' replied Savage, leaving a long silence, trying to gauge Sarah's reaction. When she didn't speak he was forced to continue. 'A long habit, apparently. Cleaned up three years ago and nothing since. Unstable background. Mother killed in car crash, father committed suicide several years later. Blew his brains out. Redford found the body.'

'Oh no.' For an instant Sarah was blinded by the image of her parents, dead, slumped in the front of their car while she and her brother lay trapped and wounded in the back. Sarah knew Redford's pain, knew there never would be any getting over it. No amount of drugs, adulation or adrenaline would ever be enough.

'You think he's clean?' Savage asked, unwittingly giving her something to focus on.

'Looks incredibly healthy. I'd be very surprised if he were using. I'll keep an eye out. Is it a problem with you?'

'I don't think so – I hope not. He's a rock star, drugs are par for the course, and he appears to be off them now at any rate. If we find out he's back on them, we'll have to reconsider whether we can live with that or not.'

'Zamaroh's cool?'

'She's right behind him.'

Sarah thought of the Iranian's dead father. *Here we all are, united by death.*

'Breden came up with the drugs stuff, I suppose?'

'He did.'

'Is he in Goldsteins today?' Dick Breden enjoyed the rare privilege of use of an office on the chief executive's floor.

'He is. Would you like to speak to him?'

'Please.'

'Allow me to put you through,' said Savage sarcastically.

For someone who even got his secretary to dial his wife for him, this was, Sarah supposed, a great service.

'Yes, Sarah. How are you?' Breden asked energetically.

'Knackered – unlike you. Look, I don't know what I'm following up here, but there's a guy on the Redford entourage, Jim O'Cleary, head of security. Something seems odd about him, about who he is. Can't be more specific than that. It's just a feeling, but you couldn't use one of your innumerable contacts and run a check on him, could you?'

'For you, and your feelings, anything.'

A knock at the door disturbed her as she formulated her response, tempted to be sharp, but aware that she was seeking cooperation here.

'Er, look, someone at the door. Gotta go – thanks, Dick.' She hung up and hurried across the room. A bellboy waited with an envelope.

'For Sarah Jensen. Urgent,' he said, handing it over. Sarah handed over what was left of her cash and closed the door. She ripped open the envelope. A single piece of paper floated out. It bore seven simple, typewritten words:

To Sarah Jensen

Carry on and Die

She sank down on the sofa, the note in her hand. Her heart beat fast and her skin pricked with adrenaline that made her feel nauseous. She wanted to scrunch up the note and throw it in the bin. Ignore it with a *fuck you* defiance. But she couldn't muster rebellion. She was too scared.

She waited until the fear abated, replaced with fury that a piece of paper, and some coward hiding behind it, could reduce her to such a state. Who the hell was responsible? Her mind toyed with options. Some loony playing with a free morning; some loony with her name, warning her off. Off what? Off her investigation? But no one outside Goldsteins knew of it, only Jacob, and he would never have told anyone about her true mission. Inside Goldsteins, only Savage, Zamaroh and Breden knew, and none of them would have any incentive to expose her.

But if someone *had* exposed her, who was threatening her – and why? It couldn't be Redford. The note seemed offbeat, adolescent almost. If Redford was trying to cover something up, warning Sarah off would merely act as a signal to dig deeper. Anyway, he wanted the deal, he needed it, and he needed Sarah on side. If he was hiding something, his best bet would be a cover-up, not intimidation. Anyway, this note wasn't his style. She could never imagine him making anonymous threats.

She threw down the note and rubbed her eyes. Christ, talk about mind-spin. The trouble with her job was that the range of human behaviour was so absurdly wide and unpredictable that analysing it could drive you nuts; searching for ever more complex interpretations when sometimes the simplest and most obvious was the right one, seeing demons all around, always looking for the bad in people.

She stared at the note. Perhaps it *was* from a deranged fan who'd seen her and Redford together. She thought of Ray Waters. He'd assumed she was Redford's *Tottie.* Who else did? All of Redford's crew must have seen her yesterday afternoon at the Beacon with Strone. Gossip would spread like a virus amongst the incestuous crew. It could have been any one of them, or a jealous groupie. Could it even have been Strone himself, warning her off his star? Extremely unlikely. First because it didn't seem in keeping with what she was slowly learning about the manager's personality, and secondly because, as Redford's manager, Strone would get ten per cent of the proceeds of the bond issue. Potentially a cool ten million.

Then an odd thought struck her. Maybe it was the Leaker. After all, members of the trading team flew in and out of New York every few weeks. Perhaps her trap had been made known to him. Shit, it could be anyone.

She thought of Strone's words, *Who would miss you if you went*? and suppressed a shiver.

Chapter Thirty-four

Sarah counted out four thousand three hundred and thirty-five dollars in cash while the hotel cashier watched her with distaste. The money was in twenties, collected by Sarah to settle her bill half an hour earlier from Citibank down the block.

John Redford materialised silently behind her and whispered in her ear. 'You a drug runner?'

Whipping round, she glared at him. Standing beside her, hands wedged in the pockets of a worn leather jacket, he was suddenly human again, the God-like performer left behind on the stage.

'Don't *do* that!' she hissed. 'You nearly gave me a heart attack. What is it with you and Strone? He did the same to me yesterday.'

Redford smiled. 'What's with the cash?'

'I had my wallet stolen,' she snapped.

Redford turned suddenly serious. 'When? Where from?'

'An upmarket pickpocket. She knocked over my bag in the loo, the night we went out for dinner.'

'How d' you know it was her?'

'I can't be sure – I just have a feeling. I hardly left my bag alone any time, so I'm sure it was no one in the hotel,' she whispered, not wanting to get any innocent maids into trouble. The snooty cashier was now bestowing a vastly more friendly look on Sarah and was craning to hear the conversation.

'What did you lose?'

Sarah studied Redford, puzzled by the intensity of his questioning.

'About five hundred quid in cash, a thousand dollars, driving licence and credit cards. Worse than that, I lost pictures of my—' *Jesus.* She stopped herself just in time.

'Pictures of your what?' asked Redford with a frown.

'Naked pictures of all my lovers,' replied Sarah with a flash of inspiration.

'Yeah, right.'

'Anyway. It was a bloody pain in the arse, but I got funds transferred, I'm solvent, so let's forget it.'

A small, curious crowd of hotel guests was gathering, all with apparently pressing reason to congregate close to the cashier. Sarah nodded in their direction.

'Shall we?'

'Shall we what?' Redford asked mischievously.

'Get the hell out of here,' Sarah said crossly.

The limousine waited outside. Strone was already seated, talking on his mobile. He nodded at Sarah, glanced at Redford, and went back to his conversation.

'Forward or back?' asked Redford, indicating the seats.

'Why, forward please,' replied Sarah archly to his courtesy.

'Get car sick?'

'No, I just hate going backwards.'

'Ah.'

'Ah what?'

'Control freak.'

'Says who?'

'Says any right-minded psychiatrist.'

'And what do *you* know about psychiatrists?'

'Well now, I don't want to give away any advantages, do I?'

Sarah smiled and filed that one away. Part of her was struck again by the absurdity of her situation, sitting in a limo with the father of her child, getting to know him. She studied him. Redford looked tired but elated, as if he were glad to be on his way.

She leaned towards him. 'I'm sure you've heard this many times before, but you were amazing last night.'

'Thank you.' He seemed genuinely gratified by her praise.

'It was an incredible feeling, watching you, being part of your songs almost.'

'Is that how it felt to you, that you were part of the songs?'

'Absolutely, me and everyone else there. The music just seemed to flow through us. I almost felt suspended in it, like a sea of sound and feeling.'

Redford nodded thoughtfully.

'How does it feel,' asked Sarah, 'to be at the centre of all that?'

Redford smiled and his eyes became sensual and contemplative. 'It's the biggest high there is.' His eyes hardened. 'And the biggest mind-fuck you'll ever get.'

'How so?'

'What d'you do for an encore? The coming down is hell.'

'How do you come down?'

His eyes flickered on hers and away, and that was all she got for an answer. As he reached forward to a cabinet and took out a bottle of Evian, Sarah noticed the bandage on his right hand.

'What happened to you?' she asked, nodding at his hand. Redford looked vaguely embarrassed and seemed to weigh something up before he spoke.

'I hit a wall,' he said, almost in a whisper.

'You what?' exclaimed Sarah.

'You heard me.'

'Why in God's name would you do that?'

Strone suddenly clicked off his mobile phone and switched on to their conversation.

'Hey, ease up, would you,' he said with feeling.

'I was only asking,' said Sarah, looking from Strone to Redford. 'It's not some bloody state secret, is it, and 'scuse my saying this, but in my book it's a pretty strange thing to do, to hit a wall.'

Strone leaned toward her. 'Yeah well, you've never been a rock star, have you? You've never had the pressure of coming down after a concert. You've never had all that stored-up adrenaline coursing round your body with nowhere to go. So for Chrissakes ease up.'

Sarah raised her hands in surrender. 'I'm sorry. Forget I ever said anything.' Redford was watching her with troubled eyes. She turned to look out of the window, trying and failing to push the image of Redford slamming his fist into a wall, with all that implied about his stability, from her mind.

Chapter Thirty-five

Redford sat next to Sarah on the plane to Paris. Strone sat two seats behind them, seemingly preoccupied with a million details for the European leg of the tour. Sarah gazed round. All the other passengers must have flown first-class many times. They all looked jaded. It seemed to Sarah it was in this spirit, rather than out of respect for his privacy, that they limited their scrutiny of John Redford to the odd sidelong glance. Perhaps they were afraid of him in this confined space, fearing an outburst of rock-star-type violence if they pushed him. As the plane powered into the sky Sarah felt her spirits soar. The threatening note seemed small, trivial – a prankster's jest.

The stewardess came round as soon as they had reached their cruising altitude of thirty thousand feet. She gave Redford caviar, black grapes, and mineral water. Sarah asked for the same, and munched away in pleasure. Redford said little, spending most of the flight engrossed in a book about wolves. He seemed to Sarah desperately tired, but wired at the same time. He surprised her when he finally spoke.

'Tell me about your purse again.'

'My wallet,' Sarah corrected, crashing down from her high. 'And there's nothing else to tell.'

'You didn't report it?'

'I probably should have, but I couldn't be bothered. I had a few hours off and all I wanted to do was spend them quietly on my own, not standing in line in some grotty police station filling out five thousand forms. Look, I'm touched by your concern, and don't think me ungrateful, but what's it to you? You're worrying at it like a dog with a bone.'

'No reason. Does there always have to be a reason?'

'Always.'

'I'm on edge, I guess.'

'Why?' asked Sarah sharply, tuning in.

Redford ran his hands through his hair, looked up to the ceiling and blew out his breath slowly.

'Jim O'Cleary, our head of security, has disappeared.'

'Disappeared?'

'Failed to show at the AA flight to Paris an hour ago.'

'Maybe he just slept in.'

Redford shook his head. 'Not his style.'

'Everyone makes mistakes. Maybe he forgot to set his alarm clock.'

'Uh, uh.'

'You're very hands-on,' said Sarah. 'I wouldn't have thought you'd get involved in details.'

'Head of security's not a detail. Our lives could be in his hands.'

Sarah looked at Redford in surprise. 'How so?'

'You never heard of crazed fans, mob scenes, kidnap?'

Sarah thought of her note and could suddenly imagine this all too clearly. 'Yeah, I see your point. But they're all theoretical risks, aren't they? I mean, there's no risk from anyone specific is there?'

'No, there's not,' Redford replied almost angrily. 'O'Cleary's job is to keep the theoretical from getting practical. That's why his disappearing like this is so annoying.'

He turned abruptly back to his book. Sarah asked for a cup of tea. She took a long, warming drink.

'Do you enjoy touring?' she asked abruptly.

He looked up with quick interest. 'Why d'you ask?'

'Because I'd like to know. It seems a difficult way to live.'

'It is, I hate it.'

'Do you? Not the performing?'

'Nah, I love that, but like I said, it's a dangerous drug. Anyone who's stood up there and felt that pure adulation, that connection with so many people stripped bare, they're shit scared of it. It's like corruption. You can feel it licking at your soul.'

'Why corruption?'

'Because there's an awesome power you can abuse if you're not careful. You've got to keep it pure.'

Sarah watched him, trying to understand.

'You can take your audience any emotional place you want. It's like brainwashing. If you do it with an evil soul, you can fill their minds with poison, hatred, anger.'

'You filled my mind with joy and melancholy. And passion,' she added quietly.

Redford looked long and hard at Sarah. She fought to keep her equanimity under such an all-seeing gaze. She saw the mirror of her memories in his eyes.

'That's what I sing about,' he answered slowly. 'That's what I do, but you see what I mean, you see how it could turn bad?'

'Yes, I see. But why should it?' Sarah felt herself searching and coming close to touching something hidden in Redford's soul.

'Because it could.'

'I could climb to the top of a mountain and throw myself off, but just because I could, doesn't mean I will,' said Sarah.

'But you might think about it, the thought might enter your head and once it's there, what do you do?'

'Climb down quickly,' replied Sarah. She paused a while before asking carefully, 'Is that what the bandaged hand is all about?'

Redford looked away. 'It's about frustration, about feeling trapped.'

'You'd like to quit,' Sarah said in sudden comprehension.

Redford looked quietly appalled, as if Sarah had spoken the worst blasphemy.

'It's not heresy to me,' she said, replying to his thoughts. 'You've made it, you've been at the top for twenty years. Why not give it up?'

'It's not as simple as that. I love to sing, I love to perform, I love to write music.'

'Love hate,' commented Sarah.

'Exactly.'

'Sooner or later one wins, or you snap from the tension.'

A shadow flitted across Redford's face.

'Is that why you want the bond issue? You want to get out now, before anything happens?' Sarah knew she was in danger of pushing too hard, but she could sense some kind of revelation and she just had to keep going and risk Redford suddenly shutting down to get to it.

'Anything happens? Like what?' asked Redford tautly.

'You tell me.'

'No, *you* tell me. It's your trip.'

'I don't know. Nervous breakdown?'

'Had one of those. You get over it,' he said tartly.

'Drug addiction?'

'Had drug problems. Used to be so drugged up I wouldn't know what I was doing, but those days are long gone. Got over that too.'

'Sex addiction?' tried Sarah with a smile.

'I'm a monk. I'm celibate. These days.'

'Oh yeah?'

'Look, I've had the groupie thing. It wore off a long time ago.' His eyes probed hers angrily.

'There's sex without groupies,' observed Sarah, now completely confused as to where the personal finished and the professional started.

'Yeah, well meeting and keeping the right woman seems to be a problem for me.' He gave Sarah an acid look.

'Money addiction?' They were playing a game now, and both knew it.

'Why do you do what you do?' asked Redford. 'You seem to be just a tad conflicted by it yourself.'

'I am. But it's all I'm fit to do. It's what I know, I'm good at it. It's nice to be good at something, to be appreciated, to get paid for it.'

'But you said you can pick and choose, that you're not an impoverished merchant banker.'

'I'm not impoverished, but I still need the money.'

'Why? What for? Sometimes I look at you and get the feeling you're on a mission.'

Because I want to give your son the best that I can, she thought, dangerously entertaining the truth.

Sarah smiled. 'It's called *fuck you* money. Freedom money.'

'Yeah, yeah, I'm familiar with the concept. No ambition, beyond that?'

Sarah pondered the question. 'Yes, once upon a time. Beyond money, I wanted success.'

'And what happened?'

'I got what I thought I wanted.'

'And it wasn't enough?'

'It was good, a hell of a lot better than failure and impoverishment. I've come close enough to those two to know I never want another round.'

'So what was the problem?'

'Does there have to be a problem?'

'It's in your eyes, Sarah.'

'We were talking about you,' she said, as if dragging her mind back from a great distance.

'We've talked enough for now. I'm tired,' said Redford, a flash of the rock star in his eyes before he closed them and reclined his seat.

Chapter Thirty-six

A black Mercedes bore them to the Hotel Costes on rue St Honoré, round the corner from the Place Vendome. Rock music pumped at them as they walked into the dark, ornate foyer. Sarah got an impression of palms, incense, tasselled lights, red velvet brocade and a dazzling courtyard, lit by the sun, peopled by Grecian statues, gods looking down while their subjects played. It took her back instantly to her childhood in New Orleans. She almost swooned as the memories ambushed her. Redford looked round with anticipation, avoiding eye-contact with the other hotel patrons who were discreetly watching him.

'This is good. I like it.'

Strone stayed at Reception, apparently renegotiating their room rates in fluent French. With great ceremony, Sarah and Redford were led to their rooms. They passed bowls of roses, red, pink and white, love seats, umbrellas. They ascended in a dramatically slow and intimately small lift, breathed the incense, looked at paintings of limply abandoned beauties, caving in under the weight of their own *tristesse*.

Sarah's suite had its own flower-strewn balcony with roses, clematis and wisteria. She stood, gazing out over the rooftops in delight. Her bed was a four-poster, hung with rich tapestries. Her bathroom was tiled ornately, like a pasha's throne room, with gold taps and a luxuriously long and deep bath, big enough for two. The heady smell of incense lingered, exotic and suggestive, redolent of hot nights in a harem. I'm in a harem of one, she thought with amusement. She took a long, lazy shower, dried herself off and rubbed the hotel's body lotion into her skin. She pulled on a crocheted silk dress. The fabric was like a caress against her bare skin. There was a light rat tat tat at her door. She was about to open it without checking when she remembered the note. She'd almost certainly left the nutter who sent it behind in New York, but even so. There was no peephole.

'Yes?'

'Room service,' said a melodic voice. 'Came to ask if you might like some dinner.'

'That's rather forward of room service,' said Sarah, opening the door with a smile. Redford stood before her in jeans, white T-shirt and bare feet. Sarah felt her heart constrict. Oh Jesus. She'd like to kiss him now, just push him down on the hotel carpet and get on with it.

'Where does room service plan to deliver?' she asked instead.

'My suite, just down the hall. There's a little table set up on the balcony.'

Sarah must have looked dubious, for Redford grinned and reassured her. 'The whole of Paris will hear if you scream.'

'Am I in danger then?'

'Only if you want to be.'

Sarah turned away. 'Give me a second.'

She left Redford waiting on the threshold. In the bathroom she brushed her hair, shoved it behind her ears, and sprayed on some scent. She stared at herself in the mirror. Her eyes betrayed her excitement. She was breathing deeply, her chest rising and falling sharply, her cleavage visible in the V of her neckline. She took a last look and rejoined Redford.

'Lead the way.'

They stood side by side on the terrace, watching the sun set over the rooftops.

'Not bad, is it?' said Redford.

'Not bad at all.'

'For the little boy from Wyoming.'

'For the little girl from New Orleans,' agreed Sarah.

'It's so much sexier, New Orleans,' said Redford. 'Down and dirty and exotic.'

'Yeah, but Wyoming is good and pure and beautiful.'

Redford turned to face her. At that moment something flashed in the near distance. Sarah glanced towards the light, but then looked back at Redford, who didn't seem to have noticed anything. He was studying Sarah, apparently lost in his own thoughts. Sarah rubbed her arms.

'I'm hungry,' she said.

He smiled at her. 'Then we must eat.'

The table was set with the finest silver and crystal. The napkin was longer than some of Sarah's skirts. They ate asparagus, and drank a crisp white wine so smooth that Sarah almost swooned. In the last flush of sunset the lights of Paris came on. Soon the moon rose and shone down on them. It was one of those evenings which survive in the memory as a slice of perfection, an offering from the gods.

'Tell me about yourself, Sarah Jensen.'

'What's to tell. Your life is much more interesting.'

'I doubt it.'

'I'm not good at self-revelation.'

'I'll bet.'

'And what's that supposed to mean?'

'No one who hides things wants to let them go.'

'And I hide things?' asked Sarah.

'We both know you do.'

'So do you.'

'I don't deny it.'

'So what do we do then?' asked Sarah.

'How 'bout a trade?'

'What kind of trade?'

'Don't sound so nervous. You're a trader, aren't you? You told me yourself, a gambler.'

'So?'

'A question for a question. I ask you, you ask me. The only condition is truth.'

'No limits?'

'No limits.'

'How do I trust you? It'd be easy to lie.'

'Would it? Do you lie well?'

'That's your call, isn't it?'

'Mmm. Well then, Sarah. Shall we? Do or die.'

This is crazy, she thought, like a game of Russian Roulette. They both had too many secrets. Her only hope was that hers were too well hidden for him to even sense the relevant questions.

'How many questions?' she asked.

'We can call it quits any time.'

'No,' said Sarah. 'Three questions, no more no less. Make them count.'

Redford reached out his hand. 'Deal.'

Sarah shook. 'I start. Why d'you need the money from the bond issue?'

'So I can quit, *if* I want to. Gives me the choice.' He took a drink of water. 'What's the worst thing you've ever done?'

Sarah raked her hands through her hair. 'Oh Jesus.'

'Answer, Sarah. The truth.'

For a long time she looked out of the window at the Parisian night. Finally she turned back to Redford.

'Taking revenge,' she said quietly. She cut off another question with a raised hand. 'What's the worst thing *you* ever did?'

He must have had his answer ready because he came straight back with it.

'Abuse my power.' Then: 'What thing has hurt you the most?' he asked.

'That's easy. The death of my parents. And you?'

'The same. What are you afraid of?' he asked quickly, getting into a rhythm.

'Ah.' Sarah slowed down. 'Violence to those I love.'

'Not to yourself?'

'Don't break the rules. It's my turn,' said Sarah, ignoring her three-question limit. 'What are *you* afraid of?'

'A random killer. Walking out of this hotel tomorrow morning in the sunshine, heading off to some bistro for a café au lait and some loony tune coming out of a side street and blowing it all away. Another John Lennon.'

'Jesus.' His vision was so powerful, Sarah felt his fear as if it were hers. 'Are you expecting something like that?'

'My turn,' he said quietly. 'What excites you?'

'Speed. Racing down a ski slope at full pelt, fast cars, fast boats, fast horses, body-surfing a huge wave. Being a little out of control.'

He smiled, as if at a private thought.

'What makes you happy?' asked Sarah.

'Riding my horses in Wyoming. Hiking in the Tetons, camping under the stars.' His eyes rested on hers. 'What makes you happy?'

'Living.'

He studied her. 'Have you come so close to death, have you lost so many people?'

'That's two questions and it's my turn. What excites you?'

'Performing.' He gave Sarah an ambiguous smile.

Sarah had a sense that they should stop now. They'd gone beyond the three questions they'd agreed upon. She hadn't had to lie to him. All the while she feared a question about her true purpose here, and she was surprised to have evaded it.

'All right,' she said. 'Last question. Make it count.'

He took a long drink of water, leaned across the table and looked into her eyes, giving her no room for escape. 'Why did you run out on me?'

Chapter Thirty-seven

Bright sunshine gleamed against the white courtyard when Sarah went down to breakfast. She took refuge in the rococo dining room, amid the deep velvet sofas and dark corners. A waiter brought her a café Americain while she scanned the menu. She chose fried eggs and bacon, then sat back to gaze around her, tuning in and out of the fractured conversations of neighbouring tables. They all seemed to be comparing the excesses of the night before. There could have been something of the air of a brothel in the sensual opulence of the place, in the beauty of the waiters, but somehow it escaped that. The hotel had an air of gravitas that co-existed with the sex which pulsed through it like a bass beat. This was not a hotel of high-priced but cheap assignations. The place had sophistication, without trying too hard or too obviously for it. It also had a soul and somehow attracted a sophisticated, soulful clientèle.

When Sarah's breakfast arrived, she snapped out of her reverie, noticing for the first time that she was attracting more than her usual share of attention – a mixture of interest, admiration and envy. She could imagine the whispers. John Redford was staying, and this woman with her luscious long dark hair, black combats, tight T-shirt and knowing eyes, was the consort of the rock star. She wanted to sit and have an anonymous breakfast, but she was on display and she loathed it.

She quickly finished her food, and headed for her room. The phone was ringing when she entered.

'Hello?'

'Sarah, it's James.' Savage sounded angry.

'What is it?'

'Wake up,' he demanded. 'You sound half-asleep.'

She took a deep breath. 'Why don't you tell me who bit you in the arse and why.'

'Someone called Roddy Clark, a City journo creep on *The Word*.'

'Ah.' Savage was notorious for his loathing of the press. 'Didn't you have a run-in with him before? I seem to remember reading a retraction or something on an article he'd written on Goldsteins last year. Something about Helen Jenks, a derivatives trader.'

'Wild girl, you'd like her. Libelled along with us. We sued the bastards and won, but now Roddy bloody Clark's got a bee in his tiny bonnet about the City and particularly about us. There's talk in his club of him ranting and raving about bringing down a City firm, preferably Goldsteins.'

'Oh please. And he's a serious journalist?'

'Serious enough to be employed by *The Word* and to keep his job after we sued. God knows why.'

'So what's he said?'

'That we're acting for Redford, securitising his back catalogue, that a deal is imminent. I'm surprised he didn't name terms and give an investor list.'

'Shit!'

'Quite.'

'Could you have it faxed through, please?'

'On its way.'

'How'd he find out?'

'That's the question, isn't it? *I* don't know. You haven't said anything, have you?'

Savage was met by silence.

Then 'I can't believe you asked me that!'

'Oh come on, Sarah, don't get so shirty. I didn't think you would say anything, but—'

'Then spare me the haphazard wanderings of your mind.'

'Sarah, I indulge your temper, but others might not.'

'That's their lookout.'

'It doesn't help you, my dear.'

'No doubt. But I'm stuck with it. And so are you, so don't provoke me.'

'I've lost track of what provokes you. Don't you think you might try to deal with it?'

'Deal with it? How?'

'Get some help.'

'What *are* you talking about?'

'Therapy.'

'*Therapy*?'

'Why not?'

'I'm not hearing this. Have you gone weird on me?' Jesus, thought Sarah, Machiavelli in therapy.

'It's a good suggestion.'

'I'd rather not know what's going on in my subconscious.'

'Then you'll be a slave to it all your life.'

'My God. You've turned into a therapy groupie. You're supposed to hate all that.'

'People grow older and wiser.'

'But not mellower. You still loathe the press and I seem to remember that was the subject of this conversation, and to answer you calmly and rationally, I did *not* speak to the press. I like to keep a low profile, as you well know, so I would never speak to them.'

'D'you think Strone or Redford might have?'

'Redford wouldn't waste his time, but he might have let something slip inadvertently. Strone is quite capable of it. Let me speak to him.'

'ASAP, and read him the riot act if he has blabbed. Politely.'

'Could it be the Leaker?' asked Sarah.

'Could be, but not his style is it, to speak to the press.'

'Not so far it isn't. Breden still got the cameras running?'

'He has. Zamaroh's getting a bit fed up, invasion of her privacy and all that.'

'Keep them running. We have to get to the bottom of this.'

'We are. Got anything for me?'

'I'm getting close to something, but nothing tangible as yet. Just hints, spectres in the mist. I'll wait until I've got something more real before I start worrying you about it.'

'Nothing bad, is it?'

'No, James, I don't think so.'

'Nothing that bloody Roddy Clark could get hold of and twist?'

'No.'

'Nothing that would threaten the deal?'

'Not so far.'

'What are you not telling me?'

'Look, James, just let me do my job, will you? I can't give you blanket assurances and I never will be able to, but so far there's no evidence of anything horrific, OK? I'm getting to know the guy. What I'm finding out are the kind of lurgies we all have, the hopes and fears and weaknesses. None of us would like to see our private torments and dreams written up in *The Word*. The trouble with our client is that, for him, nothing's sacred as far as the media is concerned.'

'You don't need to convince me, but his privacy's ours for the taking as far as this deal is concerned.'

'No, James, the only things relevant to us are things that might threaten the deal. There's a hell of a lot that's private which isn't relevant to that. I'm not going to share that with anyone.'

'Not going native, are you?'

'Trust me, James, I know how to do my job.'

'Don't play God. If you know something bad, you tell us.'

'If it threatens the deal, James, I will tell you.'

'I'll decide if it threatens the deal, not you. I want you back here tomorrow, Sarah.'

And before she could retaliate, Savage hung up.

Sarah slammed down the receiver and strode across the room. A note was stuck under the door. She paused uneasily and looked at it for a moment before stooping to pick it up. There was no envelope, merely her name typed on the outside. She unfolded the note and read:

Will you never learn? Time's running out bitch. Back off or die.

I will not react, she thought. I will go about my normal morning ritual. I will not be poisoned by some loony tune. She recoiled suddenly as she remembered Redford coldly outlining his fear. *Some loony tune lurking outside on a sunny day*. Just like today.

She reached for the phone and tried to ring Redford. The operator told her all his calls were put on hold, that no one was to get through. Sarah rang Strone.

'Yup?'

'Strone, it's Sarah. I need to speak to John.'

'No can do. It's show day.'

'It's important.'

'Nothing's as important as show day.'

Sarah breathed a sigh of frustration.

'Speak to *me*,' said Strone.

'No. It's something for John.'

Strone became all ears. 'Nothing's just for him. We're a team, Redford and Strone. What he knows I know.'

'Oh, for God's sake, cut it out. It's personal.'

That bought Sarah an electric silence.

'How personal?'

'Are there shades of personal? What's he doing all day? Won't he have five minutes somewhere? I need to tell him something.' Sarah realised she sounded dangerously like a pining supplicant, and rebelled against the thought.

'He does his yoga for hours. His breathing. He centres himself. You charging in there with whatever the hell it is you have to tell him will uncentre him, so you will not have access. You will not speak to him today.'

Strone spoke in an aggressive tone that would have normally sent Sarah off the deep end but, mindful of Savage's suggestion of therapy, she held back, just to prove to herself that she could. It so happened, too, that Strone was right. The last thing Redford needed to hear about, if he was trying to get centred, was his worst fear, his loony tune, even if he or she was stalking not him, but Sarah. The word made Sarah balk. Savage would say, in his new argot, that she was *in denial*.

'Right,' said Sarah. 'I need to talk to you anyway. When can we get together?'

'Come on, Sarah. You a slow learner or something? It's concert day. I'm just a tad busy.'

'Five minutes. Right fucking now.' Sarah slammed down the phone, shaking. *Will you never learn? You a slow learner*?

'Who the hell do you think you are?' Strone barged his way in through Sarah's door.

It couldn't be him, she thought, watching him pass. He'd be too clever to make a mistake like that, to betray himself by his words, even if he did have a motive, which she couldn't possibly see, given the ten million dollars he'd get if the deal closed. She turned to face him.

'Please excuse my temper. It's contagious. I've just been bawled out by James Savage.' She stalked over to her fax machine and swiped up a one-page fax which she thrust at him. 'Know anything about this?'

He read the article in *The Word*, then scanned Sarah's face as if noticing it for the first time.

'What's to know?'

'You didn't by any chance speak to the journo, did you?'

'I speak to journos all the time. What's new?'

'Did you speak to *this* journo, about *our* deal?'

Strone began to look awkward.

'You did,' said Sarah.

'What's the problem?'

'Confidentiality. The whole methodology of running a deal. Everything happens to a carefully worked-out schedule. There is no ad libbing, no casual chats with the press, or anyone else outside of the designated people, and that's me, Savage, Zamaroh, Breden, you and Redford and the one or two business people on your side who absolutely have to know what's going on. Namely your lawyers.'

'Aw, come on. It's not exactly state secrets here.'

'It'd better be, or else your deal goes belly-up – and you know what? You're responsible. First of all, there are a whole load of laws that govern the way investment business is carried out, and we, Goldsteins, and you, our client, have to respect them. Second, there's the right way and there's the wrong way to present this deal to potential takers. Investors are wary creatures. They like everything to run smoothly, to follow a pre-set pattern. Any divergence from the norm is cause for concern. If something goes wrong down the road they like to be able to point backwards and say to their superiors, "but hey, look, there were no warning signs, nothing odd, nothing abnormal, nothing to suggest this might all turn to ratshit". They need a well-managed deal, and that's what we have to give them. A well-managed deal breeds confidence, it isn't some optional extra. There's a very strict choreography to this. You don't go bumbling onto the financial stage and rewrite it, any more than James Savage, Zaha Zamaroh or I would go crashing onto Redford's stage and try to sing a quartet with him.'

Strone listened in silence. 'All right,' he said stiffly, 'I won't speak to the press again. Satisfied?'

'Satisfied,' said Sarah. 'But just so's I know, what exactly did you tell the journo, and who made contact with whom?'

'The guy rang me out of the blue, said he'd heard that we were gonna securitise the back catalogue, that Goldsteins were running the deal.'

'Then what?'

'I said yeah, that was correct, we were gonna do the biggest bond issue a rock star has ever done—'

'Shit,' groaned Sarah.

'What's wrong with that?'

'We don't know how big the deal's going to be yet, we're still working on the financials. It's totally premature to go round stating sizes. This isn't a case of mine's bigger than yours. You go for something too big and you'll have a flop, get it?'

Strone smirked.

'It's not a joke when it happens to you,' said Sarah.

'Does it happen to you a lot? I imagine you'd terrify most men.'

Sarah moved forward till she was in Strone's face. 'Listen buster, it's gonna happen to you, and to your star, big time, if you don't start engaging your brain and tying a knot in your ego.'

Strone headed for the door. 'You know you have one hell of a temper. You really ought to try—'

'Please,' interrupted Sarah, 'don't suggest therapy.'

'How d'you know I was gonna suggest therapy?'

' 'Cos you're the second person in one day to suggest it.'

'Maybe that should tell you something.'

'It does. I'm in the wrong business.'

Strone laughed. 'You coming to the concert tonight?'

'Wouldn't miss it for the world.'

Chapter Thirty-eight

Sarah changed into her suit trousers and a white cotton T-shirt. She threw a lavender-coloured pashmina shawl around her shoulders and was about to head out to the concert when she noticed another envelope stuck under her door. She yanked open the door, eyes raking the corridor, but there was no sign of anyone. Her name, typed, the envelope gummed shut. She ripped it open. A photograph fell out. Sarah and Redford were standing on his balcony, faces tinted gold by the setting sun, his turned toward her, hers facing forward, inquisitive. She remembered the flash, remembered a movement, fast, sniper-like. Her face was bisected by a red slash, gummy to the touch, blood or lipstick. She shuddered, terrified and enraged in equal measure. The note, in the now familiar type face, read:

If you won't stay away from Redford, you must pay. Get ready to die.

She stared at the note and then at the photograph as if trying to make them diminish in the power of her gaze, but their message of hostility would not shrink. She could ignore them no longer. She hated unfinished business, to be controlled by others, especially invisible stalkers, but her rational side told her she had no choice. She wasn't ready to leave Redford, he was unfinished business, and always would be, but her love of Georgie pulled her with an astonishing force back home. Before Georgie, risking her life was a selfish game. She never courted it, but if jeopardy went with the route she had chosen, she didn't divert. Now, all routes led back to her son. To abandon him was unthinkable. She *had* to take the stalker seriously.

She thought back to last night and Redford's final question. She had considered her answer long and hard, her eyes lingering over his body, remembering a pleasure more intense than any she had experienced before. Then she had smiled and said simply: *Because I had to.* Before she could weaken, she had risen from the sofa, and left him.

Later in bed, she had dreamed, awake, of how it might have been to make love again with this man, the father of her child, to slip into his mind, to feel his golden skin, to lie eye to eye with him, to feel the power and the thrill of him.

She stared at the note, seeing into the mind of its author. You think he's yours, she thought. You are filled with hate, filled with rage, and you would destroy me. She put it on a side table and walked out into the hall. I will watch you tonight, John Redford, she decided, in all your splendour, and tomorrow I will leave you to your crazed fan.

She sat in a private box in Parc des Princes listening to the roar of the crowd. Strone had escorted her to the box and then disappeared. She was glad. She didn't want his eyes on her as she looked upon Redford for the last time.

As she watched him run onto the stage, she could see his smile, the way his eyes were shining, could feel the thrill he both loved and dreaded as the crowd took him into their hearts, individually and collectively. Out there, somewhere, was the hate, but for now it was kept at bay. She watched him move, all loose-limbed and sinuous, watched him caress his mike, and she listened to him sing 'Come To Me'.

'Walk away now, or come to me,
Turn your face, or kiss me,
Button your coat, or let it fall,
Come to me and let me love you,
Let it begin, let me look at you,
And see you, let me kiss you,
And taste you, let me love you,
With all of me, every sinew, every breath,
Every heartbeat.

I want to talk with you,
I want to walk with you,
I want to know you,
I want to love you.'

He sang his way into her mind, into her blood. She wanted to hear his voice talking just for her. She wanted to see him open, she wanted him to show himself to her and she wanted to provoke him and feel his need. She wanted that first, knowing touch, not the accidental brushing by, nor the hand of assistance easing on a jacket, but a stroke, a caress, a hand reaching out with a question, and she yearned to yield in response. She hated the thought that she was losing control, but desire had her in its teeth. She had to have this man again. She craved him with a ferocity that frightened her. She vowed to herself she would have him again, to love, to possess for one night, and to be possessed by him. One more perfect night, but not now, not under these circumstances, when she was his entrapper, sent to unpick his soul and find his faults and his skeletons. If it happened it must be some time in the future, she decided. The fates had thrown them together twice. If it was meant to be, they would throw them together a third time. She watched him, and dreamed, while he sang 'Breathe No More'.

'You bring me the taste of faraway places,
Your looks unknowable,
You keep your fears and hopes like private dancers,
Dressed up in the dark.
You never show what moves or tears you, but Baby,
I can feel your despair.
The touch of other lovers lingers on your skin,
You will never be theirs, nor mine to have,
And to hold, and the saddest thing, Baby,
You will never be yours.

You are the mystery to my prayer,
You are my fourteen-year-old's dream
I saw you when I ate dust, when I couldn't sleep,
When the summer nights were so hot,
You came to me like a genie, and you touched my temple
With your cool hand.

Now your hand is on fire, and not even
All my tears can put it out.
I can't drown your pain,
I can't be your breath,
But I can love you
Till I breathe no more.'

Chapter Thirty-nine

Sarah sat alone on a wooden chair on her terrace, looking out over the silent rooftops. She couldn't have slept and she hadn't tried to. She decided to sit out here in the dark, with the smell of incense wafting over her skin like a caress, and watch the night turn to dawn. She loved this feeling, of being up when the world slept around you. She felt protected by the darkness. If there was hate out there, it couldn't touch her now; if pain awaited her, she couldn't feel it now; if sadness lay beyond the dawn, no shadows of it fell on her now. She felt purged. Redford had sung out her hopes and her fears and her pain, their shared pain. He had touched her with the beauty of his soul, her and fifty thousand others and, despite his fears, they all went home with their souls lifted. If he had the power to poison them, he didn't use it now. Sarah glanced at her watch. It was three. Pitch dark, dawn still hours away. She reached for her glass of whisky and paused halfway. There was a knock at the door. Silently she rose and padded across the room. Tap, tap, the knock sounded again.

'Who's there?' she whispered.

'It's John.'

Her heart gave a leap and beat faster. Her mouth turned dry.

Slowly, she swung open the door. He stood before her in his jeans and white T-shirt, barefoot again. He looked spent, ravished almost, as if he had relived all the pain and loss he sang about with every word, as if every chord played at his memory and plucked him from any safe place he might try to run to.

He looked at her and in answer she stood back to let him pass.

'I was sitting on my terrace, just watching the night,' she said. 'Will you sit with me?'

He smiled and nodded and followed her through the room and out onto the balcony. He pulled up a chair and sat next to her.

'Are you thirsty?' Sarah asked.

'I could drink a river. I downed all the Evian in my suite.'

'Here, let me get you some.' She got to her feet and returned with four little bottles. She watched Redford drink three of them.

'Your performance,' she said, reaching out to touch his wrist, 'was one of the most beautiful things I've ever seen. It was too beautiful to sleep on. I just wanted to sit up all night and watch the dawn.'

'Can I keep you company? All night, until morning?'

'I'd love you to.' She looked at him, long and lingeringly. She was unable to look away. He kept his eyes on hers, leaned across the divide and touched her face. He traced his fingers over her eyelids, down her cheeks, over her lips. All her resolutions fell away. She kissed his fingers, leaned toward him, and kissed his mouth.

It felt like a dream, a memory recalled, with every sense sharper than ever. His taste was as she remembered, only better. His kiss was as she remembered, only more passionate. He pulled her to her feet, drew her into him, and the dream became reality in his embrace. He led her gently to her bed, watched her lie down. He lay beside her, his fingers moving over her body with increasing heat. He pulled up her dress, stroked the bare skin of her thigh. She pushed against him, pulled him on top of her, opened her legs until she felt him pressing against her. She tugged at his jeans, unzipping them, pushing them off. When he made love to her, she gave herself to him in complete surrender.

Afterwards they lay in one another's arms, together in silence and love. There was too much to say to know where to start, so they said nothing, neither of them wanting to break the spell. Sarah must have fallen asleep finally, because she woke to see Redford standing before her, grim-faced. Her eyes travelled to the photograph and the note clenched in his hand.

'Ah.'

'Is that all you can say?' His voice was tight with the effort at self-control.

'What am I supposed to say?'

'Were you going to tell me?'

She got out of bed and pulled on her towelling robe. She tied it tightly round her and curled up in an armchair, legs pulled into her chest. 'I tried to this morning. Strone said you weren't to be disturbed.'

'Did you tell him?'

'No. I wanted to talk to you first. What's going on, John? It's happening to you, too, isn't it?'

He sank down on the bed. 'For the last six weeks. I've had a note almost every day, different words, but always the same meaning; *enjoy it while it lasts, ashes to ashes, dust to dust.*'

'Any idea who it might be?'

Redford shook his head. 'Could be anyone, couldn't it, any mad bastard seeking their destiny in killing me. Short cut to their own fame.'

'It's a jealous woman, that's pretty obvious.'

'Still an open field.'

'I can imagine.'

'How many notes have you had?'

'Three. One in New York, the day after we'd been out to dinner, then one this morning, then another with the photograph, just before I left for the concert.'

'Have you told Goldsteins?'

'Not yet.'

'You will?'

'I have to.'

'What'll they do?'

'Demand that I retire gracefully from your deal.'

'And will you?'

'I don't want to. I don't know,' she answered woodenly.

'What happens to the deal if you tell them?'

'I just don't know.' She tried to still the turmoil in her mind. She got up and poured herself a large whisky. She took three big gulps, feeling some semblance of clarity burn into her. 'Maybe they can be persuaded that the stalker is incidental to the deal, but it'll be a tough sell. They won't like it. They won't want the kind of publicity that could go with a stalker, if it got out. Maybe they'll worry that this nutter will turn her attentions to them.' She paused for a moment. 'I take it you haven't gone to the police?'

He shook his head, as if the idea were impossible.

'Why not?'

'Because it'll leak out, the media'll go mad with the story, and I'll become a stalker magnet.'

'There must be a way of investigating it discreetly,' said Sarah.

'You tell me.'

She was about to tell him, but caught herself in time. 'I don't know, it's not my field. You should consult an expert. Look, I have to fly back to London tomorrow. I have to tell Goldsteins. I could ask them, they'll know people. They could help you, I'm sure.'

'Not my style. Look, Sarah, is there any way you can *not* tell Goldsteins?'

'Why?'

'I don't want to stir up a hornet's nest. I'd rather just get out, go home to Wyoming.'

'Be driven out, you mean?'

Redford shrugged.

'You can't let this person rule your life.' Sarah got to her feet in frustration and paced around.

'I'm not. It's time to get out, anyway.'

'Why?'

'Quit at the top.'

'You could have many more years at the top.'

'Maybe.'

'The stalker's the real reason, isn't she?' Sarah said, suddenly inspired. '*That's* why you want the bond issue – to escape her. That's also why you don't want me to tell Goldsteins about her, because you're worried they'll pull the deal and block your escape.'

She saw confirmation in his eyes. 'But why d'you need the bond issue to escape?' she asked, mystified. 'You must have already made a mint, more than enough to retire on. I know we've gone over this before, but I can't quite believe you don't have enough dosh to quit now.'

'You'd be surprised. My records have grossed hundreds of millions of dollars, my tours hundreds more, but there are so many rip-offs coming out of that, so many legitimate expenses, so many parasites.' He looked weary at the thought. 'Part of it's my fault too. I pissed away a lot in my twenties.'

'How?'

'Aw, you know – the rock 'n' roll cliché, sex and drugs and excess of all kinds. Motorboats I'd give away, parties with everything on tap. I had it all and did it all.'

'And now you're punishing yourself.'

Redford looked surprised. 'How's that?'

'You're allowing a stalker to make one of the biggest decisions of your career for you. What is it, some kind of quid pro quo? I was guilty of excess, now I must pay?'

'Sarah, it's not that simple. I'm tired of being me, the public me, and yes, I'll admit it, I'm frightened. Hate like that, it gets to you.'

'It's got to me and it's only been going on for a few days.' Sarah took another gulp of whisky. 'Why doesn't she come out and fight in the open?'

'You seem very sure it's a woman, don't you?'

'It's sly and nasty and bitchy. Possessive too. You don't think she could be an ex-girlfriend?'

Redford looked momentarily startled. 'None of them hates me, far as I know. Might be pissed with me, but not enough to follow me round on tour for six weeks typing out notes.'

'She must be rich to fly around like that. She doesn't work, or else she's got some job that allows her to take six weeks off. Perhaps she's self-employed. Whatever she is, she's obsessive, determined, and out of her tiny mind.'

Redford got up and took hold of Sarah's hand in his. 'I'm sorry. I'm forgetting you in all this. Are you frightened?'

'Of course I am, and I hate it. I hate the whole idea of being stalked. Like your nightmare, you walk into the sunshine, right into the sights of some mad sniper. Bang bang, you're dead.'

Chapter Forty

Sarah got the first flight back to London and headed straight for Carlyle Square. Jacob was waiting on the doorstep when Sarah's cab drew up, with Georgie in his arms. She rushed up to them.

'Oh Georgie, Jacob. My passions. How are you both?'

Jacob grinned. The baby giggled with joy when he saw his mother, reaching out his arms to her. She took him, buried her face in his neck, breathed him in, kissed him over and over before she drew breath, carried him inside and down into the kitchen. She snuggled into her favourite armchair, and nursed him in her lap as she chatted to Jacob.

'How's it all been?'

'Fine, sweetie. He's such a good baby, so easy and loving. We've had a good time, him 'n' me.'

'Oh, Jacob. Thanks so much for all this. I couldn't do it without you.'

The old man smiled shyly, his eyes glowing with pleasure, and Sarah realised that her baby had rejuvenated him. 'Any time. I mean that. Now how's it going your end? You look well,' he observed, suspiciously, it seemed to Sarah.

'Do I?' she said airily. 'Can't think why. Didn't get much sleep – what with the early flight,' she added quickly. 'But it's going OK. In fact, I might not have to do any more travelling. That side of things might be wound up soon.'

'That'd be good, wouldn't it?'

'Yeah, it would. All depends on what Goldsteins say today, whether they're satisfied with my due diligence on John Redford or not.'

'What did you come up with?'

'Nothing, really. Guy's almost squeaky clean. No skeletons as far as I can find.'

'Everyone has skeletons, you know that.'

'Yeah, they do, but I suppose as long as no one finds his, whatever they might be, then the deal won't be threatened, so it all amounts to the same thing, doesn't it?'

'Which is?'

'That I end my assignment and Goldsteins do the deal.'

'Why do I get the feeling it's not going to be as simple as that?'

Sarah stayed for an hour, then charged off to the King's Road and hailed a taxi.

'The City,' she said. 'Broadgate Circle, please, fast as you can. I'm late.'

'What d'you think I am, then?' the cabbie asked good-naturedly. 'A magician?'

Sarah grinned, gathered her papers from her briefcase and buried her head in them before the cabby thought to strike up a conversation. He got her to Goldsteins almost on time for her meeting. She tipped him extravagantly, and headed to her temporary office to check for messages. Jezza was loitering inside. Sarah stopped on the threshold in surprise and irritation.

She forced a smile. 'Hi, Jezza. What's up?'

'Just wondering where you'd been. Not seen you for a while.'

'Yeah well, I feel like I haven't seen myself too. Research, flying here, there, you know how it is.'

'No, I don't,' he said, taking a seat. 'Tell me.'

'Love to, but I can't. Got a meeting with Savage and I'm eight minutes late.'

Jezza got lazily to his feet. 'My God, we can't have that, can we? Can't disappoint the great man himself.' He scratched his nose thoughtfully. 'It's not everyone on the trading floor who has access to old Savage features. You might want to watch yourself.'

Sarah stiffened. 'What's that supposed to mean?' she asked sharply.

'Hey, cool it. I'm saying this for your own interests, so don't bite the messenger.'

'Look, Jezza, for God's sake stop talking in riddles. I don't have all day.'

Jezza glanced around then beckoned Sarah closer. 'Walls have ears,' he said.

'What?'

He beckoned again. With a heavy sigh, Sarah walked closer.

'Let's put it this way,' he said in a stagily confessional voice. 'I don't think all's exactly cosy on the domestic front.'

'Meaning?'

'I think Mrs Savage might be playing away.'

'What makes you think that?'

'Because I saw her one day. I was taking a sickie, saw her in the street with a toy boy.'

God, sickies seemed to be endemic on the trading floor. She remembered PJ's comments about Fiona Savage, the suggestion of afternoon delight. She felt moved to defend her, for her husband's sake, if nothing else. 'Oh come on. He was probably her son.'

'In that case I'd say she had an unhealthily physical relationship with her son, because she was breathing into his ear.'

She felt a wave of distaste. 'Look, Jezza, this really isn't any of your business, or mine. Why are you telling me this?'

Jezza dropped the staginess and snapped in irritation.

'For God's sake, Sarah, wise up! Savage is probably looking for consolation. And who better than some new babe on his payroll?'

Sarah stepped away, glaring at Jezza with outrage.

'Get out of my way, you tosspot. I've wasted enough time on you.'

She stormed past and headed for the back stairs. Alone in the stairwell she paused for a moment, trying to collect herself, trying to shake the feeling of sleaze that travelled with Jezza, that always lay just beneath the surface on the trading floor.

Chapter Forty-one

'Tell me,' said Zaha Zamaroh, slinking around the meeting room until she came to rest leaning down over Dick Breden's chair, half-inquisitor, half-seductress, 'what do you know of Sarah Jensen?'

Breden gave her a conspiratorial smile. 'What's it to you?'

'Mere curiosity.' Zamaroh stood straight again, and stretched luxuriously, her breasts rising under her scarlet silk shirt. 'You're curious, too, admit it.'

Breden shrugged, pretending indifference. 'I'm curious as to what she delivers, how she goes about her work.'

'Not about her history?'

'What history?'

'Well . . .' Zamaroh leaned forward across the conference table. 'As I'm sure you know, she worked in the City for four years, all the time for Findlays, became their top producer, underpaid because all those British banks are cheapskates, and she's a woman and that hardly helps. Then she jumped, suddenly, into the rather nasty ocean of Inter-Continental Bank. Within a matter of weeks, the head of trading was murdered, the chief executive was murdered, and Sarah quit. Quit ICB, quit the City, disappeared for a long time. Then she reappears after three years, as James Savage's special investigator. Rather an eventful life, don't you think?'

Breden smiled. 'What do you want, Zaha?'

Zamaroh narrowed her eyes. Why did he have to be so crass and obvious? Did he know nothing of the ritual of trading, the dance of seduction it invariably involved, even for the one night stands of traders, the day traders who took and invariably abandoned positions the same day?

'I want to know what happened, how she was connected, because she must have been. That must be evident, even to you.'

'And why should I either seek this information, or provide you with it?'

'You'll seek it, if you don't already have it, because you would like to see Sarah Jensen fall from grace. She's untrained in your business, she has unparalleled access to Savage, and she's unbearably bolshy in a business where women should still be seen and not heard. You'll provide me with the information because I am your occasional paymaster. It's a simple concept, Dick. It's called a trade.'

Breden mused on this for a while. 'Why do you want to know?'

'Knowledge is power.'

The door swung open, making them both jump.

'Sarah, how nice,' intoned Zamaroh.

Sarah eyed her suspiciously, making Zamaroh wonder if she might have heard any snippets of conversation through the heavy mahogany doors.

'You're late,' she added.

'I am, aren't I?'

Zaha thought Sarah looked magnificent. She was wearing what seemed to be her new uniform of man's suit, high heels, and a plain white T-shirt with a string of lumpy, luminescent, obviously real, wild pearls at her neck, with another pair as stud earrings.

'I love your pearls,' Zamaroh couldn't resist saying. 'South Sea?'

Sarah nodded, aware that Zaha was admiring their price tag as well as their innate beauty. They were worth a fortune, but Sarah had no idea of their exact cost. They were a present from Jacob to celebrate Georgie's birth. He could have bought them then, he could have acquired them during his safe-cracking years, Sarah never asked, didn't want to know, but the thought that they might be illicit never detracted from their beauty.

Zamaroh was clearly a fan of real jewellery. She wore a huge diamond ring on the middle finger of her left hand, plus a glittering pair of studs, but it occurred to Sarah that she wore them almost angrily, as if she had bought them herself, and that their value, either monetary or emotional, was reduced by that.

The air quivered as James Savage walked in.

'Sarah, Dick, Zaha,' he nodded to them all, the king to his court. He received a bone china cup of espresso from Fred who followed him in silently, and he drank it back like a snifter.

'This room clean?' he snapped at Breden.

'Yep.'

'Still nothing on the Leaker?'

Breden shook his head. 'Very elusive. The investigation's going nowhere fast. It doesn't make sense. I know we're missing something, some key, and if we could just get that, we'd have a chance.'

Savage raised his eyebrows with displeasure and turned to Sarah. 'Do you have anything?'

'I do.' She felt the air quicken around her. 'First of all, it was Strone Cawdor who spoke to Roddy Clark.'

'The idiot,' shouted Zamaroh.

'Stupid tosser,' spat Savage.

'I pretty much told him that, if it makes you both feel any better,' replied Sarah, provoking a grin from Savage.

'If you expressed yourself with your customary lack of restraint that does give me a measure of consolation.'

'Who initiated the contact?' asked Breden.

'Strone said Clark rang him, and I've no reason to disbelieve him, so the real question is, who the hell put Clark on to the scent?'

'You did,' answered Zamaroh smugly.

Sarah gazed at her with the look of wary disbelief you give a psycho weaving down the street towards you shouting insanities.

'I'm *sorry*?'

'You and your little stunt, taking Redford down to the trading floor. Might as well have taken out an ad in *The Times*.'

Sarah smiled sweetly. 'The point is, Zaha, that talking to journos is strictly off-limits, without managerial clearance. I assume you have attempted to make that clear to your people downstairs. Problem is, you must have failed, because one of them sure as hell tipped Roddy Clark off. I mean, he's not exactly going to hang around outside Goldsteins every night quizzing employees who came in that day.'

'And?' asked Zamaroh. 'Are we going anywhere with this, other than some weak attempt to slag me off?'

'Let me put it simply,' replied Sarah. 'Whoever tipped off Clark is likely to be our Leaker.'

Zamaroh gazed woodenly at the ceiling as if waiting for Sarah to finish her floor show. She looked back down with a gleam in her eye. 'So, now you know that, how do you propose finding out who that person is? Are you going to tail Clark twenty-four seven? That's the kind of thing you're paid for, isn't it? It'll give you a chance to earn your money for once. Think of the satisfaction in that.'

'Oh shut up bitching, will you both,' said Savage. 'Saints pre*serve* us from women.' He shook his head. 'How are you going to follow this up, Sarah?'

'We've got one strand now. We keep digging around until we find another.'

'Sounds a bit vague.' He turned to Breden. 'Any ideas, Dick?'

He gave an elegant shrug. 'Like Sarah says, we keep looking for another strand. At least we've got something to go on now.'

Sarah turned to Dick. 'D'you think we should get a profile on Clark?'

He rubbed his chin. 'I think we should. Never know what we might find in his phone records. Your dirty raincoat, or mine?'

Savage and Zamaroh listened bemused.

'Mine, I think,' replied Sarah with a smile.

'Well, get bloody going on it then,' answered Savage with an outsider's pique. 'You're both being paid enough.' He got to his feet.

'Hold on a second,' said Sarah. Savage focused down on her.

'What is it? I've got another meeting in five minutes.'

Sarah reached for the coffee pot in the middle of the table, poured herself a half-cup of espresso and drank it down. Her audience waited.

She laid her cup back in its saucer with a clink and raised her eyes to meet Savage's. 'Redford's being stalked.'

There was a collective intake of breath.

'It's been going on for the last six weeks. Wherever he goes, west coast, east coast, the stalker follows, sending him threatening letters; "*Enjoy it while you can. Ashes to ashes*". The kind of stuff that lunatics get off on. He has no idea who it is.'

'Shit!' said Zamaroh.

Breden leaned across the board table, frowning.

'Bugger,' said Savage. 'Bloody bugger wild card. What the hell do we do about this?'

'Is he frightened?' asked Breden, the only one to remain cool.

'Terrified. He has this recurring fear of walking out of his hotel one sunny morning, as some nutter waits with a pistol and blows him away.'

'And you,' asked Breden, 'do *you* have any idea who it might be?'

'I think it's a jealous woman.'

'Why? How can you know that?' he asked.

'Because I'm being stalked too.'

Chapter Forty-two

Savage sent his apologies to his next meeting and commenced an hour-long interrogation of Sarah. At the end of it, she felt utterly spent and was desperate to get home again to Georgie. She'd filled them in on every last salient detail of the stalking, repeating answers to repeated questions.

'What I still don't understand, and what you haven't sufficiently answered,' said Savage with ill-disguised impatience, 'is why *you* are being stalked?'

'Jesus, I don't know,' snapped Sarah. 'Ask the bloody stalker.'

'Stalker, leaker, we're being plagued by fruitcakes,' observed Zamaroh, who seemed to Sarah to be enjoying the spectacle of her discomfort.

'I'm asking you, Sarah,' persisted Savage, shooting Zamaroh a scowl. 'Make a guess – we're paying you enough for a guess, surely.'

Sarah gave a theatrical sigh. 'All right. Two theories. One is, as I said, a jealous woman. The reason she's jealous of me is that she thinks Redford and I have a thing going. Apparently some of the band think that, too. I've suddenly joined the entourage, staying in the same hotel as Redford, something which none of his band or team is allowed to do, only Strone, and I can hardly explain my real reason for being there, so they assume, to quote one of them, that I'm *tottie*.'

She grimaced over the word. Zamaroh tried unsuccessfully to stifle a giggle. Savage had the good grace to look embarrassed on Sarah's account; Breden merely watched her with his inscrutable detachment.

'The only hole in the theory is why be jealous of me if she hates Redford as she seems to?' continued Sarah.

'Love hate?' offered Zamaroh. 'The thin line and all that?'

'Could be,' said Sarah.

'What's the second theory?' asked Breden.

'That it's someone who knows my real purpose and doesn't want me to discover something which might threaten the deal. But that doesn't make sense either, because the threats would only make me want to dig deeper to find out what's being hidden. And, anyway, who knows my real purpose? No one close to the deal should, unless the Leaker's been at work again.'

'It's so bloody labyrinthine, this whole thing,' said Savage.

'Is there anyone who would benefit from the deal being pulled?' asked Breden.

'You mean someone might be doing this just to put us off?' asked Sarah.

'Could be,' suggested Breden.

'I can't think of anyone who would benefit, unless they bore us a grudge. We make fees, Strone, the manager, gets a share of Redford's income, so he'd get a nice cut of the deal. Maybe the band don't want the deal done. There's one guy, Ray Waters, seems like a real jerk.' Sarah paused to think. 'No, the stalker's too vehement, too intimate. I'm sure it has to be a woman. I'd go with the love hate jealousy scenario.'

Savage narrowed his eyes at Sarah. 'You're not getting too close to Redford, are you?'

'What's that supposed to mean?'

'Well, you know,' Savage squirmed awkwardly. 'Going native.'

Sarah glared at him. 'I'm spending as much time as I can with him, to find out as much as I can about him. That's why it might appear to a deranged stalker that something is going on.'

'And is it?' persisted Savage.

'No, it isn't,' said Sarah quietly and, she hoped, calmly, trying to keep images of the night before, and of a night a year and a half ago from her mind, lest Savage read even a shadow of the truth.

'So what do we do now?' he asked. 'This has really thrown a spanner in the works.'

Sarah got to her feet. 'I'm going home.'

'What do you mean?' Savage stared at her.

'Just what I said. We can't take this any further right now, and I've got things to do.'

'What things?'

'Private things, James. A life. I have one. I know it's unfashionable in these circles, but so be it.' Sarah headed for the door.

'You're not going to be scared off by this stalker, are you?' asked Savage in surprise.

Sarah stopped. 'Wouldn't you be?'

' 'Course I bloody well would be, but I'm not you. You'd never have been frightened like this in the past.'

'Maybe it's age and wisdom. Besides, who said I was frightened?'

'You've got that distant stubborn look in your eyes, like you're on the way out of this already.'

'Maybe I am, I don't know. I need some time to think.' Sarah turned and walked from the room and headed home.

'Strange,' observed Breden as the door clicked shut. 'I've never seen her like that before. Scared and vulnerable.'

Sarah bolted into the back of a taxi feeling as if she were beginning to fragment. There were too many pieces in her life and the effort of holding them all together was fraying her. She forced herself to concentrate on mechanical tasks, seeking refuge in a list of things she could create, tick off and erase. She rang Teddy Skelton on her mobile. The lawyer was in a meeting but Sarah hooked him out on a plea of urgency.

'Sarah, hi.'

'Hi, Teddy. Sorry to do this to you.'

'Aren't you always, dearie. Matters not a jot. Just between you, me and the grapevine, I've got a coked-up head hunter in there trying to sue the merchant bank he placed a candidate with after they refused to pay him. It turned out after a week that their brand spanking sparkling new employee was also a cokehead.'

'I would have thought that was more a prerequisite of employment than a hindrance in certain firms,' observed Sarah.

'Not when they piss all over the head of the trading floor's desk just because he refuses to increase their trading limit.'

'Ah, yes, that is a tad antisocial, even by trading-floor standards.'

'So what's so wonderfully urgent this time?'

'Nice little thumbnail sketch.'

'Want to meet up and discuss it?'

'Love to, but too urgent.' She lowered her voice and intoned just two words: *Roddy Clark.*

'Ah,' said Skelton.

'You know who I mean?'

'The scribbler, who doesn't seem to like your lot very much, if memory serves.'

'The very same.'

'Cost no object then?'

'I wouldn't go that far. Let's start with a basic quick and dirty and take it from there.'

Skelton smiled. 'I'd be delighted.'

Sarah's list of things to do petered out there. She sank back against the black cracked vinyl seats and closed her eyes.

'Oh my sweet, oh my love.' She hugged Georgie, lips against his soft plump cheek. She held him at arm's length to study him. He reached out to her face. God, he looked so like his father. She cuddled him again.

'Oh, he's being so lovely,' said Sarah to Jacob. 'I'd thought he might have ignored me for going away.'

'They do that all right,' said Mrs V, who appeared with a pile of ironing in her arms. 'You've got off light there.'

'I have, haven't I?' said Sarah, burying her nose in Georgie's neck, kissing him, tickling him.

'So, how'd the meeting go?' asked Jacob.

'I don't know,' answered Sarah. 'There was all this stuff going on. Savage and I have to work out a few things. Right now I don't want to think about it.'

'Why not? What's come up?' asked Jacob. 'Do they want more due diligence?'

'They're not sure. *I'm* not sure – added to which I really don't want to leave Georgie again.'

'Savage'll throw a fit if you quit and he wants you to continue.'

'Yeah well, tough for Savage if that's what I decide,' answered Sarah. 'I'll just take Georgie out for a walk,' she said, before Jacob got into the swing of his inquisition. 'He's had his lunch, right?' she checked.

'He has. Steamed sweet potato, salmon and broccoli.'

'Yum.'

'You eaten?' asked Jacob.

'I'll get a sarnie on my walk.'

'Need more than a sarnie to keep you going.'

Sarah smiled. 'I've got plenty of fat reserves. Stop worrying.'

She returned two hours later, fed Georgie and put him to bed. She was just boiling the kettle to make some tea when the phone rang. Jacob got it.

'Someone called John,' he said, with a quick look of disapproval. He handed Sarah the phone, and took over the tea, suddenly making the whole process as time-consuming and ritualistic as if he were a Japanese geisha.

'How are you, gorgeous?' asked Redford.

Sarah smiled. 'I'm fine, Mr Redford, how are you?'

'My, aren't we formal today. Can't talk?'

'That's it.'

'Who's listening?'

'An audience.'

'Ah, well maybe I should do the talking, tell you how completely luscious and—'

'Is that a fact,' interrupted Sarah, glancing round at Jacob. He looked up from his tea ceremony and strove to give her an innocent smile.

Georgie chose that moment to let out a wailing sob that the baby listener broadcast into the kitchen.

'What was that?' asked Redford.

'My uncle just stepped on my kitten's tail,' said Sarah, quickly turning down the baby listener as Jacob crept up the stairs to check on Georgie.

'Look,' said Redford, serious now, 'I thought you should know. Another note came. A fax, this time, sent from London, from Kall Kwik, whoever they are. It was pushed under my door.'

'Jesus. What's it say?'

'It says that I should tell you to stay away from me, that if you don't, Georgie and Jacob will die.'

Somehow she managed to speak. 'I have to go.'

'Who are Georgie and Jacob?'

'Please. I have to go.' She hung up.

She had never felt a rage like this before. If the stalker had wanted to engage her, she had her full attention now. With her cowardly threat, she had unleashed the full force of Sarah's maternal instinct coupled with her orphan's love for Jacob. These, along with her bond with Alex, were the purest, greatest loves Sarah had ever felt, and if the stalker were before her now, she would have ripped the woman apart. A line from one of Kipling's poems shot through her mind. 'The female of the species is more deadly than the male, engined for survival.' Too right. She would kill without blinking to protect her loved ones. How did the stalker know about Georgie and Jacob? How could she *possibly* know?

With an awful clarity the answer came to Sarah. She must have followed her, all the way from Paris to Carlyle Square, watched her on the doorstep, heard her call out to her child and to her uncle.

Sarah clung to the bars of the basement window and gazed up at the street. She would not live in fear. She would not have her life and Georgie's and Jacob's contaminated by it. She prowled back and forth in the kitchen, trying to breathe in calm, to think clearly what she had to do. Instinct told her, but she had to convince herself that reason backed her too.

She had decided, had sealed her vow with the cold fury of her resolve by the time Jacob came back downstairs five minutes later, with her son smiling in his arms. She took hold of Georgie, hugged him tight, breathed him in. She handed him to Jacob a long time later, and called Eva Cunningham.

'Eva, Sarah. There's something I need to discuss with you, urgently. Could you come round? Oh, and Eva, pretend it's just run-of-the-mill business, would you?'

Eva appeared fifteen minutes later. Sarah let her in. Jacob poked his head out from the sitting room.

'Hello, Eva,' he said warmly. 'How are you?'

'Hi, Jacob.' She went up to him and planted a smacking kiss on his cheek. 'I'm well, thank you. How're you doing?'

'Holding up. Not too bad. Fancy a cup of tea?'

'Love one, but I've got to be a bit anti-social, I'm afraid. Your lovely niece wants to pick my brain about something, and since she's going to have to pay through the nose for it, I'd better closet myself away in her office and give her her money's worth.'

'Bubble bubble, toil and trouble . . .' he said with a grin. 'I'll be up in a minute with your brew.'

Jacob deposited a large teapot, two mugs, and a selection of biscuits to copious thanks, and disappeared discreetly.

Eva took a sip of scalding tea, seemed not to notice, and turned to Sarah with a look of sharp interest. 'So what's up?'

Sarah gazed back at her friend, her eyes heavy with intent.

'I have to go away tomorrow morning, for two nights. I need to have twenty-four-hour-a-day protection on Georgie and Jacob, and it has to be invisible.'

Eva blew out a long breath. 'Jesus, Sarah, you don't ask much, do you? Perhaps you'd better tell me what's going on.'

Sarah told Eva about the stalker, and the threats. She told her about the deal with Redford. Since the rock star was integral to the stalking, she had no choice. She explained that various members of Redford's entourage thought – incorrectly, she emphasised – that she was his tottie, and that she might accordingly be being stalked out of jealousy.

'Shit. Your son and your uncle,' said Eva with a heavy exhalation, after she'd listened for half an hour. 'So why are you going to Venice? I hope it's not to do what I think it might be.'

Sarah mirrored the gravity in Eva's face. 'Wouldn't you do exactly the same?'

Eva smiled strangely. For a moment her eyes seemed to relive another life, then she said merely, 'For God's sake be careful.'

Sarah hesitated. 'You can do it then, the full-time cover, from first thing tomorrow?'

Eva shrugged. 'What choice do I have?'

Sarah started at a gentle knock at the door. Jacob popped his head round. 'Georgie's sleeping, and I'm just off to the shops. We need a giant stock-up.'

Sarah smiled. 'Oh Jacob. I kept meaning to go myself.'

'And what'll we live on in the meantime?' he asked good-naturedly. He blew the women a kiss and disappeared quietly.

'I'd better ring Savage,' said Sarah, 'before you get on to your people. I need to persuade him that going to Venice won't be so dangerous after all.'

She was put through to the chief executive just as he came out of a meeting.

'I've been thinking about it, and I've decided we're in danger of overplaying the stalker thing,' she said, her voice emotionless. 'Every rock star gets threatening letters by the bagful. It's practically a trophy thing; the more nutters in your collection, the more kudos you have. I don't think we should let one nutter get in the way of our deal. I'll fly out to Venice tomorrow morning.'

His response was galvanic and a furious argument ensued.

'Under no circumstances will you carry on,' said Savage, still raging, five minutes after Sarah's declaration. 'I've been thinking about the whole thing after you waltzed out this morning, discussing it with Dick. Look what happened to John Lennon. To George Harrison.'

'I'm well aware of what happened to them.'

'So start taking this stalker seriously!'

'Don't worry, James. I'll give her the respect she deserves.'

Savage paused and asked suspiciously, 'What do you mean by that?'

'I'll behave appropriately to the level of threat I perceive.'

'You could get your head blown off. Redford could get his head blown off. Haven't you seen enough death?' asked Savage, almost losing control.

'Believe me, James, I will do everything in my power to stay alive.'

'I don't doubt that,' said Savage, sobered by the quiet vehemence of her voice, 'but you're not invincible.'

'No, but I have my own armoury,' *and it's called maternal love*, she added silently.

'All right, Sarah, I don't have the time or the energy to fight you. My wife's on the other line – I have to go. Do what you insist you must, just don't expect me to weep at your funeral.'

Sarah pushed her hair wearily behind her ears. 'I'm going,' she told Eva.

'So I gather. I'd better start getting people mobilised.' Eva got to her feet. Sarah's phone rang as she did so. Savage's voice rose up from the answerphone, morose and maudlin. 'Sarah? Are you there?'

'Sorry, Eva. Can I just get this?' Sarah snatched up the receiver. 'I'm here.'

'Look, I just wanted to say I didn't mean what I said. I'm sorry. I . . . I . . .'

Sarah saved him as he struggled for words. 'It's all right, James. Sometimes people say the opposite of what they mean. Don't give it another thought.'

There was a pause and when he spoke his voice sounded brighter. 'Thanks, Sarah. That makes me feel a lot better.'

'I'm not going to die. You don't have to make your peace with me. We'll still be at each other's throats for years to come.'

He laughed. 'I'm glad there'll be some constancy in my life.'

'What d'you mean?'

'Sorry, Sarah, Fiona's still on the other line.'

'Absolution?' asked Eva as Sarah hung up.

'You got it,' replied Sarah.

'Do you mind if I have a look round your house?'

'Go ahead.'

Sarah watched Eva slink from the room. Eva wouldn't be checking the interior design, thought Sarah, half wryly, half bitterly. She'd be looking for points of ingress into the house, seeking out its weak spots. She did her checking quietly. With Georgie still asleep, the house rang with silence.

Sarah lay back in her armchair. She should have been happy that she had got her way, but Savage's reaction frightened her. She wanted to lock the doors for a week, sleep in her own bed, with Georgie blissfully, safely close, escape the insanity of the rock-star life, of stalkers and leakers. She wanted no drama, no fear, no lust or love inflaming her, just peace and quiet, and freedom from fear, and Georgie and Jacob.

Unease crept into her stomach. She got up and paced around her study, mind working furiously. She replayed her conversations with Savage. Teatime. Savage's wife on the phone, something someone had said about Savage's wife and teatime. She stifled a shout. It was PJ. In her sly little insinuating tones she'd made some comment about Savage's wife having a busy teatime agenda. Then there was Jezza's comment about the toyboy. She glanced at her watch. Three-thirty. Her fabled instincts were screaming. She had to go and follow them up now.

She sought out Eva, found her examining the bars on the window in the kitchen. Eva looked round questioningly.

'I need a favour,' said Sarah quickly. 'Now. Just for an hour until Jacob gets home, can you watch over Georgie? He'll be sleeping anyway.'

Eva raised her eyebrows.

'Can you do all your phoning here?' continued Sarah. 'I won't go if it'll delay you.'

'Don't worry. I always take my little black book with me. I can call from your study. That's not what worries me.'

'Georgie? Don't worry about him. Just give him a kiss and a cuddle if he does wake up before Jacob's back, change his nappy, and play with him. You'll be fine.'

Then Sarah rushed off, as if the scent of some hidden quarry were calling her.

Fifteen minutes later, slouched down in the driver's seat of her old BMW, in a quiet street in the Boltons, Sarah was in position. She didn't know how long she'd have to wait, just that if she waited long enough, she was sure she'd have her answer.

Half an hour later, a man walked up the street and stopped in front of number forty-three. He eased his slim frame through the jammed gate and ran quickly up a flight of stairs to the front door. He rang the bell, glancing around as he waited on the doorstep. A few moments later, Sarah saw the door open, caught a glimpse of a blonde head, then the man disappeared. A feeling of revulsion swamped her. She sat grimly in her car until, almost to the hour, the man emerged.

She eased from her car, closed the door quietly, and followed the man. His hair was unruffled, his immaculate City suit uncreased, his grin, as he stopped to cross the road, glancing left and right, was sickeningly self-congratulatory. Through the streets Sarah shadowed him, and as he tripped elegantly down the steps of South Kensington underground, his expensive shoes beating out a tattoo as he went.

He bought a copy of the *Evening Standard*, took his seat, and sat, concealed from Sarah by his newspaper. She placed herself out of his line of sight, checking on him as every stop came up. He got out, as she had known he would, in the City, at Liverpool Street station. She followed him up the steps and out into the familiar terrain: Old Broad Street, Threadneedle Street, past the Bank of England. He turned into Throgmorton Street. Sarah hurried, gaining on him. She was just at his shoulder when he moved to turn into the portalled doors of Uriah's, one of the most successful of the City investment banks, a touted rival to Goldsteins, and winner of the three deals Goldsteins had recently lost. Sarah reached out, all smiles, touched his shoulder.

'It's Mark, isn't it?'

The man swung round. Young, lean face and body, around thirty. Young enough to play the toyboy to Mrs James Savage's fifty. Black hair, blue eyes, cold but amused. He eyed Sarah up and down before answering. She resisted the temptation to knee him in the balls.

'No, it's not Mark,' he answered slowly, appraisingly.

'You must have a brother, a twin,' said Sarah coyly. 'I refuse to believe you're not Mark.'

'I'm sorry to disappoint you,' he said smoothly, 'but I don't have a brother, and I'm not Mark.'

'Who are you then?' she asked, teasingly.

'I'm Richard Deane. And you are?'

Sarah leaned close to his face. 'That's for you to find out. Meet me here, on the steps, tonight at eight.' Before he could answer, she had wheeled around and walked away.

She took out her mobile, made a quick call, and then felt like vomiting when her question was answered.

Chapter Forty-three

Sarah sat in Savage's office, waiting for him to return from a meeting. He looked surprised to see her when he arrived ten minutes later.

'Sarah, hello. What is it?'

She nodded at his door. He closed it.

'Breden's not taping this office, is he?'

Savage shook his head. 'What's going on?'

'I think I've found your Leaker.'

'That was quick.'

Sarah shook her head. 'This isn't anything to do with Roddy Clark.'

Savage frowned in confusion at Sarah's sombre tone. 'Who is it?' he asked quickly.

'I'm sorry, James. There's no easy way to say this.'

'Just bloody say it, will you, whatever it is.'

Sarah looked at Savage from under brows lowered in apology. 'It's your wife.'

He didn't protest. There was no outrage, no instant dismissal. There was just shame. Savage hung his head. He'd allowed Sarah only one glimpse into his eyes, now he would veil them for ever. For a long time he didn't speak. He stood by the window and stared out. Finally he turned back to Sarah.

'You're sure? There's no mistake?'

'I don't have documentary proof, James, just circumstantial. Judge for yourself.'

'All right then. Spit it out.'

She wasn't going to mention Jezza. Wasn't going to subject Savage to fears of the contagion of trading-floor gossip. 'Well, it started with something you said, about continuity. You hinted things were difficult with your wife, and suddenly the profile fit; disaffected wife, tries to hurt her husband and get her revenge on him. I went to your house, on a hunch, sat opposite in my car and waited. I hadn't expected to get a result so quickly, but after half an hour, she had a visitor, a man. He stayed for an hour. I followed him after he left her. He came here, to the City, to Uriah's. I staged an encounter with him. His name's Richard Deane. I rang Uriah's switchboard, asked for his title. He's a director in capital markets. He's on the team that won all the mandates that were stolen from Goldsteins.'

Savage put his hands to his face. He rubbed violently at his eyes then turned to face Sarah. Rage began to burn through his shock.

'That's the last time I'll mention the Leaker,' Sarah said. 'Not Breden, not Zamaroh, no one will know of this.'

'I'd like to kill the bastard,' whispered Savage.

'In case you're interested,' Sarah said casually, 'I told him I'd meet him on the steps outside Uriah's tonight at eight. I won't be anywhere near there, of course, but if you were to take one look at him, you'd see he's not worth your trouble. He's a gigolo, and a sleaze.'

She knew Savage would want to look over his rival, and she also knew, from the appraising look in his eyes, that Deane would be there, waiting for her. Seeing the man suffer the humiliation of being stood up would be some consolation to Savage before he went home to face his wife.

Sarah got home at eight. She walked into a happy scene of devastation in the kitchen. Georgie was sitting on the floor, surrounded by an array of saucepans, salad driers, wooden bowls, in fact the entire contents of one large storage cupboard. Opposite him sat Eva Cunningham, blonde hair jammed behind her ears, and a desperate expression on her face.

She got to her feet as Sarah walked in. 'Ah, you're back. Right, well . . .'

Sarah burst out laughing. She negotiated the mine field of saucepans and scooped up Georgie in her arms.

'What's so bloody funny?' demanded Eva, hands on hips.

'You,' answered Sarah, through her gusts of laughter. 'I've never seen you look anything other than one hundred per cent self-possessed.'

'Yeah? Well, you too might be a little frazzled in my place.'

'Where's Jacob?' asked Sarah.

'He left a message on your answerphone. I happened to hear it,' Eva said innocently. 'He said he'd run into one of his mates and was going to have a half pint or two with him.'

Sarah gave an awkward smile. 'Sorry, Eva. He wasn't to know you'd be stranded here. Was it all OK? You had my mobile number. You should have called.'

It was Eva's turn to smile. 'I managed – don't ask me how. Your little treasure woke about an hour after you left. We've been playing with his cartloads of toys ever since. I dug out every last one of them, but in the last half hour he started getting fractious, so I tried the saucepans.' She shrugged uncertainly.

'Well, they seem to have worked.'

'They were running out of steam,' replied Eva. 'Believe you me, I'm bloody glad you turned up when you did.' She paused. 'I gave him some banana and a rice cake. I hope that's OK?'

'You've been a star, Eva.'

'I've been terrified. I had no idea babies were quite so frightening.'

Sarah gave her a wry look. 'You're not wrong. It's only now I'm beginning to get the knack of him. For the first six months I was absolutely petrified that I'd do something wrong.'

'Yeah well, you both seem to have survived.'

Sarah kissed Georgie's cheek. 'Listen, a million thanks for this.'

Eva smiled. 'You're welcome. I won't say any time, but in an emergency I'll help if I can.' She paused for a moment. 'How'd it go anyway?'

'I was chasing a hunch. Unfortunately I was proved right.'

'Bad news?'

'Very.'

Eva shrugged. 'Shit happens.'

Sarah gave a heavy sigh. 'Doesn't it just. How d'you get on with your preparations?'

'I'm getting there. Most of it's set up, the rest will be by tomorrow morning. Don't you worry.'

Sarah fed Georgie, bathed him and put him to bed. Jacob came back from a heavy session of reminiscences, with the car left in Sainsbury's car park. He ordered takeaway curries, and he and Sarah sat up eating their feast and chatting.

The night passed too quickly. Sarah had just finished breakfast when the doorbell rang. It was Eva again, this time with an overnight bag. She kissed Sarah effusively.

'Will you be my white knight for a few days?' she asked, convincingly.

'The hot-water heater broke down last night. Andrew's away, and the bloody plumber won't be here till tomorrow.' She shrugged. 'You know me and my creature comforts.'

Jacob had appeared in the hall in time to hear the bulk of Eva's story.

' 'Course you can stay,' he said with a smile of delight. 'We'd be delighted, me and George.'

Eva smiled. 'But not your niece?'

'She's off, isn't she? Venice, no less.'

'Lunchtime,' said Sarah. 'I won't be back for a couple of days.' She took Eva's bag. 'Come on, you can stay in Alex's room. Hey,' she shouted over her shoulder as she ascended the stairs, 'you can help Jacob out with babysitting Georgie.'

Her friend pulled a face. 'Give me a chance to get over yesterday first!'

Sarah headed for the third floor, her face creased in a huge smile of relief.

Lunchtime came and the taxi waited outside, diesel engine throbbing remorselessly. Sarah held Georgie in her arms, trying not to cry. Jacob watched her, compassion etched on his face.

'I love you, my sweetheart.' She kissed her son's downy cheek and handed him to Jacob. 'I love you too,' she said, raising a shy smile on the old man's face. 'I'll be home soon.' She kissed them both one more time, and prayed that her words were true

She turned to Eva, who stood back tactfully, letting her say her most precious goodbyes. The look which passed between them said it all. Eva eased past Jacob and Georgie and escorted Sarah to the taxi.

'Take care of them,' said Sarah, her voice faltering. 'Without them . . .'

Eva squeezed her hand. 'I've got four people on this, besides me. And I'll guard them with my life.'

Sarah knew that she would too.

Chapter Forty-four

Sarah sat in Garfunkel's coffee bar in Heathrow's Terminal One, sipping a cappuccino, wondering what the hell she was doing there. She thought of Georgie, at home with Jacob, smiling his smiles, playing his little games, rolling over onto his tummy, unseen by her. All she wanted was to be with him through the daily cycle of his life, of waking, playing, eating, sleeping, everything bathed in contentment and certainty. Sarah pushed back her hair. Certainty, that she didn't have. Not since the stalker bitch had prowled into her life, threatening her and Jacob, threatening Georgie, following her all the way from Paris, seeing her child with her psychotic eyes. This was obsession. Extreme obsession, and it stained the woman's threats with the reality of madness.

There was no refuge in denial, not where Georgie's safety was concerned. They couldn't hide at home, but Sarah knew that any outing with her son would be polluted by fear, and would be courting a very real risk. So she would go to Venice, let this thing play itself out, help it along a little. Her only comfort was Eva. Eva would contrive to stick to Georgie and Jacob day and night; she'd have a team of people posted in vans with blacked-out windows and on foot. Together, they would do everything possible to secure Georgie and Jacob's safety, without alerting Jacob to their presence, and terrifying him, not for his own sake, but for the little boy that he too loved above his own life.

They flew over the body of the Alps. Blue ridges stretched out like waves on a stormy sea until they blended with the endless sky. Mists shrouded unseen valleys, lakes of mercury ice lay cold and serene beneath Sarah's sombre gaze.

The minutes slipped by as she moved from her real life, to her masquerade. She gave a rueful smile. Venice was, after all, the city of masks. In the guide book she had picked up in the airport, masked white faces stared up at her from the glossy pages, cat's eyes cut into the fine plaster. Long, beaked noses protruded with a mocking air. These, she read, were the doctors' plague masks. They evolved during the epidemic that hit Venice in 1630. The long beaks were filled with medicinal herbs which the doctors hoped would protect them. Sarah imagined their fear as they treated the contaminated ones.

On arrival, Sarah walked from the aeroplane, through the airport and out to where the water taxis waited, cherrywood gleaming in the sun. Taking the proffered hand of one Venetian taxi driver, she stepped lightly off the dock and down the steps into his boat. She bent double and walked through the covered inner part to the small back deck, where she stood leaning against the closed doors to the cabin as the boat reversed out, swung around, and then with a heady burst of power, accelerated into the lagoon.

She gripped the side rail as the boat skimmed along, furrowing the water into banks of spume. They cut past the end of the runway where brilliant lights flashed like giant diamonds. Tripods of ancient wood flanked their passage, like flames along a grand avenue. They roared past a tiny island with terracotta-coloured buildings, cypress trees and palms.

Anticipation quickened in Sarah. She had never been to Venice. She'd been saving it up for the man of her dreams. Now she went to join the man who might play that role in her dreams. John Redford isn't him, she told herself, before her mind could begin its games. He's so far from it, it's not even funny. The man of her dreams was not a rock star, was not public property, would be hers, and hers alone. He would not snake-charm the millions. He would be a quiet man, wild, courageous and private.

But, oh God, this was the perfect place. The boat slowed, and sank down deeper in the water as they entered what felt like the inner portals of the city. The beauty of it hit her like a fist. There was nothing slowly captivating about the outrageous beauty of St Mark's Square from the lagoon. The grandeur, the symmetry, the setting, all magnified the power of the Basilica, of the Doge's Palace. She thought of all the seaborne expeditions launched from here, of the Doge himself who set off for the Crusades, of the boats piled high with spices and treasures of the Orient which found their way back here laden with bounty for the great ruler of the Serene Republic. She imagined the visiting dignitaries catching their breath in wonder as she did now before St Mark's. It demanded homage of the eyes and of the heart. The boat eased along the Grand Canal, under the gaze of the palazzos which had watched so many supplicants enter their watery domain.

Here, beauty and domesticity existed side by side. Glancing down an adjacent canal, Sarah saw clothes lines draped with men's capacious white underpants, hanging in the still air.

They eased under a bridge so low that Sarah ducked with fear for her head. The reflection of the light on the water spangled the underside of the bridge so that it seemed alive as skin.

When they drew level with the landing dock at the Hotel Principe, they were flanked by what looked like giant barbers' poles, striped red and black, protruding from the water to a height of eight feet. Sarah paid off the river taxi, an exorbitant hundred and fifty thousand lire, close to fifty quid, and carried her small case up the steps and on to the terrace of the hotel, stopping for a moment to gaze at its elegant facade, brilliant pink in the afternoon sun. She checked in, then returned to the terrace, where she ordered a whisky sour and sat at an ornate white metal table, sipping and gazing out across the canal. A passenger boat went by, laden down. A message written in English along the side of it caught her eye and made her laugh: *You just hope that there is hope.* A cryptic existentialist message that seemed to be meant just for her.

She couldn't quite believe she was really here. She felt as if she had entered a living painting. Venice was thrilling and exciting on some visceral level. Maybe it was the water, lapping the buildings with a lover's tongue. She had always loved water; could never see an expanse of water without wanting to hurl herself in. She imagined the indigo lake embracing her as she leapt in and yielded and ebbed and flowed with it. The water stirred long fronds of algae on the steps down into the canal, and she pictured it as her hair. Suddenly she felt eyes on her and whirled round, but there was no one.

Chapter Forty-five

It was a perfectly nice hotel, she thought, as the bellboy led her to her room, but not one she would have expected John Redford to stay in before a concert, or at any other time, for that matter. Four stars to the Danieli and Cipriani's five. She was still pondering Redford's choice when the man himself stole up.

'How did you know I was here? You got your spies out for me?' she asked.

He smiled. 'Everywhere.' The smile left his eyes. 'I wasn't sure I'd see you again.'

She drew him into her room, closed the door, and walked over to the window. She pulled back the net curtain and glanced up and down Lista di Spagna.

'I wasn't sure either.'

'So what made up your mind?'

'Well, put it this way, I won't allow the stalker bitch to rule my life.'

Redford watched her with concern. 'Can't you just drop it, pretend she doesn't exist?'

'What, you mean like you do,' she said, bridling. 'Looking for spectres everywhere you go, staying in different hotels from your crew.'

'I don't want to live, sleep, shit where I work. It's not because of her.'

'Maybe, but it's more than just privacy. You don't trust your crew, do you? One of them could so easily be your stalker. After all, they get to travel to the same places you do. It'd be a pretty dedicated stalker who flies round on her own account.'

'Or rich. Shit, I don't know. Sarah, let's don't give her airtime, huh?'

'Why not?'

'So I can live my illusions. I don't want her to cast a shadow over us.'

'Denial.'

'Is that so bad? I'll bet you deny things too.'

'All the time,' she gave a wry smile, 'but then I'm not the model of how to live your life.'

'Seem to be doing all right to me. Come on, let's deny the bitch and go explore.'

They walked from the hotel and turned left on Lista di Spagna, heading towards one of the few bridges that spanned the Grand Canal. They crossed the bridge, along with throngs of tourists and busy Venetians heading home, stopping halfway across to gaze around. Gondolas went by beneath them, lights illuminating their prows. The boats seemed like the pedestrians, lively, intent on their way.

Sarah noticed that the Venetians seemed to wear a uniform of red, blue or green padded equestrian-type jackets that wouldn't have looked out of place at a Home Counties gymkhana. They looked friendly. Gondolier, mailboat man, office worker, executive – all met your eye if you looked at them, and returned a gaze at once amiable, curious and proud. A couple passed, lost in conversation, arms flapping like seagulls. Sarah felt a momentary pang, envied the pair their ordinariness. Redford had a baseball cap pulled low over his forehead and so far no one seemed to recognise him, but for all they might skirt normality, it would always remain beyond them.

Darkness was falling as they left the Grand Canal and detoured down a myriad of side streets. The canals which criss-crossed their way were now slick, inky black, reflecting lights as if touched by an Impressionist's paintbrush. Seven o'clock and the air was rent with the ringing of bells, long, short, frantic. It was almost as if some great warning was being sounded. The echo of the bells lingered in Sarah's ears long after the sound had died. The new silence didn't last long. As they snaked round the narrow streets, Sarah heard snatches of song, and then, as they neared the singer, a long, parlayed lament. They stopped atop a bridge to listen. Redford slipped his arm around Sarah, and drew her to him with a smile. Sarah stood slightly rigid for a few seconds, before her body prevailed over her mind, and sank into his.

A gondolier came into view, switching the lone oar. He sang no more, and suddenly the night was silent again as he moved his craft toward them. A sole woman rode in the gondola. She wore a dark hat, and her face was dropped to her chest, as if she was sleeping. Arms around each other, Sarah and Redford walked on. On impulse, Sarah glanced back over her shoulder, and saw that the woman was looking up, directly at her, but the gondola had moved into a patch of darkness which veiled the watcher's features so that she could only see her eyes. Redford's motion drew her on, but the image of long hair, a broad-brimmed hat, and features masked by dark, stayed with Sarah.

Redford stopped suddenly, pulled a map from his jeans pocket, screwed up his eyes in the dark, seemed to satisfy himself, then took Sarah's arm and walked on. Sarah felt quietly impressed as he led them confidently through the maze. She wondered where they were going, but didn't ask. It didn't matter with a journey so beautiful. Always there were vistas, suggestions of hidden delights and mysteries just round the corner.

A few more turns brought them out again on the Grand Canal. A barge went by, with a Westie dog balancing assuredly on the deck. The little dog craned his neck and barked at the sky, three loud, happy barks, as if saluting an old friend. It seemed so strange that there were no cars. The feeling of being cast back in time hit Sarah. The only modern legacy that jarred was the smell of diesel hanging in the fetid air. A fisherman sat on the bank, rod dangling hopefully over the murky water.

'Wouldn't fancy his catch,' Sarah said to Redford, 'would you?'

'Don't judge yet. Might be your dinner.'

They crossed the Rialto Bridge. A flurry of boats scurried by like busy animals on a trail. They reminded Sarah of the hordes of bicycles in Vietnam, speeding this way and that, all miraculously avoiding collision. Sarah trailed her hand along the white marble balustrade of the bridge. It felt incredibly smooth, like cold skin, caressed to fineness by centuries of touch. It made her think of Redford's skin, silk over the hard stone of his muscles. Her eyes met his. He gave a wry smile, as if he could read her. She turned away, eyes finding refuge in the palazzos, uplit, mysterious and regal in the night. She glimpsed the glow of a chandelier, and a ruby red wall, imagined a brocade-swathed bed below, herself and Redford lying on it.

'I wonder who lives there now,' she mused. 'It must have been quite something to have been one of the noblemen who built these palaces.'

'Would you like to have lived then?' asked Redford.

'Oh no,' said Sarah, shaking her head. 'I'm very happy where I am.' She wanted no more to travel in time than in place if it meant leaving Georgie. She felt the warmth of his father's arm pulling her close. What would it be like, she wondered, to have them all together, to see Redford's face when he looked at his son. She smashed the dream, reprimanding herself. He would be appalled. Or, worse, what if he wanted Georgie – what if he tried to take him from her? Redford must have felt the current of her thoughts. He turned to her. 'You OK?'

'Yeah, yeah,' she said, releasing her hold on him, and freeing herself, ostensibly to push her hair back from her face. 'Just thinking about home.'

The soft look vanished from Redford's face. 'Missing someone?'

'Don't we all?'

'Georgie and Jacob,' he said, an observation rather than a question.

Sarah retreated into silence. Redford didn't break it. He stopped suddenly before a shop full of masks. Sarah stopped beside him. He took her hand.

'Come on. Let's go in.'

The shop was tiny. Every available surface was covered with masks. More hung from the ceiling. Sarah almost felt as if they were watching her. An elderly shopkeeper regarded her and Redford with indulgent detachment. Sarah turned to Redford, who had picked a mask off a shelf and held it over his face. The nose was long and pointed. The doctor's mask. It seemed to reek of death, not of healing. How the dying must have trembled when that alabaster face attended them. Sarah suppressed a shudder. Redford had been transformed into something sinister. She turned away, and went out into the night. Moments later she felt his hand on her shoulder.

'Are you sure you're all right? You seem jumpy tonight.'

Sarah gazed up at his naked face. The fear conjured by his masked face had gone.

'It's just that stalker bitch. She's getting to me, I suppose.'

He took her arm. 'Come on. Let's try and put her out of our minds.'

They turned into St Mark's Square and stopped before the Doge's Palace. Close up, the Basilica and the Doge's Palace were even more magnificent than when seen from the water. The Basilica looked like a fairy-tale castle, with its paintings of heroic scenes, and Christ being taken down from the cross. Here was a muscled warrior about to slay a cowering supplicant, there a gargoyle saying *attack me if you dare*, and another blowing away evil spirits with jovial power. They walked through the crowds back to the water.

Redford stopped and looked down a side canal. He gestured at an enclosed bridge. 'The Bridge of Sighs.' He turned to Sarah. 'Know why it was called that?'

'Tell me.'

'Not because lovers went by underneath, gazing up at its beauty and sighing with pleasure. It connected the old prisons to the court offices in the Doge's Palace. It was used to bring prisoners to trial.'

'So they gazed out of those tiny lattice windows, glimpsed free Venice, and sighed,' said Sarah. 'Ever been to prison?'

Redford split sharply from his reverie. He studied Sarah carefully. 'Why d'you ask? Have you?'

'Nope.'

'I was thrown in for two nights, back in my teens.'

'What for?'

'Drinking. Out of control, you know.'

'No, I don't. Out of control in what way?'

'I serenaded Main Street. At four in the morning, and let me tell you, the good old citizens of Cook County were *not* fans.'

Sarah smiled. 'Didn't know what they were listening to.' She stopped for a moment. 'Was it bad?'

Redford lapsed into silence. Sarah watched the shadows cross his face. 'I'm a claustrophobic. How do you think it felt?'

'I didn't know,' Sarah said simply, chilled by the bitterness that even the decades hadn't washed away. 'It must have been hell.'

Redford gave a slow nod. 'Put it this way. I won't go there again.'

'No more drunk and disorderly,' she said, trying to lighten the mood.

'Hell no. Just don't get caught.' He offered Sarah one of his wicked smiles which danced, as always, somewhere between truth and irony. He took her arm, and led her on.

They walked along the Riva deglia Shiavoni and turned into the Danieli. In the bar, the lights were soft, red brocade hung on the walls, a pianist played slow, lascivious jazz, and they ordered caipirinas – drinks of an almost hallucinogenic mix of Brazilian cane-sugar rum and fresh lime juice. It would have been so easy, so blissfully right to yield to the mood, to allow what should have been inevitable to happen, but in her mind she saw the notes with their bland, disjointed and terrifying lettering, she saw Georgie's face, she imagined a hooded stalker in pursuit, crooked, deformed by evil like the villains of fairy tales, then she looked into the candle-lit faces in the bar and wished that in real life the stigmata of evil was so visible.

She ate the ice, left the drink, and pretended to sip her way through another. Redford drank slowly but steadily. They moved onto the rooftop restaurant, and dined on the terrace, gazing out over Venice by night.

Sarah's eyes settled upon a dome, which glowed like skin in the moonlight. It was adorned by balustrades and finely carved statuary that gazed back at them across the Grand Canal.

'God, that's beautiful.'

'Santa Maria della Salute,' replied Redford. 'The Venetians' favourite church. Built in 1631 as a thank you to the Virgin for saving them from the plague, after, incidentally, half of them had been wiped out.'

'You cynic, John Redford.'

'You think so?'

'I don't really. I think you're a desperate romantic.'

He laughed. 'Yeah, maybe. And what about you, the elusive Sarah Jensen? Who does she believe will rescue her?'

She thought of the stalker, she thought of Georgie and Jacob. 'Myself,' she said firmly.

'With no help from the gods?'

'With all the help they can give me.'

Chapter Forty-six

They returned to the hotel at midnight. The air shimmered between them. Sarah longed to stay with him, to spend the night in his arms. She could see the yearning in his eyes, knew it showed in hers. She turned away abruptly.

'I have to go.'

He looked surprised. He veiled the hurt that showed only briefly. 'Do you?'

She nodded.

He looked at her a while before speaking, then he leaned across and kissed her.

'Good night, then.'

She kissed him back, then pulled away before heat seared her whole body and she was lost.

Breathing hard, she let herself into her suite. As she had hoped, and feared, a note was awaiting her under the door.

> Your life is on its way out. Then your son.
> Begin counting.
>
> Ten . . .

Rage almost blinded her. She stormed back and forth in her room, eyes burning ahead, seeing nothing save a hidden face. Now the face was veiled by the white Venetian mask, showing only the gleam of demented eyes. What did she have – ten hours, ten days, ten minutes? She walked to her window and looked out at Lista di Spagna. Then she kicked off her high slingbacks, dragged off her stockings and pulled on combats, her black rubber-soled lace-up boots and a dark parka. She grabbed a miniature bottle of whisky from the minibar and, before even a drop of her rage dissipated, let herself out of her room.

She walked down the empty staircase and into the foyer, where she glanced around. A few couples sat, heads close, or far away, happy and sad at the circular tables; a solitary man in his fifties toyed with a balloon glass of brandy; a rakishly beautiful woman, who must have been a model, walked in with an older woman who looked like her mother. Sarah left her key with Reception and walked out onto the street.

Trying to escape the throngs still coursing down the busy concourse, she turned right, and walked down Calle dela Misericordia. The street was so narrow she could almost span the blood-red walls with outstretched arms. The wash of sound from Lista di Spagna soon ebbed away. She listened intently, but heard only the faintest hint of birdsong, a nightingale singing in the distance. She walked past the two-star Hotel Atlantide, then the one-star Casa Hilbert. This was the lair of cheap hotels, where nobody asked any questions, where no evil would be seen, heard, or spoken. She had gone no more than two hundred yards from Lista di Spagna, but she might have been in the centre of a graveyard. All she could hear was the gentle pad of her boots on the moonwashed streets. She wanted to stop and turn around, check over her shoulder at the very least, but forced herself to continue the masquerade, meandering slowly as if simply out for a jaunt, enjoying the night air and the silence.

She jumped at the sight of her own shadow, snaking along before her, then stopped, pretended to take a tissue from her pocket and delicately blew her nose, waiting for the sound of the blood pounding in her ears to ease. Behind her came the faintest suggestion of footsteps, then nothing, as if they had stopped. *Put away your handkerchief, walk on, do not even think about looking back. Keep your movements fluid, even if your legs are beginning to shake.* The night sky was bitumen black ahead of her. There were street-lights dotted here and there, but all they served to do was highlight the darkness. She passed padlocked gates, behind which a garden glowed darkly. To her left stood a tall apartment block. Sheets hung from a balcony, ghostly against the terracotta walls. Cast like fragments of lace onto stone was the shadow of the filigree gates that cut her off from the homes and the safety within.

When Sarah emerged from the narrow confines of these streets, and the inky blackness of the Canal Regio, relief swept over her as she rejoined a world of lights, people and open vistas. The footsteps she'd heard were probably nothing more than a late diner returning home. She passed red lanterns, strung outside a Chinese restaurant; they looked homely and comforting, and the smells warmed her. The lights of Lista di Spagna beckoned her and she walked quickly towards them, but only for a moment. Before she could give into the temptation to go back to the hotel, she forced herself to turn right on to Calle Vergola.

Here was a sign for the entrance to a park, and she followed it, walking further from the lights and the noise, until she was surrounded by darkness and silence once more. She found the park. Tall, locked gates barred her entry. She turned left into an unmarked street, and carried on, up to a green door. Just before the door there was a recess in the wall, and Sarah instinctively made for it. This time, she could definitely hear the sound of footsteps. She shrank back into the recess, stood frozen as the footsteps approached, slowing down, slowing down as they grew closer still. Then a shadow pooled onto the green door, rising like a miasma before her eyes, growing, growing until the body behind it came fully into view, with the hooded head turning. Terror flooded her body. She leapt from her hiding place, stifling her scream.

A voice screamed back at her. Black hair tumbled in her fists; nails scrabbled at her face. Their bodies crashed to the ground. Sarah forced herself on top, swung a violent punch at the face, saw the nose explode with blood, and again the woman screamed and writhed. Sarah grabbed her wrists, fury giving her strength, and held her still. She leaned down till her face was only inches from the woman's.

'OK, you bitch. Give me one good reason not to break your neck.'

The woman spat in her face. Sarah yelled, let go of her wrists, wiped the spittle from her skin. Then, in one smooth movement, she seized the woman's right arm and dragged her to her feet and slammed her into the wall. As the woman began to slump, Sarah grabbed her and held her up.

'You threatened me, you sick bitch, that's one thing, but you also threatened my son, and my uncle.' Sarah fought for breath as rage swamped her again. 'I should kill you for that.' She slammed her prisoner into the wall again.

The woman went limp and dropped to the ground with a moan. She curled into a foetal position and, to Sarah's horror, she began to cry.

Sarah paced beside her, anger ebbing as she felt an unexpected jolt of pity. 'Oh Jesus, stop that.' The soft sobbing continued, plaintive, bereft – there was something utterly heart-wrenching in it. Sarah found herself bending down over the woman. 'Come on, get up.'

After another minute of quiet sobbing, the woman turned to stare up at Sarah. She looked to be in her late thirties, skinny, sparrow-like. The remnants of beauty showed in the fragile face, crumpled with tears. She was a complete, trembling mess.

Shit, what now? thought Sarah. She couldn't leave her pursuer here. She hooked her arm through the other woman's, pulled her to her feet.

'Come on. I'm going to take you back to my hotel. Find out what the fuck this is all about.' The woman looked at her with a rabbit's terrified eyes, but said nothing, just allowed herself to be helped down the street.

At the hotel, Sarah gave the night concierge a brief explanation of an accident, followed by copious assurances that neither the police nor the hospital were required. As the woman tottered beside her, dabbing at her nose, which refused to stop bleeding, Sarah prayed she was right about the hospital.

She sat the woman in a deep armchair and went to get cold water and two face cloths from the bathroom. After wiping away the rest of the blood, she handed over the clean face cloth, wrung out in water.

'Here, hold this against your nose,' she said roughly. 'It should stop bleeding soon.' The woman took it, with a quick glance at Sarah. Fear, sorrow and a kind of madness showed in her eyes. She gripped the cloth to her nose, her knuckles white, and she started to sob again.

Oh God. Sarah sank back on her bed, trembling herself now, with delayed shock. This wasn't how it was supposed to be. In her mind, she would catch the stalker, vent her fury, beat her half-senseless – and then what? She'd never got beyond that in her planning, so consumed was she by maternal rage. Now, sitting before her, this woman looked pathetic, a threat to no one. Probably how half the captured murderers in the world appear, paper tigers, but no less lethal for it.

She hardened herself. She took a whisky from her minibar, knocked it back, and began to pace around the room, eyes on the woman. Something about her nagged at Sarah. She felt sure she had seen her before.

'What's your name?'

The sobbing eased. 'Carla. Carla Parton.' The accent was American, with the soft lilt of the south. The fearful eyes that searched hers like a captive animal's, were intelligent.

Sarah stopped in front of the woman, bent over her. 'Why were you following me? Why did you threaten me and my family?' A flash of rage inflamed her again. She knew what she was capable of. For some time she had thought, hoped, that her capacity for violent revenge would have waned. Now she knew it hadn't. Having a child had added ferocious new instincts to her existing motivations, and she knew the cocktail was potentially lethal. So, from the look in her eyes, did Carla. She was mute with fear.

Sarah wheeled around and grabbed the note from the mantelpiece. She hurled it at Carla.

'You wrote this, you bitch. I want to know why.'

'What are you going to do with me?' The voice trembled.

'I don't know. I haven't decided, but I want some answers in the meantime, so get talking.'

Carla's face collapsed again as she began to sob. This was not the quiet sobbing of before. This was great, heaving convulsions as if she were giving birth to some unspeakable pain. Sarah watched, horrified.

The sobbing carried on so long, with such abject misery, that Sarah felt flayed. Finally, the crying abated to a series of great, dry gulps.

'Talk to me,' said Sarah, handing over a glass of brandy, followed by a toothmug of water.

Carla took a long drink of water, rubbed her hands over her face, and began to speak.

Chapter Forty-seven

'It all started thirty years ago, when my folks 'n' I moved from Georgia to Wyoming. That was when I first met John Redford. Lord, he was beautiful, and so hurt you could see it oozing out of him. It was just after his mamma died. We all fell in love with him, me 'n' all the other girls – their mommas too, I reckon. Anyways, he wouldn't let any of us close to him, just went on his own way, riding his horse, playing his guitar.'

Carla's eyes began to glaze over, and her voice became distant, almost childlike, as if she had stepped back in time. 'We were at the same school, same class. I used to give him sweets, then my whole packed lunch 'cos he never had any. His papa was pretty useless with his own grief. John didn't come to school much, so he was kept in the same grade two years running, and we sorta lost touch, until fifteen years later. I was in my mid-twenties by then, living in New York, your standard struggling actress.' She gave a pained smile.

'I was working as a waitress – in a real dive on the Upper West Side. One evening, on my way to work, I see the posters. John Redford's in town, performing live at Madison Square Gardens. I was working, of course, but I thought if I hurried I might just catch the end of the show, so I got off my shift early, didn't even take the time to change out of my uniform, and I just hared on down there. But the concert was over. I was so disappointed, I burst into tears. I told security I was an old friend of John's and they must have believed me, 'cos they let me in backstage. I was so happy I could have flown,' she said bitterly.

'Anyways, they sent me in the direction of his changing room, said I should knock, say who I was. So I wandered around, found his room and knocked. He said to come in, but when I went in, he was behind some kind of screen; I could hear him moving about. So I sat down, waited, and I felt eyes on me, you know. And I began to get frightened. Something wasn't right. I was just about to get up and go, when the lights went off. Before I could even scream, he had grabbed me, pushed me from the chair, and got on top of me.' Her voice faltered; she rubbed tears from her eyes and grief hovered on her lips. 'I tried to force him off. I pushed him and I tried to hit him. I scratched his face. He caught my hands, pinned me down.' Her eyes looked up from the ground and locked on to Sarah's. 'He told me if I made a sound, he'd kill me. I believed him. Then he raped me.'

Sarah looked back, struggling to stay steady.

'Finally he walked out. I heard voices outside, a sort of hurried discussion, then someone came in. It wasn't him, this man felt different. Heavier. He grabbed me, tied me up, pulled some kind of scarf over my eyes, and gagged me. I remember sitting there in the darkness for what seemed like hours, until everything went quiet. Then the man picked me up, literally carried me out, down loads of stairs, and pushed me into a car. He locked the doors, then punched me so hard in the face I passed out. Next thing I know, the car's accelerating, I hear a door opening, and he pushes me out.' The eyes tested Sarah's again, then flickered away. 'A construction worker found me next mornin', lying in some back street up in Harlem. He took me to hospital. I had ten ribs broken, broken nose, broken jaw, and I got pneumonia. I was in hospital for six weeks. Three weeks in, they discovered I was pregnant. Anyways, I terminated it. I killed it.' Her voice died.

'Oh Jesus.' Sarah struggled to stop herself breaking down. She forced out a question, a lifeline, anything to hang onto, to keep Carla's sobbing at bay. 'Did you go to the police?'

'They came to me. I told 'em nothing. They tried to coax me. I didn't speak a word to them, not even hello.'

'Why not?'

'I wanted my nightmare to end. I wanted it to be over.'

'So what happened?'

'Well, I had to get plastic surgery. My face was wrecked. I had four operations over eighteen months. I gave up trying to be an actress. My insurance company paid for all the treatment, and they had to pay me a settlement too, 'cos I'd taken out a policy on my face. Got four million dollars for my face – not bad, huh?' She attempted a smile that nearly broke Sarah's heart. Sarah got to her feet and returned with the bottle of brandy. She filled up their glasses, set hers down and rubbed her eyes.

'That was fifteen years ago. What did you do in all that time?'

'Therapy for three years. Really sorted me, you know. I met a man and I married him. We were happy for six years. Then we tried for a baby.' The tears started to roll. 'We tried for years. Nothing happened. Finally I went to have myself checked out. You see,' her voice broke; she paused to collect herself and struggled on, 'the termination had gone bad, left me scarred. I'm infertile. I'll never have a child.'

Sarah couldn't hold herself in any longer. Tears rained down her face.

Carla went on. 'When they told me that in the fertility clinic, I broke down. I told my husband about the rape. I didn't say who it was, just a strange man.' Her eyes found Sarah's. 'You know what he did?'

Sarah shook her head.

'He left me.'

Sarah nodded, as everything became clear. 'So you decided it was time to make John Redford, and anyone he looked like having a relationship with, pay,' she said grimly.

'Wouldn't you?'

Sarah locked her rage away in a compartment of her heart, with all her other rages. She, almost more than anyone, knew the power of revenge, how it lured you in, the most powerful of drugs, and how, like all drugs, it promised everything and delivered only the great lie. Revenge was no cure for the original crime. There was no remedy for that pain, other than the seeming poison of acceptance. Lift the cup of your pain to your lips and drink. She still gagged at the thought. When she was twenty-one, armed with a pistol, she had killed the man who, thirteen years before, had killed her parents, the man who had laughed at her and her seven-year-old brother when he walked free from court. Though it had brought her no solace, she would have done it again, with all the hindsight she now possessed. She was in the grip of her rage, as Carla was in hers.

She took the woman's hand. 'Go to bed – sleep in mine.' Carla followed her meekly, all rage spent.

'What're you going to do?'

'I'm going to get my head straight. Don't worry about me, just try to get some rest.' Sarah sat and watched Carla until she saw that sleep had her in its grip. Her face in repose assumed a kind of peace, betrayed only when her eyes suddenly flinched, or her lips pursed. Sarah recognised the woman in the restaurant lavatory in New York, who had brushed up against her and stolen her purse. She had worn a red wig to cover her long black hair, which was itself obviously dyed. It hung in stark contrast to Carla's pale skin. She had disguised her accent, worn a mask of metropolitan cool. It was the same woman, but almost a different incarnation. The sleeping form on the bed seemed like a broken child, burdened with the ultimate sorrow of a grown woman. Sarah watched over her another hour, knowing that this was the way you watch a baby; an ecstasy that John Redford had forever denied Carla Parton.

How could he have done this, the man who had fathered her child, the man who made such tender, passionate love, who sang such heart-rending songs? Everything had been perfect; John, the perfect lover who, even though he did not know it, had given her the perfect child. Georgie would always remain that. Nothing could sully his perfection, but Sarah's memory of Redford had been destroyed. She had thought she knew him; she was wrong. She remembered his fears of corrupting the audience. The bandaged hand he had slammed into a wall with uncontained rage. No wonder he feared himself and what he was capable of.

She took her key, and marched up to his door. Heedless of the other guests, she banged upon it, balled her hands into fists and knocked as hard as she could till her knuckles were bruised. When Redford appeared, tousled-haired, alarmed, Sarah pushed past him and strode into his suite.

'What the hell's going on?' He followed her, angry and uncomprehending.

She turned upon him. 'Don't speak to me, you bastard. Just sit down and listen.' She pushed him at a chair. He fell into it then leapt to his feet again. He took two steps toward Sarah, before her words stopped him.

'Are you going to hit me now? Or is rape still your style, all these years on?'

It was as if she had struck him a blow.

'What are you talking about?'

'Oh, please. Don't come the innocent with me.'

'I'm not coming anything. I don't know what the fuck you're talking about.'

'Let me tell you then,' said Sarah, pacing the room, eyes never leaving Redford's face. 'Why don't you sit down, get comfortable. It's a long story.'

She watched while Redford picked his way to a chair, sat down delicately as if his whole body was wracked. She saw the hurt in his eyes, the confusion, but also a profound weariness, and the odd flash of what seemed like fear. But all his emotions were as flimsy as a masquerade compared with Carla's crippling sorrow.

'Rape,' said Sarah, her voice haggard. 'One perpetrator, you. One victim, but I'll bet there were more. Raping a woman is never a one-off, is it? It's an attitude of mind that allows you to do that. I know who your stalker is, you bastard. Her name is Carla Parton. She was at school with you, shared her lunches with you, tried to give you solace when you were twelve years old and your mother had just been killed. Then she grew up, slim and beautiful, and the big time beckoned. She went to New York, tried to become an actress, worked as a waitress. Now one day she sees that John Redford's in town, her old schoolfriend, so she turns up at the end of the concert, and her charm or her beauty gets her backstage. The security guards point her in the direction of your dressing room, the way they must have done for hundreds of other girls, in tens of other cities. So she goes in. You're behind a screen, so she sits down to wait. Then you kill the lights, and rape her. Then you leave her, and get one of your henchmen to clean up after you. He blindfolds her, takes her into his car, knocks her out and, for a finale, chucks her from his speeding car into some back street like a bag of garbage.'

Redford looked away.

'Watch me, you bastard. You *will* watch me and hear every last word. A construction worker picked her up, took her to hospital. She had ten broken ribs, a broken nose and a broken jaw. Oh, and by the by, she was pregnant with your child. She aborted this child, and years later, when she tries to have children with her husband, when she thinks she's finally laid to rest the traumas you put her through, she discovers that the abortion fatally scarred her, that she will never have children. So she breaks down and she tells her husband. And you know what? He leaves her.'

She walked slowly up to Redford's chair. 'How could you do this? Who are you?' she whispered.

He made no excuses. He didn't speak; he just stared out into space, utter desolation in every feature.

Chapter Forty-eight

Dawn broke and Sarah went back to her room. She let herself in and closed the door. When Carla stirred, Sarah sat on the bed beside her and took her hand.

'Do you want to end this thing now?' she asked. 'Get it out of your system for once and for all?'

Carla looked up at her with clouded eyes, at once hopeful and fearful. 'How?'

'I told Redford everything you told me. Go and see him now.'

Carla's hands went to her throat.

'It's all right, you don't have to see him.'

Carla forced herself up. Sarah saw to her shame that the other woman's nose was bruised and swollen. 'Let me get myself straight,' she asked quietly. 'Give me five minutes.'

A short while later, Sarah knocked on Redford's door. He opened it, grey-faced.

'Will you see her? You can do that, at least.'

Redford looked at Sarah with immense sorrow. 'Go get her, then. Let's play this thing out.'

Sarah fetched Carla. 'I'll be outside if you need me,' she said.

Redford's door was open. Carla skirted round it, as if expecting an ambush, then uncertainly went in and closed it behind her. Sarah moved down the corridor, away from the low murmur of voices. She leaned against the wall and waited. Half an hour later Carla opened the door and called her in.

Redford sat slumped in an armchair. He looked utterly alone, and lost. Perched on the edge of a table, Carla was smiling with a kind of unstable relief.

'I'm going home today,' she told Sarah. 'There'll be no more stalking. It's not worth it.'

'How did you get to that?' asked Sarah.

'Part of me will always hate this man. Part of me will always want to kill him, to see that he never gets any peace or happiness, to kill the things *he* loves – but when I look at him now, he's the little boy I used to know again. He's not that monster who raped me, took my life away, murdered my dreams. If you gave me a gun now, I wouldn't use it on him. I just couldn't.' Carla turned to look at Redford. 'Knowledge is your punishment. You won't hear from me again. I won't stalk you, but I'll stalk your dreams.'

Carla walked defiantly from the room, neck tilted back, taut with self-control, with the pyrrhic victory she had won. Redford watched her go, then dropped his head in his hands. When he looked up there was anger in his eyes.

'Just answer me this. Where do you get off being judge and executioner?'

'I don't get off. I'm sickened.'

'Have you never messed up? Have you never done anything terrible in your whole perfect life?'

'I wouldn't call my life, or the way I've led it, perfect,' said Sarah. 'And I've done my share of terrible things. The better part of me would undo them if I could, but some part of me would do them again. I sicken myself too, so don't feel lonely.'

'That's my epitaph, is it? I sicken you?'

'What do you care what I think? You sicken yourself, that's the real point, isn't it?'

'The real point is, I don't know what to think,' said Redford softly.

'Let me help you then. You're guilty. You should feel guilt, and remorse.'

Redford looked up. 'Am I? Should I? How do you know?'

'Because of Carla. Don't try to say she was making it up. No one could simulate her emotions.'

Redford looked at the ground.

'So?' interrogated Sarah. 'What do you have to say?'

She needed to hear his contrition, to salvage something from him to show that he understood the enormity of what he had done. Her craving for justice would allow her no less.

Wearily he looked at her. 'I might have done it. I might not have done it. The awful thing is, I don't know.'

'*How* can you not know?'

'Because there were whole nights, and days, when I was so out of it on coke and booze I wasn't sure what I was doing. I was hardly conscious, hardly functioning. I managed to perform onstage, I made records, that's the only tangible legacy of about ten years of my life.'

'Oh come *on*! Surely you would remember something like a rape, for God's sake.'

Redford shook his head. 'No, I wouldn't. I had blackouts, periods sometimes for a night and a day when I couldn't remember a thing. I would wake up in strange places and have no memory of how I got there. I wouldn't recognise the people milling around, or the woman I was with. I woke amongst strangers, with a night of my life gone. So, yes, I could have raped her, and God knows, I hope to high heaven I didn't. But I might have done. I remember hearing backstage talk, in the days after one of the New York concerts, years ago, about some woman who was bundled out into a car.' His features carved into shame. 'A piece of trash, she was called. Causing trouble, and dumped somewhere. The roadies were whispering about it. I didn't think much of it at the time, there are always incidents with groupies throwing themselves at you, sometimes getting violent, but something about this must have stuck in my mind. It rings some sort of bell. So it could have been me. Yeah, it might have been me. And don't you think that appals me? I keep thinking of my mother. I have an image of her face. What would she have thought of me? I would have broken her heart. And that poor girl.' His pain showed in the eyelid of his left eye, which flickered with tiny paroxysms of emotion. 'If I am responsible, I'd do anything to take it back. I'd offer up everything I own to give that woman back her life, but I can't.'

'So, do something that *is* in your power,' Sarah said gently.

'Like what?'

'I don't know. There must be a thousand good causes you could rescue. Give five million to help out battered women and children.'

'It's not that simple. I already give away a lot of money. It doesn't buy me absolution.'

'Stop thinking of yourself. This isn't about *your* absolution. Only God can do that for you. This is about helping someone else. Call it making amends, if you like. Five mill would buy houses, pay for healthcare, food, staff. You could do a hell of a lot of good with that.'

'I don't have five mill in loose change.'

'You soon will. If the bond issue goes ahead you'll have a hundred.'

'How can it go ahead now, with you knowing what you know? Goldsteins would drop me in a second, and don't think I haven't worked out that you're some kind of spy for them. You never were just checking out the numbers, were you?'

'What if I wasn't?'

'Either way, you know the worst, whether it's true or not, and as you say, Carla can't have faked that emotion. No one could. So I have to assume I did do it. You clearly do.'

'What if I keep silent?' asked Sarah, falling, with horror, into a trap of her own making.

'What, lie to Goldsteins?'

Sarah thought of Carla, thought of all the Carlas who lived with their abusers, who tried to protect their children, shackled to a life of violence, their narrow exits blocked by sheer loss of hope. Five million could buy these women a haven, a passport to a new life.

'Yes,' replied Sarah slowly. 'I could lie to Goldsteins.'

'Your choice,' said Redford.

'If I lie, will you give five million to a charity for battered women, one of my choice?'

'This is beginning to sound like blackmail.'

'It's not blackmail, it's the closest thing you'll get to absolution on this earth. Like I said, call it amends. You're looking for a way to right your wrongs: I'm offering it to you. Take it or leave it.' Sarah turned away, affecting the trader's indifference, her heart raging all the while with hope of what she could do. But another voice whispered in her mind, What if Redford was lying? What if he *had* raped before, and since? Her connivance in his guilt might sentence more women to violation.

His voice broke through her hopes and fears.

'All right, Sarah. You've got your deal.'

Chapter Forty-nine

Sarah caught the first available flight back to London. Just before she boarded in Venice, she rang Jacob and told him she was on her way.

'I thought you weren't coming back till tomorrow,' he said, pleased and surprised.

'I wasn't supposed to be, but what the heck? It's only business. John Redford and his entourage can do without me, but I can't do without you and George.' She could sense Jacob's smile. He loved her little rebellions against the corporate world, so fell easily for her lie. As always, she loathed fibbing to him, but telling him the truth with all its myriad complexities and revelations was unthinkable.

Redford was performing tonight on the mainland, several miles from Venice, in an open-air concert at Jesolo. She had always intended to be there, but now she couldn't get away fast enough. As her plane pierced the leaden skies, she attempted to summon up a sense of relief, that she had found, trapped and stopped the stalker, as she still called Carla to herself, and that she was now escaping Redford. But her spirit remained as heavy as the sky.

A few hours later, she was welcomed home by a reception party of Georgie, Jacob and Eva. Georgie and Jacob gazed at her with love, Eva with relief and a fatigue she was clearly attempting to mask. Sarah guessed she'd been up all night keeping watch over the household.

After a prolonged cuddle and play session with Georgie, and an expansive gossip with Jacob, Sarah contrived some time alone with Eva in her study.

'All clear,' said Eva, before Sarah could ask. 'Neither I, nor any of my team, picked up anything remotely suspicious.'

Sarah leaned forward and kissed her friend, much to Eva's surprise. Eva herself was rarely demonstrative, unless playing a part. Emotion, especially the depth of gratitude registered in Sarah's eyes was, according to Eva's schema, best kept under firm control. Sarah knew this and smiled at her friend.

'How'd it go in Venice?' Eva asked, moving onto surer ground. 'I was worried when Jacob told me you were on your way back a day early, but you seem relatively unscathed.'

'I did what you thought I'd do. There was no point hanging around after that.'

'You got the stalker?' asked Eva quickly.

Sarah nodded.

'And?' Eva prompted, surprised at Sarah's reticence.

'Long story. But I don't think she'll be a problem any more.'

'Something's a problem though,' observed Eva.

'Yeah, it is, but this one I can do nothing about,' replied Sarah sadly.

Eva got to her feet, knowing not to push further. 'I'd better go. I told Jacob my water heater's been fixed.'

Sarah reached into her desk drawer. 'What do I owe you?'

Eva winced. 'Two shifts of four guys, nine hours each. Fifty pounds an hour. Comes to three thousand six hundred.'

'What about you?'

Eva gestured into the air. 'You can babysit for me sometime, when I have my own kids.'

'Happily, but in the meantime I want to pay you for this.'

Eva smiled. 'Don't waste your breath. I won't take it, Sare. It's expensive enough as it is.'

'Oh, Eva. Thank you. It's worth every single penny,' said Sarah, recognising Eva's intransigence, and closing her cheque book.

'Yeah,' agreed her friend. 'And at least you won't have to worry about your stalker any more.'

Sarah conjured up Carla's face, wondered why she couldn't shake her feeling of foreboding.

She saw Eva to the door and said her goodbyes, attended by Jacob and Georgie. After that she carried her son down to the kitchen, sat him on her knee and gazed at him, eating him with her eyes, feeling that strange amalgam of love and fear she sometimes experienced when she looked at him. Love for everything he was, fear for the pain that could strike him, rebound on her a thousand times more sharply. Please God, he was the love not just of her life, but of her eternity. Please keep him safe.

She brewed up some extra strong coffee, bit back a mouthful, got to her feet, and tried to summon the necessary resolution for her meeting with Goldsteins.

Chapter Fifty

James Savage looked limp with grief. He drank his bitter espressos, one after the other, shaking them back with quick jolts of the head as if they were shots of vodka. They seemed to elevate his grief to anger.

'Still alive?' he barked at Sarah.

'So far,' she answered evenly, smoothing down the folds of linen as her skirt rucked up her thigh. She'd lost weight at last over the past few days, as her appetite deserted her. Savage eyed the movement with despair.

'What news of the stalker?'

'No news. Seems to have gone silent,' said Sarah.

'That's strange,' answered Breden. 'He/she's made contact in every other location over the past few weeks, no?'

'Yes,' answered Sarah, 'but nothing in Venice.' She kept her eyes bland.

'Why?' asked Breden.

Sarah shrugged. 'Beats me. Maybe she had to go back to work, or ran out of money. It'll be interesting to see if either Redford or I get a note here.'

Breden looked at Sarah long after she had finished speaking. She attempted to appear nonchalant under his scrutiny, wondering if that were the right approach.

'Maybe she's found someone better to persecute,' said Savage bitterly.

'Maybe,' replied Sarah. 'Let's hope so. You got anything, Dick?'

'Nothing dodgy. No more drug problems. Lives a simple life in his place in Wyoming when he's not touring. Lonely guy. No known girlfriend, but no groupies either. Does a lot of yoga, rides his horses, gives a lot of money to charity.'

'Does he? How much?'

'Over thirty million dollars.'

'Jesus!' exclaimed Sarah.

'You didn't think he was the charitable type?'

'I had no idea. Who's he give it to?'

'Mental health charities, orphaned children.'

Sarah swallowed, trying to compose herself. 'How's the deal going?' she asked Zamaroh, hoping her voice didn't sound as strained as she feared.

'Well. The numbers look great. I'm confident we can raise the full monty.'

'A hundred?' asked Sarah.

Zamaroh nodded. 'We want to take the whole lot.'

'We're *thinking* of taking the whole lot,' corrected Savage.

'It's perfect for our fund management side,' insisted Zamaroh. 'Low risk, single A, but yielding two hundred basis points above comparable single As. We've got to take it all.'

'We've *got* to do nothing,' snapped Savage.

Sarah watched Zamaroh. Her temper was beginning to bubble.

'We cannot sit on the fence, James, however much you happen to like that particular position.'

'We can if I want to.'

'If we want to lose the deal we can sit on the fence from here to eternity. Or till our Leaker blows this deal.'

Sarah and Savage studiously avoided each other's eyes.

'Any news on that front, Dick?' asked Zamaroh.

'Nothing. Like Sarah's stalker, seems to have gone strangely quiet.'

Breden watched Sarah as he spoke. She became engrossed in her coffee.

'Do you think you could take those blasted cameras and mikes out of my office now then?' demanded Zamaroh. 'I can't even fart without an audience.'

Sarah and Breden guffawed with laughter.

Zamaroh flashed a quick smile then resumed her attack on Savage. 'So, can we drop the spying?'

Savage gave a vague wave of his hand, as if brushing away an irritating fly. 'Why not?'

'And what about my deal?' continued Zamaroh. 'Do I have to wait till hell freezes over?'

'Not that long,' said Savage, as if he could imagine a date sometime soon when that would come to pass. 'Just till I'm confident that Sarah has nothing nasty hidden.'

'Me?' asked Sarah. 'What are you talking about?'

'Your stalker,' responded Savage, deceptively casual, 'and any other little matters that might not have come to light yet.' His eyes were upon her, dulled by grief, but still fearsomely sharp.

It was make-your-mind-up time. Lie, or tell the truth. Sarah saw Carla's crumpled face, her broken dreams, saw, too, havens for perhaps thousands of women. Five million dollars' worth of havens. *This is not your job*, said her rational voice. *It's not for you to play God. Do your job, tell the truth.* Goldsteins could see a hundred million sliding rapidly into the red if she had miscalculated, if Redford had committed not just the one rape, or if Carla's story came out. It was all or nothing. She couldn't advise Savage to do the deal but to take only part of the hundred million themselves. He would see her qualification as evidence that she knew something she wasn't sharing. It seemed to her suddenly ridiculous that after the science of valuation models, the nihilistic ruthlessness of the trading floor, the fate of one hundred million dollars, and of all those touched by it, should rest with her, upon a lie concocted from hopes, forgiveness and redemption. But then she'd always dabbled, interfered, played God, or His antithesis. She paused for just a moment before answering with a light smile.

'There are no "other little matters", James. The stalker's not ideal, but we can't pull a deal for something so intangible. I'd go for it, take the whole hundred.'

Zamaroh grinned with delight. Breden looked on with his customary mask of polite interest. Savage seemed to be retreating fast from the debate.

'Fine.' He waved his hand again. 'We'll take it all. You deal with it, Zaha.' He pushed himself up from the table and walked out of the room. Then he paused midway and wheeled round to Sarah. 'You'd better be right.'

Sarah, Breden and Zamaroh watched him walk away in silence. When he had disappeared from view, Sarah let out a long sigh.

'Great. He's just hung the entire success or failure of the whole bloody deal on me.'

'Not the success, Sarah,' corrected Zamaroh, 'that would be his. Just the failure.'

Sarah laughed. 'Official scapegoat. I wonder if I can get goat money. I didn't get danger money for the stalker, but perhaps I could get scapegoat money. I think I'll put in a claim.'

'Did you need it?' asked Breden.

'Need what?' asked Sarah disingenuously.

'Danger money,' Breden answered levelly.

'Apparently not. I seem to be pretty unscathed, don't I?' Sarah got to her feet, bade them goodbye and walked out.

'So,' Breden said to Zamaroh after Sarah had closed the door behind her, 'you've got what you wanted.'

'What have I got?' enquired the Iranian crisply.

'Your deal. Sarah gave Redford a clean bill of health.'

'So did you.'

'Ye-e-es, and I hate to be modest, but it wasn't *my* approval Savage was looking for. Sarah swung it, we both know that.'

'She has a real hold over him, that's what gets me,' grumbled Zamaroh.

'Don't knock it. Like I said, it got you your deal.'

'The deal should be *got*. It's not Sarah's doing.'

'I'm not so sure about that.'

'What do you mean?' asked Zamaroh, quick as a knife.

'I think she's covering something up.'

'Something big?'

'Something that would blow the deal if we found out.'

'Why would she do that?'

'Maybe she's fallen for Redford. He's a rock star, women find him irresistible.'

Zamaroh shook her head. 'No. Not her style to compromise herself like that.'

'You think she's incapable of lying?'

'On the contrary, I think she'd need a better reason than sex to lie.'

'What about love?'

'Does she look like a woman in love?' asked Zamaroh.

'No,' Breden admitted, 'she doesn't. But she looks like a woman who's got a lot on her mind.'

'So what do we do? Savage's obviously got some kind of personal crisis going on, he's no help. We whisper something like this and he'd pull the deal, the mood he's in.'

'He probably would.'

'You know, it just drives me mad. If it were me, if I had personal problems, it'd be, "Women can't compartmentalise, they are over-emotional, unstable, never make a fighter pilot, *sniff*, PMT and all that", but when it's the chief executive, and a man to boot, we all make exceptions. It's written off as some kind of eccentricity, almost seen as a good thing – "the man can feel, he hurts, he's human like the rest of us". His wandering round like a zombie makes him one of the boys. It's enough to make you sick.'

Breden shrugged. 'Come the revolution.' Oh God. He almost bit off his tongue as soon as he said it.

The blood drained from Zamaroh's face. 'What are you going to do about Jensen?' she asked in a burst of staccato.

'Pay her a visit at home, have a little chat.'

Chapter Fifty-one

Sarah awoke swathed in the luxury of her own duvet. She stretched, raised her feet up and jack-knifed out of bed, pulled on sweat pants and a skimpy, sleeveless T-shirt and went in to Georgie. She changed and fed him, played with him for half an hour, then carried him across the King's Road to buy the papers.

The sun was shining brightly. The day was unseasonably warm. It must have been more than twenty degrees. The air was crystalline after a heavy rainfall overnight, and Sarah felt relief steal over her as she put John Redford and Goldsteins from her mind. She returned with an armful of papers and a black coffee.

Up on her roof terrace, she settled Georgie in his mobile playpen beside her, with his favourite red and black striped cloth spider, and spread out her papers on the wooden trestle table in the splendour of the autumn sun.

The Redford retinue, she read, were moving to London on a wave of plaudits. She practically choked on the PR. 'Redford's tours are magical experiences where an angel swoops down to entertain us for a few golden hours,' said a somewhat overcome critic for *The Times*. The *Sun*'s verdict was more earthy: 'sex on legs is back!' The *Independent* rather more soberly described the world tour as one of the biggest-grossing tours of all time. 'Hundreds of thousands of loyal followers flock to the concerts. Millions more buy the CDs. John Redford's star is riding as high as ever.'

Sarah could shoot that star down. Or let it shine on, untarnished. She had not spoken to Redford since she made her deal with him, but she hadn't escaped him. She yearned for him, as he had been, before she knew the truth about him; and with her new knowledge, she despised him. She was not good at giving people second chances, but she fought to now. She knew well enough that once her mind was made up, once she had damned someone, they stayed condemned. There was no court of appeal in her heart, no reversal possible, but this man was her son's father, even if he didn't know it, and she had loved him. Despite her rage, part of her loved him still. He had done something vile, made more terrible by the consequences which had unfolded over time, like some coiled-up curse, slow to act, lethal when started. All these time bombs we plant, never knowing it, Sarah mused. Decisions we make, places we go, jobs we take, people we collide with. Perhaps we have some slight presentiment, but really, we're fucking fate and we never know what offspring she will present us with down the road.

She turned back to the papers and, as if in a vain attempt to exorcise the man from her mind, she tore out the pages with the Redford coverage, and dropped them onto the floor. Georgie caught a stray one, sent his way by a sharp, fluttering breeze. He grasped it with delight, tearing into shreds the column inches of lies.

He gurgled with pleasure, finches in the garden square serenaded them, Jacob slept downstairs in his room, and Sarah didn't want to move. Not now or ever. She wanted to be here, with her baby, in their home, basking in the benign presence of her uncle. She wanted no more part in the deal. To hear Redford's name, to have to intone it coolly, professionally, to lie and cover up his true character, was more than she thought she would be able to do. But she hadn't been paid yet. She needed the money, and so did all the women Redford was going to help if she lied for him.

She reached out for her coffee cup, and flicked through the rest of the papers, pausing as an article caught her eye.

> *INTERPOL AND FBI HUNT SERIAL RAPIST.*
> *A rapist who appears to have struck in at least ten US cities over the past four months now seems to have moved to Europe. Interpol and local police, helped by the FBI, are now investigating rapes in Paris and Venice which they believe may have been committed by the same man.*

There followed a list of the US cities in which the serial rapist had struck. Sarah got up slowly and deliberately, as if unsure that her body would obey her commands, and went to her study. She fished out a sheet of paper from her desk and returned to the terrace, moving like an automaton. She looked from the piece of paper to the article and back again, then she jumped to her feet, knocking over her cup. She rocked back and forth on her heels, hugging her arms around her, making a low keening sound. The coffee spread like blood over the newsprint till the words were obscured. It dripped from the table and pooled on the floor. Georgie watched the flow approaching him, looked up at his mother's face, and screamed.

The doorbell rang. Sarah swallowed back the taste of vomit in her mouth, picked up her baby and soothed him. 'It's all right, darling. Mama got a shock, that's all. Doesn't matter, doesn't matter. Nasty coffee spilled, that's all. Didn't touch Georgie. Georgie's fine.' She kissed his silken hair as she carried him downstairs. Her mind elsewhere, unthinking, she threw open the door.

Dick Breden stood there. His customary half-smile vanished as he took in Sarah and Georgie. Her hair was wild as if she had raked her fingers back and forth through it. The expression on her face flickered between fear, anger and helplessness. Breden had caught her, as if naked. There was nothing she could do to cloak her emotions now.

She glared at him, furious that he had broken in on her, that he had seen the secret she tried so hard to hide.

'Please go, Dick. I don't know why you're here, but whatever it is can keep. I need to be alone right now. Please go. And please forget you came here today.'

Breden looked from her to the child in her arms. 'Your baby?'

'Yes. My son.'

'He's beautiful.'

'Yes. He is.'

'Why didn't you tell us?'

'It's none of your business.'

'Most people shout it from the rooftops.'

'He's my private joy, and none the less loved for that, and anyway, it's still none of your business.'

Breden gazed steadily at her, trying to read the secrets in her eyes. 'Something's happened. What?'

'Leave it.'

'May I help?'

She shook her head violently. 'Help by going.'

'Can I come back later?'

'No.'

'Sarah, we need to talk.'

'About what? About Georgie? He's got nothing to do with anything.'

Breden gave her a strange look. 'Not about Georgie. As you say, he's none of my business, and look, you needn't worry that I'll say anything about him to anyone, because I won't.'

'Thank you,' said Sarah. 'I would really appreciate that.'

Breden looked at her gently. 'No problem. But we still need to talk.'

'Why? What's going on?'

'Name a time, I'll come back,' said Breden.

'Oh God, you will too. All right, eight o'clock tonight. Georgie'll be in bed. We can talk, but there's nothing to talk about.'

'See you then,' said Breden.

Sarah closed the door on him, walked into the hall and leaned back against the wall, Georgie like a hot bundle in her arms. She glanced at her watch. She'd got nine hours before Breden came back. Nine hours to decide what the hell she was going to do. It was only 11 a.m., too early for a drink. She looked in on Jacob. The old man was still fast asleep, recovering from the rigours of childcare. She pulled on her trainers, put Georgie in his pushchair and headed for Battersea Park, hoping the walk would clear her head.

She walked beneath the red cedars, past the throngs of feeding pigeons; she strolled around the zoo, skirting dancing squirrels; she counted out the minutes, she counted out the rapes. Ten in the States, two in Europe. Twelve rapes, all committed in the cities where John Redford had toured and, she was willing to bet, at the same time as the Redford entourage had hit town. And she had believed him. She had made her five-million-dollar pact with him. Five million for one rape. Absolution on earth. A haven for many, bought from one woman's pain. A price put on something that was priceless.

Only it wasn't five for one. It was five for twelve, and who knows how many other women had kept their own vows of silence, had tried to put an end to a nightmare that wouldn't be exorcised by silence? She had got it wrong, she had been blinded by dreams of what five million could do.

And, far worse, she had been blinded by her desire *not* to see. She had wanted to believe that it had been a one-off, an aberration, and that he deserved another chance. Her own inner voice had been right. *Do your job, do not even attempt to play God. Fate spins you the cards. Play your hand, don't attempt to doctor it, whatever your motives.*

She paced round the lake, past the Henry Moores, looming in brooding bronze amidst the trees. What now? She headed for home, put the sleepy Georgie into his cot for a nap, and submerged herself in the shower. *Oh God, what now*? She dried off and sat alone, staring round at the four walls of her study, sentencing herself to immobility until she had found a solution.

Chapter Fifty-two

Breden arrived promptly at eight. Sarah greeted him, wearing khaki combats and a clinging brown T-shirt. She had piled her hair on top of her head. Wisps escaped and framed her face. She wore no make-up, just a flash of heady scent that smelled of jasmine on a hot night. Her skin was pale, but her eyes were resolute.

She led Breden through her house, up the stairs and out onto her verdant terrace. She put the baby listener down on the table where it sat hissing with interference as a plane flew overhead.

As Breden sat down, she studied him, unselfconsciously, as if she were seeing him for the first time. She knew he was forty-five, but he looked less than forty. He had the bearing, colour and musculature of someone who worked out a lot. He moved freely and powerfully, no macho swaggering. She knew he had been in the army, and suddenly liked the thought. He was a man of the world, of many worlds, and he would have occupied them all, not merely passed through, marking time. He was watching her now, not with his normal sardonic smile, but with open interest, as a man might look at a woman. It was as if both of them had come to an understanding without the need to express it. It was a laying down of arms, an openness to go down some unnamed path, together.

'Would you like a drink?'

'Please. Vodka.'

Sarah returned with a bottle of whisky, a bottle of vodka, an ice bucket and two glasses. She took a seat opposite Breden and poured their drinks. For a while both of them sipped, eyeing each other as the silence and the night gathered around them. Breden said nothing. He didn't ask her questions she wouldn't have answered about Georgie, and she respected him the more for his silence. In fact, it seemed to her that she saw an increased respect in his eyes, and a gentleness that hadn't been there before.

'I think I may have made an awful mistake,' Sarah said finally. 'I lied about the stalker. I set a trap in Venice, caught her, confronted her, got her story.' Her voice dull with suppressed emotion, she told Breden that story. He listened in silence, sipping his vodka. When she had finished speaking, he just gazed into the night. Then she showed him the article in *The Times*. She refilled their glasses, took a long pull of whisky.

'I have a horrible feeling Redford's the serial rapist.'

Breden took a while to respond. 'So what's your dilemma?'

'Part of me can't believe it – refuses to believe it.'

'Your fabled instinct?'

'Yes.' Sarah raked her hair off her face. 'I mean, why would he need to rape someone? He's got so many women hurling themselves at him.'

'It's not about sex, is it, rape? It's more about power. And maybe all that consensual sex on tap has bored him. Maybe he needs resistance, a fight, to make it feel real, to make it a proper conquest.'

'How totally sick.'

Breden nodded. 'You said it. But one thing I don't understand,' he added slowly.

'What's that?'

'Why tell *me* all this?'

Sarah didn't hesitate. 'Because I want you to help me find out if it is him.'

'And if it is?'

'We throw him to the wolves.'

'And if it isn't?'

'We keep his secret, the deal goes ahead.' Sarah didn't mention the five million going to charity; she didn't want Breden to think it clouded her judgment.

'And how do I help?'

'You use your sources in the police, Interpol, FBI – I know you have them. You get all the details of the rapes, the modus operandi, why the cops think the cases are linked, the exact time they were committed. I'll check on Redford's movements. If he was performing onstage, or was at a dinner somewhere public, he's in the clear.'

'What about Savage?'

'There's no need for him to know about this until we have our answer.'

'We run our own private investigation?'

'Yes. I'll pay your side.'

'I don't want your money, Sarah.'

She shrugged.

'Tell me, why would I do this?'

'Because if he's guilty, we stand a reasonable chance of proving it, and if he's innocent, and if it got out that we thought he might be a serial rapist, that might stick. Savage wouldn't leak, but we can't be sure that the Goldsteins Leaker wouldn't get onto it.'

'Who is the Leaker? I've a feeling you know more than you're telling about that, too.'

'Don't ask me.'

'I am asking.'

'I can't tell you. Please, it's not relevant.'

'Does Savage know?'

'Yes, he knows.'

Breden nodded. 'All right, I'll let it go. For now. But as for going off on some clandestine investigation, if Savage finds out we've both gone AWOL he'll throw a pink fit. He's my biggest client – I can't afford to lose him. And the other thing that bothers me is the feeling that I'm wearing a blindfold. There's so much that's being covered up here, omissions if not lies.'

Sarah gazed across the table. 'I'm guilty on both counts. What can I say? I have my reasons, none of which are to harm anyone. Just the opposite.'

'Ok. Just give *me* one good reason why I should get involved?'

'I'm asking for your trust, and for your help, Dick. That's the best reason I can give.'

Chapter Fifty-three

The doorbell rang the next morning at ten. Sarah was sitting at her desk paying long overdue bills while Jacob drank tea in the kitchen and Georgie napped. She hurried downstairs and opened the door. A motorcycle messenger, sinisterly concealed behind his helmet, thrust an envelope at her, then a clipboard to sign.

She returned to her study and ripped open the envelope. An information snapshot of Roddy Clark tumbled out – phone records, bank statements from Coutts, a brief biography. He lived in Camden Hill Square, was born in St Mary's Paddington 1968, educated at the Dragon School, then Eton, then Oxford. Travelled the world for four years before becoming a staff writer on *The Word*, made meteoric progress to news editor at twenty-nine, then seemingly burned out after a few years as he became a general reporter, always on the trail of scandal. On the trail of Goldsteins, Sarah mused. She'd have to dig up the articles from the year before, when he libelled the company. Perhaps he had had an inside source at that time. Something tickled away at her, some connection. She began to scan the phone records when her own phone rang.

She grabbed it, irritated. 'Yes?'

'Hi, it's Strone.'

She groaned.

'I got some more financials 'n' stuff for you. Want to come and go over them?'

Oh God no, anything but. More snaking columns of numbers, more eyestrain, more headaches. More Redford. When would she ever wrap this thing up? When you get paid, her voice of reason chastised her.

'Where are you?' she asked.

'The Portobello Hotel.'

'All right. See you in half an hour.' She left Roddy Clark forgotten on her desk and set off.

The Portobello was so discreet that Sarah passed it by first time. It was in one of Notting Hill's elegant streets, a place of white stucco, polished brass, with an air of order and quiet well-being. Sarah asked for Strone Cawdor and was sent up to his room. She knocked and sucked in her breath when Redford answered the door. He looked like he hadn't slept for days.

'Er, sorry,' said Sarah. 'They must have sent me to the wrong room. I'm here to see Strone.'

'This is his room,' said Redford coldly. 'He just had to step out to see someone. Be back in five minutes. He didn't tell me *you* were coming.'

'Yeah well, that puts us both at an equal disadvantage, doesn't it?'

'So this is the way it's going to be, huh?'

Sarah crossed to the window. She didn't want to look at him, didn't want him to see the questions in her mind, the suspicion that had taken root. 'Innocent until proven guilty,' she kept repeating to herself, fighting for equanimity. Carla's face fought too, rising up through her consciousness like an avenger.

Redford walked up to the window and stood beside Sarah. She wheeled around to face him. 'How do I know how anything's going to be! All I know is, it's all fucked up.'

They stood, braced, questions flaring in their angry eyes, words unspoken freezing on their lips.

Strone walked into the room. 'Am I interrupting?'

Sarah and Redford stepped apart.

'Hello Strone,' said Sarah wearily.

'Looking pretty hot and bothered there.'

'And you're looking rude and boorish as usual.'

Strone ignored this and turned to Redford. 'The in—' he cut himself short. 'The geezer who saw you yesterday's here again. Waiting downstairs.'

Redford tensed suddenly. 'He can wait.'

Strone shook his head. 'Anticipated that. Says he will see you *now*. Busy man and all that.'

'Fuck it!' Redford dragged his fingers through his hair and marched out without saying goodbye.

'What's up with you two? Had a lovers' tiff?'

'What? You know, you really have an over-fetid imagination.'

'Do I now? I also know John Redford.'

'And what do you know?'

'I know that he's fallen in love with someone, and that someone has done something to hurt him very badly,' replied Strone, his voice unexpectedly gentle. Sarah turned away from him, tears burning her eyes. She coughed, wiped the tears away, gained time by feigning fascination with the empty street below.

'When's it all gonna happen then?' asked Strone, casting her a lifeline. 'I must have biked round half a ton of paper, and still your Zamaroh woman asks for more.'

'All these deals are paper nightmares,' said Sarah, turning to him, grateful to be back on the solid ground of numbers. 'You wouldn't believe the documentation. I'd imagine we're getting quite close to closing,' she said, as much to placate him as from any knowledge that the issue was imminent. 'The next consideration then is market conditions. You've got to launch your boat on a favourable tide.'

'We *are* the tide,' countered Strone, with a smile.

'Yeah, and don't tell me, you can hold it back, just like King Canute. Ever heard of hubris?'

'Is that a warning?' The smile faded.

'Let's call it a piece of life-enhancing advice.'

'I want this deal done quickly, do you understand?'

'You'll get the deal when it's ready, not a moment before. Do *you* understand? Now what are these papers you've got for me?'

Strone handed her a sheaf of documents. 'Shall we go over them then?' he asked.

'I'll ring you if I have a problem with them,' replied Sarah. 'I mean, they're not exactly rocket science, are they?'

Strone smiled. 'Beware your own words.'

'What?'

'Hubris and all that. Pride and fall.'

'I'd better watch my step then, hadn't I?' Sarah walked out and shut the door behind her with relief. On impulse, she took a seat in the foyer, pulled out her newspaper, and pretended to read. There was only one other person waiting in the foyer. A man in his forties. Something about him radiated authority, despite his crumpled suit.

As if feeling Sarah's scrutiny, he raised jaundiced eyes to her. A few minutes later, her patience was rewarded when the receptionist sashayed up to the man and said with great import: 'Mr Redford will see you now.'

The man grunted and walked to the stairs. He was the in—, the geezer, as Strone preferred to call him, borrowing the English slang. Insurgent? Insurer? Interested party? What was he to Redford that he must be seen so urgently, and why did he disturb him so?

Chapter Fifty-four

Sarah returned to an empty house. Georgie and Jacob must have gone out for a walk in the autumn sunshine. God, wouldn't that be nice. Ditch all the crap waiting for her and piss off into the sun. She made herself a monstrously strong pot of coffee, dejectedly climbed the stairs and shut herself in her study. Roddy Clark lay before her. She picked over his credit-card statements. The man was a dandy, tailors in London, tailors in Windsor, where all the old Etonians were outfitted as boys. Touchingly loyal. Then Sarah began to feel the hot wire of a connection burning in her brain. School, loyal, schoolboy, Eton . . . come on, come on, spit it out, you're close, you're just teasing me, she urged her brain. She could feel it working. Bingo! She jumped up. Eton. *Jezza.*

Fingers fumbling with excitement she pulled out her desk drawer and the Jezza file, quickly flicked through it to the bio. Born 1968. She removed the phone records and compared them with Clark's, running her finger down the column of numbers dialled. There was Clark's number, rung by Jezza on 23 September, two days before Clark wrote the article on Goldsteins and Redford. She checked back over nine months to see how often the two men had spoken by phone. Just two other times. Not by any means regularly enough for the call on the twenty-third to be mere coincidence. Sarah smiled. *Gotcha, you bastard.* Her sense of triumph quickly faded. Why had Jezza done it? What could he possibly have to gain? And how could he have been so stupid as to think he would get away with it? The phone records were circumstantial evidence, yes, but then he wasn't going to be tried under the more liberal auspices of a courtroom, but in the fiefdom of a trading floor.

Sarah caught a cab to the City. She took out her mobile and convened a meeting with Savage, Zamaroh and Breden for an hour's time, but first she met Zaha on her own.

The head of the trading floor was coiled in her seat, talking into her telephone headset when Sarah arrived. With an air of disdain, the Iranian watched her visitor sit down. Sarah saw the look and ignored it. Part of her felt too sad to play games. The Iranian concluded her conversation with a, 'Well, see to it!' command and removed her headset with a frown.

'Sarah. What can I do for you?'

Sarah eyed her evenly. 'I have reasonably strong evidence as to who leaked the Redford deal to Roddy Clark,' she said, toning down her certainty.

Zamaroh's face tightened. 'Who?' she whispered.

'Jeremy St James.'

Zamaroh jumped to her feet. 'I knew it – I just knew it! The bastard!' She began to pace, head down, staring at the carpet, building herself up like a cyclone.

'Just a sec there, Zaha. Have a look at the evidence first.' Sarah showed Zamaroh the telephone records, explained the Eton connection.

'It's good enough for me,' concluded Zamaroh.

'It's circumstantial, not proof,' warned Sarah.

Zamaroh turned on her. 'You want proof?'

Sarah nodded dubiously.

'Get St James in here.'

'Get him yourself,' said Sarah, walking from Zamaroh's office back to her own. She wanted no part of what she feared was coming. It took only about a minute. From her office, she heard Zamaroh's voice, starting quietly enough, hissingly sibilant, punctuated by Jezza's lower tones. These interruptions just seemed to inflame Zamaroh, for her voice rose in pitch and volume, and Sarah couldn't help but hear her words.

'Why? Just tell me *why*! I gave you everything. You flourished under me, way beyond your limited capacity. I brought you on. I gave you the chance. I bailed you out when you fucked up, and for the past eight months you've been existing here on my grace, *my* sayso, although I should have fired you back then when you dumped eight million in one spectacularly moronic performance.'

Sarah rubbed her face, as if attempting to slough off Zamaroh's words. The Iranian sounded for all the world like a lover scorned.

'Why? *Just tell me*!' she screamed. The trading floor had fallen strangely silent. Jezza's humiliation had become a public hanging.

'What makes you think I've done anything?' shot back Jezza in a doomed voice.

'See this?' demanded Zamaroh shrilly. 'See this? Black and white proof. You're not only disloyal, you're stupid. Did you really think you could get away with this?'

'With what?'

Sarah cringed. The longer Jezza held out, the worse would be his inevitable fall. The poor guy still thought he could escape.

'You did it. We have more proof in the wings. You betrayed me, you betrayed the whole floor. Now tell me why. Come on, just say it, admit it like a man and I'll consider saving your miserable hide.'

There was a long silence, then Jezza's voice, dripping desperation. 'I didn't want to cause any trouble. There was no malice in it.'

'Then why?'

'I wanted to give Roddy something. I wanted to sound plugged in, like I was part of the decision-making process here, not just another slave at the coal face.' There was a long silence. Sarah could almost feel Jezza willing Zamaroh to give him another chance. She added her silent voice to his.

All hopes were smashed by the hammer of Zamaroh's laughter.

'Get out, you little shit.'

There was another silence and Sarah could imagine Jezza looking at his boss in confusion. Zamaroh's voice again.

'Security? It's Miss Zamaroh here. There's someone up here I'd like you to escort from the premises, please.'

Oh God no, the bitch.

Sarah saw St James walking from Zamaroh's office, head bowed, utterly humiliated. He glanced up, their eyes met. Sarah tried to veil the pity in hers, and the guilt. Jezza slumped into his seat. Then two security men appeared.

'All right, sir,' said one of them, a six-foot-three rugby player by the look of him. 'Like to come with us?'

'Give me five minutes, would you?' he hissed.

Zamaroh walked up behind him. 'You know the rules. Out now.'

Jezza got to his feet and stared at her in sheer hate. He turned away and began to open his desk drawers, picking up tennis shoes, some correspondence.

'Leave all that,' said Zamaroh. '*You know the rules.*'

'These are personal items,' said St James.

'We'll be the judge of that. Now go!' She nodded to the security men who took one arm each and pulled Jezza from his desk. His gaze roved around desperately over the rapidly assembling throng. Again, he met Sarah's eyes. She tried to impart some message of strength. She could see how close he was to losing control.

'Oh, for God's sake let him walk freely!' shouted Sarah, walking from her office. 'He's not some bloody murderer.'

The security guards looked embarrassed. Zamaroh turned and walked away, as if bored by the spectacle. The spectators waited.

'And get back to work, you bunch of bloody pirhanas,' said Sarah, before returning to her office, slamming the door and drawing the blinds over her glass windows, sickened.

Chapter Fifty-five

Sarah met Zamaroh again thirty minutes later, together with Dick Breden, in Savage's office. She felt as if the two men were all that stood between her and grabbing Zamaroh's neck.

'Er Sarah, I just need to go over something with you,' said Savage, nodding at the door. Sarah got to her feet and followed him into his personal bathroom. Savage closed the door behind them and leaned back against the marble sink. Sarah closed the loo seat and sat on it.

'I took your advice,' he said with a gleam in his eye.

'With respect to what?' asked Sarah with a smile.

'That little shit, Richard Deane. I didn't tell you yesterday. I must have been struck by conscience or something, felt a bit ashamed of myself, but the more I think of it, the better I feel.'

'What did you do?' asked Sarah, delighted by the animation that had returned to Savage's face.

The chief executive grinned. 'I had my driver go via Uriah's, eight o'clock that same night you told me. Deane was there, primping and preening himself, cocky bastard. Anyway . . . I got out of the car, walked up to him and gave him a whacking great punch.'

Sarah burst out laughing, horrified and thrilled at the same time.

'Good for you!' she exclaimed. 'What happened then?'

'He staggered back, sat down on the steps, blood all over his Brooks Brothers' shirt. I gave him a look, turned and walked back to my car and drove off.'

'Did anyone see?'

'Several people must have. I was in too much of a daze myself to pay them much attention.'

'Shit. But no one's contacted you about it since?'

Savage smiled. 'No law suits, if that's what you mean.'

Sarah visualised the scene. 'Well done.'

Savage's smile faded. 'Yeah well, we take our small victories where we can.'

Sarah wanted to ask if Fiona had broken off the affair, but feared she had heard the answer in the despair that suddenly seeped through Savage's voice.

They walked back together into the boardroom, to curious looks from Breden and Zamaroh.

'Strone gave me these this morning,' Sarah said to Zamaroh, still delighting in the image of Savage flooring his rival. She launched the paperwork down the board table with a vicious spin so that Zamaroh had to scrabble about to collect it. 'He wants the money,' continued Sarah. 'He really pushed me. What's the timetable on this thing?'

'We're working as fast as we can,' said Zamaroh, quickly scanning the documents. She looked up at Sarah. 'If we take the whole issue, it really speeds everything up.'

'I thought you'd already agreed to take the whole thing?' Sarah said to Savage.

'He's wavering,' Zamaroh grunted with thinly disguised contempt.

Savage directed a look at the Iranian that might have turned her to stone.

It was good to see him angry, thought Sarah, better than despairing.

'So?' she asked him. 'What's your thinking?'

'Will we go the whole bloody way?' Savage pondered, as if toying with some philosophical dilemma.

Sarah watched, trying not to hold her breath. She could feel Breden's tension as he looked out of the window, eyes casual, lips tight.

'Will we, Sarah?' Savage turned his eyes on her like a weapon.

She shrugged. 'Not my money, James. It's your call, isn't it? Yours and Zaha's.'

'And if it *were* your money?' Savage persisted.

'If I had Goldsteins' balance sheet, I dare say I could swallow a hundred and not even notice it. If it's for your pension funds, it's a tad racy, but a tad richer than their normal fare, so I'd probably eat it there too.'

'Then let's eat,' said Savage.

Zamaroh looked delighted.

'When,' asked Sarah, 'do we eat?'

'It'll take another couple of months to close,' replied Zamaroh. 'It's the rating agencies that are the main constraining factor. I must say in that control freak Strone's favour, he runs a good ship, reporting wise. The documentation from him has been first-rate. Really helped things along.'

Sarah listened in mute surprise to Zamaroh's unexpected outburst of generosity.

'Say nine weeks to be absolutely safe,' Zamaroh told her.

'By early December then,' concluded Savage. 'Tell Mr Strone that the deal launches then, barring any unforeseen problems.'

Chapter Fifty-six

Breden arrived at eleven that night.

'Sorry I'm so late. I was at a dinner. Went on for ever.'

'You don't need to explain your social life to me,' said Sarah, a touch sharply. It was late, she was tired, and though Breden was helping her, she was sad and furious that it had come to this, that Redford had made this necessary.

'It wasn't social,' replied Breden, with his usual equanimity. 'It was business, some old rozzer pals of mine.'

'Anything on the rapes?'

'I've just asked them. It'll take a few days for them to get back to me, and a coupla hundred.'

'Did you pay?'

'Absolutely. They wanted to know what it was to me.'

'So what d'you say?'

'Touched my nose. They wouldn't expect an answer, but they wouldn't be coppers if they didn't ask.'

'If the press got hold of this . . .' said Sarah.

'You don't have to warn me, I'm being as careful as I can.'

Sarah frowned. 'I know. Tell me as soon as they get back to you.'

'I've got something else too.'

Sarah looked at him with interest.

'That Jim O'Cleary character you asked me about?'

'Yeah, the head of security who disappeared.'

'He's ex-CIA. Left three years ago under a bit of a cloud – something about drugs. Nothing was ever proved, far as I know, but there were serious suspicions that he was working some anti-narcotics operation both ways, taking the big boys' silver, and liberally helping himself to their product.'

'Really. I wonder if Redford knows anything about that?'

'Strone Cawdor's the one who employed him. Apparently O'Cleary either suddenly became open about his drug problem, or developed one for real after he started working with Redford Inc, because Strone paid for him to go into rehab for two months.'

'Yeah, paid for him with Redford's money no doubt.'

'No – with his own, I heard. Apparently the manager's very loyal to his people.'

'Huh! You live and learn. I wonder if O'Cleary's shown up again. Maybe he fell off the wagon?'

'Why don't you ask Strone?'

'I will.'

'What does Strone make of the Carla thing?'

'He knows nothing about Carla. At least, I'm assuming he doesn't.'

'Maybe his CIA guy does. A professional digger of dirt.'

'I think he's more there to protect Redford from stalkers. He got really nervous when O'Cleary disappeared.'

Breden got to his feet. 'Find out if he's reappeared. And I'll call you when I have something.'

'I'll keep my mobile on me.'

'By the way, a word of caution.'

'Yes?'

'Zamaroh is convinced you're hiding something. She's keen enough at the best of times to get something on you.'

'Why? What have I ever done to her?'

'You make her nervous.'

'Of what?'

'Everyone has something to hide. I think she fears you might investigate her, discover her secrets, use them against her.'

'I have no possible interest in doing that. The woman's paranoid.'

'Paranoid, bloody and ruthless, a worthy descendant of her Moghul forebears. Look at how she treated that poor twit, Jezza.'

'She needn't have humiliated him. But it's different with me. She doesn't have any power over me,' she added defiantly.

'Just be careful, Sarah. That's all I'm saying.'

'Why are you telling me this? She's obviously confided in you.'

'Because you and I are working as a team now, and Zamaroh could trip you up if you're not careful.'

Chapter Fifty-seven

The next day Sarah resolved to push Goldsteins, Redford, Carla, and the entire outside world from her mind. Jacob had gone home to Rotherwick Road for a day of necessary solitude, broken by card sessions with his old gang, leaving Sarah with some long overdue time alone with her baby.

It was ten in the morning, and Sarah had been up with Georgie since five-thirty. He was now blissfully sleeping off his ultra-early start, leaving his mother reeling. She gazed wistfully at her bed, deciding if she got into it she'd never get out. She changed out of her pyjamas into the acceptable daytime version – sweat pants and a T-shirt. It might not be acceptable outside in Carlyle Square, but here, in her home, it was the hautest couture she could face. Her eye was caught by her ficus tree, leaves furled with thirst. Before she did anything else, she had to see to it. She filled a large watering can, added a dash of plant food, and watered the ficus and all her plants.

Next she needed to tend to herself. What little sleep she had grabbed the night before had been tense, and she'd woken with her whole body aching. She desperately needed to do ten minutes of yoga, free up her spine or else she'd soon be cooking up one hell of a headache. She went downstairs, flicked through her CDs and chose Gloria Estefan. Gloria sang of hopes and dreams, of better days and nights full of love. Sarah turned up the volume, and sang along as she fell into her routine, carried out religiously every day until she gave birth, grabbed again perhaps five times since. Her body punished her neglect. It also dimly registered that in her early thirties, she was no longer blessed with the ability to ignore or abuse her body that she had taken for granted for so long. Just as she was finishing, the intercom rang once, a mercifully brief buzz. Anyone who woke Georgie wasn't likely to forget it in a while.

Dick Breden was waiting for her on her doorstep. So much for escape.

'Whatever it is will have to wait till I've eaten. I've got low blood sugar and I'll be ruined if I don't eat right now,' said Sarah.

'Fair enough. I don't want to constitute ruination.'

'Oh, I never said that. Although I'd imagine that for quite a lot of people you're walking ruination.' Sarah glanced round her pantry. She decided she needed pancakes.

'You hungry?'

'Depends what you're offering.'

'Pancakes.'

'Then I'm definitely hungry.'

Only after Sarah had made eight and consumed four pancakes topped with brown sugar and lemon did she decide she could hear Breden's news. She took a long swig of her black coffee.

'All right, tell me.'

Breden took a folded sheet of paper from his pocket.

'Here's a list of where the rapes were carried out, and the approximate times. Some of the victims were so traumatised, they couldn't say exactly what time the rapes happened.'

He put the paper on the table. Sarah scanned it, then collected the tour itinerary from her study. The conclusion screamed up at her. All the rapes took place in cities where Redford toured, and during his stay.

'Did you get a description?'

'I did. Thirty to forty. Five elevenish, fit, hard body.'

'And,' interrupted Sarah, 'what about his face?'

'He wore a hood – get this, a black hood that was stuck to his skin so it couldn't be pulled off. Several women tried and got nowhere save a few more punches.'

'Jesus.' Sarah raked her hair back off her face. 'Redford must be five ten, fit, lean body. He would have to wear a mask. Everyone knows his face. I'll kill the bastard.'

'Slow down, Sarah. The rapist doesn't have to be Redford. How many people's he got on tour with him?'

'I don't know. Say a hundred. Of that, about eighty men.'

'It could be any one of them.'

'It could also be Redford. Says here all these rapes are committed after midnight and before nine a.m. He was well finished performing by then.' She paused as another thought bubbled up. 'He's wired for hours after a concert. He has big problems coming down. Strone referred to the whole performance thing as a mind-fuck, as something dangerous. I know Redford fears it too, he's told me as much. After his last New York show, he appeared with a bandage on his fist, said he'd smashed it into a wall. Maybe he rapes to burn up all his adrenaline after a concert, and maybe he hurt his fist raping someone.'

Breden consulted his notes. 'What was the date of the last New York concert?'

Sarah told him.

Breden grimaced. 'There was a rape in the early hours of the next morning.'

Sarah buried her face in her hands, trying to block out all knowledge.

'What about in Paris and Venice?' asked Breden. 'Were you with him at all late at night?'

'I was,' Sarah replied with a heavy voice, 'but not on the nights of the rapes. Got anything else?' she asked quickly.

'There's a pattern to the rapes. They were all committed in sleazy parts of town, and all the women were waitresses or cooks at late-night cafés. He picked 'em off when they finished work, all after midnight, some as late as four in the morning, followed them some way, then pounced.'

Sarah felt as if she were going to vomit. A low moan issued from her.

Breden took hold of her arm in alarm. 'What is it?'

'I didn't tell you. It seemed like an insignificant detail. Carla Parton was a waitress. She turned up at Redford's concert after her shift, still in uniform. He raped her in her waitress's outfit. It must have started some kind of fetish.'

Breden blew out a long breath. 'It's not looking good for him.'

'It *all* points to him,' said Sarah. 'He, above all people, needs a disguise. Everyone knows his face. Did the rapist say anything?'

'Not a word, apparently. The police have no voice, no accent to go on.'

For a while they stared at each other in silence.

'So what now?' Breden finally asked.

A plan began to form slowly in Sarah's mind. 'I've got something. Call it a long shot.'

Chapter Fifty-eight

Breden must have seen the vague outlines of Sarah's plan in her eyes for he suddenly tensed.

'I could be the waitress. I could be the bait. You could organise back-up. Our rapist takes the bait, jumps me, you jump *him*. Bingo!'

Breden's response was deceptively mild. 'It's never quite that simple. And how are you proposing to trap him? He could pick any fast-food joint or late-night bar anywhere in London – outside London, for that matter.'

Sarah smiled. 'We follow him.'

'And I suppose we have to disguise you. He's not going to rape someone he knows, is he, especially not you? You're his passport to a hundred mill.'

'I'll get myself a wig. I can make myself up to look very different. I'll wear a short skirt, high heels—'

'And he won't be able to resist,' offered Breden.

'That's the plan,' said Sarah with a sheepish smile. 'You got a better one?'

'Nope, but I don't go a bundle on this one. Too much could go wrong.'

'Like what?'

'He jumps you, he could do a lot of damage before I get to him. For the trap to work, I'd have to hang back out of sight. Could take me a minute to get to you. That's long enough for him to inflict some serious injury, physical and psychological.'

'Were they hurt, the women he raped?' Sarah asked.

'If they resisted, yes.'

'How badly?'

'Anything from black eyes to busted ribs, a punctured lung, fractured jaw, broken wrist. Guy seems to enjoy violence.'

Sarah swallowed. 'Does he carry any weapons?'

'He hasn't used any so far besides his fists and his penis, but he might carry one all the same. If we do go down this road, I'll need to do a lot of checking first. Rape can escalate into murder, Sarah. One thing I didn't mention, the police reckon the guy's beginning to decompensate. The rapes are increasing in frequency. The rapist needs more of the same to get his old kick. Soon rape might not be enough for him.'

'That's comforting.'

'You should know the arena you're proposing to walk into. Have you ever experienced violence?'

Sarah looked away. She didn't answer. When she turned back there were tears in her eyes.

'Right, that's it, we stop this now,' said Breden.

'We go on,' said Sarah, her mouth tight with determination. 'I can handle the future; it's the past that sometimes gives me a bit of trouble.'

'You can't handle the past, you can't handle the future, is my experience,' observed Breden, laconic again. Sarah was at once comforted and enraged by his insistence on de-dramatising the situation.

'I can handle violence to me, all right. Being bait for the rapist doesn't faze me,' she insisted.

'Not now, maybe. Sitting here in your beautiful house, the door locked. Try it out on the street, at four in the morning, teetering along on your heels, hearing footsteps behind you, accelerating; maybe you try to run but he runs faster, catches you up, hurls you to the ground. Rips your skirt up, forces your legs apart.'

'Shut up! Don't you think every woman has imagined what it must be like to be raped? It's a fear we all confront. We've all walked back home late at night, or on a dark afternoon and heard those footsteps. Sometimes they turned out to be innocent, but for the unlucky ones they weren't. So don't feel you have to spell it out for me, I've gone down that road in my mind many times.'

'I'm sure you have, but now you're proposing to go down that road for real.'

'Tell me a better way and I'll do it.'

'There must be a better way. You seem too ready to throw yourself into the firing line. I don't get it. Seems almost personal to me.'

'It is,' said Sarah, mixing truth with a lie. 'I decided to play God. I was wrong. Now I've got to try to make it right.'

'What about your son? If something goes wrong, you're not the only one affected.'

'The reason I'm still in this is him. The last letter the stalker, Carla, sent me, threatened Georgie and my Uncle Jacob. That's why I flew to Venice and went after her. I couldn't leave Georgie and Jacob exposed.'

Breden raised his eyebrows in sudden comprehension. 'That explains your behaviour. One minute you were going to drop the whole thing, the next you were insisting you should go.' Breden rubbed his eyes. 'So you made your son safe by exposing her?'

'Yeah. I don't think she'll bother me any more, or Redford for that matter.' She paused. 'I could always be wrong, but I don't think I am this time.'

'No one ever does. Not till after.'

'Leave it. Don't try to scare me.'

'I'm just presenting the facts as I see them. You still haven't explained why you want to use yourself as bait, despite the repercussions to your son if anything happens to you.'

'Nothing's going to happen,' said Sarah through clenched teeth. 'Look, I've got the best survival mechanism there is. Maternal love. I love that boy more than the whole world, more than my life, but I'm selfish, yeah. I want to stay alive to love him, to be loved by him. All those stories about mothers lifting lorries to save their children, that's the power of mother love. There is nothing more powerful than that on this planet. Not the lust of a rapist. Nothing.'

Breden looked away, hiding the sorrow in his eyes.

'So help me,' demanded Sarah, sensing his fears for her. 'Help me defend myself.'

'How?'

'Teach me some tips to fight him off.'

'The women who fought back got hurt worst of all, Sarah. I wouldn't advocate that. Unless you're a black belt, fighting this kind of guy'll only make it worse.'

'So what's your advice then?'

'Don't do it. But if you must, we'll plan it like a military campaign.' He suddenly looked resigned. 'Oh, all right. I'll teach you a few dirty fighting tricks, things you can pick up in a couple of days. Might immobilise the guy until I can get there.'

'Don't go thinking you're the cavalry.'

'Would I? You're a cavalry all on your own.'

'We all need help.'

'What are you up to this weekend? Will you be here if I ring?'

'I'll be here, hanging out with Georgie. And I suppose I might go and visit Redford. See if I can find anything out, snitch an old diary, whatever.'

'Looks like the prospect doesn't fill you with much enthusiasm.'

'Pilfering, pick-pocketing someone's soul? No, I'm not exactly keen on it.'

Chapter Fifty-nine

Sarah was playing downstairs in the kitchen with Georgie when the intercom rang on Saturday morning. She was still in her nightie, an old favourite in honey-coloured cotton, washed translucent over the years; her hair was wild and unbrushed, and she hadn't yet washed the sleep from her eyes. Georgie looked quite happy where he was, and he was not yet crawling, so she left him on the kitchen floor and, muttering darkly, headed upstairs for the door. She threw it open and there was Redford. He was standing, backlit by the sun, in jeans and a leather jacket, and despite everything, he took her breath away.

Looking at him, she felt as though she were waking from a dream, light and happy, until she remembered the nightmare.

'*John.*'

She said his name like a lamentation. He looked at her in silence, naked awareness in his eyes. After a few moments he turned and picked up from behind him a gardenia plant, radiant with white scented flowers.

He held it as if to carry it in for her. She reached out, took it from him, then glanced involuntarily over her shoulder, as if Georgie might suddenly have learned the art of crawling and climbing and made his way up the stairs to meet his father.

Redford followed her gaze. Sarah could feel him taking in the tumble of her hair, her sleepy eyes shadowed by dark circles, drawing the inevitable, and wrong conclusion. He gave her a sad smile.

'I'll be on my way, then.'

'Look, it's chaos inside,' said Sarah hurriedly. 'I'd invite you in, I just—'

'No need to explain,' he said. 'You told me yourself that we were all entitled to secrets. I won't intrude on yours.' He turned to go.

'Wait, John. Let's get together later, do something simple, just walk and talk.' Looking at him now, despite everything she suspected, she still couldn't believe he was the serial rapist.

Redford paused, indecision flickering in his normally resolute gaze.

'As it happens, I was planning just that for this evening. A long walk, maybe stop at a bar, find some music.'

Sarah waited.

'We can walk together,' Redford said, half as a question.

'What time?'

'Ten o'clock?'

Sarah gulped. Way past when she'd rather be in bed.

'I'll come to the Portobello.'

She rang Jacob on the mobile he had purchased when Georgie was born.

'Hello, sweetie. Everything all right?'

'Everything's fine.' She paused. 'I was just wondering . . .'

'What time would you like me?' he asked, a smile in his voice.

She tried to reach Breden all day. He'd said he'd be around, might call on her to start her crash course in dirty fighting. Where the hell was he when she needed him? At nine she gave up, leaving a long message explaining her evening as her insurance policy. She'd just have to go with Redford, take her chances. If he was the rapist, as someone known to him she wouldn't be his target, according to past form, at least the past form the police were aware of and had passed on. But then there was Carla, a victim known to the rapist, even though he'd forgotten the connection, or was too out of his head to notice. And what else had Breden said? Something about the rapist decompensating. She knew that meant losing control, breaking out of the previous pattern, committing crimes more frequently and frenziedly, almost seeking a way out, capture or complete insanity, or both.

So why was she going? To salvage something from the wreck of a relationship, or to hasten its demise? She was no wiser as the time came for her to leave. Her thoughts were clouded, she knew, by her overwhelming wish that Georgie's father were not a rapist. It seemed impossible, when she thought of him as her son's father, and not as the rock star, that he *could* be the guilty party. But she knew too, that wishing alone wouldn't make it so.

She dressed for comfort, and for speed. She wore her black combats and trainers, with a white T-shirt and a black leather jacket into which she had crammed her money, mobile phone and a can of Mace.

She looked in on Georgie, kissed Jacob goodbye.

'Take care, girl, whatever you're up to.'

'More snooping,' she said with a miserable frown.

'When will this be over?' asked Jacob.

'As soon as I'm paid,' replied Sarah hopefully.

She set off for the King's Road and hailed a taxi. Sinking back into the seat, she suddenly wondered how Redford had found her address. She'd never given it to him, she thought with a pang of suspicion. *Deal list*, she realised with a curse. On any deal, the major participants are given a list of one another's home phone numbers and addresses. Jesus, it had been close this morning. She could so easily have answered the door with Georgie in her arms. She didn't want him within a million miles of her child. That wasn't entirely true, she knew that. In one of her waking dreams, she showed her son to his father, bursting with pride at the miracle she had grown inside her.

The John Redford who had made love to her with such dizzying passion and tenderness might stroke a child's face with the same exquisite intensity. Redford could feel all right, could feel and love from the tip of his head down to his boots. If he could hate with half the intensity with which he loved . . . Sarah couldn't finish the thought. She shuddered, rubbed her arms, trying to grab back a piece of reality. She felt a pang of conscience at the vehemence of her emotion. Guilty of the serial rapes or not, Redford would always be guilty of the terrible attack on Carla, and part of Sarah could never forgive him. She thought about his dead mother, about him walking in on his father's shot-gunned corpse, and the compassion flowed.

She arrived at the Portobello at ten, went up to Redford's room and knocked. The door swung open. He stood barefoot, a half-smile on his face.

'Hi. Come on in.'

She stuck her hands in her pockets, sidled past him, avoiding the issue of a more formal, or intimate, hello.

'Thanks for the gardenia,' she said over her shoulder. 'I've put it in my drawing room, by the window so it gets plenty of light. It's filled the whole room with the most delicious scent.'

'Good. I was walking along the King's Road, went into the Chelsea

Gardener, someplace like that, saw it and thought of you.'

Sarah smiled. 'I'm glad it wasn't a cactus.'

'Wasn't my first choice,' said Redford, 'but they were all out of Venus Fly Traps.'

'Ha, Ha.'

Every word closed the distance between them by an inch, and increased the magnitude of Sarah's spying betrayal by a mile.

'So, you ready for a walk?' asked Redford, still grinning.

'Walking?' said Sarah with a jolt, as if he'd invited her to jump from a plane without a parachute.

'Yeah, walking. Like we planned.'

'Seems to be a theme, your walking.'

'It is. Every city I choose someplace that appeals to me, and take a walk.'

'Like where?'

'In Paris I like St Germain, though I didn't do it this time round. Just walk the streets, stop at a bar or a club for a few drinks to soak up the atmosphere. Walking around, you own a place. Always did it – took off by myself, in the day, late at night, see the city as a native does.'

'Why didn't you do Paris this time round?'

'The stalker.'

'Ah. That reminds me, did your head of security turn up? What was his name?' asked Sarah, feigning vagueness.

'Jim O'Cleary,' answered Redford. 'Bastard did turn up, day late, claimed he had some personal emergency he had to sort out.'

Sarah shrugged. 'Everybody has them.'

'He has them too often. I'd have fired his ass if Strone hadn't of stepped in.' He mused for a while. 'Maybe I still will.'

'Not good, having a head of security you don't trust,' observed Sarah.

'Yeah well, guess I'll have to take care of myself.'

Sarah pondered that for a while. 'All this walking around in cities . . . wouldn't you get mobbed, especially without someone like O'Cleary around to protect you?'

'Uh, uh. Mostly I wear a wig, even a bit of make-up occasionally. Don't get recognised, by and large.'

Sarah felt her heart chill. She bent down, pretended to tie her laces, waited until she felt the shock had crept from her face before she straightened up.

'So, where're we going?' she asked.

'Somewhere in the East End. I like all the tiny streets around Smithfield Market, the all-night cafés. I think there might be a few clubs somewhere round there. We could go and get a drink, listen to a band. Think about nothing for a while.'

'Bit sleazy round there, isn't it?' said Sarah, jolted by her own words.

Redford smiled. 'What's wrong with a bit of sleaze? Thought you liked that sort of thing. Uptown girl meets downtown girl.'

'Sleaze can be fine, that doesn't worry me. Could be a bit dangerous, though, wandering round that area late at night.'

'Dangerous? Not when you're with me.'

Sarah turned away, sought refuge in an assortment of guide books and an enlarged *A to Z* of London which littered the sofa.

'D'you know the Spitalfields area?' asked Redford, as Sarah picked up a book.

'Not really.'

'Then allow me to be your guide.' He squatted down by the books, indicating their route. 'We could end up at the Tower of London,' he concluded, 'if we've got the energy. Sound good?'

'Sounds fine, but what about your disguise?'

'Wait there.'

Redford disappeared into the bathroom, giving Sarah time to study the maps and his route, checking for dead-end streets, searching for the nearest police stations. A sound made her look up. Redford had approached silently and was standing over her – at least, she presumed it was Redford. This man had a mousy brown mop, where Redford's hair was sleek and dark. This man had pouches to the sides of his mouth, where Redford's skin was smooth. This man had brown eyes, where Redford had blue.

'It's me,' said the familiar melodious voice.

'Sure as hell doesn't look it. How on earth did you do that?'

'Wig's obvious, contact lenses're obvious, dental pads not so. I've got two lots of pads taped to my gums, gives me a nice jowly look, just like an English gentleman.'

Sarah laughed, despite herself. 'Not like any of the English gentlemen *I* hang out with.'

'Can you bear it? One night of slipping standards?'

'I'll have to, won't I?'

They took a taxi to the City. 'I like to start in the heart of riches, move through, back to the rough places.'

'Like a reverse journey through your life.'

'Yeah, kind of.'

Like walking through one of his songs, thought Sarah, recalling 'Heart of Riches', his song about a lonely boy's walk through life, the orphan's unacknowledged journey.

I want to go back before the start of the game,
Get back what I had of old.
I'll trade success, I'll trade fame,
The heart of riches is cold.

I walk all the old paths,
I sing all the old songs,
I've searched the whole world
Looking for what I had.

Sarah's heart went out to him. She knew too well that routeless search. There was no validation at the end of it. The only sane way was to seek out another path. That path had been given to her. That path was Georgie. Her mind lingered on her son, and the spell of compassion was broken. She was no longer the orphan, but the mother of a child. Inside her jacket pockets her hands clenched around the Mace.

A taxi deposited them in the heart of the City. They walked through the canyons of the temples of Mammon, empty now of human traffic. Sarah looked around. Who would hear her scream in these abandoned streets? The City after ten was a ghost town during the week, let alone the weekend. Was that Redford's design? She glanced across at him. He looked back steadily at her, his gaze filled with unspoken questions.

They walked up Bishopsgate, towards Spitalfields. The East End came to life as they turned into Brick Lane, and Sarah felt herself relax. The air was rich with the sweet, acrid tang of curry, the street-lamps were a glorious Pakistani rococo. They turned down Hanbury Street, reeled into the sudden roar of traffic on Commercial Street, regained peace on Lamb Street. Sarah read the street name and suppressed a sudden shudder as the words came unbidden into her mind; *like a lamb to the slaughter*. She was glad when they saw the portals of the old Spitalfields Market looming up before them, for cries of life rang from the ancient arches. Inside, on fields of Astroturf, a series of games of five-a-side football were taking place.

Redford watched the players with interest, a slight smile on his face. He was loving this, thought Sarah, retreating into his own world, just as she normally did when she walked, but couldn't do tonight. They moved on, past columns of blue-and-white striped awnings set up over rows of tables that would have groaned hours earlier with the weight of fresh fruit for sale. They stopped before a row of shops, eyes drawn to the names.

'Roughneck and Thug,' said Redford with a chuckle. 'What the hell do they sell? C'mon, let's take a look.'

Together they peered into the window that was filled with posters and postcards, concealing whatever lay within. 'Who are these people?' asked Redford, studying the elaborately adorned figures frolicking on the posters.

'Looks like the whole pantheon of the Indian gods,' said Sarah.

'I'm impressed,' said Redford, straightening up.

'Yeah well, don't ask me any more 'cos my knowledge runs out there.'

Restaurants lit with orange-burning oil lamps spilled out customers replete with good food, plentiful wine, and abundant conversation. Sarah felt more conscious than ever of the gulf between her and Redford. There was so much she couldn't say to him and, no doubt, he too had his secrets. What they might be, she didn't want to think. So they walked on, alone in their silence, out of Spitalfields, into the night.

Sarah checked the street names, tried and failed to recall the map in her mind. They walked past an underground car park, the entrance to which was protected by huge iron gates which swung open suddenly as they passed, emitting an enormous, sleek silver Mercedes that purred away, leaving them alone and in silence again, as they walked deeper down Lamb Street.

They passed Spitalfields Crypt. From within a bright light shone, illuminating a ragged procession of people exiting, their hands wrapped tightly round cartons of steaming food, faces smiling. The homeless at their soup kitchen.

They turned into Fournier Street. Sarah gazed up at the elegant facades of a row of Georgian houses.

'This is where the Huguenots came when they fled France,' said Redford suddenly. 'They were master weavers and dyers, they made damasks, brocades and silks, and they used their new-found wealth to build these houses.'

'Now *I'm* impressed,' said Sarah.

'Guide books are a wonderful thing,' he grinned.

As they rejoined Brick Lane, a low haunting cry issued from the mosque on the corner of Fournier Street, a muezzin calling the faithful to late prayer. The sound followed them like a wraith. Sarah stopped abruptly before the window of a Metropolitan police station. The glass was covered with posters, betraying the sad currency of the criminal underworld. There were at least five posters announcing: MURDER. *Can you help*? Or SERIOUS SEXUAL ASSAULT. *Did you witness anything*? TERRORISM. POSTAL BOMBS. BE ALERT. *Do you have any information? Call the incident room.* It was a grim reminder of the nature of the area in which they now walked. This was a long way from Carlyle Square. Redford led them off Brick Lane, into a narrow side street.

'Yes, this is it,' he said softly, almost to himself. Sarah was about to ask him what he meant when her eye was caught by a black Landcruiser approaching at speed.

'Jesus Christ.' Sarah flattened herself against the wall. There was no pavement here, and the road was so narrow there was scarcely room for the Landcruiser, let alone pedestrians. With a squeal of rubber on tarmac, the car slowed, passed them at a crawl. The windows were blacked out, heightening Sarah's sense that she was being watched by hostile forces inside. With a thump of bass beat that would have had the speakers jumping inside, and a sudden roar of acceleration, the car was gone, and they were left alone once more in silence. Sarah glanced around uneasily. The street echoed to their lonely footsteps.

'Did you know Jack the Ripper stalked these streets?' asked Redford, turning to Sarah. 'His first known victim was found here, in Gunthorpe Street.'

'Jesus Christ. Let's get out of here.' Sarah hoped her voice came out level. Show no fear. Her fingers snaked round her can of Mace.

Redford stopped. Sarah braced herself.

'Hey, you all right?' asked Redford, reaching out to touch Sarah's arm.

'Did you hear that?' she asked, stepping back, looking around.

'What?'

'Footsteps,' answered Sarah, seeking any imagined diversion.

'You spooked?' asked Redford.

'Of course I'm bloody spooked. You bring me out here, and start talking about Jack the Ripper.'

Redford looked hard into Sarah's face, as if searching her for the truth. For those moments neither of them moved and Sarah could imagine that anything was possible, so charged were his eyes. The scrutiny ended; Redford's eyes retreated. He turned around.

'Let's go. I'll take you to where you can find a taxi.'

'What's wrong?'

He wheeled round. 'What's wrong?' he snapped. 'Don't pretend. Don't patronise me. You don't trust me, do you? What d'you think I'm going to do to you? Take you out here, rape you? I can see it in your eyes. The dark, lonely streets – something I thought romantic, you think sinister. Trouble is, everything I do will be sinister. You've got me tarred and all you see is black.'

Sarah didn't answer, couldn't answer. Redford spoke the truth. She no longer felt fear, but a great weariness.

Redford started a slow walk. 'Come on, let's get a taxi.'

'You go on,' replied Sarah. 'I'll find my own way. I'm sorry it turned out like this, John.'

'Not half as sorry as I am.'

Chapter Sixty

The taxi finally dropped Sarah in Carlyle Square. Relieved to be once more in her familiar world, she paid off the driver and was walking the steps to her front door when the slam of a car door made her pause. She wheeled around. Dick Breden crossed the street and came at her.

'What the *hell* were you thinking?'

'I tried to ring you. You didn't answer.'

'And you thought leaving some idiotic message on my phone would protect you.'

'Shh,' said Sarah. 'Don't shout.'

'What – you worried I'll wake your baby? Your little baby's lucky to have a mother, even if she is as irresponsible and thoughtless as you.'

Sarah's hand came out like a flick-knife. The air cracked as she slapped Breden's cheek. Tears streamed down her face.

'Don't you even think that. This is hard enough without someone who doesn't have the faintest idea what he's on about sticking his bloody oar in. You're right – I *was* stupid. I shouldn't have done it, don't you think I know that? But I'm home now, and all I want to do is creep upstairs, crouch beside my baby's cot and listen to him breathe.'

She fumbled with her keys and burst sobbing into her house. She leaned against the wall for a few moments, cramming her hand in her mouth to stifle her sobs, until slowly she got herself under control again.

Breden had followed her in. He stood behind her in the hall, his anger washed away by her tears.

He stood waiting for her while she walked upstairs. Georgie was fast asleep, arms thrown out to his sides in confident abandon. A light burned in the hallway. Sarah peeped through the open door of the next bedroom and saw Jacob curled on his side, breathing the slow, rhythmic cadence of deep sleep. Quietly, she unplugged the baby listener from his bedside table and carried it back downstairs.

'Who looks after your baby when you're not here?' asked Breden.

'You think I leave him alone?'

'No, of course I don't.'

Sarah led the way downstairs to the kitchen. Breden followed her. She plugged in the listener, swiped a bottle of whisky off a shelf, opened it and poured out two quadruples.

'My Uncle Jacob looks after Georgie. I'd trust him with my life. I *have* trusted him with my life.'

'Sarah, hold on. It's all right. You don't need to explain yourself to me.'

She gave a mirthless laugh. 'That's exactly what you wanted. Well, you've got your explanation now, so stop judging me. I'm a good mother. I do the best I can. I do what I have to do. It's not easy. It's full of conflicts. You do something, you get sucked into the consequences. I have to do lots of things I don't want to but I have my reasons. *My* reasons, get it?'

'All right, I'm sorry. I was frightened for you. It was fear talking, not judgement, not criticism. I've seen the way you look at your child. I've seen the way he looks at you. It's like a forcefield. It shook me. I've never seen anything like it.'

Sarah smiled. 'You don't know many mothers, then.'

'No. I don't.'

'How long were you waiting?' she asked, gentling now.

'A while.'

'How long would you have waited?'

'As long as it took.'

Sarah gave a sad smile. She wasn't sure what Breden was saying. In another time and place she might have pushed it along, seen where it went, but right now there was no room in her heart.

'What happened tonight?' asked Breden, with an abrupt change of tone, as if he'd read Sarah's mind.

She relayed the night's events to him as he listened in taut silence.

'I thought you could act better than that, cover your tracks.'

'So did I,' replied Sarah, stung.

'You shouldn't put yourself in that position if you don't think you can carry it off.'

'I thought I could.'

'No, you didn't. You were gambling.'

'Shit, maybe I was, but I could normally get away with it.'

'Not with Redford. He gets through to you. It's as if the two of you are bound together somehow.'

'I empathise with his past,' said Sarah quickly, as if she could cover the truth with speed. 'We're both orphans. You don't get much more of a bond than that. Whatever he has or hasn't done, I still feel for that little boy who lost his mother, who walked in on his father's dead body.'

'That empathy makes you vulnerable. He empathises with you too. He cares about you. It matters to him deeply what you think. If he's innocent, you're really putting him through the wringer. If he's guilty, you're lucky you got off so lightly.'

'But he's not innocent, is he?'

'Does one rape make him a rapist?'

'Doesn't it?' asked Sarah. *Did one killing, even though it was in self-defence, make her a murderer*?

'We're not here to ponder that one.'

'Why d'you say I got off lightly? After all, it's not the rapist's modus operandi to attack people he knows. Or at least we're assuming that.'

'If he is guilty, you're getting much too close for comfort. He came near to losing his self-image completely in your eyes. If you think of him as evil, what does he have to lose, if he *is* our rapist? Like I said, he cares deeply about your good opinion. Now he knows he's lost it. And you're the only other person alive, apart from Carla, who knows about the rape. Just you and she stand between him and his good name and a hundred million dollars.'

Sarah wondered how Breden would react if he knew she'd got Redford to commit five million of that to a charity of her choosing. 'What are you saying?' she asked.

'I'm saying that if he *is* guilty, killing you begins to look like a better and better option. He has motive, and tonight he had the opportunity. And what worries me most, he was in disguise. No witnesses, no faces watching from a bedroom window would be able to clock him.'

'So why didn't he try?' asked Sarah, suppressing a shudder.

'Perhaps your ruse about hearing footsteps put him off.'

'Pretty thin ruse.'

'Not if you're contemplating killing someone. And he could, of course, be innocent.'

'But the whole walk, the empty streets, late at night, the disguise, it *sounds* so like the rapist.'

'It does,' replied Breden. 'And I got two new lots of info today which deeply trouble me. Firstly, I was in Lyons until this evening, at Interpol HQ. Before we go ahead with our entrapment, I wanted to make sure I knew as much as I could. I've a friend there, high up, and the only way to prise the facts out of him was to do it face to face. That's why you couldn't reach me.'

Sarah felt a pulse of excitement. 'What did you find out?'

'Details. The guy's right-handed. Smells of lemons, wears rubber gloves, uses a condom—'

'That's considerate,' interrupted Sarah with heavy irony.

'To prevent collection of DNA. The mask covers his hair, he makes damn sure the minimum traces get from him to his victims.'

'What traces have they picked up?'

'Clothing, taxicab seats. Nothing else.'

'He never speaks?'

'No, so we've got no voice, or language.'

Sarah thought for a while. 'He must grunt, sigh, make some sound.'

'None. Completely silent.'

'Incredible control.'

'Of himself. Of his victims. Apparently, he is utterly convincing, totally terrifying. His eyes are "merciless, cold, evil" – I quote. Until after it's over, then he looks desolate.'

'Post-coital tristesse. My heart bleeds. But the silence – that's another thing that points to Redford. The man with the golden voice, known to millions.'

'Do you think his singing voice sounds like his spoken voice?'

Sarah thought for a while, suddenly recalling the night they stayed up together at the Hotel Costes, sitting on the terrace as the moon shone down.

'His spoken voice is even better in some ways, when he's mellow, dreamy. The more time I spend with him, the more I can hear the two voices overlapping, but I suppose at first it might have been difficult to do a blindfold test on them.'

'But the rapist is a perfectionist, obsessed that no detail will give him away. If it *is* Redford, veiling his voice would be essential to his modus operandi.'

'He's like a chess player,' said Sarah. 'Planning every last detail.'

'Or a musician. Writing music is a mathematical skill.'

'Oh, Jesus, it all points to him. Is there no other detail? Nothing we could get him on?'

'Resistance loosens his control, elicits violence. We knew that. But my friend thinks the violence isn't just to control his victim, it's rage that his smoothly orchestrated campaign is being resisted. Guy's a control freak.'

'That's half of London.'

Breden gave a grim smile. 'True.'

'Where does he hide his gloves and mask before and after the attack?'

'No report on that, but the guy usually wears a jacket, so . . .'

'What kind?'

'Sometimes leather, sometimes a Puffa type, sometimes denim.'

'What else does he wear?'

'Jeans, trainers. Your typical urban uniform.'

'Watches, jewellery?'

'No reports of either.'

Sarah stared into space in frustration.

'One thing my friend says mirrors my own personal feeling.'

Sarah looked up, startled by Breden's tone.

'The guy's been raping his way around the world. The Far East, South America, North America, now Europe. The papers haven't picked up on the Far East or South America. I've checked the concert schedule, before you ask, and yes, we have overlap. Back then, nearly a year ago, the rapes were less frequent, perhaps one every three weeks. Now it's down to one a week. The guy is definitely coming apart. He's getting more dangerous by the day. With each rape, he has less to lose. The next step will be getting smaller and smaller in his mind.'

'And what step is that?' asked Sarah dully.

'Murder.'

'Oh great.' She lapsed into silence, wondering if the whole tragic, sorry disaster could get any worse. 'You said there were two things you came up with today. What's the second?'

'Redford's bank account. I've had people going over all the accounts we have access to with a fine-toothed comb. Yesterday a cheque was presented to his bank, made payable to one Carla Parton, for one million dollars.'

'Oh no. He did it,' said Sarah, her voice groaning with agony. 'I can't believe it. He did it.' But she could believe it. Now she had no choice. She felt dazed by a kind of factual vertigo. Evidence against Redford was now towering up all around her.

'Do you want to go on with this?' asked Breden, his voice cutting through her confusion.

She looked up at him, taking a while to focus on his concerned features.

'I don't know. I suppose there's no point unless I think there's a reasonable chance he's innocent. If we know he's guilty, we might just as well hand him over to the police now.'

'We don't know he's guilty yet, Sarah. It doesn't look good for him, but all we have so far is circumstantial evidence. We've no concrete proof.'

'Apart from Carla's word.'

'True, but that was for one rape, not a series.'

'A series of waitresses, after raping his first waitress, Carla. I don't think you can explain that away as coincidence.'

'No, I don't either. If we went to the police, they'd have to mount some sort of sting operation, try to trap him to get the evidence they need. What we have just won't cut it, Sarah.'

Her face took on a grim resolution. 'Then we continue. *We* sting him.'

Breden nodded slowly. He studied Sarah for a while before speaking, as if assuring himself of the certainty of her intent.

'What's the chances of getting close to him tomorrow?' he asked.

Sarah paused, trying to gather herself together. 'Extremely slim. We didn't exactly part on good terms, and anyway, he always goes into a kind of purdah on concert day. Sees no one.'

'I wanted you to swipe him with a tag, just a tiny sticker that gives off a pulse. Makes it easier to tail him.'

'Even if I could get close, he showers after the concert, I assume, and he'd certainly change.'

'Could you see him after the concert?'

'I suppose I could. I could ask Strone for a backstage pass. Then I could show up, congratulate him on the concert, try to clear the air. He should be either on a high, or depressed the performance is over. Either way he's likely to be more receptive.'

'That's if we decide to go that route. Tomorrow's not just concert day, Sarah. Late tomorrow night, or early next morning, is Rape Day. We're counting down. You can step out at any moment, but if you're going to do it, I need to start the clock now.'

Sarah looked out into the night for a long time, then she turned to Breden.

'Start counting.'

Chapter Sixty-one

'OK, we'll start with my staying here. I'll sleep on your sofa if you don't mind.'

'Why?'

'If Redford is our guy, your performance tonight might just have set him off. I don't want him deciding to pay you a nocturnal visit.'

'Jacob's upstairs. I'm not exactly alone.'

Breden paused. 'Your uncle?'

'Yes.'

'And how old is Jacob?'

Sarah looked pained. 'In his seventies.'

'No offence, Sarah, to you or Jacob, but I don't want to take any chances.'

'All right,' she replied slowly. 'But there's no need for you to sleep on the sofa. I have a perfectly good guest room upstairs.'

The night passed quietly. No one tried to break in. If anyone crouched in the bushes in the garden square, gazing at the sleeping house, Sarah was unaware of their sinister vigil. She collapsed into the leaden sleep where the body seems to crash, unable to face the nightly chore of maintenance and repair. She awoke the next morning to her son's happy greetings to another day and lay awhile, listening to him, revelling in the joy of him, before pulling on a wrap and padding through to his room. She gathered him up in her arms to outrageous gurgles of pleasure, changed him, and carried him downstairs. On the way she checked on Breden, whose door was ajar. The private eye was prone on the floor, doing some kind of static press-up, wearing nothing but a pair of boxer shorts. After an impressively long time he collapsed, groaning. He recovered for a moment then pushed himself to his feet.

'Not bad,' observed Sarah.

'The plank,' he explained. 'Form of torture.' He walked across to them. 'Morning, Georgie. How are you, little one? Sleep well?'

'Yes, thank you. He did,' said Sarah. 'And thanks to him, his mama did too.'

'I'm glad you did.'

'You didn't?'

'No. Too much to think about.'

'Well, I won't think about it now. Not with Georgie in my arms,' said Sarah fiercely. 'He picks everything up like a little sponge. I don't want him to feel Mama's fear.'

'Fine,' said Breden, raising a hand in surrender. He lowered the hand, and tagged Georgie's bare feet. Sarah watched him run his fingers over the tiny, perfectly formed toes, saw the awe in his eyes, felt tears spring to hers.

'Who's this then?'

They spun round at the crusty voice. Jacob stood wrapped in a thick tartan robe, arms crossed defensively.

'Jacob, this is Dick Breden. He came to discuss the case last night. We stayed up much later than we planned and he stayed.' Sarah felt the need to gesture at the guest room. To her equal amusement and disquiet, she felt sixteen again.

'Hmm.' Jacob eyed Breden's boxer shorts with distaste. 'Right then. Whatever you say. I'll just get dressed and take over your boy. If your case kept you up half the night, I dare say you'd best be getting on with it.' He turned with one last, warning look at Breden and slammed the door to his bedroom.

'My uncle. He pretty much brought me up,' Sarah said, eyes on the slammed door. 'Bark's worse than his bite.'

Breden shrugged. 'He's just protecting you. I'd do the same in his shoes.'

'Don't, whatever you do, let on about the trap. He'd go loco.'

Breden looked as if he'd like to go loco too. 'I can imagine.'

Sarah dressed Georgie, handed him over to Jacob and quickly dressed herself.

'Bye, my boys.' She kissed Georgie and Jacob. The old man melted slightly as Sarah squeezed his hand and gave him a reassuring look.

They took a corner table at Oriel in Sloane Square, and ordered. Brown toast and black coffee for Breden, a full cooked breakfast for Sarah.

'You always eat like that?' asked Breden.

Sarah nodded.

'How the hell d'you stay so slim?'

'Nerves, and breastfeeding, but I'm not exactly slim at the moment.'

Breden skimmed his eyes up and down her, the look of admiration unmissable and shook his head.

'I still find it amazing that Sarah Jensen is a mother.'

'Why? What's so unnatural about that?'

'Nothing in the world,' said Breden, with a touch of wistfulness. 'Seeing you with him, it seems so obvious.'

'It is.'

'You really love him.'

'With all my heart. Unconditionally and for ever.'

'Lucky boy.' Breden got to his feet, walked to the bar and came back with two newspapers. He handed *The Times* to Sarah, kept the *Telegraph* for himself.

'D'you mind?' he asked, nodding at the papers. 'Old habits die hard. If I don't read the papers at breakfast, I never do.'

'Be my guest. You're a paper and breakfast man, why not admit it?'

'Ever met a guy who isn't?'

She thought of John Redford. She picked up the paper and read. Their breakfasts were delivered by a waitress with a pierced nose who gazed with hungry eyes at Dick Breden as she laid down his plate with a flourish. Breden thanked her absently, and she repaid Sarah, the presumed cause of his indifference, with a, 'Here's yours, luv,' and a crash of china upon marble. Sarah flinched and, glancing at Breden, blinkers removed for a moment, saw all too easily what the waitress saw. A good-looking man in his forties, an oasis of strength, someone who would hold you through your nightmares and solve all your problems. She laughed out loud.

Breden looked at her in surprise. 'What?'

Sarah wiped the mirth from her face. 'Nothing, just fairytales and dragons.'

Breden stared at her, bemused, then applied himself to scraping the thinnest layer of butter on his brown toast.

For a while they ate and read in companionable silence. Suddenly Sarah slammed down the paper.

'Shit!'

'What?' asked Breden.

Sarah read out loud: ' "The menace of stalking grows. It is rumoured that a major pop star is currently the victim of an allegedly deranged stalker," writes Roddy Clark. "The star, at the peak of his profession after many years of success, has reportedly been stalked for the past few months, but refuses to increase his personal security. Sources indicate however, that he believes his life to be in danger and has modified his behaviour. However, public exposure is the oxygen on which all performers must live, and the musician in question is one of the world's biggest touring attractions, regularly drawing hundreds of thousands of fans to his concerts. The police deny any knowledge of the stalking, but it is believed that the rock star does not wish to inform them. The most famous musician to be stalked was of course John Lennon. The former Beatle was gunned down outside the entrance to his . . ." ' Sarah interrupted herself. 'We know the rest of *that* story. Dammitalltohell!'

Breden looked grave. 'Who knew? You, me, Savage, Zamaroh, and Carla. Anyone else?'

'You're aware of what happened with Jeremy St James?'

'Of course. But he couldn't have heard of the stalker unless one of the inner circle leaked. He'd certainly have the incentive to leak after Zaha fired him.'

'Publicly eviscerated him, you mean. Yes, he had the motive all right, but, as you say, there's no reason why he would have known in the first place.'

'Who then?' asked Breden.

Savage's wife. She could have told Lover Boy, and Lover Boy, perhaps in an act of vengeance against Savage, could have sought out Clark, whom he knew was on his own Goldsteins vendetta, and fed him the story. But Sarah said nothing.

'The secret Leaker again?' asked Breden.

She gave the slightest nod.

'You know this really pisses me off,' said Breden angrily.

'I know,' said Sarah, 'and I'm sorry, but I still can't say anything. If you knew you'd understand why, so please, let's just drop it.'

'This person no longer works for Goldsteins, I take it? They're in no position to do any more harm?' asked Breden.

'Right on both counts,' replied Sarah, praying she was correct.

Breden threw up his hands as if in surrender. 'All right, all right. I get the message. Let's put aside who leaked and look at what the effect of the leak will be. If Redford *is* our rapist,' he continued, 'this will make him decompensate more. The spotlight will really be on him now. His secret's in danger of unravelling. He's got less to lose. He could decide to try to eliminate the loose ends, you and Carla, or he could just decide it's all too difficult, subconsciously wish to be caught.' Breden paused to assess the effect of his words on Sarah. She gazed back, resolutely.

'My advice,' said Breden, 'is back out now.'

Sarah shook her head. 'This is our one chance to get him. We've got to have our answer now.'

'Or what? The deal falls apart. Is that the end of the world?'

'It is for Redford, and if he's innocent he just doesn't deserve that. We're only suspecting him because of Carla. We've got to give him a chance.' The five million flashed through her mind. She knew it was colouring her reason, could not blank it out. For that reason alone, she should disqualify herself.

'We go ahead, Dick. The sooner we set the trap, the sooner we catch the rapist, the sooner we stop him claiming any more victims. If it is Redford. That's my last word.' She *had* to know if the father of her child was a serial rapist.

'It could be one of your last words, Sarah. If your plan was dangerous before, it's suicidal now.'

Chapter Sixty-two

Dick Breden lived in Battersea, just over the Albert Bridge, in the penthouse of a glass, metal and concrete block six stories high. At any other time, Sarah would have indulged her curiosity and wandered around this ascetic temple to minimalism, but she could already feel the tunnel-vision kicking in. Analysing Breden, the man he appeared to be, versus the man he was, would have to wait. John Redford and the trap became Sarah's focal point. But agonisingly, she had first to keep Savage and Zamaroh at bay. Breden handed her a phone. They both spent the next two hours trading calls with Zamaroh and Savage, arguing their case. Both had to maintain it was impossible for them to come into the office. Both received severe flak from Savage and Zamaroh. When they reconvened, they looked slightly battered.

'Could have done without that,' said Breden. 'They both complained vehemently that neither of their top security people were available, that it just wasn't good enough.'

'Yeah, I got the same theme tune too,' said Sarah ruefully.

'Now we forget them,' said Breden. 'Let's get to work. We start focusing on our operation. Nothing else gets in the way, OK?'

Sarah welcomed the steel in his eyes which belied the gentle tone of his voice.

'OK.'

Breden's drawing room was perfect. Huge and bare, save sofas and a glass table, which he pushed to the windows. He explained what he was going to do, then in three easy strides, he moved in and threw Sarah across the room. She did her best to roll on the mattress he'd pulled from his bed, but came up bruised and hurting.

'All right?' asked Breden, concerned.

'I'll live.'

'See how easy it is.'

'For you. With all your training.'

'How d'you know the rapist doesn't have training? Besides, it's not difficult for a man to throw a woman, Sarah; that's not training, just superior weight and power. I'm going to show you something that'll help you put him down – three quick moves you can practise on me.'

Breden drilled Sarah for an hour, leaving her smiling through the rivulets of sweat that ran down her face. She fought free of his arms, striking as he'd shown her, writhing for freedom if she got it wrong and he tightened his grip in punishment. So close she could smell him. Jesus, what was she doing? She pulled herself up. Redford had reawakened her sexuality; she felt suddenly like a hunting animal. The better to trap him, she thought with a pang.

'Only use the moves if you have no choice,' cautioned Breden, holding Sarah's wrists, keeping her from hurting him, 'and then use them with extreme aggression. You can't go in pussyfooting.' He hid a smile of his own; he couldn't imagine Sarah pussyfooting around anything.

'I've got eight men assembled for the back-up team,' he went on, letting her go. 'This is what we're going to do.'

'What's all this going to cost?' asked Sarah, when Breden had finished recounting his plan. 'An eight man back-up team, and you. It'll cost a fortune.'

'It will, I'm afraid,' he nodded. 'I'm not going to charge you anything, but I'll have to pay the other guys. It depends what happens, how long the whole thing takes, but you won't get much change from four grand.'

Sarah grimaced. 'Hopefully Savage'll pay me soon.'

'Since it would appear you caught his Leaker for him, I'd imagine he owes you big time.'

Sarah smiled awkwardly.

Breden left at lunchtime to mastermind the operation from his office. Sarah stayed at his flat. She couldn't go home. Jacob and Georgie would pick up her nerves, she'd frighten them, and they'd distract her. She felt a new ruthlessness come over her, for their sake, and for that of the women who had been violated.

She rang Strone. 'Hi, it's Sarah. Look, could I have a backstage pass for tonight?'

Strone sounded harried and angry, but promised to leave one at

Reception in the Portobello. Sarah hung up and paced around Breden's flat, trying to lose the tension that was breeding in her like an infection. She forced herself to eat a large lunch of pasta with a basil and tomato sauce from his well-stocked kitchen, knowing that she needed to store away as much energy as possible. Extreme stress always exhausted her and she hadn't slept much the night before. After lunch she took herself off to the guest bedroom to try to steal a couple of hours' sleep.

She woke feverish and sweating in the midst of a nightmare. The echoes of a sound seemed to reverberate around the bedroom. It sounded like a scream, or a shout. It was her own voice, she realised, calling out in terror. She pushed herself out of bed, more exhausted than when she had climbed in. The alarm clock showed six o'clock. Shit, she'd slept far longer than she'd meant to, must have slept through the alarm she'd set for four-thirty. She stood under a hot shower for five minutes then turned it to cold for one long blast. Adrenaline switching through her body, she towelled herself dry, dressed and took a taxi home.

Jacob was bathing Georgie. Both of them were mercifully distracted. She ducked her head round the corner of the door, blew kisses at them both.

'Hello, you gorgeous little beast, and you lovely big old thing. Can't stop, I've literally got to change and run out again. I'll be back late, Jacob, so don't wait up.'

With a steadying arm round Georgie's back, the old man looked up at her with questioning eyes. Sarah was all too aware that he knew she was concealing something. She crossed the room in two fast paces, kissed his cheek, stroked her baby's head, then hurried out. 'Got to go. Late already.'

Seeking sanctuary in her bedroom, she closed the door behind her, and sank back against it, still seeing two sets of concerned eyes scrutinising her: her child's infant, but sometimes seemingly ancient, regard; her uncle's look of troubled love. Quick, she had to get out of here before she threw it all in. She paused for one more moment, sipping at the idea of abandoning it all, locking herself in here with the two of her three loves. Only her brother was outside her orbit. She knew this for a lie as soon as she thought it.

There were four men she loved. Redford had infected her with his love, that was how she saw it. She wanted to hate him, or at least rise above him to the plateau of indifference, but still she felt the tumult of love for him, still her temperature rose when she came face to face with him, and when she remembered their love-making she felt herself burn. She was in thrall to him, tormented by love and doubts, her passionate love for her son cementing something that should have been eroded long ago by all the blows inflicted; absence, suspicion, betrayal, Carla, and who else on his list of victims? She had betrayed him by spying on him, and now, if he was innocent, she had the chance to make it right. If he was guilty, she could be rid of him, and retreat to a life over which she had control, just her and Georgie.

She moved away from the door and paused before her wardrobe, fingered through the velvets and silks like a woman casting charms, and made up her mind. Part of her wanted to wear comfort clothes, old jeans, a sweatshirt and trainers, another part wanted to dress as if she were attending her own funeral, a final fling, a last dazzling dance. She picked out a red and salmon-coloured silk and velvet dress, long, figure-hugging, low-cut, and high, red, strappy sandals. She piled her hair on her head, applied full make-up, finished off with a blast of Fracas. She surveyed herself in the mirror, one final glance, then set off without a goodbye.

Chapter Sixty-three

Sarah sat alone in her VIP box at Wembley Arena, looking down at the stage. She longed for a cigarette, cursed herself for ever thinking she could do without them. She bit at her nails, and waited for Redford to appear.

John Redford stalked onto the stage like the pro he was. Blue denim, the loose-limbed walk, fluid and powerful and infinitely sexy. She remembered his hands on her body and shuddered. He had been all tenderness, violence subdued, but still near, dizzyingly, excitingly near. He launched into the first of a whole string of rocking anthems; his voice, so rich and powerful, vibrated through her. She could see him working the crowd into its inevitable frenzy, but before the audience lost control, he switched to a ballad, a new song, just him and his guitar, no backing. The spotlight shone on him alone; he looked into the crowd, and although it would have been impossible to pick her out, unless he knew exactly where she was sitting, she could have sworn he was looking directly at her. He strummed up the intro, then began to sing.

'One dark night,
One sin, without redemption,
Body and soul broken
Time bomb set.

What do I have to do to say sorry?
Aren't we all allowed just one mistake?
God only knows I'd give everything I own,
To take it back, but not even God can do that.

I see only suspicion
In your eyes,

You are my judge
And you'd hang me out to dry.

What do I have to do to say sorry?
Aren't we all allowed just one mistake?
God only knows I'd give everything I own.
To take it back, but not even God can do that.

Is there another road
We can go down?
Or have we come to
The end?'

The audience stayed silent after the last chords of the song had died with the echoes of Redford's voice. Then the applause started, a small wave that grew into an ocean. The audience knew this was some kind of testament, with all of them as witnesses, and they were on his side.

Redford took his bow.

'Thank you. That was my "Song for Sarah".'

John Redford sat alone in his dressing room. Sarah entered with a knock. He wheeled round at the sound of her voice.

'Hello, Sarah.'

'Hello, John.'

There was peace in his eyes, as if he had come to some kind of personal exorcism.

'Your song was beautiful.'

'Thank you. A bit out of date now, but what the hell, it's a nice tune.'

Sarah looked at him in puzzlement. 'What d' you mean?'

He shook his head. 'Doesn't matter.' He shrugged, and Sarah was struck by how often the most painful words were said in a way or setting which was banal. Perhaps that was how we kept our sanity.

'Strone said you wanted to see me,' continued Redford in his monotone. 'Why?'

'To say goodbye,' said Sarah.

'Ah.'

'And to wish you luck.' She opened her arms. He looked at her for a few moments, his face unreadable, before he stood up and went to her. She had the electronic tag on the tip of her index finger; she pressed it to the underside of the collar of his denim shirt as Redford hugged her to him.

'Goodbye, Sarah. You know, I had hopes for us.'

Sarah hugged him hard. She drew back, holding his arms. 'I wouldn't have been good for you.'

'You can't know that.'

'Oh yes, I can.'

She let go, kissed his cheek, and left before he saw the tears teeming down her cheeks.

Chapter Sixty-four

Sarah found Breden's van parked exactly where he'd said it would be. She took great comfort from this. Breden was a man who would run his side like clockwork. He had no choice, as he'd put it. Her life was at stake.

The rear door opened as she approached. Awkward in her tight dress and high heels, she clambered in. Breden's eyes widened fractionally.

'You look beautiful.'

'Thank you.'

'Why so desolate?'

'I just said goodbye to Redford. I put the tag on him as he was hugging me. He wrote and sang a song for me, Dick, asking my forgiveness, asking if it was the end. It frightened me. He was acting as if he'd made his mind up about something.'

'About what?'

'I don't know.' She hesitated, unwilling to voice her fears. 'It was like he'd come to his own end. When I walked into his dressing room I wasn't intending to say goodbye, it just came out. I felt like it was goodbye.'

'Maybe we should forget this whole thing. You can back out even now, Sarah.'

'No, I can't. Let's see it through.'

Breden gave Sarah an outfit that a waitress might wear, a short white starched coat. She wore it with beige tights and her own high heels. A gnarled, Oriental make-up artist worked on her face and hair. He didn't say a word, just tilted her head this way and that, fingers surprisingly soft and strong. When he had finished, Sarah, under a blonde wig, was transformed into a trampy vamp.

Breden studied her. He nodded at the make-up artist. 'Good job. See you round.'

The man nodded back, then turned slowly to Sarah. Before, when he had studied her face, it was with a professional's eye; she had been nothing more than a mannequin. Now his sombre regard frightened her. He bowed to her, then opened the rear door of the van and jumped out, landing on silent feet.

'I hope we don't have to wait long,' said Sarah as the door slammed shut with a thump.

Breden nodded. 'That's the worst bit, the waiting. That's what undoes people. Greatly underestimated talent.'

'Waiting?'

'Lying still as a log, peeing into your camouflages, throat tickling, gagging for a cough or a sneeze.'

'At least I don't have to stay silent.' Sarah looked round in alarm. 'What do I do if I want to pee?'

Breden reached under his seat and pulled out a bowl. Sarah burst out laughing.

'Can you manage?' he asked.

'You're talking to a woman who can pee standing up. Yeah, I'll manage.'

There was a tapping on the darkened window separating the back of the van from the front. Breden slid it back.

'On the move,' said a voice from the front seat. Sarah caught a glimpse of dark curly hair, tanned skin. 'Moving steadily, walking, probably heading for his car.' Breden peered through the gap at a monitor. Sarah saw a small white dot pulsing, and moving north. Breden checked a tiny earpiece in his ear, and spoke into a small mike attached to his shirt collar.

'Got movement, two?' he asked. 'Good. Stay ready.' He repeated his question twice more.

'How many vehicles have we got?' asked Sarah.

'Four including this one, two men in each.'

The white dot stopped.

'About to move?' asked Breden into his mouthpiece. 'I'm guessing he's just got into his car.'

The dot suddenly began to move again, faster now, going south this time. Breden watched the movement. 'Strap yourself in,' he said to Sarah. She did so, then craned forward, watching the dot.

'He's coming toward us,' said Breden. 'Number two will take him, repeat, number two will take him. Three, get behind me, four, try to get ahead of him.' As the dot came closer, the curly-haired man started up the engine, as the dot turned abruptly right, he got into gear and slid out into the traffic.

'Anyone got visual?' asked Breden. 'Number four? Good. What's his vehicle? Got a driver? Anyone else with him?' He listened then turned to Sarah.

'He's in a Range Rover, blacked-out windows. There seem to be two of them in there, he's probably got a driver. My guys can't see Redford, but he's in there.'

'A driver would complicate things,' said Sarah.

'He'll probably drop Redford off somewhere. If he is our rapist, he'll want to be dropped some way from his chosen hunting ground, unless the driver's an accomplice.'

'That'd be a twist. I can't imagine he'd risk letting anyone else in on his secret.'

'Neither can I. My guess is the driver'll drop him off, and he'll walk.'

'He loves to walk the city at night,' said Sarah. 'He told me so. He could go miles.'

'Then we'll have to be ready to do the same.' Breden spoke into his mike. 'Be ready to devehicle. Target might go on a long ramble.'

'And he might be wearing his disguise,' Sarah added. 'He hates to be recognised at the best of times.'

'Sandy, wavy wig, jaw-length, and jowls?' checked Breden. Sarah nodded.

'Target might be in disguise, as discussed,' Breden intoned into his mike. 'Could be sandy wig, jowly, could be anything.'

Sarah tried to imagine what Redford might be feeling. Had he stripped off the personality she knew, exposed a hidden, putrefying side? She couldn't imagine it, but knew well enough there was no comfort in that. If rapists, child molesters and killers were so easy to spot, their neighbours would turn them in. The most successful criminals were the best dissemblers. And Redford was nothing if not a performer. He knew what people wanted, and he gave it to them. Sarah shuddered.

They drove along Harrow Road, heading south-east, on to Western Avenue, over the Westway, at speed. Sarah gazed out of the darkened windows, listening to Breden crooning into his mike, a low drawl.

'Number four, slip back, number two, take up advance position.' Marylebone, Euston, King's Cross. Nice and seedy. She saw the hookers eyeing their car, food for their crack habits. The white dot stopped. They stopped. Sarah eyed the screen.

'Number two, got visual?' asked Breden. He listened intently. 'Passenger two, devehicle. Go after him on foot. Car two, stay with his car. All passengers, devehicle, follow on foot with your hand monitors. Drivers three and four, move forward at intervals, don't let him get more than a quarter of a mile from you.'

Breden turned to Sarah. 'He's on foot.'

'What happens now?' She picked at her fingernails, eyes flickering over his face.

'You and I follow by car, till we get a better handle on what he's up to. As far as we know, all the rapist's victims have been waitresses or cooks, working in late-night joints. My guess is, he'll walk until he finds somewhere suitable, then he'll go into hiding. It's when he stops moving we have to be ready.'

Sarah nodded, her stomach sick. They parked, waited. The dot moved on, along Pentonville Road. Breden's eyes flickered in silent calculation as he listened to the voices murmuring into his earpiece.

'There's two of them,' he said to Sarah. 'Redford and another guy – at least, they think it's Redford. He's wearing a leather jacket with the collar turned up, and a baseball cap.'

'Anyone made a definite ID?' asked Sarah.

Breden shook his head. 'They don't want to get too close. The rapist is highly intelligent, our assessment is that he'd spot any clumsy surveillance. We have to hang back. We don't get closer than eighty feet, and we can't be sure from there. The guys have binoculars, but they have to be careful not to be clocked using them; that would wreck the whole thing at one stroke.'

Breden turned alert again, listening to his earpiece. 'He's turned onto City Road. There's still two of them.'

'Any idea who the other guy is?' asked Sarah.

'Around six foot, medium build, white, baseball cap, baggy jacket, trainers.'

Sarah shook her head. 'Don't know him.'

'Let's get closer,' Breden said to the driver.

Sarah stared out of the window as their car started up. They drove to

City Road, turned off and parked in a side street. Sarah checked the name and laughed.

'What's up?' asked Breden.

Sarah nodded at the street sign. 'Micawber Street. As in Mr Micawber, therefore something must turn up. I always thought the gods had a sense of irony. They're obviously ready for some sport this evening.'

Breden returned her wry look, wondering at her gallows humour. In a strange way, she reminded him of his soldiers, joking their way to death before an op.

Sarah gazed out of the window at a street of pretty Georgian houses, uncomfortable neighbours with a harsh yuppie development, the lamp-lit, speed-bumped tarmac, the soulless council houses decamped a little way back from the road, and the bleak warehouses on neighbouring Taplow Street; an urban wasteland of anonymity and bleak functionality. She felt the tentacles of exhaustion begin to wind themselves around her. Only adrenaline kept her awake.

The dot moved on relentlessly, down Great Eastern Street. Redford had been walking over forty minutes now.

'He's heading for Spitalfields,' said Sarah in horror. 'Maybe last night was just a recce.'

'Would he risk taking you to a future crime scene?' asked Breden.

'Maybe he really does want to be caught.' Sarah and Breden stared at the flashing dot, as its bearer turned into Commercial Street and on into Grey Eagle Street. Then it stopped.

'Who's got visual?' Breden asked sharply. 'Number two, what's happening?' He turned back to Sarah. 'Redford and his friend have gone into a bar. Let's go,' he said to the driver. He took Sarah's hand. 'You ready for this?'

She nodded. He handed her an earpiece, and fixed a microphone to her collar. 'Remember, I'm number five, you're number one. All working?'

Sarah pushed in her earpiece, spoke and listened. 'This is number one. You all hear me?' A chorus of voices answered *Yes.*

Breden traced his finger over Sarah's face. 'Your disguise is good. He won't clock you until he's on top of you, as it were. Don't speak to him until I get to you. I don't want him recognising your voice and bolting.' Or killing you, he thought to himself.

'Silent as the grave,' said Sarah, managing a smile.

Breden suddenly hugged her. 'Good luck.'

Sarah hugged him back. 'Thanks.' She thought he was bound to feel her heart pounding, as if it had doubled in size. He would sense her terror, hold her back, abort the whole thing, but he just released her.

'You call for me, I'll be there in a sprint. In an emergency, call Mayday. Keep up a running commentary, keep your mouth as immobile as you can. Speak softly. The mikes are so sensitive they'll broadcast your breathing.'

The van parked on Grey Eagle Street, a long, empty corridor of urban decay. Sarah and Breden slipped out. It was 1 a.m. The street-lights glowed orange; falling rain cast a miasma round the light. The bar was called The Fallen Angel. They skirted around until they found the back entrance. Breden led Sarah in.

A man with a ponytail blocked their way. 'What's your game?' he asked, hard-voiced.

'Who am I talking to?' asked Breden.

'I'm the soddin' owner. Who the fuck are *you*?'

'Police,' replied Breden. 'I'm going to reach in my pocket and show you, OK?'

The man flicked his head in a dismissive nod. Breden produced a laminated police pass, stating that he was Detective Inspector Dick Evans of the Metropolitan Police. The owner took the pass and studied it with an unimpressed air.

'What d'you want?'

'We want to use your premises for surveillance. We'd like to wait somewhere quiet then, we're not sure when, we'll need to have my Constable here,' he nodded at Sarah, 'show her face in the bar, just for a minute. We'll want you to speak to her, say, "Good night," act as if she's your new, temporary short-order cook, just covering for one night as a favour.'

The man's gaze flickered from Sarah to Breden. 'Don't look like a cook to me.'

Sarah gave him a tight smile.

'She's a cook,' said Breden tightly. 'Play along.'

The man raised his eyebrows. 'Why should I?'

Breden looked at him for a few moments before answering. 'Never needed any favours?'

'Don't we all.'

'Well, let's call it earning some credit, then.'

The owner nodded slowly, as if weighing up his different options, taking his time, saving his face.

'You owe me then.'

'I owe you. But only if you don't mess up.'

'And how would I do that?'

'You won't if you do what I say.'

The owner seemed to think he'd done enough posturing because he suddenly became more businesslike.

'Better come to my office.'

'Just the Constable,' said Breden. 'I'll hang round out here.'

'Please yourself.'

Sarah turned, took one last look at Breden, and followed the owner into The Fallen Angel.

Chapter Sixty-five

The place reeked of smoke, piss and fried onions. A juke box played rock, something by Bon Jovi: 'You Give Love a Bad Name'. Yeah, right, thought Sarah. The owner led her up some rickety back stairs. Her legs trembled as she climbed. The man took a key from his pocket and unlocked his office. He opened the door, stood back, gestured to Sarah to go in.

'Thanks.' She took a seat on a battered sofa. The owner walked in after her.

'So what happens now?' he asked.

'You leave me here alone, get on with your own business, and wait for the Detective Inspector's instructions.'

'That simple?'

Sarah nodded. 'That simple.' Just leave, please. Just leave, she prayed. As if reading her thoughts, the man ambled slowly back across the room. With a quick glance around, as if checking his inventory, he walked out wordlessly. Sarah bolted the door behind him, spied a bottle of whisky and a glass on his desk, poured herself a double, then slumped back into the sofa. She stared into the glass as if at some magic potion. *Giver of Dutch courage, don't fail me now.* She sipped it slowly, letting it burn its way down her throat, imagining Redford in the bar downstairs. The voices chattered away in her ear.

'Number three here,' said a soft Irish brogue. 'I'm with number four, in the bar. We've got visual. Two men at the bar, one of them is the one tagged, but he's not Redford.'

'*What*?' Breden's voice rasped into her ear.

'Hang on,' cried Sarah. 'What's he look like?'

'Five ten, eleven maybe, dark wavy hair, brown eyes.'

'Jowly?'

'Yeah. Hi, my friend – sorry, am I in your way?' Sarah heard the scraping of chairs, a responding voice, then the slurping of a drink and the munching of crisps.

'Sorry 'bout that, someone came a bit close. Jowly, yeah, he's heavy round the mouth, I'd say jowly.'

'That's Redford,' whispered Sarah. 'It's his disguise, just like last night. Different wig, that's all.' She picked up her whisky glass. It was empty. She put it, unseeing, on the edge of the small side table. It toppled to the floor and smashed.

'What was that?' said Breden sharply.

'Dropped a glass,' said Sarah. 'Everything's fine. What's the other guy look like?'

'Same height as Redford. Baseball cap, straggly blond hair, smoking.'

'Know him?' asked Breden.

'Nope,' replied Sarah. 'What're they drinking?'

'The blond straggly one's drinking a short, looks like whisky,' said number three. 'Other one's drinking a pint of something white and fizzy, could be water, could be lemonade. Eating crisps. Looks ravenous.'

'I'm sure it's Redford,' said Sarah. 'He's always thirsty and starving after a concert.'

'Has to be him,' said Breden. 'Unless he gave his denim shirt away.'

'Yeah, that's likely, isn't it?' said Sarah sarcastically. 'And gave it to someone who came to exactly the same place he did the night before? No,' she muttered. 'It's Redford. I'm sure of it.'

'Bloody good disguise,' said number three.

'He's got access to the best make-up artists in the world,' said Sarah. 'It's no problem for him. Besides, he almost had me fooled last night.'

The voices lapsed into silence. Sarah lay back, her breathing shallow. Perhaps nothing would happen. Perhaps Redford would get in the car and go home. She lost herself in her reverie and jumped when number three's soft Irish brogue spoke low and rapidly into her ear.

'Unidentified man is off to the Gents. I think they're gonna move soon. Repeat, looks like they're gonna move.'

'Right,' came Breden's voice. 'Number one, be ready. I'm going in.'

Sarah flinched. She heard footsteps, then a door opening and closing, then Breden speaking to the owner. 'I'm going to go and get my Constable.

Here's fifty quid. Give it to her, say thanks for her cooking, for helping out, all low key, don't overdo it.'

'Not my style,' replied the man laconically.

Sarah heard footsteps, then a knock on the door.

'Open up, it's me.'

She opened the door to Breden.

'All right?'

She nodded, her throat dry.

'Off you go. Good luck.'

She gave him one last glance, then walked down the stairs to the hallway where the owner was waiting. She felt as if her legs would buckle. Her whole body trembled, and sweat coursed down her back.

The owner set off towards the bar. He opened the door and strode in. Sarah held the door, partly concealing her face, peeking round the edge. The owner muttered as he walked up to the till. He counted out five tens and handed them over to Sarah.

'Fifty quid for a short-order cook. Bloody rip-off merchant.'

'Oh, spare me,' said Sarah, in somebody else's voice. The two men pulling on their jackets at the bar swung round to follow the voice. Sarah looked for just long enough to register Redford's eyes on hers, before glancing away, as if shy, or just flirtatious. She stared at her feet. She dared not look again and check out the other man. She made a quick show of counting and pocketing her cash, mumbled goodbye to the owner, and walked to the door. She let the door slam behind her. Then she set off slowly.

'Walking north up Grey Eagle Street,' she whispered to the surveillance team. God, it was bleak. The cracking tarmac was strewn with litter. High concrete walls, corrugated iron tinted nuclear-orange by the pall of the few street-lights that hadn't been smashed. A break in the iron curtain exposed tumbledown flats, long since evacuated by anyone with either sense or choice. But still there was the detritus of human visits, a broken chair, beer cans, it had the air of occupation. Squatters would choose somewhere better. This had to be a crack house. Sarah moved on quickly.

'They're leaving the bar,' said number three. She heard a door slam, resisted the urge to turn around. 'They're watching you, number one, the both of them,' said a different voice in her ear. She walked on, slow on her high heels. 'They're talking, looking round. Wait, a car's coming up, looks like a mini-cab. Car's stopped, target's approaching, talking to the driver. He's getting in. Repeat, target getting in car. Red Volvo estate. Reg number CST 45P. Repeat, red Volvo estate. Reg number CST 45P. Target's car's pulling away, going north along Grey Eagle.'

'Numbers two, three and four, take up pursuit of car. Repeat, take up pursuit of car,' commanded Breden. 'Number one, stay cool. Keep walking.'

Sarah braced herself as she heard the car approach. 'Car approaching me, changing gear, he's accelerating,' she glanced at the car, saw Redford looking out, straight at her. Christ, the eyes were like a flash of lasers. Did he recognise her? 'He's passing, turning right fifty yards ahead of me,' she continued, voice strung tight. 'I can still hear the car, going away, getting fainter,' she said, relief and confusion sweeping over her.

'Target car going east on Cheshire Street,' said a voice.

'Number four, get ahead of target,' said Breden. 'Number three, take up the rear, stay out of sight. Anyone with visual?'

'I got a glimpse,' answered a Welsh accent. 'Pakistani driver, target in back.'

'What happens now?' asked Sarah.

'Go left into Quaker Street,' replied Breden, 'then take another left into Commercial Street. Walk down to the junction with Hanbury Street. I'll be there waiting for you.'

'On my way,' said Sarah.

Chapter Sixty-six

She walked awkwardly in her high heels, nearly slipping on the rough streets. Christ, what a way to spend the night! Now that the drama was over and the danger had passed, she felt an overwhelming weariness, as well as confusion. What had gone wrong? Why had Redford gone off? Perhaps he was seeking out other hunting grounds. Maybe he was innocent, after all. But then who was the rapist, if not him?

She turned into Quaker Street. Jesus Christ. Away from The Fallen Angel, polluted by the noise of the traffic on Commercial Street, the silence descended like fog. She could hear her own footsteps, but no one, she realised, would hear her scream. She didn't think it was possible for the urban landscape to get worse, but this was the stuff of nightmares. An empty road ran alongside a railway siding. High mesh wiring prevented any vandalism, or perhaps it was to foil any suicides on the track. An empty car park lay strewn with rubbish; dim lights from station arches across the track cast a pall over pock-marked concrete. Desolate yards full of scrap were illuminated briefly as a red BMW roared past, pulsing with music. It was a good place to score drugs, for those who want it, Sarah thought. For a moment she feared the car would slam on its brakes and stop, but it carried on as if oblivious to her. She felt herself holding her breath until the car disappeared from sight, then she walked on, now totally alone.

Something made her stop, a strange, squishing sound. She listened, her heart suddenly pounding. It was the sound of footsteps, of trainers on the wet street, getting closer. She began to move, faster in her high heels. The junction with Commercial Street was a mere fifty yards away now, and she willed herself closer to it. She wanted to run, she had an overwhelming urge to run. *Stay calm, it's just someone on their way home, Redford's gone*, she told herself. She listened to the voices in her ear, keeping up their commentary. Redford was now on Great Eastern Street, heading west. She was nearly at the junction, just another twenty yards, when suddenly there was a rush of sound behind her. She wheeled round; a man was running at her full pelt.

A scream ripped from her. '*Nooooooo!*' She began to run. The man was closing, she tried to run faster, the voices shouted urgently in her ear.

Breden's voice, 'Where are you, number one? What's happening?'

'Help me! Help me! I'm on—' She slipped, her ankle turned and buckled and she crashed to the ground.

She screamed in pain and terror and tried to get to her feet. She was nearly there when the man caught up with her, and flung himself down on top of her. She felt her head slam into the rough ground. The man grabbed her wrists; his fingers encircled them like a band of steel. A wave of nausea flooded her and bright beads of red flashed before her eyes. She shook her head, desperately fighting to remain conscious. Through the haze of red, she saw the man looming over her. He wore a black hood, with slits for his eyes. He smelled of lemons. He said not a word, as he stared at her. The only sound was the rasping of his breath, which came in quick, excited sucks.

Time slowed suddenly, as in a dream, when you try to escape and find your legs trapped in mire while a predator gains on you. Here the only difference was that the predator knelt over her, crushing her wrists against the ground. She could feel the grit grinding into her skin; could taste blood in her mouth. She must have bitten her lip when she hit the ground. Dimly, on the peripheries, she saw the disused railway siding. She heard traffic; it seemed to be far away, as if it belonged to a different world. As it did. The world she had been snatched from by this man was one she had created. A world where there was no violence, where there was only goodness, and good things. Where there was Georgie. Her child, her son, her love.

As she pictured him she felt a surge of strength and heaved with all her might to loosen the man's grip. He responded by punching her in the face. Her head snapped back against the road again, and she felt herself beginning to lose consciousness. Oh no, oh God no, this can't be happening. She fought against it. She grabbed hold of everything good. *Georgie, my baby, Georgie, I love you. Nothing can happen to me. Nothing will happen to Mama.* She saw her baby in her mind, reaching for her, arms outstretched in supplication. Tears streamed down her face. She tried to remember what Breden had taught her.

Heedless of the last punch, she tried again to fight off the man. The response was another blow to her head. Oh God, any more of this and she wouldn't be able to hold on. It wasn't meant to be like this. She remembered Breden telling her things always went wrong. Where was he, where was he? Where the fuck was he? The man began to drag Sarah off the street towards the railway siding. Her calves scraped the rough ground. She could feel the blood begin to run as the skin seared off. 'Help me. HELP ME!' she screamed into the mike, but no one came. She was abandoned to this man. Each moment stretched into an infinity of terror. She felt herself begin to detach. Saw herself lying on the filthy ground, prey to the predator looming above her. She could almost see the scene unfold, as if she were watching it happen to someone else. *Oh Georgie, I can't let this happen to Mama. I can't let this man . . .*

Rage flooded her. She squirmed away and tried to get up. She bent her knees up, till she got both feet under the man's ribs, and then she lunged at him with all her force. He grunted and fell back. Slowed by the blows to her head, she struggled up. The man leapt to his feet, swinging his fists. One caught Sarah another blow to the side of the head. It seemed to loosen something inside her, and she punched back, not how Breden had taught her, with the blade of her hand, but with bareknuckled fists.

She could hardly see what she was hitting; a film of rage covered her eyes. She was just conscious of punching his face, of taking blows herself which rocked her, of one almighty punch, of stars exploding in her head, of falling backwards. The man wouldn't stop now; she knew that. She had unleashed a torrent of violence. She remembered Breden telling her that the rapist was getting more violent, and the more his victims resisted, the more he punished them. She didn't think it was possible to feel more fear, but suddenly her fear seemed to flare like a fire out of control when another pair of arms grabbed her from behind. She screamed in abject terror. She could hardly hear now, so loud was the roaring of the blood in her ears, but slowly, in fragments, words pierced her consciousness.

'Sarah, Sarah, it's all right, it's me. It's Dick. It's all right, Sarah. I've got you. You're safe now.'

The masked man spun round and lurched away. Breden very gently and quickly laid Sarah on the ground, and ran after him. '*Catch him. Please God, catch him,*' Sarah whispered, before a great black wave flooded over her and she thought no more.

Chapter Sixty-seven

Linoleum floors, police milling around, the smell of cigarette smoke, low voices talking.

'Have a look at her. Possibly severe head injury, concussion, lost a lot of blood. I'd rather get her straight to Casualty.

'Doctor's on his way. He'll be here within five minutes. If she needs to go, she'll go.'

Words rained down on her like blows, and she tried to remember why that frightened her. Then it all came back, and with it her full consciousness. She sat up and vomited.

Hands went around her, steadied her, held her head.

'Easy there. It's all right. Cough it up, that's right, that's better,' murmured a voice rich with compassion, a voice her mother might have used. At that another jag of pain, and up came the vomit again.

The same voice speaking sharply. 'Clean towels, one dry, one dampened with cold water. *Now*, please.' And she felt herself being sponged down. The water ran down her face, and with it something else, acrid, sick-making. She put her fingers to her head and brought them before her eyes; great gobs of blood. Then her own voice.

'I'm hurt, I'm hurt.'

'It's all right, Sarah.' Someone took her hand. 'You'll be fine.'

She looked up, trying to focus, and dimly made out the face of Dick Breden. 'It's you. What happened?' Then, more urgently, 'Did you catch him? Please tell me you caught him. You did, didn't you?'

'I caught him.'

'Who is it, who is it? Tell me.'

'I don't know. He won't say who he is, and there's apparently no ID on him.'

'It's not Redford,' said Sarah, trying to remember why she thought it wasn't.

'No. Not Redford.'

'Who then?'

Another voice, a man bending over her.

'I'm Detective Inspector Harding, Miss Jensen. That's what we'd like to ask you, Miss. Do you think you're able to take a look at him?'

She saw Breden looking from her to the Inspector with doubtful eyes.

'Where's that bloody doctor?' demanded Breden to the air. 'She needs to be seen now.'

'We'll have her examined as soon as he gets here,' the Inspector promised. He bent forward toward Sarah. 'How d'you feel? You up to looking at this man? He won't see you, don't worry.'

Sarah wiped her mouth with the back of her hand. 'Yes, I want to see him. And I want *him* to see me.'

The Inspector led her along a narrow corridor lined with more posters of the type she had seen the other day: MURDER, RAPE, TERRORISM, DISAPPEARANCE. Now she was part of it, and one of the perpetrators was waiting in a cell for her. Dick Breden walked beside her, arm around her, holding her up. Their feet beat out a slurred tattoo. They descended a flight of stairs and paused. The Inspector turned to Sarah. 'You sure you're ready for this?'

She nodded.

He gave her a quizzical look, before turning and leading them round a corner. A group of cells lined the wall. They stopped before the first one. A man sat on the floor, with his back to them.

'Get up, you bastard,' said Harding. 'There's someone here to see you.'

That did it. The man slowly unwound, got up, and turned to face them. It was Strone.

Chapter Sixty-eight

It was gone four by the time Sarah left the police station. She'd been checked there by the doctor. He'd cleaned her grazed calves and dressed them. The cut to her head was superficial, a small gash to her scalp. The doctor had dosed her up on painkillers and put in two stitches but, more seriously, he diagnosed bad concussion, and wished to admit her to hospital for observation. Sarah, however, wanted to go home. Insisted on going home. She had to see her son, and no one was going to keep her from him. The doctor and Breden relented, against their better judgement, only when Sarah promised that there would be someone to watch over her. Jacob, as always.

A uniformed Constable drove her home. Breden had to stay in the station, explaining himself to a DTI screaming about entrapment. Strone had been locked up, that much she knew and no more. Please God he would stay locked up for ever. She shuddered uncontrollably at what had nearly happened to her, at the thought of what had happened to all the victims who did not have a surveillance team ready to bail them out. She rubbed at her face with her sleeve, trying to gouge all the make-up off her face. Her blonde wig lay in the back of Breden's car, removed before they turned up at the station.

The journey home seemed to take for ever, and she was left alone too long with her thoughts. She had always kidded herself that she was invincible. Now the last of her illusions had been shattered and she would never look at the world in the same way again. She knew, as if by ancient instinct, that the legacy of violence would be a small kernel of fear that would never go away.

The Constable saw her to her door. Sarah paused a while before putting her key into the lock. She didn't want to bring the contamination of the night into her home. She didn't want to pollute it with her fear, with the violence wrought upon her. Finally, on the fifth attempt, she managed to control her shaking hands enough to negotiate the lock. On tremulous legs, she tiptoed upstairs to her room, shedding her clothes, heading for the shower. Following the doctor's instructions, she gingerly put a shower cap over her head before immersing herself in the jet of water. She stood under it for ten minutes, until she could remain upright no more. Then she pulled on her oldest pyjamas and crept from her room. The hall light was on, and when she pushed open the door to her son's room, the light seeped round, casting a faint glow upon the sleeping infant's features. She crouched down beside him, gazing at him through the bars of his cot, listening to the sound of his breath, watching his tiny chest rise and fall under the blankets, smelling the milky, bready smell of him and weeping silently. Her fingers reached out through the bars seeking his sleeping body.

Jacob was waiting for her at her bedroom door. He looked old and frail, wrapped in his tattered tartan bathrobe, white stubble grazing his chin, hair unkempt, fear in his eyes.

'Oh my God. Oh Lord above. What happened to you? What happened to you?' he wailed, his voice a lament. He reached forward, fingers brushing the swollen contours of her face. 'God in His heaven, I'll kill the bastard who did this. Was it that Breden? Was it him? I'll—'

'He saved me, Jacob. He saved me.'

Together they went downstairs, sitting beside the Aga for warmth, a whisky for Jacob, and milky, sugary tea for Sarah, while she told him what had happened.

Chapter Sixty-nine

The ringing of the alarm hit her head like a percussion of hammers. She stumbled to her feet, rushed for the bathroom, and threw up in the sink. Concussion, shock, painkillers and exhaustion made a toxic cocktail. She raised her head, splashed water over her skin, flinched, peered through swollen eyes at the havoc wrought upon her face. She gently touched the black eye, the swollen lips, the grazed cheek. The image of Strone's masked face, eyes black slits, staring down at her with undiluted evil filled her mind. She vomited again. Fifteen minutes in the shower and she felt marginally less like death. She dried herself hurriedly, pulled on clean clothes. It was nine. Georgie had long since woken, been given his breakfast by Jacob, and was already into the first of his morning naps. Sarah looked in on him, drank in the goodness of him, the feeling of her love, then closed the door softly behind her.

Jacob was in the kitchen, drinking tea. His eyes as he took her in spoke of his hurt. She was his child, in all but biology, and her pain was magnified a hundred times in his heart and soul. That he could not bear it for her, that she had not shared her plots and plans with him, given him the chance to help her, if not to stop her, was a wound that would heal far more slowly than Sarah's battered face.

'How're you feeling?' he asked stiffly.

'All the better for seeing you and my baby,' she answered.

'Yes, well. Lucky you are to be seeing anything if you—'

'I know, you told me last night. I'm stupid, irresponsible, a negligent mother, I shouldn't be allowed—'

'Stop. I was wrong to say those things. You're a wonderful mother. I'd never say otherwise, unless I was out of my mind with worry, but stupid, yes. You were stupid. I still don't understand why you put yourself at risk like that. It doesn't make sense. There's something you're not telling me.' He looked at her with his wounded eyes.

Sarah went to him and took his hand. 'Jacob, I've told you everything I can. Please, let it go. I have my reasons: allow me those. I'm a big girl. I don't choose to have secrets from you for a whim. Please, trust me.'

He dropped his hand from hers and got to his feet. 'I'm going to make you some breakfast, sweetie. You're as white as a sheet – where you're not black and blue, that is.'

It was ten-fifteen by the time Sarah got to the Portobello. John Redford's face was sleepy with surprise when she knocked at his door.

She held onto the doorpost, almost crippled by exhaustion. Redford opened the door, dazed by sleep, eyes barely open.

'Sarah. Come in.' He brushed his hair from his eyes. He was wearing the hotel bathrobe; his bare feet looked pale and strangely vulnerable. Sarah saw again what had been there all along – the little boy, the strange innocence. He didn't know. No one had told him yet.

The sitting room was in darkness. Heavy curtains kept out the light. Redford sank into an armchair. Sarah took a seat opposite on the sofa.

'I've got some bad news,' she said softly. 'It's about Strone.'

'Jesus, what? I was with him coupla hours ago.'

'We believe he's guilty of over twenty rapes, in South America, North America, the Far East, now Europe.'

'What?' Redford jolted awake. '*Who* believes? Strone is never a rapist. This is not some obsessive game, Sarah. Dammit all, you're talking about people's lives, reputations.'

She stood up, switched on the lights and turned to Redford.

'Shit! What happened to you?' He got up and went to her. He traced his fingers over the livid bruises colouring Sarah's face. She flinched and pushed him away.

'This serial rapist has raped in almost every place that you did a show, always in the early morning after a performance,' she said, standing at arm's length from Redford, her eyes never leaving his.

'When I heard about Carla, and then learned about the serial rapist and his itinerary of rape, I thought it might be you. I had to know for sure, so I and my team studied the rapist's modus operandi, and decided to set a trap, with me as bait. I tagged your shirt with a surveillance beeper when I went to your changing room. I and a back-up team trailed you to The

Fallen Angel. I was the woman in the blonde wig and the waitress outfit. That's the type the rapist always went for. I left the club the same time as you. You even looked at me. You were in your disguise, I was in mine. You went off in a red Volvo; I thought the danger had passed. I took a walk round the block. Someone came after me. A man wearing a black hood, with slits for his eyes.' Her voice, at first cold and devoid of emotion now began to tremble. 'He jumped me, I tried to fight back, so he hit me. He only had me there for around forty-five seconds, but it felt like an eternity. He must have hit me six times before my back-up team arrived, chased him, caught him. I passed out, woke at the police station on Brick Lane. They took me to see the man my team had brought in. It was Strone.'

Redford sank his face into his hands.

'Dear God, Sarah, I'm sorry. I'm sorry you went through that. Christ, it must have been hell.'

'It was.'

Redford backed away and began to pace.

'I can't take this in. He told me he just wanted to walk. He always does, in every city; he goes off walking – that's what got *me* into it. But he has his anonymity, he can go anywhere. It became a joke between us, his walks, his slumming. And when we went out together, he thought it was a blast to put on a disguise too. I thought maybe it was whores he was after, never pushed that much.'

He stopped before Sarah. 'My mind feels like it's gonna burst. Strone, a serial rapist, and you . . . "Back-up team, surveillance tags". Getting yourself in danger like that. Who the hell *are* you?'

'A woman making a living.'

'I said once you were a spy for Goldsteins. That's all you are, isn't it? The numbers stuff was just a ruse to spy on me.'

'It wasn't just a ruse, but part of it was, yeah, sure. Someone had to check for skeletons in your closet. Goldsteins decided that someone was me.'

'How could you do this? To me, to you, to us?'

'Oh John. Don't do this, please. I can't deal with it now.'

'Answer me, Sarah. You can't walk in here, dump what you've been doing for the past months on me and expect me to sit here like some patsy and just nod. This is real life, not some financial game, with me as a pawn. This is something that affects real people. Like us.'

'There is no us, John,' Sarah said slowly. 'There never was.'

'You believe that?'

'I believe what I have to.'

'And is that why you slept with me? Just doing your job?'

Sarah slapped his face. Redford rubbed his reddening skin, looking almost pleased he'd elicited some passion from Sarah.

'What do you think?' she said.

'How do I know *what* to think? You lied to me from the first.'

'Not in Wyoming,' she said softly. 'And after that, over here, I did everything I could *not* to sleep with you. When I did it had nothing to do with the job, believe me.'

Redford gave a bitter laugh. 'Belief's a pretty scarce commodity round here. You believed I was a serial rapist.'

'I was wrong, but you raped once; it didn't look good for you.'

Redford dragged his hand through his hair. 'The police have been to see me. A Detective Inspector.'

Sarah looked up sharply.

The insurgent, the insurer. A *Police Inspector.* She should have guessed from the man's bearing, the crumpled suit, the cutting through the rock star's defences.

'Wanted to see me about a Miss Carla Parton,' said Redford, in a deliberately emotionless drawl. 'Alias Jenni White, alias D.D. Simmonds.'

Sarah felt her knees wobble. The assault, the concussion, her fear and exhaustion, and now the sense that some other terrible thing was going to be flung at her made her almost pass out. She sat on the sofa, hugged her knees to her for comfort.

'Carla Parton, failed actress, sometime resident of various psychiatric wards where she was treated for psychotic behaviour, is wanted across five states in connection with stalking, blackmail and extortion,' intoned Redford. 'A certain rock star, I'm not at liberty to say who, challenged her when she accused him of raping her when he was in a drugged-out haze. He called in the cops, his security people kept Miss White as she called herself, on the premises. Cops printed her, and the prints came up with a rap sheet long as her legs. She's tried it on three other performers before me. All three paid up, compensated her for fucking up her life. So believable was her tale, and she picked her victims so cleverly, just enough possibility of guilt.'

Sarah dropped her face into her hands. She sat there, her breath hot against the backs of her fingers, seeing Carla's face, hearing her voice, the tears, the pain. She had wanted to believe Carla, had wanted to judge Redford, to see the worst, all so that she could be free of him, could break the love that bound her to him, all so that she could keep her son from him, would feel no obligation to share her child with a rapist. She had seen everything through the distortion of her own love and need. Then another thought struck her.

'Maybe Carla was telling the truth the first time. Perhaps she really was raped, not by you, but by Strone.'

Redford watched her in grim silence.

'She never saw who she claimed raped her after your concert,' continued Sarah. 'Security directed her to a dressing room. She walked in, and whoever was in the room was hidden behind a screen. Next thing she knew, the light was turned off, and someone jumped her. She never saw who it was, but just assumed it had to be you, since it was your dressing room.'

'Strone always has his own room too, to chill out in, to *mastermind operations*, as he puts it,' said Redford tightly.

'She was dressed in her waitress uniform. All the women we think were raped by Strone wore waitress uniforms. Carla wouldn't have known a detail like that. If she were raped by Strone, then maybe it dislodged something in her brain and she thought all the other rock stars she blackmailed had really raped her too.' Sarah dropped her head into her hands.

'Maybe. Whatever,' said Redford. 'She's convincing as hell, whether or not she's convinced herself. She fooled me. I paid her a million dollars,' he added in a tone of self-disgust.

Sarah decided not to tell him she already knew about this. She paced around Redford's room, her mind a maelstrom. She stopped and turned to him.

'Why didn't you tell me about this?'

Redford gave a derisive laugh. 'It was too late, wasn't it, Sarah? You'd already made up your mind about me.'

Sarah began to weep. She got to her feet and ran from the room.

Chapter Seventy

She caught a taxi on Kensington Park Road and headed for Goldsteins. James Savage was the next person to be faced. Just as the taxi was approaching Liverpool Street, her mobile rang. It was Breden. Once he had ascertained that Sarah was relatively OK, his voice became excited.

'I just spoke to the Old Bill. Strone's confessed.'

The shock rendered Sarah silent for a while. 'Confessed? I never thought he would. I thought he'd stick it out in grim silence.'

'Nope. Confessed a few hours ago, wouldn't shut up apparently. It all came tumbling out. I mentioned before that the view was that he was decompensating, that he almost wanted to be caught. It seems it was almost a relief, and even more of a relief to confess.'

Sarah's mind raced. 'Did he say anything about Carla?'

'He did. Apparently she was the first one.'

'That was so long ago! How many times must he have raped in the meantime?' For a moment, the horror of it all threatened to engulf her.

'You stopped him, Sarah,' said Breden. 'Your courage stopped him.'

'Yeah well, I'll need some more of it now. I'm just going to see Savage and tell him everything.'

'Good luck,' said Breden.

'Do you want me to keep you out of it?' asked Sarah. 'He'll be mad as hell with you.'

'He will be, but no, don't worry. The truth'll come out sooner or later. I'll just brace myself for a rocket.'

When Evangeline saw Sarah's face, and heard her grim request to see her boss immediately, she interrupted Savage halfway through a meeting with a new prospective client. Savage's choleric air vanished as soon as he saw Sarah.

'What in heaven's name happened to you?' He reached out to her impulsively, then withdrew his hand as if even a gentle touch might inflict more damage upon her.

'Can we sit down?' asked Sarah, suddenly reeling from another onslaught of nausea. Savage reached out with certainty this time, gripped her arm, led her into his office and sat her down on his sofa.

'Evangeline,' he called over his shoulder. 'Bring a glass of water, would you.'

Sarah gently sipped the water Evangeline had brought her, and began to gather herself. Savage watched her with concerned eyes.

'Just tell me,' he whispered between gritted teeth, 'who did this.'

'Back up,' said Sarah, raising a weary hand. 'It's a long story. I'd better start at the beginning.'

It took her an hour, and two more glasses of water. She told him how she had decided to set a trap and catch the stalker. She told him how she had caught Carla, and all about Carla's awful story, then about the serial rapes in *The Times*, and her suspicion about John Redford. Finally she told him about how she had acted as bait for the rapist, with Breden as back-up.

'So if it wasn't Redford, who the hell was it?' shouted Savage as she came to the end of her story.

'It was Strone.'

'Bloody hell and damn it all,' said Savage, getting to his feet. 'And I thought I was on top of things, and all the while, this insanity is going on.' He marched up to Sarah and bent over her. 'You could have got yourself killed. Why, for crying out loud, did you do all this? First with the stalker, then with the rapist? Have you got a death wish or something?'

Sarah bit her lip. Her heart trembled as she tried to separate what she would tell Savage.

'I had my reasons.'

'What reasons? What could possibly justify all this?'

'The stalker didn't just threaten me,' said Sarah in a dull voice. 'She threatened my uncle, and my child.'

Savage paused. He looked at Sarah with renewed shock. 'Your child?'

'I have a nine-month-old son. He's the reason I took this work, he's the reason I played hardball with what you paid me, he's the reason I set out to trap the stalker. She wrote that she would kill Georgie.' Tears began to spill down Sarah's face as she spoke her son's name. She brushed them away and carried on. 'How could I just let that go? I got full-time surveillance and protection on my uncle and my son, and went off to Venice to set a trap.'

Savage blew out a heavy breath. 'You were behaving so strangely about so many things. I couldn't understand what had got into you, but it all makes sense now. Especially Venice. One minute you didn't want to go, the next you were insistent that you did go.'

'In between she threatened Georgie and Jacob.'

Savage nodded. 'Why didn't you tell me any of this?'

'I don't know. You had your own problems, and I thought I could sort it out on my own.'

'Playing God.'

'If you like.'

'I always knew you were holding back on something. Bloody hell, Sarah, I can hardly think straight. This is too much to take in during one sitting. You're really run amok this time.'

'Have I?' asked Sarah, anger building. 'You wanted me to dig around, drag the bloody skeletons out of every cupboard, and I've done that for you. I found your Leaker, I found out that Redford was being stalked, I found the stalker, and I found out that Strone is a serial rapist. Now your precious deal is safe. It'll be messy with a prosecution of Strone, but Redford's innocence is what counts.'

'You think I should go along with this deal now?' Savage asked incredulously.

'Why the hell not? If you don't, everything I've done, all the risks I've taken, will have been in vain.'

Savage drew in a number of deep breaths as if trying to fight down his own nausea.

'You are unbelievable. I suppose you suborned Breden into helping you?'

'I made it difficult for him to refuse. He didn't want to go behind your back, I can assure you.'

Savage gave a bark of laughter. 'Don't worry, I won't hold it against Dick. I'll give him a bloody bollocking, but the poor guy wouldn't have stood a chance.'

'What do you mean?' asked Sarah.

'He's nuts about you,' said Savage. 'Don't tell me Miss Super Instinct didn't know.'

'I *didn't* know,' replied Sarah angrily. 'And I'm sure you're wrong.'

Savage sat down behind his desk and brought out a cheque book. He tore out a cheque, filled it in and handed it to Sarah.

'Here you are. I can't say you don't deserve this, but I wish to high heaven you hadn't taken all the risks you did.'

'There *was* no risk-free way of doing this, James. You must know that, deep down. You'd just rather not know too much about our methods, but you still push for the results.'

Savage paused for a moment before handing over the cheque.

'Maybe you're right. Anyway, here's one hundred K for the Redford work, and fifty for finding the Leaker. That should about cover it all, don't you think?'

Sarah pocketed the cheque. 'Thank you, James. It will. Just one question. Will you employ me again?'

Savage raised his eyebrows. 'Great time to ask me when I'm still in shock.'

'I have to know.'

'So that you can support your son?'

'Yes.'

Savage smiled with surprising gentleness. 'Get yourself better, enjoy some time with your boy. And don't worry.'

'And the deal?' She thought about Redford and his dreams of retiring. 'Will you go ahead?'

Savage took a while to answer. 'I just don't know. I'll have to think about it. It's so damn messy. Externally, the press'll be all over us, and internally, I'll have Zamaroh to contend with. How the hell do I explain any of this to her? Or try to keep it from her? She'll be like a walking volcano.'

'Do it, James,' said Sarah, heading for the door. 'It's the right thing to do, and you know it. The mess is in the past.'

'Is it?' asked Savage, slowly. 'I wonder.'

Chapter Seventy-one

Sarah hailed a taxi on Liverpool Street and slumped in the seat. Her mind went back to her meeting with Redford, to his revelation of Carla's blackmail, and Breden's subsequent news of Strone's confession. How had she got it all so wrong? How could she have believed so quickly that Redford was guilty? The personal and the professional blurred until she could see nothing but her own ineptitude, her own guilt. She had loved John Redford, despite the fact that he was a rock star. Why was she so frightened of her own motives in loving him? She didn't want fame. Money, maybe. But she would never have chosen someone in the public arena, let alone with a face recognised around the globe. She loved anonymity. She loved the man, not the rock star, but the rock star frightened her, and so she destroyed him in her mind, killed their love.

She got home, close to collapse, face red with tears, took Georgie from a surprised Jacob.

'What's happened now?'

'I've been an idiot,' she gasped, trying desperately not to cry for Georgie's sake. 'I've messed up so badly, you wouldn't believe. I've—' The ringing of the buzzer drowned out her words. 'Oh, who the bloody hell is *that*?' She strode down the hall and flung open the door. John Redford stood on the threshold. Sarah let out an anguished cry. She turned her body away from him, trying unsuccessfully to shield Georgie from his gaze.

'Who the devil are you?' demanded Jacob, appearing at Sarah's shoulder. 'Shall I get rid of him?' he asked Sarah, squaring up.

Sarah looked at Jacob, turned slowly to look at Redford, whose incredulous eyes flitted from Georgie's face to hers.

'No. No need for that.' She spoke heavily to Redford. 'You'd better come in.'

Sarah sat on the sofa and hugged Georgie to her. Redford stood opposite her. Jacob hovered uncertainly in the doorway.

'How old is he?' asked Redford, his normally smooth voice shaken.

'Nine and a bit months,' answered Sarah. She could see Redford doing the calculations.

'Do I need to ask you anything else?' he said slowly.

Sarah had never felt so utterly open, so defenceless. 'No,' she said, her voice a whisper. 'You don't.'

Redford buried his head in his hands. 'Why didn't you tell me?' he asked, anguished. 'How could you do this?'

'Do what?' asked Sarah, voice tight with sudden terror. 'You mean not have an abortion?'

'No, *damn* you. How could you not tell me? How could you keep him from me? How could you do what you did?'

She stared into his face and saw, blazing in his eyes, the same ferocity she had seen in Wyoming. Then it was passion, now anger, but through the anger, just a trace of something good showed.

'Oh dear God,' said Jacob. '*You're* Georgie's father?'

Both he and Redford looked to Sarah to confirm the truth they saw all too clearly in the baby's blue eyes.

Sarah turned to Redford, answered the question directly to him.

'Yes. You're Georgie's father.'

Chapter Seventy-two

The following year

Extracts from The Word

> *3 June*
> *The sensational trial of the Rock Rapist as he has become known, ended today as Strone Cawdor was found guilty by the jury at the Old Bailey. Strone, the manager of rock star John Redford, was found guilty of a specimen count of fifteen rapes carried out over an eighteen-month period during the world tour of John Redford. Interpol, the FBI, and the police forces of over twelve countries were searching for the serial rapist, but he was eventually caught by the efforts of a financial consultant and a private investigator. Sarah Jensen, a former foreign exchange trader at InterContinental Bank, and now attached to Goldsteins International as a freelance consultant, was walking home from a visit to The Fallen Angel bar near Spitalfields Market in the early morning of 4 October last year when Strone, wearing a black hood, stepped out of the shadows and attacked her. Dick Breden, who had also been at The Fallen Angel, heard Jensen's screams and went to her aid. Breden then performed a citizen's arrest upon Strone and called the police. Sarah Jensen, formerly known as one of the City's top FX traders, is no stranger to violence. She left ICB four years ago after a series of high-profile murders rocked the leading City firm. It was suggested at the time . . .*

Sarah threw down the paper. 'Roddy Clark keeps digging, he'll hit Australia soon.'

4 June
Following the sentencing yesterday of Strone Cawdor, the Rock Rapist, for fifteen rapes across the world, Jim O'Cleary, the head of security for John Redford, was sentenced to eight years in prison for perverting the course of justice. O'Cleary was found guilty of attempting to intimidate key witnesses in the trial of Strone Cawdor. He was also charged and found guilty as an accessory to rape. Evidence showed that he knew of at least some of the rapes carried out by Cawdor, but kept the information to himself out of a misplaced sense of loyalty.

Sarah stopped reading in disgust.

7 June
Goldsteins International launched the largest 'Bowie Bond' the industry has seen when they securitised the back catalogue of rock legend John Redford. Goldsteins raised one hundred and ten million dollars for Redford. The bonds, rated Single A by Moody's, were taken up by ten institutional investors. Redford does not seem to have suffered adversely from the scandal surrounding his former manager Strone Cawdor, sentenced last week to twenty-two years in prison for serial rape. In fact, Redford's record sales seem to have benefited from all the publicity generated by the trial when the star was called to the stand four times to give evidence against his former manager.

More, see Concrete Jungle Grapevine.

7 June
Concrete Jungle Grapevine, *by Roddy Clark*
Goldsteins' Imperious chief executive, James Savage, has divorced Fiona, his wife of twenty-eight years. Fiona Savage has moved in with Richard Deane, a rising young turk with Goldsteins' rivals Uriah's. One wonders what passes for pillow talk . . .

Silly cow, thought Sarah.

10 June
'Women in Crisis', an international charity that covers a wide range of activities, from providing reconstructive surgery for women who have been subjected to clitorodectomies, to building havens for battered women and their children, is reeling with delight after an anonymous benefactor donated five million dollars to the organisation.

'A beautiful dark-haired woman came in with an envelope. She waited in our hallway for half an hour, after asking to see the Director, Lydia Priors, then she just handed her the envelope and said: "Use it well," and disappeared. The Director left the envelope unopened on her desk and it was only after lunch that she remembered it,' reports secretary to the Director, Lindsay McManners. McManners said she heard a whoop and ran into Lydia Priors's office to find her boss leaping around with joy and brandishing a cheque for a cool five million.

Sarah put down the newspaper with a smile. She bent over Georgie and kissed his cheek.

'D'you want to come out for a bit of fresh air before we bath you and put you to bed?' she asked.

He shook his head violently and enunciated a perfect and definitive 'No!' before turning back to his puzzle.

Sarah smiled. 'OK, my angel. I'll just be five minutes.' She glanced around the room, making sure everything was as baby-safe as it could be, then she secured the door, walked out onto the balcony and breathed in the bracing air. Summer had come suddenly to the mountains, and brought with it a feeling of euphoria.

Each day, the snow that had coated the Tetons like a thick cape just two weeks ago, unravelled a little bit further and faster. Now it just covered the deepest crevices. The sun was beginning to set, casting the rock terracotta red, leaving the identical image, upside down, shimmering in the lake that rose each day with the snow melt. Sarah walked down the wooden steps from the balcony, out onto the thickly growing grass. She strolled the twenty yards to the lake, and climbed up upon a mossy rock. There she lifted her face to the sun, catching the last of the day's warmth, before it dropped like a meteor behind the towering horizon of stone. She could already smell the cold in the air, the freshness of moss and the clean tang of the lake.

From her vantage point she could see down the valley to the plains beyond, with the mountains framing her view to left and right. She saw a moose pick its way delicately from a clump of trees, and head toward another. It stopped halfway across. Its ears flicked back and forth, then it turned in her direction. It must have been thirty yards away. She stayed quite still. Moose could be dangerous, but she had a feeling this one just wanted to be on its way. It suddenly turned its head in the opposite direction and seemed to be looking hard at something. It took Sarah a while to spot the source of its interest. Then, slowly, she picked out a moving dot, which grew into a horse mounted by a tall rider in a cowboy hat. The horse was the same terracotta red as the sun-burnished mountains. She could see even from the distance of half a mile or so the elegance and surefootedness of its carriage as it cantered gently toward her. The moose watched its approach with grave interest, before slowly high-stepping away into the trees.

Sarah climbed down from her rock and walked back to the cabin. Georgie was still playing happily. She gathered him up into her arms and went outside with him. The horse slowed and now slow-trotted towards them. Ten yards away, the rider slipped from the saddle, hooked his reins around the pommel, and walked towards them with arms outstretched. Georgie wriggled in his mother's arms until she put him down on the ground. He toddled towards the smiling man, and said one word, over and over again.

'Dada.'